MICHAEL WEBB

Rise of the Shadow

Books by Michael Webb

THE LAST SHADOW KNIGHT

RISE OF THE SHADOW

SHADOW OF DESTINY

Contents

Land of Terrenor
North Sea
Bryveld
Nortris
Noravorre River
Daratill
Norshewa
Korob Mountains
Rydland
Gap of Thardor
Molyaigh
Kyrd Forest
Kärondir
Westfale Ocean
Karad
Bromhill
Feldor
Nasco
Tienn
Kandis
Benavorre River
Felting
Rynor
Straith Mountains
Felavorre River
Lorranis
Palenting
Isle of Paratill
Tarnvorre River
Tarving
Tarphan
Portris
Searis
Marris
Gulf of Tartis
Parathan Ocean
N
Parthe Mountains

I

Restarting

1

Attack

Drumming filled his ears in time with his heartbeat. Veron followed the wall, slinking through the shadows, breath heavy with anticipation. He glanced back to Chelci, who nodded, her sword still and ready.

After peering around the corner, Veron left the darkness's safety for the exposed entry hall. Moonlight peering through the windows at the far end splashed onto the smooth, marble floor. There was nowhere to hide. Veron and Chelci soundlessly padded across the floor. As they arrived on the other side, Veron stopped in his tracks, sword balanced in front of him. Chelci bumped into his back as two men clothed in black stepped out of the shadows. They stood a full head above him, glaring back with fixed jaws. One rested a massive sword against his shoulder, and the other held dueling daggers.

"Stand back," Veron said over his shoulder before stepping closer to the men. A glint from Farrathan's hard steel caught his eye as he readied his weapon and pulled origine from the well inside of him. His body tingled, and his thoughts sharpened. Power flowed from the energy waiting to be unleashed.

The two began to move, but Veron struck down the sword-bearer before the man's weapon left his shoulder. The one with daggers remained frozen. His face had hardly registered the attack when Veron kicked him in the chest, sending him flying against the stone wall. The blades flew from his hands as his head cracked into the rock. His body collapsed limp on the cold marble.

"Veron," Chelci said hesitantly as he released his energy source. He turned to find ten men with weapons blocking the room at the far end.

Veron pulled on her shoulder. "Run."

He turned the other way and froze—another ten men. He looked at the grand staircase leading to the second story, but a dozen more waited at the top.

"We're trapped," Chelci said, her voice catching.

"Stand to my back," Veron said with forced calm as he faced the closest group. Sweat beaded on his forehead. He knew what he could do, but it was a lot of men. Suddenly, the sight before him grew hazy, as if his eyes struggled to focus. He blinked quickly and shook his head, clearing the fog.

With a pull of origine, Veron whirled into their midst. His sword sang as it cut through the air. Flesh and bone broke under the blade's sharp sting. He ducked under the opposing weapons and spun out of their reach. He took a man by the arm and propelled his body into several others, sending weapons and armored bodies clattering across the floor. He jumped and kicked several in succession, knocking each into the stone wall. He and his sword twirled between the four remaining men, cutting them down before they had time to react. The bodies lay in a disheveled pile, strewn around his half of the room.

Chelci! He turned and ran to join her, breathing deeply to recover his energy. She had fought off two but couldn't hope to defeat them all. Veron admired her tenacity as she held her sword up and glared, taunting them with fierce confidence. The remaining men hesitated, clearly unprepared for the fight she gave them. Veron took advantage of the brief lull, stepping between her and the attackers. He tightened the grip on his weapon, pulled from the origine, and struck.

The fight was a blur. Moving without thinking, he cut down man after man. He held his sword's hilt and slammed both fists into one, sending him flying into the air and another into the wall. No one even moved to defend.

As the last man fell, a cry behind him turned his blood to ice. He spun, and his stomach lurched to see men from upstairs holding Chelci with a knife wrapped around her neck. "Leave her alone!" he shouted.

"Drop your sword or she dies!" yelled her captor.

Veron stepped closer, but a fresh cry from Chelci stopped him short as the blade bit into her neck. His vision blurred again, and he wiped his eyes forcibly.

"What is this?" an indignant voice shouted from atop the stairs. "Release her at once! Who are you all? What are you doing in my house?"

Lady Luciana had arrived. Chelci's mother was an imposing force, but the half-dozen men at the top of the stairs didn't appear intimidated. They surrounded the lady of the house, blocking her from Veron's view just before a bone-chilling scream filled the hall. Veron winced as he heard a body slump from above. The men turned to head downstairs, leaving Luciana's limp arm hanging over the top step.

"No!" Chelci screamed as she strained against the man holding her.

"Stop this!" Veron yelled. "It's me you want!"

"Put down your sword, or she's next!" the man shouted back. His words were strange, sounding as if a blanket covered everyone's mouths and muffled their speech.

Veron locked eyes with Chelci. Her tears welled up, glistening in the moonlight. He gritted his teeth as he set down his blade and pushed it away. Men surrounded him with swords and knives. Veron scanned the crowd as they approached.

The men charged at once. Time slowed as Veron pulled from the origine, ducking under two swords then whirling out of the way of the next. His arms and legs blasted with force, sending men flying. Those remaining on the ground desperately slashed but found nothing but air.

Chelci again cried out. Slowing his attack, he clenched his jaw and glared at her captor while stepping in her direction. Suddenly, his body jolted as a searing white fire pierced him from behind. When the sword pulled out of his back, two more blades struck him in the front—one in his gut, and one in his chest.

Veron's eyes bugged as he staggered. His nerves screamed in protest. He glanced down at the weapons sticking out of him before looking to Chelci. Her mouth hung open, paralyzed with shock.

The attackers pulled out their swords, and Veron collapsed to his knees. His eyes lost focus. He pressed against his chest wounds. Blood seeped between his fingers, laughing at his futile attempt to stop it. Weakness spread, and his limbs shivered.

"You can't hide from Edmund Bale," the man holding Chelci sneered. The hazy words slurred together and echoed through Veron's mind.

As his head hit the stone floor, darkness pulled at his mind. He tried to fight it, but the weight was more than he could bear. His eyes closed.

With a start, Veron sat up in his bed. Sweat drenched his face, and his sheet clung to his bare chest. His hands flew to his body, but he found no injury. He glanced around the room. *What was that?* His breath heaved, and his pulse thundered in his ears as he sought a waiting enemy. The moonlight flooding in illuminated how alone he was.

He grasped the Shadow Knights medallion around his neck and forced his muscles to relax. Soon, his breathing evened. It was his first night as a servant in the Marlow house, and it was the first time he'd ever had a Dream.

2

Servant Greetings

A knock sounded on the door as footsteps and voices echoed in the hallway. "Time to wake!" a muffled voice proclaimed. Veron was already awake, staring at the dark ceiling as a faint whisper of light crept in from the window. He couldn't sleep since the Dream. *A glimpse of the future, huh?* he pondered. He'd never known anyone to have one. *But how could it be possible? I can't use the origine. I barely know Chelci. And Bale . . .* He sighed. *Bale will be looking for me.* He rose to dress with a lingering feeling of dread. The time had come to find out what a servant's life was like for a nineteen-year-old in the Marlow house.

In the dimly lit hall, dozens of men and women marched toward the stairs with slumped shoulders and downcast faces. No one greeted Veron or glanced in his direction. Veron followed the silent crowd as they made their way down three flights of stairs to the basement. He remembered this place from the previous night. He had met Luciana Marlow next to the stairs, and she tried to intimidate him into submission. He smirked, recalling her expression when he stood against her, yet the feeling softened as he remembered the Dream's prediction of her future.

The welcome smell of sausages and herbs brought him back to the present, and his stomach grumbled with anticipation. The surrounding servants were hard at work, preparing to feed a small army.

"You! New boy! Come here!"

From across the kitchen, the diminutive house steward, Tessa, motioned him to join her. Her scowling face was one of the few he recognized, so seeing her was oddly comforting. Veron dodged cooks carrying pots and servants hauling crates to reach the older woman.

"This is Tatiana," she said, nodding to the woman next to her. "She's the head housekeeper here and who you report to."

"Veron," he said, offering a slight bow to the middle-aged woman. Wrinkles lined her face, a black dress fringed with white covered her plump frame, and her dark brown hair curled into a tight bun.

Tatiana angled her head to the floor, where the metal anklet stuck out from Veron's woolen pants. She sniffed as she raised her nose. "Come with me," she said, surprising him with the gravelly timbre of her voice. As he followed her down a basement hallway, he noticed her ankles, peeking out from her dress, were bare.

She spoke over her shoulder as they moved. "You'll work in the housekeeping department. I give the orders, and you obey them. Understood?"

"Yes, I understand."

"The housekeepers' principal job is to keep the house clean. You wash the clothes, scrub the floors, empty the ashboxes, clean out the privies and chamber pots, and do anything else I tell you to. If you do well, after a few years, you may progress into other jobs."

"What other jobs? Cleaning is fine, but I ran a large business before I was forced to come here. I could be useful elsewhere, too," Veron said hopefully.

Tatiana stopped walking. "Being a servant of justice, speaking of your past life and the reason you are here is forbidden. Two years ago, one pleaded to Jackson—the Marlows' son—that someone wrongfully sold him and asked for Jackson's help. They took the servant to the whipping post, and he received eight lashes." She raised an eyebrow as she leaned in. "He couldn't walk for two weeks."

Veron swallowed hard, remembering the previous night when he met Chelci, the Marlows' daughter, in the sparring room. Her friendly demeanor made her easy to talk to. They even practiced sword fighting together.

"Don't make the same mistake he did. In fact, don't speak at all to family members unless spoken to." Tatiana's glare forced him to nod before she turned back down the hall. "As a servant in the Marlow house, you must do certain things. Keep yourself clean and presentable. You will bathe once per week but clean your face and hands daily. The family does not want dirty servants running around. Make yourself invisible as you work. Clean rooms when people aren't around, and avoid the family as you move through the house."

Veron glanced in the rooms they passed—storage rooms, mostly. Crates and bags stacked the floor and lined the shelves. Dim lanterns lit the hall, reminding him of the dungeon underneath the castle in Karad. The memory made him shudder.

Tatiana stopped at a dingy room on the basement's far side. The sickly-sweet smell of mold assaulted Veron as he entered. Three large, empty basins filled one side of the room, and baskets of unfinished laundry surrounded them. On the other side, piles of firewood stacked from floor to ceiling, and multiple wires strung wall to wall.

"Today is laundry day, but before it begins, you must fill the basins."

A dozen empty wooden buckets sitting in the corner caught his eye as another servant, a young man around his age, came up behind them.

"Nathaniel, Veron is new. Show him what to do." She didn't wait for a response before she returned down the hallway they had come through.

Nathaniel smiled and extended his arm to shake. His callused, cracked hand revealed the years of physical labor the servant had already experienced. "Hi, Veron," he said. "Today's your first day?" Veron nodded, and Nathaniel offered a grim smile. "Welcome to the housekeeping crew. It's not glamorous, but at least we know what's expected. Grab a yoke and two buckets and come with me."

Following Nathaniel's example, Veron selected a pair of buckets connected to a wooden yoke and followed down the hall and out the door to the side of the kitchen. The crisp early morning air hit him as he stepped outside.

A high wall surrounded the estate. Only the tallest of nearby buildings were visible. Just over the wall, a faint, orange light grew in the eastern sky, giving the air a warm glow. Balancing the empty buckets, Veron and the young man walked side by side around the back of the house.

In the outdoor light, Nathaniel looked a few years older than Veron. He was around the same height and build, but his brown hair was shorter. Veron squinted at his face. *He looks familiar. Do I know him from somewhere?*

"What's your story?" Nathaniel asked.

Veron pursed his lips. "Um . . . Tatiana said I'm not supposed to talk about my past." He stopped and pulled up the hem of his pants to show the metal ring identifying him as a servant of justice.

Nathaniel chuckled. "Sure . . . if you're talking with the family or one of the department heads. No one else cares." He pulled up his own pant leg to show a similar anklet. Veron raised his eyebrows. "So what brings you here?"

Veron scoffed. "I barely understand it myself. I ran a market in

Karad, where I lived for most of my life until a friend betrayed me. He was jealous . . . I guess. He threw me in prison and shipped me off as a slave . . . well . . . a *servant*. What about you?"

Nathaniel spoke as they continued walking. "I stole something. Well . . . they caught me stealing something. I stole for years before that."

"Here in Felting?"

"Yeah, I've been on the streets most of my life. I grew up in an orphanage. They kicked me out when I turned fifteen."

Veron snapped his fingers. "That's it! That's how I know you! I was there, too. I guess it was eleven or twelve years ago when I ran away."

Nathaniel stopped and tilted his head. "Yeah, you do look familiar. You left with Fend, right?"

Pain struck Veron at the mention of his old friend. He nodded.

"He was a friend of mine before he left. Whatever happened to him?"

Veron grimaced as the memory of soldiers killing Fend flooded his mind. "He didn't make it."

"That's too bad," Nathaniel said as he shook his head and resumed walking down the path.

Although in the middle of the city, the Marlows' house and yard seemed more like a wooded estate. The trees surrounding the property were as thick as a forest. Veron would have thought they were somewhere in the Feldor countryside if not for the neighboring buildings visible through the tree limbs.

To the side of the path, an enormous vegetable garden—ten times larger than the one at Artimus's house—came into view. The familiar produce reminded Veron of the four years he spent training with the old man, and a smile inched on his face.

Three men tended to the plants but glanced in their direction. "What's this? You have a new friend?" a man with a thick beard said as they walked past. "That's great . . . now you can polish each other's anklets." All three burst into laughter as a clump of weeds sailed toward Veron and Nathaniel.

Veron reddened as he ducked, and the weeds passed just over his head. Nathaniel continued walking without even turning his head. "Ignore them," the older servant mumbled.

The laughter faded as Veron and Nathaniel reached the end of the garden where a circular ring of stacked stones rose off the ground. Nathaniel unloaded his yoke and lifted a lid off the well before lowering down a bucket.

"Well, I'm glad to have another ankler around the house."

Veron cocked his head as he set down his buckets. "Ankler?"

"These metal decorations we wear. Very few servants have them. Most are proud to serve by choice. Since us anklers are 'criminals,' the rest of the workers want nothing to do with us."

"But, I'm not even a criminal," Veron protested as Nathaniel poured a full bucket of water from the well into one of his empty ones.

"It doesn't matter. A servant's station is so low that whenever they find someone lower, it helps them feel better about themselves." He let the bucket back down into the well as he continued. "Maren and Baker are the only other anklers. With you here, it makes four of us. Those men in the garden have been known to purposely track mud over floors we just cleaned. One of them tripped Baker once, and he spilled a bowl of soup onto a dinner guest. The guards whipped him for it at the post."

"They whipped . . . the person who tripped him?"

"No, Baker." Looking back at the house, Nathaniel pointed to a wooden post fixed to the side of the house they passed a moment before. "They only use that punishment for anklers."

Veron gulped. "So, are all the servants mean like those guys?" he asked, nodding toward the garden.

"Oh no. Overall, it's not too bad. I assume you met the house steward, Tessa."

"The short one? Yeah."

"She's always unpleasant and grumpy. Avoid her whenever you can. Tatiana is over all housekeeping, but she's not too bad. Just make sure you clean things well, and you won't have any problems. Then, there's Jensen. He's the head attendant over the wardmen, choremen, carriagemaster, and guards. He does his job well but isn't very friendly. Corbus is the head chef. He mostly keeps to the kitchen and shouts orders to people. As long as you don't mess up his food or complain about what you get, you'll get along fine. He's in charge of all the cooks and servers. The last house lead is Hugar, the head craftsman. He's over the mason, carpenter, landscapers, and gardener. Hugar is a great guy, but the landscapers, James and Montgomery, and the gardener, Tristan—the men you just met—"

"Let me guess," Veron said. ". . . don't like anklers?"

"Nasty," agreed Nathaniel. "None of them are particularly great at their jobs, but somehow they stay around. They pick on anyone they can."

"Why? I haven't done anything to them."

"Because you're a servant of justice. Because you're tall. Because they don't like your face. Take your pick."

"What's wrong with my face?" Veron asked, faking a scowl and causing Nathaniel to laugh.

"When they pick on someone, it makes them feel like they're better than them . . . I guess," Nathaniel said. "Just don't fight back. They've been known to seek vengeance if someone tries to one-up them."

"Noted. Thanks."

After their buckets were filled to the brim, Veron lifted the yoke to his shoulder. The heavy containers balanced on either side of his body, and they made their way back to the house.

By the time they returned, Veron's shoulders ached from the wooden crosspiece's pressure. They sidled themselves carefully down the basement hallway until they entered the laundry room, where they poured the buckets into the waiting basin. Veron groaned when he noticed the four buckets they emptied barely made a dent.

Veron lost track of how many trips they took. The sun was high in the sky by the time they finished filling up the third basin. Another housekeeper named Enith had already built a fire underneath the first container, while a young woman named Rysalee loaded linens and stirred the water with some sort of cleaning agent.

Veron held his shoulder and lifted his arm in a circular motion while the two walked down the dim hallway.

"Don't worry, it gets easier," Nathaniel said.

Veron shrugged off the fatigue. "It's been a bit since I've carried things on my shoulders, but I'll be fine. What's next?"

"Breakfast. The family will have eaten by now."

Veron sighed with relief. His stomach growled through most of the water carrying, and he felt a bit light-headed.

They returned to the kitchen, and Veron looked for the source of the lingering smell of sausage. His heart sank as Nathaniel led the way to a cook who ladled a scoop of mushy porridge into two bowls and handed them over.

Next to the kitchen, two long tables filled a medium-sized room functioning as the servants' dining room. Several sat, eating and talking, and Veron joined Nathaniel at the table's end.

As they sat, the other servants' conversations grew quieter and they shot furtive glances in their direction. Veron was suddenly keenly aware of the metal anklet, which seemed to increase in weight as the whispers surrounded them.

"The servants eat in shifts based on when they finish their morning chores, but always after the family," Nathaniel said.

"What happened to the sausage?" Veron asked, refusing to give up hope.

Nathaniel laughed. "I'm sure that's long run out. Whatever the family doesn't finish goes to the servants, but that's usually gone by the time the housekeeping crew eats."

Veron hung his head before lifting a spoonful of the porridge. It didn't even steam. The gruel was cold and slimy as it slid down his throat, but he wasn't one to complain.

After breakfast, Veron stretched his shoulders and followed Nathaniel to check in with Tatiana. The portly woman scowled as they approached. "Nathaniel, help Rysalee," Tatiana ordered. "Piles of laundry need to be brought down for cleaning." Nathaniel nodded as she turned to Veron. "I trust you're able to move water on your own now?" She peered forward and lifted her eyebrows, waiting for confirmation.

Veron quickly nodded his head. "Yes, I can."

"The kitchen basins need filling. Once you're done, find Fern. She'll teach you how to scrub the floors and empty the ashboxes."

"Sure, I can do that." Veron almost cringed at the prospect of hauling more water. Instead, he beamed a needless bright smile, as Tatiana had already moved away. He turned back to Nathaniel. "She isn't one for small talk, is she?"

The other servant laughed. "No, she's not. You know what to do?"

"Yeah, I think so."

"It's these basins over here." Nathaniel crossed the room and pointed out two large tubs against the kitchen's far wall.

"Who's Fern?"

"Another housekeeper. She'll probably be around the living quarters on the second floor."

"What does she look like?" Veron asked.

Nathaniel smiled. "It's easy to pick her out. She weighs about as much as a fern. You'll find her on her hands and knees with her hair tied back, scrubbing the floor."

Veron returned to the laundry room and grabbed a bucket yoke to work on the kitchen basins, dreading the shoulder impact. The weather had warmed, and it felt pleasant as he followed the familiar path to the well. When he passed the garden, only the bearded man remained, tending vegetables. Veron ignored him.

While he pulled up buckets of water, some movement drew his attention. Next to the vegetable garden, a flower and plant garden ran alongside the house. The path to the sparring room Veron had followed the previous night meandered next to the vegetable garden and passed the well. Veron's heart beat faster when he recognized the movement's source. Chelci strolled down the path. Her flowing, light-green dress was a marked change from the pants and shabby tunic she sported the previous night. Her long, brown hair bounced behind, matching her face's joy.

"Welcome home, Chelci!" a boisterous voice called from the vegetable garden—the gardener.

Chelci stopped walking and looked toward the bearded man. She half-lifted her hand then nodded before continuing along the path.

"Wait!" he called as he ran to the edge between the two gardens, bringing him closer to Chelci and Veron. She stopped and turned back to the insistent servant.

I thought we couldn't talk with the family? Veron thought.

"You probably don't remember me, but I was here when you left. Tristan's my name."

Chelci shifted her legs and glanced around quickly, as if she wanted to keep walking. She shook her head.

"I wouldn't think you would," Tristan said. "That's okay. You were young then, but wow, how you've grown! You're a woman now."

Veron's blood boiled as the gardener surveyed her, leering at her body. *What a jerk! I should teach him some manners!*

Even though there was plenty of space between the two, Chelci took a hesitant step backward and covered her chest with her arms. Then, seeming to change her mind, she stepped into the garden.

Veron's hand hurt, and he let go of the bucket handle. He hadn't noticed how tightly he gripped it. He couldn't hear their voices as Chelci stopped an arm's length away from the gardener, but Tristan's eyes grew as she spoke. Veron clenched his teeth but stopped as Chelci turned away from Tristan and continued down the path, bringing her closer to him. His heart raced as she gracefully moved and drew near.

Suddenly, her eyes found his, and he sharply inhaled. She caught herself mid-stride. Her face's scowl immediately melted into a grin as she bounced a few steps in his direction.

"Veron! Hi!"

He tried to lower his head out of deference, but her face's magnetic draw refused to allow his eyes to leave hers. He wanted to reply, but the words froze in his throat.

I'm not supposed to talk. But if she's talking to me, it's rude to not respond, right? The gardener didn't hesitate to talk, but it didn't seem to go well for him. Chelci shifted her weight as Veron stared dumbly. *Come on, just say something!*

"Chelci! Chelci, come here, please!" a voice called from the house.

She glanced back at the house before turning back to Veron. "I've got to go, and I know you're working . . . but it's good to see you, Veron. I'm sure I'll see you around." She smiled and waved as she backtracked a few steps before turning toward the house.

"Bye," Veron whispered when she was well out of earshot.

A grin covered his face as he watched her walk away. After a moment, another presence shook him to his senses. Tristan leaned on his shovel from the garden, glaring in his direction. Veron cleared his throat and focused on his buckets.

He didn't know how many trips it took him to fill the basins, but the work felt easy. The entire time his steps were light and the yoke felt soft. He spent the time thinking of Chelci, wishing for another nighttime sparring session.

3

Lessons Learned

After filling the basins and returning the buckets, Veron walked up the stairs in search of Fern. He poked his head into a few open doorways to look for a girl the size of a fern scrubbing floors.

"What do you think, Elliot? Would it work?" asked a voice from inside one of the rooms.

"I'm not sure," another replied. "If they paid estimated taxes for the upcoming season instead of waiting until the end, it would be the same overall amount to the businesses. I don't see why it would be a problem."

Veron peered through the doorway. A large mahogany desk filled most of the room. A window to the side lit up the space with a small bookshelf and a safe against the back wall. The richly-dressed man sitting behind the desk was surely High Lord Marlow. Which made the man sitting opposite him Elliot, his wardman.

"I'm sorry, but are you thinking of having businesses pay taxes at the beginning of each season instead of the end?" Veron blurted before covering his mouth with his hand. "I'm so sorry. I shouldn't have spoken," he mumbled with wide eyes as he backed away.

"Wait, hold on," Marlow said, holding a hand out. "Who are you?"

Veron tentatively stepped back to the door frame. "I'm a new servant. I just started yesterday. I forgot we weren't supposed to speak to the family."

"Do you have thoughts on the issue?"

Veron glanced at the wardman, whose nostrils flared and eyes bored a hole into him. "How would they know how much to pay?" Veron asked, turning back to the high lord.

"It would be estimated by their sales from the previous season."

"What if they ended up over or under?"

"They'd make up the difference or take it off the next season's payment."

"What about businesses just starting?"

Marlow cocked his head. "What about them?"

"Would they get a pass their first season? Or would they double up at the end of that period? Or would you estimate it based on the size of their license fee?"

Marlow leaned back in his chair and whistled. "I hadn't thought that through yet. Those are good ideas, though," the high lord said. Veron pursed his lips, and Marlow raised an eyebrow. "What is it?"

"It wouldn't work," Veron said.

Elliot spoke up. "Excuse me, but who do you think you are—"

"Elliot, it's okay," Marlow said, raising a hand to quiet his wardman before turning back to Veron. "What wouldn't work? Why not?"

"I'm sorry," Veron said. "He's right. It's not my place to say."

"I insist . . . Please."

Veron bit the side of his lip. "You'd end up shutting down a lot of businesses . . . leading to fewer taxes."

Marlow raised an eyebrow. "How so?"

"Most businesses barely scrape by. They sell all season and set money aside as they go. If they had to pay an estimated tax before the season's sales, they couldn't. Plus, most new businesses struggle for the first year. If you required a prepayment when they started or a doubling up after their first season, it would likely shut them down."

"And you're a . . . *housekeeper* here?" Marlow asked. Veron nodded. A faint look of approval crept over the high lord's face. "Your concerns are the same ones I'm wrestling with—generating income for the city without jeopardizing its people. I'm simply exploring our options."

"If you *really* wanted to bring money in quicker, consider having mid-season payments from the sales so far. That wouldn't hurt the average man as much as prepayments."

Marlow raised an eyebrow and nodded slowly. "I hadn't considered that."

"But, it would still cost. You'd have to hire more workers to handle the extra tax processing. Plus, it would be more work for business owners, so it could create some unhappy Feldorians. I'm not sure the benefit would be worth it."

"Those are interesting thoughts. Thank you for your input," Marlow said, lowering his head to the papers on his desk.

Sensing he was dismissed, Veron glanced down the hall and took a step away. He bowed his head curtly toward the high lord and left the office.

From there, Veron's search to find Fern was short and easy. He turned the corner, revealing a long hall with wooden floors. He spotted the thin, short girl with her hair pulled back at the far end on her knees, scrubbing.

"You must be Fern," Veron said as he approached from behind.

The housekeeper stopped her scrubbing and looked back to Veron. She was younger than him by several years and didn't reply as he stood over her.

"I'm supposed to help you clean the floors and the ashboxes . . . I think."

The girl blinked several times before she pulled another brush from the bottom of her bucket. She let it drip for several seconds before handing it to Veron then turned her attention back to the floors.

"I guess I can just follow your example?" Veron crouched down next to her. The damp sheen and lack of dirt ahead confirmed the clean areas of the hall. The floors behind them still needed work.

He mimicked her, scrubbing the floors and rinsing the brush in the bucket. When the water grew too dirty, they dumped it outside and filled it fresh from the well—a task at which Veron was quite adept. It took hours, but they eventually scrubbed all the upstairs halls. Veron's already sore shoulders ached even more, and his knees joined with objections of their own. Fern never complained. She never even spoke. At first, Veron thought her silence odd but soon grew comfortable with the quiet.

When they finished the floors, they returned the scrubbing tools to the basement storage room. Fern had Veron carry the ashbox bin while they toured the house, cleaning out each of the nine fireplaces. The work was simple. Veron held the bin, and Fern shoveled out the ashes using a small, flat scoop.

As they entered the last room, just past the breakfast area, Veron's jaw dropped. Bookshelves stuffed with leather-bound works lined every wall of an enormous library. A spiral staircase wound up to a second floor where a balcony circled the room with another layer of shelves. Rich wooden tables and comfortable-looking chairs dotted the room. Veron's heart ached with desire toward the available knowledge just waiting for someone to discover.

The fireplace in the center of the room contained a full ashbox. Fern scooped while Veron held the bin and gawked at the space.

"Fern!" Tatiana called from the doorway to the library, causing Veron to jump. "You're needed downstairs. Veron, finish up on your own. Dump that in the chute, and be quick about it. You're needed downstairs."

"Sure," Veron said as Fern handed him the scoop. He watched as she walked silently to the door, her head looking down at the floor.

After she left, Veron finished shoveling out the ash. The bin was nearly full, but it was the last fireplace. *So, where is this chute?* He hadn't seen one in the house. *Maybe I could just dump it outside?*

Veron picked up the cumbersome, heavy bin. He made his way through the house and leaned on the back door, pushing it open with his body. Outside to the left were the walking paths among the plants, and straight ahead was the vegetable garden. Veron remembered a brushy area just past the well where he should be able to dump the ash. He waddled down the patio steps and made his way toward the well.

As he struggled down the path, the bearded man in the garden caught his eye, leaning on his shovel and staring. An uncomfortable warmth crept up Veron's neck. He tried to ignore the man, but eventually slowed and turned to him.

"Tristan, right?" Veron asked, eliciting no response from the gardener. "I'm not sure if I've done something to offend you, but . . . I'm just here trying to work."

"No, there's been no offense," Tristan said after a moment's pause, leaning his head back and staring down his nose. "We're all here just trying to work. Some of us have simply been here longer than others," he sneered.

"You wouldn't happen to know where the chute is, would you?" Veron asked.

Tristan scoffed. "Why should I tell you?"

"I could use help from someone experienced like you who's been around much longer than me. I barely even know how to find the kitchen." Veron laughed at himself, and Tristan softened a bit. "This is an impressive garden by the way. How long have you worked it?"

Tristan adjusted his stance, appearing surprised by the question. "Um . . . around four years. It used to be smaller, actually. I added those rows over there last year."

"Nice. Well, if you ever need a hand, let me know. I did some gardening a few years back and would be happy to help."

Tristan kicked at the dirt for a moment while Veron adjusted the bulky bin on his hip. "Well, you won't find the chute here in the garden," Tristan said. He pointed his head back toward the house. "Second floor. First door at the top of the east stairs."

A grin formed on Veron's face. "Thank you! I really appreciate it!" He turned to shuffle back along the path to the house. *Maybe the servants won't be bad after all?* His thoughts turned to Tatiana telling him to be quick about his job. The detour to the garden didn't help, so he hurried back to the house.

Sweat covered his forehead as he exited the second-floor staircase, struggling under the bin's weight. He paused outside the door Tristan indicated and leaned against it. He considered placing the bin on the floor, but it was bulky and would be difficult to pick back up. Holding it between his left arm and hip, he used his right to try the knob, but it felt stuck. He pushed with his legs as he pressed his shoulder against the door. It was solid. He pushed a little harder and wrenched on the knob.

Distant voices came up the staircase. *Come on, Veron. It's your first day. Get this done. Don't start on a bad foot!*

Feeling more desperate, he readjusted the ash bin, granting him more ability to push. He brought his body back a step and lunged at the door with his shoulder while pulling on the knob. As his body struck the wood, the knob suddenly turned, and the solid barrier gave way. The door's opposing force had completely disappeared as someone from the other side opened it.

Veron's stomach lurched as his legs stumbled hopelessly into the room. He desperately tried not to fall as he balanced the heavy, precarious bin of ashes. After several haphazard steps and careening off unseen furniture pieces, gravity won. His body spectacularly fell to the floor, limbs flailing while the ash bin bounced into the air, upending its contents.

As he tried to locate the flying object, a heavy pile of soot blanketed his face and most of his body. The sound of scraping furniture filled the room along with the crash of the metal bin hitting the floor. Veron turned his head and spat a mouthful of ash, sending him into a coughing fit as he struggled to take in air. When the coughing calmed, he made his way to his knees and wiped the ash off his face and eyes. Finally able to see again, he looked up, terrified to take in the scene.

Back at the door, frozen with her hand on the knob, stood the wardess, Violetta, the lady of the house's personal companion Nathaniel had earlier pointed out. Her eyes were wide, and she covered her mouth with a hand. She stared at Veron for a long moment until she finally moved her eyes up, staring at something past him.

He swallowed hard, not wanting to know what she looked at. Unable to avoid it, a turn of his head revealed the worst thing he could imagine. Lady Luciana, the cold, demanding lady of the house, stood just past him, unmoving. She stood in a tub with a towel wrapped around her and water dripping from her body. Ash covered the towel and her bare arms, legs, and shoulders. Behind the gray and black residue on her face, her eyes burned like fire as she stared at Veron. Invisible behind his own sheen of ash, Veron's face paled as his blood drained.

Two guards held Veron's arms as they marched him out the back door, while Tessa, the house steward, followed with a scowl. Veron reeled from what just happened. His shoes felt lead-lined, each step jarring his body. Around him, a crowd of servants followed, whispering at a distance while his vision spun.

"What were you thinking, busting into the washing chamber uninvited?" Tessa shouted as she marched in a lively manner to keep up. "And with a bin of ashes! You must be mad!"

"I didn't mean to spill everything," Veron insisted, talking over his shoulder. "I was just taking the ashes there like the gardener told me."

"Wait!" Tessa called to the guards, halting them on the back patio. She stepped around to speak directly to his face. "Tristan? He *told* you to take ashes into the washing chamber while Lady Luciana was bathing?" A murmur grew in the crowd.

"Well, not exactly. He—" Veron stopped as he noticed Tristan approach, carrying his shovel. "Ask him!" Veron said, gesturing with his chin toward the man in the back of the crowd.

"I did no such thing," Tristan said with a firm voice. Veron's stomach turned at the gardener's lie. "He asked me for help because it's his first day, and I told him to put the ashes in the chute . . . on the ground floor, just past the library. He inquired where the bathing chamber was because he said it would be funny to dump the ashes in there or some such foolishness. I told him he was mad and he should keep his head down and just do his job, but he didn't want to listen."

"That's right," another man added. Veron recognized him as one of the landscapers from that morning. "Montgomery and I were both there and heard it all, weren't we?" he said to the other man at his side.

"Yeah, Tristan's right," the other man said. "James and I both saw it. The boy had a crazed look in his eyes too, like something wasn't right."

"That's not true! They're all lying!" Veron struggled against the arms holding him. He felt the wideness of his eyes and realized he played right into their story.

"Enough of this," Tessa said, silencing them all before turning back to Veron. "If you weren't a servant of justice, we'd fire you for this. Since you are, you'll receive ten lashes and bread and water rations for a week."

Veron's stomach dropped, and the sound of the crowd faded to a dull roar. He glanced frantically amongst the servants, but they averted their eyes. His search for help found Tristan, Montgomery, and James staring from the back of the crowd, wicked smirks on their faces. Veron ground his teeth.

The guards pulled on his arms, leading him along. It was only twenty or so steps to the side of the house, but it seemed like an eternity. Veron felt his pulse in his ears and heard his ragged breath. The crowd followed but didn't speak for him. He hung his head, resigned to his fate.

When the guards halted, Veron looked up to find the whipping post standing ominously before him. His heart quickened. Strips of dull-gray flecked the post—blood faded by sun and time. The guards took off his ash-covered shirt before they lashed his arms around the post, exposing his bare back to the growing crowd behind. A cold wind blew over his skin, but the fear pumping through his body kept him from shivering. His face pressed against the rough wood, scratching his cheek.

Nathaniel arrived in the back of the crowd, face aghast. An instant of hope filled Veron until he realized the truth. *He can't do anything about it.*

Behind him, steps shuffled as if people backed up to create space. A low whistle hummed in the air, and Veron imagined the guard preparing a whip. The scent of ash and rotting wood filled his nose as sweat dripped into his eyes.

I could use the origine right about now, he thought, frustrated he hadn't been able to use the ability since he fought Bale's men in Karad.

Veron focused his body, attempting to tap into the energy source. He cleared his mind and flexed his stomach in the hope of the warm, tingling feeling returning, but nothing came.

Crack!

Pain seared his body as if someone stabbed him with a burning poker, dragging a reluctant yell from his throat. His nerve endings lit up as his body writhed against the post. He instinctively tried to pull his arms free to protect himself, but the lashings were too tight.

Crack!

The agony returned, somehow even more excruciating, and he again yelled. Veron desperately tried to focus his mind to find the origine, but the act was futile.

Crack!

The lashes continued one after another. Veron's mind soon became fuzzy, and his body ceased its fruitless attempt to escape. He longed to sleep—to avoid the torment, but the pain continued.

As he waited, enduring blow after blow, they finally stopped. Gradually, he loosened his clenched fists. The guards untied him, and his body fell off the post, held up by the men's rough hands under his arms. Veron couldn't feel it. His back, shoulders, and arms were completely numb, and his vision spun. The residue of pain lingered, but the agony was only a whisper of what it once was.

The guards helped Veron walk inside. His legs wouldn't cooperate. His feet caught on stones, and he would have fallen if not for the support. The two men practically carried him upstairs and led him back to his room where they dropped him unceremoniously on his bed, chest down.

As soon as they left, Fern entered the cramped space and knelt by the bed. Veron was barely aware of her presence as she wrung out a rag and used it on his back. The initial numbness had faded, and the debilitating agony quickly returned. He fought against the need to writhe and lash out against the pain. Thankful to not see the extent of his injuries, he watched her face. Her lips were tight, but she moved purposefully. *She's dealt with injuries like this before.*

Fern dabbed from near his shoulders down to his lower back, continually rinsing the cloth in the bucket while the water grew increasingly red. "I'm sorry," she said in a quiet voice. "I should have told you where to take the ashes."

The shock of her talking momentarily distracted him from the pain, but it didn't last long. He mumbled it wasn't her fault, but he could barely focus on his words.

"Someone will bring you bread and water this week, but they won't allow anything more—not that you'd be able to eat it anyway. After that, all your meals will be up here the following couple of weeks while you continue to heal."

Veron shuddered as he drew in ragged breaths, fighting against the pain. Tears filled his eyes, but he refused to give in.

After dabbing his back one more time, Fern stood and moved to leave. "That should keep the wounds clean, but unfortunately, it won't do anything for the pain. Again, I'm sorry."

Veron tried to mutter any words of appreciation, but he didn't have the strength.

After she closed the door, he lay on his bed for what seemed like an eternity. He longed to rest, but the throbbing pain refused to allow it. *This wasn't how I wanted to start,* he thought as his hand wiped the tears away.

Veron breathed several deep breaths in and out. He tried to ignore the pain, thinking about what he wanted to do and who he wanted to be as a servant. He thought about his body, how broken it was. The memory of his friends at the Karad market filled his mind. He thought of Brixton, who betrayed him along with the three men from the garden. Finally, he pictured Edmund Bale, wherever he was, and how he still had a destiny to fulfill in defeating him.

The pain flared in his back, but he didn't fight it. He focused and cleared his mind. Soon, his heart leaped as he noticed something—a warm, tingling feeling.

Is that it? Am I doing it?

Something was wrong. The feeling was faint, as if he'd swallowed a spoonful of soup and it only teased his body with comfort. He tried to use the origine and pull the energy from inside to heal his back, but something fought against him. He pulled harder. The tingling grew along with his hopes, but it threatened to slip away.

Why is it so hard? What's wrong?

Straining from the effort, his back prickled as deep cuts slowly healed, but it took all of his strength to hold on to the origine and direct the energy into his recovery. His breathing labored, and his forehead dripped with sweat. His energy drained, though he felt like he'd barely accomplished anything. Veron pulled from his core, using everything that remained. The cuts slowly mended until his energy was suddenly and entirely gone.

Veron's muscles collapsed. His exhaustion was complete, and he couldn't move. Before he closed his eyes, a sound drew his attention. He flicked his eyes and could barely see the floor in front of the door. A small, folded note rested there. He wanted to get up and read it but lacked the strength. Veron sank into his bed and was soon fast asleep.

4

Getting Reacquainted

Sunlight streamed into Chelci's room as someone flung open the window curtains. She covered her face with her arm, groaning in complaint of the sudden intrusion.

"It's time to get up, Chelci," her mother said as she flicked open the second pair of curtains. "Breakfast will be ready shortly, and you need to get dressed."

Chelci threw off the covers and rubbed her eyes before sitting up.

"Jensen picked up a couple of dresses for you. They're in the wardrobe. You'll need to shop to get more though." Luciana looked at Chelci, stared at her hair, and raised an eyebrow. "Now that you're home, we need to make sure you look presentable."

Chelci didn't feel like arguing—at least not yet. She arrived home the day before and had already told her mother of her expectations. She needed to make sure her mother didn't slip back into old habits, but she was too tired at the moment.

She had been up late the night before, visiting the sparring room. Her thoughts returned to Veron, the servant who had shown up and practiced with her. It was invigorating training with someone so skilled . . . and also so young and handsome. She hoped they could practice again soon.

After her mother left the room and closed the door, Chelci collapsed back onto the bed. The soft, warm luxury was foreign and strange. While she enjoyed the comfort, it was partially regrettable. Her old, lumpy bed back in Nasco was not comfortable, but she missed Russell and Nevi.

Chelci stood and walked to the wardrobe. Two new dresses hung from a rack—one bright yellow and the other deep blue. She skipped them and chose a third one—the light-green dress made by Nevi in Nasco she had worn the last few days. Looking past the smudges of dirt on the hem and loose threads around the collar, she smiled at its sight.

After dressing, Chelci stopped in front of her room's mirror—a rarity in Nasco. She had grown the last six years. No longer a child, she was an eighteen-year-old woman. Sharper lines framed her face, and her neck was long and slim. Her chest filled out the dress—a feature most women in the bustling capital city tried to emphasize. The thought of doing so herself brought a flush to her face.

A brand-new brush and comb sat on a small table below the mirror. She picked up the brush, which reminded her of the one she lost in the woods many years before. Looking back at her reflection, she lightly chuckled as she took in her hair's state. The long, brown strands fell haphazardly to her shoulders, reflecting the "who cares" attitude she'd held toward it over the last few years. She ran the brush through her hair and winced as she tugged at the tangles. After a few strokes, she gave up and pulled it back with a hair tie. Chelci smiled at her reflection before leaving her room.

After making her way down the stairs, Chelci followed the smell of food to the breakfast room. Her parents already sat as servants bustled around, delivering platters of eggs, sausage, cooked potatoes, fruit, and pastries. Her mouth dropped as she eyed the food. She didn't have to prepare anything. Dozens of people had been awake for hours, cooking and preparing her meal—a fact not lost on her.

"Chelci! Good morning," her father said as he stood to greet her with a hug.

The warm embrace brought her back from the food's paralyzing effect. She returned his hug, relishing his kindness and love. Her mother made no move to greet her but continued eating fresh tarrols with a fork.

"How did you sleep?" he asked as she took a seat at an empty chair next to him.

"Great—well mostly. The bed is a lot softer than what I'm used to, but it was fine." Chelci covered her mouth with her hand as she yawned.

Her mother stopped eating as she eyed her from across the table. "I would think after sleeping so late, you wouldn't wake up tired."

"Luciana, please," her father said. "She had a long trip to get here. I'm sure she needed the extra rest to recover."

Chelci was quiet. She wouldn't admit her late-night sword-fighting with the servant left her tired.

"Why are you wearing that rag instead of the new dresses we bought?" her mother asked.

Chelci's posture shrank a bit as her face turned red. "I like this dress. Someone made it for me."

"Well, um . . ." Luciana glanced briefly at Darcius. "I don't care how you got it. It's dirty, and the fabric is cheap. You can't wear things like that in Felting. After breakfast, you're to change. I will not have my daughter looking like a street urchin."

Chelci's anger slowly burned. *It's just like before. Why did I come back for this?* She recalled the feeling from the day before when she stood up to her mother. After taking a deep breath, Chelci sat up tall and looked her mother in the eyes. "No."

The response was calm and measured, but her mother's reaction was clear. The older woman's eyes grew wide as she breathed in quickly.

Chelci continued. "I like this dress. I won't wear it every day, but I will wear it. It may have frayed ends and some smudges that don't come out, but I'm alright with that. There are more important things than having the most fashionable dress."

Luciana stared for a long moment, her lips pursed together and askew. "Fine," she said after a moment, averting her eyes to return to the food.

Darcius leaned into her shoulder. "I think it looks nice," he whispered, giving a wink. Luciana's fork clanked against her plate as she glared at him.

Chelci stifled a grin and turned her attention to the food. After much deliberation, she selected a glazed, spiral-shaped pastry. It was warm and tasted like honey and nuts. As she chewed, she looked at her father. "How have things been?"

Darcius swallowed a mouthful of sausage as he turned to her. "It's been interesting recently. Did you hear about Bale's attack on Karad last week?" Chelci shook her head as her father continued. "Edmund Bale, the king of Norshewa, led his army to Karad and attacked last week. He killed Baron Rycroft and would have taken control of the city if not for Lords Fiero and Billings who stopped him with Karad's army."

Chelci's eyes widened. "That's awful."

Her father nodded his head. "King Wesley selected Raynor Fiero as the new baron, and there have been no more signs of Bale."

"Where's he now? Did his army return to Norshewa?"

"I haven't heard. I don't think anyone knows yet."

"What if he comes to Felting?"

"Let's hope that doesn't happen. But if they couldn't defeat Karad's army, I think we're safe here." He took another bite of sausage before continuing. "As far as the commerce work goes, it's been mostly uneventful. We do need to choose a new Lord of Commerce in Karad. I've been exchanging messages with Fiero about it. What about you, Chelci? Now that you're back, did you have any thoughts on what comes next?"

"She needs to get married. That's what comes next," Luciana said.

Chelci dropped her fork and turned to her mother. "What?"

"Oh, don't be naïve. You know you have to get married."

Chelci hadn't given marriage a lot of thought. She knew she probably would one day but didn't think it would be soon. "I—I don't want to be forced into marrying someone I don't like."

Her mother tilted her head. "Think about it, Chelci. You're eighteen years old. What are you going to do? You can't go around climbing trees and playing with your friends forever. And you can't live here, doing nothing. You need to find a promising suitor and get married, so you can have purpose in your life."

Chelci adjusted in her seat. She didn't know what she wanted to do, but marriage wasn't the only way she could have purpose. "You will *not* force me into marrying someone I don't like."

Luciana glared back at her, seething across the table. "Fine, but you *will* meet with suitors if we arrange it." Her mother tilted her head forward as if she expected an answer.

As much as Chelci wanted to fight back, the request was not unreasonable. "Sure, I can do that," she said. Her mother smirked. Chelci grew eager to change the subject. "So, Jackson's in the army now? I thought you always said he would never do that?"

Her father exchanged a knowing look with her mother. "Yes, well . . . he made his desires known after he graduated from King's Academy."

"The *friends* he made there convinced him to join. He's off in

Karondir—apparently a captain now," her mother added with a look of distaste.

An awkward, thick silence followed, so Chelci stood and picked up her used plate and utensils. "Father, are you finished with yours?" she said as she reached out toward his empty plate. Her mother audibly gasped across the table, and her father froze, looking at her with a raised eyebrow.

"What do you think you're doing?" Luciana asked.

Chelci shrugged. "I'm done, so I'm clearing my dishes." She added her father's plate to hers and turned to leave the room. Servants stationed by the door looked at each other, appearing unsure. She walked past, leaving behind her parents' shocked expressions.

After walking down the hall, she descended the spiral stairs leading to the kitchen. Cooks and servers quizzically stared at her as she placed the dishes next to the cleaning basin.

"Corbus, isn't it?" Chelci said to the portly man, frozen with a large bowl of chopped greens.

"Yes," the head chef replied without moving.

"Breakfast was great. I especially enjoyed the pastries. Did you make them?"

The man stared for a moment before speaking. "Um . . . Yes, I did. I'm glad you liked them."

Chelci spent much of the morning exploring the house, becoming reacquainted with old servants. Paloma, the cook, had always been nice to her. Enith, the housekeeper, gave her an enormous hug when they met. Chelci wandered through the library with a newfound respect and excitement for its books. She anticipated spending long hours there.

After walking the house, she went outside, eager to stroll through the plant garden. As a girl, it was one of her favorite places. Walking along the meandering path, the impressive limbs and colorful leaves of her sugar maple tree filled the sky at the far end. She smiled at the sight, thinking of her childhood days climbing the branches.

"Welcome home, Chelci!"

She turned toward the voice where a man hailed her from the vegetable garden. She had a vague memory of him, and it wasn't positive. She politely nodded her head and partially waved before continuing.

"Wait!" the man said.

He's not supposed to be talking with me unless I address him. I guess it doesn't hurt to be friendly, though. She stopped and turned to face him.

"You probably don't remember me, but I was here when you left. Tristan's my name."

She shook her head, pretending she didn't remember.

"I wouldn't think you would. That's okay. You were young then, but wow, how you've grown! You're a woman now." His eyes dropped and lingered as he leered at the rest of her body.

Blood rushed to her face as she stepped back and folded her arms to cover herself. Her jaw clenched as she breathed in deeply. *He is not going to treat me like this.* She stomped through the dirt to approach. The gardener's eyes widened the closer she got.

"I do remember you, Tristan." Her low voice had a rough edge as she leaned toward him. "You're the reason my favorite server, Naomi, quit years ago."

"But . . . I didn't make her—"

". . . because she was uncomfortable around you," Chelci added, silencing the gardener while narrowing her eyes. "I'm willing to overlook that crude glance this once . . . but if I ever catch you looking at me or anyone else in this house like that again, I assure you it will be the last time." The gardener didn't respond but only stared in shock. Chelci turned away and smirked as she left the garden.

While she continued along the path, another servant drawing water from the well caught her eye. She stopped mid-step as she realized who it was. "Veron! Hi!" The gardener disappeared from her mind as she broke into a spirited grin and stepped jauntily in the new servant's direction. The young man offered a shy wave and a half bow.

Her legs felt weak as she looked him in the eyes. The memory of clashing swords and sweating the night before made her heart beat quickly.

Why isn't he saying anything? Is he afraid of me or something? He continued to stare back, looking as if he wanted to say something.

"Chelci!" She turned to the house. It was her father. "Chelci, come here, please!"

She looked back at Veron. "I've got to go, and I know you're working . . . but it's good to see you. I'm sure I'll see you around."

As she walked back toward the house, a smile covered her face. She looked forward to sword fighting with him again soon.

"I have something for you," Darcius said with a grin as Chelci entered the sitting room. His eyes lit up as he handed her a small box.

"What's this?" she asked, shaking it gently.

"I'm so glad to have you home. I wanted to get you something to remember your homecoming."

The corners of her mouth turned up. She lifted the lid, and a sparkling, gold necklace with a small, gold heart fastened in the middle reflected the sun's rays. "Oh, Father! It's lovely! You didn't have to!"

"Here, let me help." Darcius lifted the necklace and walked behind her where he fastened the links.

Chelci beamed as she pressed the necklace against her chest. "Thank you, Father." She wrapped her arms around him, pulling him into a great hug. As she held him, regret washed over her, tugging on her heart. She pulled away slowly and lowered her head. "I'm sorry, Father."

"Sorry? About what?"

"About leaving. I . . . I hate that I left you—that I missed all that time."

"Oh, come now. Don't think anything about it. I'm just happy you're back."

"How about Mother?" Chelci asked. "How does she feel?"

Darcius's mouth formed a tight line. "Um . . . You know how she gets. She *is* glad you're back. She simply has a difficult time showing it."

"How are you two?"

"What do you mean?"

"Have you two been . . . okay?"

"Eh," he mumbled with a shrug. "We're here. We're together. I think that's about the best I can hope for."

Chelci sighed, appreciating her father's candor. She knowingly nodded. "Well, I'm glad to be back."

After leaving her father, Chelci found her way to the library. She pulled various books off the shelves, creating a large stack to work through. Up the spiral staircase on the second-floor balcony, she found a warm, leather chair tucked away in the corner. She piled books on the old, wooden table beside it. In the alcove, shelves surrounded her on three sides, completely hiding her from anyone below. The small, round window on the wall provided light from which to read. She propped her feet up on a matching stool as she sank into the soft leather and got to work on her stack, eventually spending much of the day hidden away in the large room.

In the early afternoon, a door opened below, rousing her from the sleep she'd fallen into. She blinked several times and picked up the book resting on her chest. Shuffling feet and the sound of scraping metal prompted her to peek around the bookshelf and over the balcony. Two servants knelt in front of the fireplace and used a flat shovel to empty the ashbox.

The sight reminded her of the six years living in Nasco. She often had to clean out the fireplace in their small, wooden house. *I wonder how Russell and Nevi are doing without me?*

"Fern!" a voice called from below, bringing her attention back to the room. "You're needed downstairs. Veron, you'll have to finish up on your own."

Chelci's breath caught at the name. Down below, he had turned toward the door, the polite smile and shaggy brown hair confirming it was him.

Chelci watched as Veron finished the job alone. He looked around, apparently figuring out what to do next. Chelci wanted to call down but didn't want him to think she was spying on him. She stifled a giggle. *That's what I am doing.* Eventually, Veron picked up the bulky metal bin and left the room.

Chelci returned to her comfortable chair and picked up the book on the lineage of Feldorian kings. A clock on the table next to her ticked the minutes away as she flipped page after page, but she was distracted. *Why do I think so much about that boy?* After several minutes of reading the same passage repeatedly, she gave up.

Carrying her stack of books, she wound through the library, placing the titles back where she had gotten them from. Once finished, she climbed the spiral staircase once more and took the door on the balcony to the estate's second-floor hall.

The house seemed quiet. A window on the left side of the hall looked out on the patio and the gardens. A large gathering of servants caught her eye through the glass. *That's strange. They must have a servants' meeting or something.*

Chelci continued down the hall to her room. Again, she marveled at the luxury of it all. The fine silk curtains probably cost enough to feed several families for an entire year. She opened her wardrobe again to examine the two new dresses. She liked the dress Nevi made, but in truth, she was excited to wear some high-quality clothes again. She took them out one at a time and tried them on to make sure they fit.

Maybe tomorrow I can go shopping with Emma for some new clothes? She looked forward to telling her friend everything about her time in Nasco—the training she went through—making it in the village guard—fighting off wolves and a valcor. *Ha! She'll never believe me about the valcor.* Chelci smirked as she thought about all she had done. *Maybe I'll tell her about practicing with Veron? No, that's silly. There's nothing to tell.*

Chelci sat at her desk and pulled out some paper and a pen with ink. Her note was short and sweet. She didn't even sign her name. Just in case someone found it, she didn't want anyone else to know who it was from. She folded it several times and placed it in her pocket.

Leaving her room, she listened attentively as she approached the eastern staircase. No one was around. She looked over her shoulder one last time before taking the stairs and walking up toward the servants' quarters.

5

Incomplete Practice

Veron's eyes slowly fluttered open. He groaned, anticipating pain as he rolled to his side, but his muscles felt fine. His mind floated in a hazy soup as he struggled to collect threads into a coherent thought. Something nagged at him, but he couldn't identify it.

I was whipped! The thought finally came to him. He'd never been whipped, so he didn't fully know what to expect in the way of healing. He figured there would be more lingering pain. *Didn't Tatiana say something about a servant not walking for two weeks after his lashes?* He rolled his shoulders and sat upright in bed. His body felt stiff, tight with scabs, but there was no pain or soreness. His heart jumped when he saw his sheets, stained with blood in a macabre display.

The origine! He recalled his battle before falling asleep. He used the energy to heal . . . but it was a fight, taking everything he had to make any progress. Still, knowing the origine hadn't completely abandoned him was encouraging.

A faint light entered his room through the small window above the bed. Outside, shadows of limbs swayed in the wind. *It must be around midnight,* he thought, observing the moon's placement.

Something else tugged at his brain, but he couldn't place it. *What am I missing?* Something felt urgent, as if a priority waited for him to act. He looked around the room until his eyes caught a small object on the floor in front of the door. *That's it!*

Veron moved quickly to pick up the note from the floor. Folded several times, the tightly creased paper released a faint scent of flowers as he opened it. His brow creased as he stared at two words on the paper— "Practice Midnight?" He flipped the paper over, expecting more, but the back was blank.

His eyes shot open as he thought of Chelci. *Does she want to meet tonight to practice again?*

His pulse quickened at the thought, and a smile crossed his lips as he stared at the paper. Rolling his shoulders and moving his arms, Veron tested his body to see how it felt. A general fatigue affected him, but there were no sharp stabs of pain or deep feelings of soreness. He slept all afternoon and part of the evening, and he felt good . . . considering.

Veron grabbed a shirt and made his way through the house. A clock in the sitting room on the ground floor confirmed it was thirty minutes past midnight. He cursed, worried he'd missed his chance. As he approached the sparring room at the garden's far end, a faint light gave him hope.

He gingerly pushed open the door to the small building. "Hello?" A lantern hung as it had the night before, but no one appeared to be there. The swords rested on the wall, and silence filled the room. Veron stepped into the middle of the chamber. "Chelci?" His voice was timid, not entirely sure it was her that left the note. A tingling sensation crawled up the back of his neck, stopping his legs and turning his head. "Hello?" he said again as his muscles tensed.

A sudden collision shook his midsection, pushing his body to the ground. He rolled over and looked up to find a backlit shadow holding a sword toward his chest. "Gotcha!" a girlish voice said triumphantly as the sword lowered and a shadowy hand reached out to replace it.

Veron took the hand and allowed himself to be helped up. Chelci's grinning face looked back at him. She wore the same white shirt and brown pants from the night before, her hair pulled back.

"What took you so long? I was about to give up and head in."

Veron dusted off his pant legs. "I'm sorry, I fell asleep and just now found your note."

"You want to practice some more? Like last night?" Her eyes sparkled as she nodded to the swords on the wall.

Veron grinned, unable to contain the excitement of being with her. He wasn't sure he could fight after what he'd been through, but he would give it a shot. He winced as he walked to the swords and reached his arm around past his shoulder. He remembered the feeling of the whip tearing his skin only hours before. Being knocked to the floor had tweaked his back and brought back a residue of pain he hoped to forget.

"Are you okay?" Chelci asked.

Veron held the part of his back he could reach. "Yeah, I'm okay. It's just . . . I injured my back earlier, but I'm fine." He selected a sword and turned to her, standing tall and strong to mask the pain.

Chelci held her sword to the ground as she stared back with narrowed eyes. "An injury from today? What happened?"

"It's nothing. I'm fine. Come on, let's practice." Veron walked to the middle of the room with his back to her.

"You're bleeding!" Chelci yelled.

Oh great, Veron thought. *The floor must have opened up the wound.*

"Here, let me see it."

Before he could protest, she lifted the back of his shirt, and a loud gasp filled the room. Veron looked over his shoulder. Her eyes were wide as she leaned away.

"What happened to you!" she said. It took a moment for her to finally avert her eyes from his back.

"Is it bad?" Veron asked.

"Bad?" Her mouth hung open, and the whites of her eyes shone in the lantern's light. "Were you whipped?"

Veron lowered his head, tearing his eyes from hers. "Yes, I was," he mumbled.

"I'm so sorry. Let me help." She released his shirt and scurried up the ladder to the loft above the room. "Take your shirt off."

"No, it's ok. I'll be fine. You don't need to do anything." Scuffling sounds came from wooden boxes in the darkness above. With a sigh, he raised his shirt and gingerly removed it. Spots of blood dotted the shirt, but it was nothing compared to the sheets on his bed.

After a minute, Chelci lowered herself back to the ground with cloth bandages in her arms. "When I knocked you down, one of your old scars must have torn open. Here, come and sit down." Chelci led him to a bench against the wall and had him sit, facing away from her.

"Really, it's not a big deal," Veron insisted, trying to look over his shoulder. The freshly-branded "24521" caught his eye on his side. Embarrassed of the marking, he tried to hide it with his arm.

"Hold still," Chelci said as she dabbed behind his shoulder. "Hmmph."

Chelci's face screwed up as if deep in thought. "This is strange," she said. "It doesn't seem . . . How old are these scars? A year?" Veron held his breath, unsure of what to say. "It's odd that scars this old would tear open from hitting the floor," she added.

"It was . . . more recent than that," Veron said finally, turning his body to see her better.

"It's too bad I don't have some barkleaf elixir. That would heal these right up. Whoever it was that did it, I'm so sorry. Be careful here though. I know my mother has had servants whipped before. I think it's awful." Veron squirmed. "So, today was your first full day, right?" she asked. "How did it go?"

She rested one hand on his bare side with the cloth and used the other to wrap the strip across his back and over his shoulder, bringing it around his chest. Her cool hand on his skin gave him goosebumps, distracting him from the pain's dull thrum.

"Yeah, it was my first day. I learned how to do things—carry water, scrub floors, clean out ashes."

"I saw you in the library," Chelci said.

"Really?" Veron tried to turn around, but Chelci's firm grip prevented him.

"Yeah, I was reading upstairs when you came in."

"Well, I found out some people here don't like anklers and gave me some bad advice that got me into trouble."

"Anklers?"

"Yeah, apparently, some other servants don't care for us that much," he said as he extended his leg to show off the metal shackle.

She pulled tight on the bandage, sending a jolt of pain through his body and causing him to wince. "Sorry," she said. "That should do it though."

Veron turned around on the bench so they could talk face-to-face again.

"What is that?" Chelci asked, pointing at his leg. "What's an ankler?"

"You know . . . the difference between a servant and a servant of justice?" Veron said, but all Chelci offered in return was a blank stare. "What do you know about the servants here?"

"Not much, I guess. Mother hires them and they work various jobs. Most stay here for many years. Some are the same since I was a little girl."

"I've only just learned this, but apparently, they can sell people in prison. Whoever buys them owns the rights to their labor."

"Like a slave?"

"Right? That's what I said. They're called servants of justice and have to wear a metal anklet like this."

Chelci hesitated before leaning her body away slightly. "So . . . you were in prison?"

Veron exhaled heavily. "Yeah. I guess."

"Why were you there?" Her voice wavered slightly.

"I—" Veron stopped as he remembered Tatiana's warning. *I'm not supposed to talk about my past. I'm actually not supposed to talk with her at all.* He was in enough trouble already with the Marlows and didn't want to risk it further. "I'd rather not talk about it."

Chelci reached out and fingered the medallion and key that hung around his neck. "What's this?"

Instinctively, Veron raised a hand to grasp the memories of his past life as he tensed. "It's nothing. Just . . . things to remember." The silence following felt awkward and reminded him he was still shirtless. Veron held it out. "Do you mind giving me a hand?"

She took the shirt. "Of course. Can you raise your arms?"

Veron lifted them gingerly. His left arm felt tight as it pulled against the fresh bandage. While he leaned forward, Chelci lifted his shirt, guiding it down his body. When her fingers brushed his chest, he felt a tingle and his heart sped up. Clothed again, he adjusted his sleeves.

"So, other servants don't like you because of your metal thing?" Chelci asked.

"I guess not. Apparently, there are four of us here. The gardener, Tristan, is particularly nasty."

"Ugh, I don't like him," Chelci said with a glower.

Veron laughed. "Yeah, that makes two of us." He brushed his shirt and the front of his pants as he stood. "Thanks for patching me up. You ready to spar now?"

"What? No!" Chelci said with a look of horror on her face. "Do you want to open up that wound again?"

Veron searched for a response but couldn't think of anything fitting. The realization that they could talk quickly replaced the disappointment of not getting to train with her.

"Alright, so tell me about yourself," Veron said. "I've never seen a girl use a sword as you do. I've never seen one use a sword at all, actually. What's your story?"

"Me?" Chelci paused for a moment. She picked up the sword leaning next to her and spun it in her hand. She shook her head, appearing conflicted.

"You don't *have* to share if you don't want to," Veron said. "I realize I'm a servant here."

"No, it's not that!" she said quickly. "I feel comfortable talking with you." Veron smiled as she continued. "I ran away when I was twelve and was gone for six years. There's a village in the woods called Nasco where a family took me in. They taught me . . . everything, I guess." She took a few swipes in the air with her blade. "I never got a chance to learn anything real when I lived here before. I trained to be in the Nasco village guard, which is where I learned to use the sword, but eventually, I decided it was time to come home."

"That's incredible," Veron said. "It takes a lot of bravery to run away on your own so young."

"Or a lot of stupidity," Chelci countered, drawing a laugh from Veron. "My mother seems bent on manipulating me, but I'm going to stand up for myself this time."

Veron's thoughts turned to his Dream and what was supposed to happen to her mother. "I met her. She seems . . ." He couldn't think of something to say that wasn't insulting.

"Awful?" Chelci suggested. "Horrible, mean, selfish?"

Despite his effort to stifle it, a small laugh escaped Veron. "I was going to say self-confident. You seem nothing like her."

Chelci tilted her head to the side and raised an eyebrow.

"You seem confident," Veron added quickly. "But not those other attributes you mentioned."

"I don't want to be like her." Chelci looked down at her sword and ran her hand down the flat part of the blade. "I want to be different."

"What do you want, then?" Veron asked as he sat back down. "What do you want from your life?"

A stunned expression covered Chelci's face. "I . . . uh . . . haven't thought about it in a while. When I was younger, I simply wanted to be myself. My mother wouldn't allow it, so I ran away. I finally got the chance to be myself in Nasco. I still want that, but my time there changed me. Now, I think my hope is to make a difference."

Veron stared intently. "What kind of difference?"

Chelci pursed her lips as her eyes drifted down to the side. "I hate the world's inequality. It's not fair I was born in this estate with every opportunity in the world, but someone else is born in a hovel in the Red Quarter. I'm given everything I could ever want while they have to fight to make it day-to-day. Many people are selfish and treat others unkindly, but I want to make other people's lives better. I'm just not sure exactly how."

Veron stared at her, in awe of her words. Everyone of high station he'd known only served their own interests. "You're an amazing girl. I've never met anyone like you before," he said, looking into her eyes.

Chelci's face turned red as she looked away, resting her hand over her chin. "Thanks, so what about you?" she asked after turning back.

"What about me?"

"Yeah. What do you want out of life?"

The question reminded him of the conversation he had with Brixton only a couple of weeks before about his goals, which seemed like a lifetime ago. His eyes drifted to the empty room as he thought through them. He learned how to tap into the origine—although he was having trouble using it. He faced Bale and survived. Paying off the market didn't matter anymore.

He looked at Chelci, a twinkle in his eyes. "I feel I'm destined to do something great. Today, I'm a servant, but that doesn't define me. I'm capable of so much more. I'll do the best I can scrubbing floors and filling tubs, but one day I'll do more. Years ago, I promised a friend I'd make something of my life. I've worked hard to do that for six years, and after all that time, here I am—just a servant. But I promise you I won't be just a servant for long."

Chelci stared back with her mouth askew and head cocked to the side. "I believe you. I have to say, you're not like anyone I've met before, Veron. And selfishly—" She leaned in closer, hunched her shoulders, and sheepishly grinned. "—part of me is hoping you stay for at least a little while."

It was his turn to blush. He smiled as he looked at the wooden plank floor while redness crept over his face. Although embarrassed, he was excited she saw him for who he truly was.

"You probably should get some rest," Chelci said, nodding back toward the house. "That cut should be much better by morning."

"Yeah, I guess so."

"You go first," Chelci said. "It's probably best no one finds us together so late."

Veron said goodnight and returned to his room. As he lay on his bed, he considered how he would explain his healing to the rest of the servants. Also, what would Chelci think when she learned his whipping had been that same day? He didn't have answers to those questions, but he knew one thing—he needed sleep. It had been quite a first day.

6

Petition to Father

Brixton grasped the red velvet hanging from the four-poster bed and rubbed it between his fingers. It was thick, draping from the rails to surround his bed on three sides. He liked his new room, which was twice the size of his old one thanks to his father's promotion. The walls were a deep grey stone. He strolled past rich, wooden furniture to the first of three square windows to gaze outside. Two stories below, the castle's large inner courtyard sprawled with walking paths, rows of plants, and a large tree-shaped fountain at its end. He looked straight ahead, over the castle wall to the city of Karad beyond. The Benevorre river flowed along the crowded city's western border with a protective wall making up the other three sides. Brixton spotted his old house. It stood out from the surrounding buildings by its height and size, though living there was nothing compared to the castle.

He turned back and faced his room with a smile. New clothes filled his wardrobe. A platter of meats and cheeses sat on a side table, brought by a servant an hour before. Even though Brixton had eaten his fill, he barely made a dent. With a full stomach and dressed in a bright blue tunic—freshly made by the in-house tailor—Brixton exited the room. He walked down the stone hallway to take the stairs to the main floor, where his father worked. He had something on his mind he wished to talk about.

When the king promoted his father, Raynor Fiero, to Baron of Karad, their family's station increased dramatically. While Brixton used to walk through the city unnoticed, now—as the baron's son—hushed voices, pointing fingers, and turned heads surrounded him everywhere he went. *All it took was Father aligning with an evil tyrant,* Brixton thought while shaking his head.

Brixton exited the staircase on the ground floor and walked through the sunroom. He didn't know if it had an official name, but that's how their family referred to it. The yellow walls and span of windows gave the room a bright, cheery feeling, but Brixton felt anything but cheer. His stomach turned as he stared at the faint, red stain on the rug by the window. He would avoid the room if he could, but getting through the castle was nearly impossible without passing through it.

Only a week before, everything fell apart in that room. He found his fiancé kissing his best friend. He revealed his plans to extort money from Veron. He stabbed and killed Hailey in a fit of rage. After that night, he tried to convince himself it was all Veron's doing, but he knew he was the one responsible. *Still, it's nothing compared to betraying your country, like Father.*

Brixton breathed deeply as he stared at the rug, trying to tear his eyes from it. He missed Hailey, but even more so . . . he missed Veron's friendship.

"Brixton, good morning!"

His mother's voice snapped him out of his trance as she walked through the room, smiling with two servants at her side. She wore a flowing dress of white and dark green, and her hair formed an elaborate mixture of curls. Since his father's promotion, she put even more effort into her appearance. A majestic glow followed her.

"Hello, Mother. Where are you headed?"

"Mila's coming by shortly. I promised to give her a tour of the castle. Would you like to join us?"

It had been several days since Brixton last saw his sister, but he had other things on his mind at the moment. He shook his head. "Not now. Have you seen Father?"

"Yes. He's in his study. He was looking for you, too. I think he had something to ask."

Brixton's posture snapped straight. "Thanks, I'll go see him." He proceeded down the hall toward the study—where his father spent most of his time since they had moved into the castle. The door was closed when he arrived, so Brixton knocked. The impact on the thick, wooden door resonated in the stone hallway.

"Come in," his father said.

Brixton opened the door to reveal Raynor Fiero poring over a stack of ledgers. "Hello, Father."

"Brixton, sit down," Raynor said without looking up.

He'd seen his father in the same position many times while at the Department of Commerce—same man, same actions—but the surroundings were much different. His desk was large and solid, made completely of warm, rich parthe wood. Four chairs for guests littered the large space. Elaborate scrollwork played over their arms and backs, accenting the plush leather cushions. Walls of faded books surrounded the room, and a few landscape paintings added color to the otherwise dark space.

Unsure if his father would speak, Brixton interrupted the silence. "I hear you were looking for me."

The newly appointed baron set down his pen and looked up. "Yes, I was. As you know, it is the baron's job to select the city's lords."

Brixton's heart skipped a beat as he fought to hold back a grin. That was what he wanted to talk with his father about. He had been head clerk in the Department of Commerce for almost two years. Since his father vacated the role of Lord of Commerce and was in charge of choosing his successor, Brixton felt he was a solid choice.

"I need to choose lords that will lead the city well and support the leadership I provide."

"Yes, Father. That is very important."

"Considering this, I will not be choosing you as Lord of Commerce."

Brixton felt as if the oxygen left the room and someone punched him in the gut. He stared dumbly at his father, his jaw drooping. "But . . . why not, Father?"

"You're too inexperienced for starters. I need someone who knows this city inside and out and has, ideally, worked in the commercial structure longer than you've been alive. Although you've worked hard and improved a lot, you're not capable of leading an organization that important. Plus, as my son, what would people say if I chose you?"

Brixton clenched his jaw as his father rattled off his reasons. "That's not fair!" he shouted as he stood, the chair scraping the floor as he shoved it backward. "If you *don't* choose me because I'm your son, that's showing prejudice *against* me. I should have the same chances as anyone else."

Raynor leaned back and lifted his chin, but he didn't respond.

"I may be young, and I know I don't have ten or twenty years of experience, but I know more about the Department of Commerce than anyone! Since Tucker left, I've handled pretty much all day-to-day office work."

His father rubbed his hand across his chin. His eyes softened a bit.

"And if you're looking for someone to support your vision as baron, you won't find anyone better than me. I've lived with you all my life. You've taught me everything I know, and we've worked together hand-in-hand for years. You say I've improved a lot? That's all due to you! You've molded me to be the man I am with the knowledge and experience I have. I owe it all to you. I'll support whatever your vision is!"

Brixton breathed heavily as he finished his desperate plea. Realizing he leaned aggressively over the desktop, looming over his father, he sank slowly back into the chair.

What surprised him most was his father—known for having a short temper—didn't immediately rage back at him. Brixton was used to having his outbursts met with verbal and physical retribution—a fact he had briefly forgotten in the heat of the moment. But, instead of the expected response, his father's face softened as he looked down at the desk.

Brixton waited as his father sat for a moment. "Please, Father," he added, leaning forward. "I've worked hard for years, and I'm still barely making any money. This would be a tremendous increase for me—the opportunity of a lifetime!"

Raynor gathered himself and looked back in Brixton's eyes. The familiar hardness had returned, strangely eliciting both unease and reassurance in Brixton.

"I would even—" Brixton stopped himself, causing his father to tilt his head. He didn't want to speak the words but worried it might be his only chance. "If you promoted me to the position, I would even be willing to give a portion of my salary back . . . to thank you."

Raynor finally spoke. "How much?"

A lump formed in Brixton's throat. His heart raced with excitement, but it also chafed him that his father would take him up on it. "Maybe . . . twenty percent?"

His father's eyes narrowed. After a moment, he pulled some papers out of his desk and wrote. Brixton's heart beat wildly while the ticking of the clock blended in with the scratching of the pen on paper. After an agonizingly long wait, his father stamped an impression on the paper and handed it to Brixton.

"Very well, Lord of Commerce Fiero," Raynor said with a smirk. "I hope you will make a wise choice selecting your head clerk replacement."

A broad grin covered Brixton's face as he took the paper. "Thank you, Father! I promise I'll make you proud!"

He stared at the paper, a Lordship Proclamation Decree establishing Brixton in the vacant post. He felt warm inside as he read the words, having desired it for years. Hailey laughed when he told her of his aspirations. Now, he would prove he could make something of himself.

Brixton stood to leave but paused as he opened the door. "Father," he said, turning back. Raynor looked up from the desk. "Why did you work with Bale?"

Raynor instantly stood and practically jumped across the room. His hand slammed against the door, closing it with a thunderous boom. Brixton jumped back, shrinking against the bookshelf.

"Never speak of that!" Raynor said as he waved his finger in Brixton's face. He restrained his voice, as if yelling through a whisper.

"I'm sorry," Brixton whimpered. "I didn't think." His body tensed as he held his breath and braced for whatever may come. Raynor breathed heavily. It wasn't until he lowered his hand that Brixton allowed himself to relax.

"Rycroft was a joke. King Wesley is weak. Bale was an opportunity." Raynor backed off. His voice was low, and he wouldn't meet Brixton's eyes. "He was going to set me up as Regent of Felting."

"Did you find out what happened to him or where he went?"

"I don't know. A contingent of soldiers must have fought his men and run him off."

"Do you think he's coming back?" Brixton asked.

Raynor exhaled heavily. "Either they returned to Norshewa or they're hiding somewhere in the woods. I don't know what he's going to do."

"Wouldn't someone notice thousands of soldiers camped in the woods?"

"Not if they're deep enough. The trees are all but impenetrable as you near the Kyrd Forest. It's twisted and overgrown. No one would find them there."

Murdering the baron was wrong, but Brixton had just killed his fiance for liking someone else, so he had little room to judge. At the same time, he respected his father's move—how he saw the opportunity and took it. "Well, if he returns and you need help in any way . . . let me know. You will have my support." He looked his father in the eye, who nodded as he stepped out of the way.

Brixton exited the study and closed the door. Alone again, he leaned against the wall. Only then did he realize his arm trembled. He held it against his chest as he exhaled a long breath, gradually calming down. The folded paper in his hand caught his eye, and a broad grin covered his face. *Brixton Fiero, Lord of Commerce. Let's see what people think of me now.*

$$7$$

Return to Commerce

Brixton stood out in his bright-blue outfit as he walked down Dock Street. Everyone he passed wore faded, torn clothing. Watching his step, he used a cloth to cover his nose against the offending smells of the city's poor area. He turned down an alley and checked the sheet of paper in his pocket. After a short walk down the damp, narrow lane, he stopped in front of a dingy doorway and knocked. A bout of coughing sounded behind the door before the hinges creaked open, revealing an emaciated Tucker Waystone.

Brixton's ex-coworker had once been robust and healthy with weight to spare. He had been friendly to Brixton since he was a boy, but now his eyes' sockets seemed hollow and his shoulders drooped. Thin clothing hung loosely on his frame, matching his sagging skin.

"Tucker?" Brixton said, unable to restrain his shocked look at the man's appearance.

Tucker forced a smile, but it stopped halfway formed. "Brixton? What are you doing here?"

The newly appointed Lord of Commerce suddenly felt out of place. He was now in charge of one of the city's most important institutions and lived in a castle. He wanted for nothing but still felt inferior around the previous head clerk. Tucker looked like a shadow of his former self, but all Brixton saw was the hard-working, intelligent, and capable man he once knew. *The man I tricked Father into firing, so I could take his place.* He shuddered inside but kept his face from giving his feelings away.

"I came to find you. How are you doing?" Brixton asked, realizing late that his pleasantries rang hollow.

Tucker hung his head. "It's been a rough last three seasons. I spent a year in prison before they released me. When I got out, I tried to find a job keeping up ledgers for the shipping companies at the docks. I volunteered my work for a few weeks to get started, but when it became apparent they never intended to pay me, I looked elsewhere. I did some odd jobs—cleaning stalls at the stables, making deliveries for an apothecary. Eventually, I ended up laboring at the docks. My older son was going to work as well, but he caught the blue fever his first week on the job." His voice caught as he covered his face. "He didn't recover."

The older man's words barely registered by the time Brixton had moved on. "That's too bad. How would you like your old job back?"

Tucker wiped his eyes and stared at Brixton as his mouth fell. "What do you mean? Your father wants me back? Did he finally realize I didn't mess up those reports or steal money?" His jaw tightened as his words developed a sharp edge.

"Uh . . . No, he's not the Lord of Commerce anymore."

Tucker's eyes widened. "What happened? Was he the one taking the money all along? Was he caught?"

Brixton shifted his weight to his other leg and fiddled with his tunic's hem. He cleared his throat to halt the dryness. "No, it's nothing like that. He . . . um . . . he's the new Baron of Karad after Rycroft's death."

The man's eyes somehow grew even wider, and he took a step

backward.

"And . . . he's appointed me Lord of Commerce to replace him."

Tucker narrowed his gaze and stared. Brixton swallowed and stood uncomfortably.

"Congratulations," Tucker said, finally. He extended his hand, yet his eyes did not match the well wishes.

"Thanks. Since I'm in charge, I get to decide who to hire for my old position. Heath's been there for years, but he doesn't have your experience and skill. Andrion's too young. I'd like to hire you back as head clerk, Tucker."

The gaunt man breathed deeply then exhaled, melting into a warm smile. He lunged forward and wrapped his bony arms around Brixton, dropping tears onto his shoulder.

"Thank you, Brixton!" he jubilantly exclaimed. "I promise I'll work hard. I won't have even a hint of foul play!"

Brixton stared hard at the man. "See that you don't." He knew Tucker would be a good worker but needed to appear suspicious. "I'll see you tomorrow morning," Brixton said as he backed away from the house. He smirked at the irony as he walked down the dirty alley, leaving the broken man to revel in appreciation toward the very man who put him in his dire situation.

* * *

Brixton stopped with his hand on the doorknob and a flutter in his stomach. He had changed outfits twice that morning, wanting to look his best on his first day as a lord. He started as a mere clerk only two years before, knowing very little about how things worked—despite his father's attempts to teach him. Now, he was in charge and expected to run the department. The task felt daunting, especially considering many of the workers under him had more knowledge and experience.

He first saw Tucker, sitting in a chair inside the entry of the Department of Commerce. "Good morning, Lord Fiero," he said as he stood with an eager expression.

Brixton nodded as he looked around the office. Andrion sat at his desk in the back corner, keeping his head down, pretending to work.

Heath stood from his desk—where he had been for eight years—with his hands on his hips. "Is it true?" He glared between Brixton and Tucker.

Brixton pulled a folded piece of paper from his cloak and walked across the office, extending it to the clerk. Heath grabbed it and read, mumbling select parts. Finally, ending with a huff, he handed the paper back to Brixton.

"And you've brought *him* back? The thief? You think he's a better choice for head clerk than someone who has worked here without blemish for eight years?"

Heath's argument was solid, but he didn't know the truth. "It's my choice," Brixton said, standing tall and stepping in close. "If you decide you can't work under these conditions, let me know. I'm sure I can make other arrangements."

He had no intention of firing Heath, who was also a good worker. Brixton needed him to keep the office operating smoothly. He hoped Heath would cower under the threat, establishing his position of authority as lord of the department. Instead, the older clerk laughed in his face.

"You want to threaten me? Fire me? Go ahead. I'd love to see your father's face when this department runs into the ground. We all know you can't manage it without me and that you only got the job because of your last name."

Brixton's face flushed, and his shoulders shrank as he backed off. Heath was right. He fumbled for the door to the back office—*his* office. "Show Tucker to his desk," he mumbled to no one in particular before retreating into the other room and closing the door behind him.

Brixton sighed as he sank into his father's old leather chair. Inside, he ached, like his chest was being squeezed slowly. He would never admit it to anyone—especially his father—but he didn't feel qualified.

Voices outside his office drew Brixton's attention, rustling him out of the sleep he had drifted into. An open ledger of historical price stipulations rested on the desk. He had been studying anything he could, but the dry subject and maze of numbers had a soporific effect. He wiped his hand across the small drool mark staining the page.

"Thank you, Tucker. I assure you, we'll make good on it," a muffled voice said in the other room.

Brixton's blood ran cold. *I know that voice.* He had loathed him for years, and the situation only grew worse when the piece of scum married his sister. A smirk ran across his face as he stood to open the door.

"Magnus Hampton," Brixton said smugly as he leaned against the doorframe to his office. "How's that lowly accountant job treating you?"

The other young man with short, blond hair didn't know, but Brixton had desperately wanted the position Magnus received when he moved to Karad three seasons before. What he *would* know was how he cheated and took advantage of Brixton in their first year at King's Academy, resulting in the humiliation of Brixton's father bailing him out. He was eager to dangle his new promotion over the young man he had despised for years.

Magnus's face turned sour as he spoke without enthusiasm. "Brixton, congratulations on your new position."

Brixton stepped forward and stood tall. "That's Lord Fiero to you!"

Magnus narrowed his eyes. "Congratulations . . . Lord Fiero," he said with his jaw fixed.

Brixton smiled and spoke with an airy tone. "So, what brings you into my office today?"

"I'm filing an extension request for Karad Lenders."

"I'm just finishing it up now," Tucker said, lifting his pen into the air.

"Oh no, this won't do!" Brixton said, taking a stack of papers off of Tucker's desk. "For a member of my family, I insist on handling it personally. Come, join me in my office, Magnus." He extended his hand and waited for his brother-in-law to obey.

Magnus's eyes grew as he glanced at Tucker, but the clerk only shrugged his shoulders. Finally, he rose and walked into the back office.

"Tell me more about this extension," Brixton said as he sat.

"Oliver Marshall sent me to request it for him. We've had a few customers default on their loans recently, so our funds are tighter than normal. The seasonal license fee is due soon, and we need an extension."

"Interesting. Let's look, shall we?" Brixton sifted through the papers detailing the history of Karad Lenders. He mumbled occasionally and disappointingly wrinkled his forehead.

"Tucker seemed to think everything was in order," Magnus said. The interruption earned him a glare from Brixton. "I thought these extensions were common and rarely an issue?"

"It's my job to make sure this office is run responsibly. If we grant extensions to anyone off the street who asks, this city would fall apart. I'm not sure I can allow this request."

"What?" Magnus yelled. "Karad Lenders is hardly 'anyone off the street.' They've been an institution in this city for almost two hundred years. How can you have a problem with that?"

Brixton set down the papers and stared at the boy he once wanted to be. Years before, the boy's friends, his brain, and his family's connections intimidated him. Now, Brixton relished the fact that he sat here, requesting mercy from the city's newest lord.

"What I have a problem with is you," Brixton said, looking down his nose.

"Me? I'm just an accountant. You can't take your petty concerns with me out on Oliver Marshall's business."

"I know Karad Lenders has many years of reputation to lean on, but you're an unknown and new to this town. How do I know you won't take advantage of this?"

Magnus leaned forward in his chair and gave an exasperated gasp. "My father is High Lord of Trade for Feldor, and I've lived in this city for over a year!"

"I've lived in this city for twenty years, and now I'm in charge!"

"Only because your father gave you the title," Magnus muttered to the side.

Brixton's stare could have shot daggers across the desk. Finally, he turned his attention to the paperwork before him. "After reviewing the request, I am officially declining it."

"That's ridiculous!"

"If Karad Lenders cannot pay their seasonal license fee by the deadline, their license will be revoked. Any business activities will be unsanctioned and punishable by time in prison."

Magnus's face softened as he rested his hands on the desk. "Brixton, please. I know we've had our differences, but you can't do this. They don't have the money yet, but they're a solid company. You could ruin many people because of this grudge you've held. That was five years ago!"

"Actions have consequences, Magnus."

"What about your sister?"

Brixton's stomach turned. He hadn't thought about her. "What about Mila?"

"If you do this, you could ruin this company, which would put me out of a job . . . which will bring shame to your sister. You may not like me, but think of her!"

"She was shamed the day she married you." Brixton's smug grin returned. "Plus, she's always welcome to come and live with us in the castle."

Magnus shook his head as he stood to leave. Before exiting, he turned back. "I'm sorry about stealing your work at the Academy—honestly. I was young and stupid, and I wish I could take it back. Don't let a grudge cause you to do something foolish."

Brixton scowled as the young man left the office. He crossed the room and slammed the door. *He will not take advantage of me again.*

8

Turba Square

Chelci paced the music room, looking out the window every few seconds. Her new deep-blue dress was longer than she was used to, the fabric tickling her ankles. Mother's wardess had arranged her hair in a popular coif, pulling it back and up. She liked the look, but the tightness was uncomfortable. Light makeup colored her face, which was something she hadn't done in years. She wanted to look nice when she saw her old friend.

"Stop pacing. You'll wear a track in the rug!" her mother called from the adjacent room.

Chelci chafed at the rebuke. *I should drag my feet while I pace,* she thought, wanting to do anything to defy her mother.

"Here she comes, miss," the choreman, Jensen, said from another window.

Chelci snapped her head. She stretched her neck forward as her eyes grew. "That can't be her," she mumbled to herself as she watched the tall, young lady walk up the path to their house.

Emma had grown considerably. In place of the girl Chelci once knew was a lady. As tall as her mother, Emma's long, red-and-white-striped dress hung nearly to the ground, and a red cloak wrapped over it. Her slender arms swung by her sides as she stepped with a lively gait. While still youthful, her face had matured over the years, and her curly, blond hair was now long and mostly straight.

Chelci stood behind the door as the other girl mounted the steps and Jensen opened the door.

"Hello, Jensen. Someone summoned me to come here today. I assume Lady Luciana?" Emma said as she entered the house with her back to Chelci.

"Hello, Emma."

Her friend turned slowly, her face twisted in confusion. Chelci smiled softly, waiting for the moment—which didn't take long to arrive. Emma's eyes grew steadily wider as her hands covered her mouth. "Chelci?"

Chelci nodded her head while grinning. The two girls collided in a hug, squeezing each other tightly while Jensen took his leave. Emma rapidly mumbled questions, but Chelci only laughed as they embraced. When they finally pulled away, Emma's eyes were desperate for answers.

"You came back?" she asked breathlessly.

Chelci nodded, wiping away tears. "Yes, it was time."

Emma's face grew serious as she leaned in closer. "I never said anything . . . to your parents. They thought someone kidnapped you. I wasn't sure if I should tell them."

"It's okay. It worked out." Chelci glanced over her shoulder to the other room. She leaned in even closer and whispered. "You should have seen the look on Mother's face." Both girls stifled a giggle.

"Come on, let's go into town as we talk," Chelci said, glancing behind once more. She wrapped herself in a cloak, and the two girls left the house.

"So . . . tell me about it!" Emma said as soon as they were outside. "What happened to you?"

"Oh, Emma, it was amazing. Well, mostly. I almost died several times." Her friend stopped and stared but resumed walking when Chelci didn't slow. "I have to say, you were right."

"About what?"

"About surviving in the woods. It's *not* easy. I can't believe I ran away like that. It rained on me. I ran out of food and got lost. I even fought off wolves."

"What!"

"Yeah, I almost died. Russell rescued me. He's from Nasco—a town in the woods, near Karad. He and his wife Nevi took me in, raising me as their daughter."

"That's amazing!"

"After a few years, they let me train with other boys to try out for their village guard. I learned how to stop invaders and sword fight. I even fought a valcor to protect the town!"

Emma narrowed her eyes and pulled Chelci to a stop. "A valcor? Come on. Is any of that real?"

"It's *all* true! Really, it is!"

Emma leaned her head down as if looking up through her eyebrows. "Either way, I'm glad you're home. What made you come back?"

Chelci sighed. "It *is* true," she muttered. "I felt it was time to come home. I missed Father . . . and you."

"And your mother?"

"Ha," Chelci scoffed as she continued walking. "I have hope though. She walked all over me when I was younger, but I can stand up for myself better now." The two girls reached the end of the drive where the main cobblestone street passed by. "Can we go to Turba Square? I need to get some new clothes and don't want to go on my own."

"Of course!" Emma replied.

The girls turned right, heading toward the town's center.

"Tell me about you," Chelci said. "Other than pining away for your lost friend, what have you been up to the last six years?" she asked with a wink.

"I'm engaged."

Chelci clapped and squealed as her face lit up. "Congratulations! Who is it?"

"Do you remember Matthew, the baker's son? You know the bakery on Ryding Street?"

"Of course! I remember going there and buying rolls just so you could wave at him."

Emma grinned sheepishly. "Well, I guess it worked. I kept visiting, and eventually, we started spending time together. He received a courting permit a few seasons ago, and now we're to be married on mid-wiether's day."

"What's he like?" Chelci asked as they walked around a cart stopped in the middle of the street.

"Oh, he's wonderful! His words are soft and kind, and he's always baking me special treats. He made a loaf of bread for me the other day with my name baked into the middle when you slice it. I have no idea how he did it. He works with his father, but he runs most of the bakery now that his father's getting older."

"How do your parents feel about him?"

Emma pursed her lips and rolled her eyes. "It took some convincing. At first, they told me I couldn't see him—his father being a baker. Eventually, they realized what he meant to me and grudgingly allowed it." Emma broke into a broad grin then grabbed Chelci's arm. "But now that they've gotten to know him, they adore him! I'm so glad you're back! Now, you can come to the wedding!"

"I'm glad, too," Chelci said.

"What about you? Did you fall in love with any woodsmen when you weren't fighting the dragon?"

"It was a valcor."

"Mmm, sorry, that's right."

Chelci sighed, frustrated her friend still didn't believe her. "No, there were some nice boys, but none I wanted to marry. I guess I'll eventually find someone here, but I'm in no rush." Chelci's mind unwittingly turned to Veron. She smiled to herself as she thought about their nights in the training room.

"What?" Emma asked.

Chelci looked to her friend, unsure of the question. "What?"

"What are you smiling about?"

Chelci scoffed. "I'm not smiling." She smiled even broader, remembering how difficult it was to hide anything from Emma.

"Who is it?"

"There's no one. I promise."

Emma stopped walking, put her hand on her hip, and raised her eyebrows.

"Emma, I promise, there's no one."

"Oh, there's someone. I may not have seen you for six years, but I can still read your thoughts." She folded her arms, signifying she wouldn't move until Chelci answered.

"There's no one I'm *in love with.*" She fought the smile threatening to turn the corner of her mouth.

Emma cocked her head and tapped her foot.

Chelci sighed. "I've been training . . . sword fighting with a servant for the last two nights."

"You're in love with a servant?" Emma's eyes widened as she lowered her arms.

"No! Not at all! We've just been training together, and it's been . . . nice."

"Whatever happened to marrying someone who had money and servants, so you didn't have to cook or clean? If I remember right, that was your top priority."

"Living in Nasco gave me an appreciation for life I never had before," Chelci said with a shrug. "Sure, money's great, but I would rather be with someone whose company I enjoy."

"Does your mother know about this servant?"

"No! She would die if—" Chelci stopped as Emma raised her eyebrows. "There's nothing for her to know about, so it doesn't matter!"

Emma laughed, eliciting a groan from Chelci as she stomped toward the square. "I'm sorry, Chelci! I'm just teasing you!"

Her friend quickly caught up and ran her arm around Chelci's as they walked. "You know I don't care, as long as he's good to you. Whoever you end up with—whether it's a lord or a servant—will be fine with me."

As the girls approached Turba Square, the street grew more congested, and the smells intensified. The scent of smoked meats, baked goods, and fresh fruit swirled together, vying for the attention of those passing by. Turba Square was the central gathering place for all of Felting. An open space in the middle of the square provided room for people to gather, although carts laden with goods filled most of it. Directly in the center, towering over the crowd, stood a statue of King Darrick, the man credited with defeating King Vitrion of Norshand hundreds of years before.

Around the perimeter of the square were storefronts of every type. Chelci and Emma headed to the northwest corner where a half-dozen clothing shops stood in a line with friendly, well-dressed owners waiting to usher patrons inside. Chelci looked at the shops, deciding where to go first. Neatly arranged fabric hung from mannequins in each shop window, displaying the styles and colors of the season. She needed a lot of clothes, and her father had given her a small fortune to shop.

"'Scuse me, miss," a man said, pulling at her sleeve.

Chelci jumped as she turned. The stench of dirt and urine immediately wrinkled her nose, and the sight of the man in front of her confirmed its source. His filthy clothes hadn't been washed in some time. He stood up, but his back's crook meant he barely reached her shoulders. His hair had mostly fallen out, and the remaining tufts stuck in whatever direction they wanted to. Dark spots speckled his few remaining teeth.

"Hello," Chelci said as Emma stepped behind her.

"I's sorry ta bother ya, but can ya spare some coin?" the man said.

Chelci kept her hand down rather than cover her nose as the odor of decay wafted to her. As a child, her parents kept her well clear of the city's beggars, but she always knew they were around. Her mother said they were dangerous and one should avoid them at all costs.

"What's your story?" Chelci asked softly.

"Chelci, come on!" Emma said as she pulled in the opposite direction.

"Hold on!" Chelci brushed off her friend and turned her attention back to the man.

"My story?" he said, leaning his head back. "Whaddya mean?"

"Yeah, what's your name? How did you get here?"

The man smiled and stood a little straighter. "Name's Wesley."

"Like the king!"

"At's right. M'wife calls me 'Your Majesty' when she's feelin' partically . . . sportin'." Wesley toothily grinned, eliciting a blush from Chelci. "I used ta work for a dyer down by the river. I hauled the fabric around for her and made deliveries. When I hurt me back, I had to stop. It's a shame. 'Twas good work. None of my wife and I can read, and I can't do the physical work now. We get by on what we can, livin' on the street in the middle of the Red Quarter. If ya can spare some coins, I'd 'preciate it."

The weight of the coins in her pocket grew. *How many outfits do I really need? Maybe I could get Wesley some food or a new outfit? I'm sure Father could give me more money.*

"You! Back away from her!" a soldier yelled as he pushed his way through the crowd, heading toward the man in rags.

Wesley turned suddenly toward the voice and stepped away from Chelci.

"No, it's okay, he's not bothering me," Chelci said, reaching her hand into her pocket. "Here, Wesley, I can give you some coins."

"That's it," the soldier said as he grabbed the poor man by the back of the neck. "How many times do I need to tell you to stay out of this square!" The soldier turned back to Chelci as he led the beggar away. "I'm sorry, miss. He won't bother you anymore."

"Stop it! He wasn't . . . You don't need to . . ."

The soldier was already out of earshot. Wesley's wide eyes stared back at her, pleading as they grew farther away and eventually disappearing around a corner.

"How dreadful," Emma said, covering her chest as she walked up beside Chelci. "It used to be much worse here in the square. The city's tried to crack down, but some still get through. I can only imagine how you felt . . . so intimidated that you were actually about to give in to that man."

"He didn't intimidate me," Chelci insisted. "He just needs someone to help him out."

"Come on." Emma pulled on Chelci's arm. "We need to forget about that. Let's get you some clothes and hopefully get that awful smell out of our noses."

Emma led her into the nearest shop, but Chelci's mind was elsewhere. Her thoughts remained with Wesley and everyone in the city facing a similar plight.

Later that day, porters delivered the clothes she purchased, and she arranged them in her wardrobe. Although generally content wearing anything, her stomach fluttered at the thought of new outfits and fine fabric. There was something about dressing up and looking pretty she still enjoyed.

She pulled out a dress she was particularly excited about—a dark, silk gown that fell to the floor in shimmering waves of crimson. The sleeves fell at an awkward length—too long on her arms—but she liked the dress enough to still purchase it. The sleeves were easily adjustable. Chelci draped the dress over her arm and left the room.

In the basement, she passed servants hard at work in the kitchen and walked down the hall to the laundry area. "Hello?" She poked her head in the rooms at the west end of the house. The washing room was empty, as was the storage room across from it. Next to it was the room she wanted. Several tables filled the area, along with a sewing machine in the middle. Light funneled in from a small window near the ceiling.

She wanted to find Tatiana to help with the alterations, but no one was around. *I don't want to wander all over the house trying to find her.* She chewed the side of her cheek. *I don't need to ask someone to do something for me when I can do it myself.*

Chelci sat in front of the machine and went to work. She tore out the current seams then measured and cut the sleeves into her desired length. Back in Nasco, she learned to make clothes from nothing but a bolt of fabric. Nevi taught her, and Chelci remembered how proud she felt the first time she wore something she made completely on her own. The memory brought back a smile as she lost herself in her work.

"What are you doing?" a voice said behind her, causing Chelci to jump, sending her line of thread askew. Enith stood in the doorway, mouth ajar, holding a pile of sheets in her arms.

"I needed to shorten these sleeves. No one was down here, so I figured I'd just take care of it."

"No, you can't do that," Enith said quickly as she tossed the sheets on a table and nudged Chelci from the chair where she sat. "You can't . . . sew your own clothes! That's our job!"

"I know you can do it, but I thought I'd help."

Enith stared, blinking several times before she broke down into a laugh. "If your mother saw you right now, she would die. Chelci, you are indeed something special."

"Thank you?" Chelci replied, raising an eyebrow, unsure if it was a compliment or not.

"I appreciate that you want to help. I think our city would be better if people like you—and your mother—could do your own work, but what would that mean for me? For all of us here? My job, my livelihood, is to sew your clothes, keep them clean, and make sure they fit. Where would I be if you did it all?"

"I didn't think about that. I'm sorry, I just didn't want to trouble you."

Enith chuckled softly again. "It's no trouble, dear. Show me what you need done."

Chelci showed Enith her partially completed work.

"This is great! How'd you learn to do this in the woods?"

It was Chelci's turn to laugh. "What do you think I did? Just hunt wolves and climb trees every day?"

Chelci left the rest of the job to Enith—who seemed more than happy to help. The older lady promised to bring it to her when she finished, so Chelci left the room, wandering back through the basement.

The cooks were busy, sweating in the kitchen. Corbus barked orders as the others jumped to obey. It was still hours until dinner, but they already baked bread and roasted chickens over the stove. It reminded her of the enjoyable time spent cooking with Nevi.

I won't be able to do everything I learned in Nasco. The realization sent a pang of regret through her. Strangely, she missed the menial tasks, the cleaning, cooking, and sewing. She enjoyed sweating as she chopped wood and trained at the academy. *I need to find a way to do what I love.*

Two servers worked on the kitchen's far side, cleaning up the midday meal's remains. They scraped and washed plates and pots. Chelci tilted her head as they repeatedly dumped food into a crate.

"What are you doing with all of this?" she asked the servers as she arrived next to them and peered into the crate. A pile of food filled it—half-eaten rolls, slices of meat, fruit that was barely touched, and even some whole cooked potatoes.

The servers stiffened and looked at each other. The older one finally spoke. "We're just doing what we're told, miss. We take the old food and toss it."

"You just toss it? As in . . . throw it away?" Chelci asked.

"Yes, miss. It's our job to clean up. We throw out whatever isn't eaten or won't keep. There's plenty more food," he said, motioning to the nearest storeroom.

The room he pointed to burst with raw grains and food. "Isn't there something else to do with it?" she asked.

"I'm sorry, miss. That's our job."

She shook her head and frowned. The servers trembled as she stood in thought. "No, don't worry about it," she said, resting her hand gently on the older servant's shoulder. "You're doing an outstanding job—following orders just as you've been told. Thank you."

Both servants exhaled, the tension melting from their bodies.

"The food was excellent today, by the way."

Smiles formed on the server's faces as they looked between each other. "Thank you, miss. I'm glad you liked it."

Chelci took her leave. Her mind spun, thinking of options as she ascended the stairs to the ground floor.

9

Garden Test

Veron awoke to voices echoing in the hallway, but no knock sounded on his door. He sat up and looked to the window, where a tinge of orange grew in the east, signifying daylight's arrival.

Why didn't they knock on my door? Veron thought, rushing to get dressed. The soreness and pain he felt the night before barely registered through the foggy haze of sleeplessness. His midnight meeting with Chelci didn't help his tiredness or the dull pain behind his eyes. The hallway was empty by the time he emerged. Veron stepped lively as he descended the spiral staircase three floors to the basement.

The kitchen was alive with a bustling crew of servants leaning over stoves, chopping food, hauling supplies, and talking. Veron smiled and waved, catching Nathaniel's eye as he spoke with Tatiana across the room. Nathaniel's jaw dropped as he stared back with a look of horror on his face.

Veron looked behind him, expecting to see some sort of monster about to attack, but there was nothing. A loud crash sounded as a stack of dishes fell to the stone floor. He turned to see shards of porcelain covering the floor, but no one moved to clean them up. The server who dropped them stood and stared. Surprised gasps echoed from different corners of the room, and Veron gradually realized everyone was frozen in place, watching him.

Unsure what to do or say, he slowly crossed the room to Nathaniel and Tatiana. "Hey. What's going on?"

"Are you okay?" Nathaniel said. "How are you up?"

Veron narrowed his eyebrows and leaned his head backward. "Yeah, I'm okay." He suddenly remembered the whipping. *I'm supposed to take weeks to heal before I'm up and around.* His mind scrambled to think of an explanation.

"Oh, yeah, the whipping. The pain is horrible, but I'm just pushing through it." He jerked his head and snapped his fingers. "Barkleaf elixir! They gave me some last night—I think that's what it was—and it helped a lot. Plus, I've always been a fast healer."

Nathaniel looked at Tatiana, who shrugged. "We need someone to haul water . . ." she said, raising an eyebrow.

"I can do it," Veron said quickly.

"Alright then. Nathaniel, make sure he's good, then help Maren hauling laundry."

The rest of the servants in the large space gradually resumed their conversations and returned to work. The server who dropped the dishes cleaned up the mess. Veron noticed several furtive glances in his direction as he followed Nathaniel to get a yoke of water buckets.

"A fast healer, huh?" Nathaniel said as the two boys walked down the hall to the western end of the basement.

Veron noticed a hint of doubt. "I think the guard took it easy on me . . . it being my first day and all."

A smile crept onto half of Nathaniel's face, and Veron relaxed. "Well, I'm glad you're okay."

After gathering his buckets and assuring his friend, Veron resumed the familiar task while Nathaniel left to do other chores. Outside, the air was crisp as the early morning light crept over the buildings to the east, just outside of the Marlows' property. Veron walked along the well-trodden path, past the vegetable garden between the house and the well. It took twice as long as the day before since Veron worked alone, but he didn't mind. Not being allowed to eat a full meal, he was happy to keep busy.

To his dismay, once the sun came out, so did the gardener. Veron felt Tristan's fiery stare the first time he passed. He avoided eye contact but noticed Tristan motioning desperately to James and Montgomery working nearby. Their whipped foe was back to work the next day, and Veron sensed the confusion across the rows of crops. Walking tall, he tried to show no sign of weakness as he passed.

When Veron walked toward the well on his last trip, the sight of Tristan working alone in the vegetable garden bent over and digging with a shovel caused him to pause. Veron set down his buckets and walked through the garden.

Tristan glanced up as Veron approached. The gardener tensed then straightened to his full height, rising a few inches above Veron. "What do you want, Ash?" Tristan said, barely opening his mouth. His legs staggered, one in front of the other, with both hands on the shovel's shaft, as if he prepared to fight.

Veron swallowed. He wasn't sure what he wanted. *Leave me alone. Leave Chelci alone. Go dig up a rock and chew on it.* He opened his mouth, unsure what would come out.

"My name's Veron."

"I'm not good with names," Tristan said with a smirk. "All I can think of is a pile of ashes."

Veron bit his lip. "I don't know why you did what you did or why you don't like me." Veron hesitated as Tristan leaned his head back and stared down his nose. "But . . . no hard feelings."

A scoff escaped the gardener's mouth. "No hard feelings, eh?" He looked around the area. "Is this a joke?"

Veron shook his head. "My offer to help in the garden stands."

"Listen here!" Tristan aggressively wagged a finger in his face. "I don't need your help! I've worked here for twenty years. My pinky knows more about gardening than your entire body!"

"I didn't say I—"

"I saw their daughter batting her eyelashes at you, but you need to learn your place. That anklet proves I'm better than you, so don't poke your nose where it doesn't belong. Leave me alone and stay out of my way. If you don't, I promise you'll regret it!"

"Well . . . still . . . let me know if you ever need anything."

"Bah!" the gardener started to wave him away but stopped. "How are you . . . up?"

Veron partially wished he acted like he still hurt. He would have avoided a lot of questions and been excused from laboring for a while. He didn't mind the work, but he couldn't tell the truth—especially not to Tristan. "I just am," he replied, glaring back down his nose.

While he stared, the row of ripening, waist-high verquash stalks between them caught his eye. It wasn't the plants themselves but the plump verquash hanging like bells from the green stalks. Each light-green, cylindrical fruit contained streaks of yellow running along the length. Veron tilted his head and leaned in closer to the plants.

"What's wrong with your verquash?" he asked.

"What? Nothing's wrong, you miserable ankler! Get back to carrying water, where you belong."

"No, but . . . the yellow. They're not supposed to be like that. They—"

"Get out of here before I summon the guards to whip you again." The gardener's face hardened as he stepped forward and tightened his grip on the shovel. Veron shrank back.

"Tristan!" a voice called from the garden's far end. Montgomery stood near the house and beckoned the gardener with his arm. "It's time to pick up the fertilizer."

Tristan scowled at Veron before turning and silently walking away to join the landscaper, who disappeared around the side of the house.

Veron exhaled loudly. *Nathaniel seems right about that one.* He turned back to the verquash plants to inspect them closer. The streaks ran all the way around, and the fruit wasn't as firm as it should be. It felt as if they were overripe, but the color wasn't dark enough.

Veron squatted to the ground and poked in the dirt with his fingers. The soil was loose with an appropriate dampness. The smell of the turned dirt returned him to his time with Artimus in the garden where the old man lectured him on gardening, weeds, and fertilizer.

He dug farther, uncovering the stalk's roots, and Veron's breath caught as he paused with his hands in the dirt. He quickly turned to other nearby stalks and checked their roots. Content with his investigation, he replaced the dirt and patted it back down firmly. He remained in a crouch, frozen in thought for a long while. Eventually, he stood and spun around, looking at the trees and bushes surrounding the vegetable garden. He stopped when he spied a young molopyr tree just past the well.

Veron walked to the tree and plucked leaves one at a time from the tangle of the lowest branches. Once he had as many as he could hold, he walked back to the garden, crumpling the leaves. *If this works, I can teach Tristan a thing or two,* he thought as a grin covered his face.

* * *

The following day, Veron began with cleaning duty. He and Fern scrubbed the kitchen and the floors of the basement. They transformed the blackened stone into a fresh, clean gray, filling Veron with a profound sense of accomplishment. It also kept him distracted from his stomach, which growled in increasing frequency, reminding him of his times on Karad's streets. The meager bread and water he received kept him alive but was hardly filling.

Later that morning, Tatiana chose him and Nathaniel for water duty. A commotion drew their attention as they rounded the corner to walk along the garden. Tristan stood with James and Montgomery. The gardener's face was red, and his voice carried a sharp edge as he gesticulated wildly. Veron's stomach dropped when he noticed Tessa's head peeking just above the crops, listening to Tristan's tirade with crossed arms.

Veron slowed as he put his arm out to stop Nathaniel. "What is it?" the other boy asked.

"Let's go around. We need to find another path."

"What do you—"

"There he is!" Tristan yelled, pointing from across the garden in his direction.

Veron's insides felt watery as he stood like a statue. Everyone stared in his direction.

"What happened?" Nathaniel asked. "What did you do?"

The soft words didn't even register as Veron thought of being whipped again, reliving the white-hot sting.

"Get over here!" Tristan yelled.

Veron felt like lead lined his shoes as he plodded across the garden to meet the ire awaiting him. Tessa's floating head scowled, and Tristan's chest rose and fell rapidly to keep up with his anger.

"He's been trying to ruin me ever since I called him out the other day. Now, he's trying to spoil our crops and make me look bad for it. But he's not just hurting me, he's hurting the entire Marlow household!"

Footsteps approached from behind Veron as he swayed, stunned from the onslaught. He turned, and his breath caught in his throat as

Luciana Marlow approached with her wardess, Violetta. He opened his mouth to speak, but his tongue was tied in a knot. His legs shook as he looked rapidly between Luciana, Tessa, and Tristan, all scowling at him.

"What's going on here?" Luciana asked Tessa in a flowing, deep voice.

The house steward turned to the gardener. "Tristan, tell Lady Luciana your accusations."

The gardener swallowed as he shifted his stance and glanced at the two landscapers. Finally, he turned to the lady of the house and cleared his voice as he stood tall. "Ash here—" he gestured to Veron "—has been upset with me since his episode the other day. I'm sure you remember, my lady."

Luciana allowed a quick, soft laugh to escape. "Ash . . . ha! Yes, I remember." She smirked as she looked at Veron.

Tristan continued, "Since then, he's been mean to me and tries to get me in trouble. Yesterday, I caught him messing with my garden, tearing things up to make me look bad. When I went into town to get fertilizer, he covered the base of some crops with these." He bent down and picked up some of the crumpled leaves Veron had strewn at the base of the plants. He held the leaves in Veron's face as he fumed. "These are molopyr leaves."

"What does that mean?" Tessa asked.

"Poison!" Tristan yelled. "He's trying to poison my verquash plants . . . *your* verquash plants!"

The lady of the house took some leaves and smelled them before turning to Veron. "Is this true?" she asked with a raised eyebrow.

"Oh, please! Of course, he's going to deny it!" Tristan interjected.

"Quiet!" Luciana said before turning back to Veron. "Did you wait until the gardener left to cover these plants with poisonous leaves?"

Veron's heart beat wildly as he looked around at the crowd.

"You're standing on very thin ice, *Ash*," she said with vitriol as she stepped closer to Veron's face. "Did you do this?"

Veron exhaled slowly as the crowd waited on him. He lifted his chin and looked lady Luciana in the eyes. "Yes, I did this."

Tessa cried out and covered her mouth as Tristan yelled in triumph. Luciana's jaw remained hard as she stared back at Veron.

Veron continued, "I came to Tristan yesterday to smooth over whatever grudge he held against me. We spoke for a moment, and I noticed the yellow lines in the verquash."

"That's right," Tristan interrupted. "He insulted your crops as if he's some sort of expert."

"But, why would you poison our food?" Tessa asked. "Surely, you understand that couldn't end well for you?"

"I didn't poison the food," Veron said, and the rest of the crowd froze in place.

Finally, Luciana spoke up. "But you just said—"

"I said I covered the plants with leaves, but these don't hurt the plants. Answer me this . . . How has your verquash tasted recently? Has it been crisp and juicy with a slightly sweet flavor as it's supposed to have? Or has it had a bitter aftertaste?"

Luciana looked at Tessa before speaking. With one eyebrow raised, she answered in an even voice, "It's been bitter."

"For the last two years, actually," Tessa added.

"When you cook it, does it end up mushy?" Veron asked. "Do your stores rot sooner than expected?"

"It's mushy," Luciana confirmed quietly.

"And they do rot quickly. We have to throw half of it out," Tessa said.

Veron stepped to the nearest plant and held one of the not-yet-picked verquash. "These yellow lines show the plants are infected."

"He doesn't know that," Tristan said. "You can't really—"

"Quiet, gardener," Luciana said, glaring at him before turning back to Veron. "If the plants are infected, why would you cover the base with poisonous leaves?"

"Here, let me show you." Veron bent down and dug in the dirt. "See here?" The crowd leaned in to get a closer look. "You see these holes in the roots? They're from borticle beetles."

"Don't listen to him. He's just making things up. I don't see any beetles," Tristan said.

Veron tilted his head. "Do you know what borticle beetles are?" he asked the gardener.

Tristan looked between the landscapers and adjusted his feet. "Why don't you teach us all?" He smirked as he offered a slight bow, extending his arm in a mock sign of respect.

Veron looked between the crowd as he explained. "Native to Tarphan, borticle beetles attack plants at their roots—verquash plants in particular. They migrated here when importers began transporting crops across Terrenor's borders. During the day, they burrow deep underground and come up at night to chew on roots. Based on the extent of the spread and the verquash quality, I'd guess they've been infecting your garden for a couple of years."

He held up one of the molopyr leaves as he continued. "You see these bite marks in the leaves? Last night, the beetles found them. The poison won't hurt the plants, but it will kill the pests. In another night or two, they will all be dead, and your plants will flourish."

"This is ridiculous," Tristan said. "What does an ankler know about all of this? He's lying to cover up what he did."

"We'll see," Luciana said, staring hard at Veron. "A night or two, you say?"

Veron swallowed as his stomach churned. "Yes, my lady. Don't disturb the leaves. In two days, you'll see a difference."

"You better hope we do," she said, stepping close enough that he felt her breath. "Clearly, the soldiers took it easy on you for your first whipping. Next time, I'll see to it they don't hold back. Or maybe I'll have to invoke your collateral to get your attention."

The color drained from Veron's face as Luciana and Tessa walked away. He glanced at Tristan's scowl before turning back to join Nathaniel, who held out the empty buckets for him.

"What was that about?" Nathaniel asked.

"I was just trying to help," Veron replied. "Now, they think I'm sabotaging the vegetables."

"Is that leaf thing gonna work?"

Veron took a deep breath and exhaled as they walked to the well. "I hope so."

* * *

When Veron awoke two days later, butterflies danced in his empty stomach. His heart sped up as he got out of bed. *The plants have to be better today, or I'm in trouble.*

The previous day, he had visited the garden to see how things were going. Tristan smugly looked on as Veron approached the verquash plants with a slack jaw. While the beetles ate many more of the leaves, the plants were also crawling with the bugs. Tristan ridiculed him for not knowing what he was doing and laughed about the beetles only coming out at night. Veron didn't have a retort, so he left without saying a word, worried his idea may not have been a bright one.

I was sure the leaves would work. Maybe they still will? Veron thought as he dressed, eager to get to the garden and see the result.

Tatiana flagged him down when he arrived in the basement. "Veron, I need you to scrub the basement floors right away."

"Would it be alright if I went out to the garden for a moment? I need to—"

"No, you can't go play in the garden."

"I'm not going to—"

"You're going to scrub the floors like I told you to. You understand?" she said. "Nathaniel will be back soon with fresh water. Grab a bucket, soap, and brush from the laundry room. I need you to clean the whole level." Veron groaned as he trudged down the hall to gather supplies.

"Nathaniel, how are the verquash?" Veron asked after his friend returned with water.

Nathaniel shook his head. "I looked, but I'm not sure what to check for. There were some bugs on the ground. I think you'll need to look for yourself."

Veron sighed. "Tatiana won't let me do anything until I scrub the downstairs floors."

"Maybe that will give them more time to improve?" Nathaniel said.

It took most of the morning to clean the rough, stone floors. Nathaniel brought him fresh buckets when the water grew too dark. After finishing the last room, dumping the filthy water, and returning the buckets, Veron hurried down the hall to exit the house.

Sunlight beat down on him as he ran around the corner. His breath caught when he came into full view of the vegetable garden. Luciana and Tessa stood together at the far end, inspecting the plants, but Tristan was nowhere to be found. Veron breathed heavily as he approached. Tessa noticed him and mumbled something to Luciana while nodding in his direction.

The lady of the house turned with a stern look. "Ash, explain to me what I'm seeing here," she said.

When Veron arrived, his eyes widened as he took in the sight. Beetles littered the dirt all along the rows of verquash stalks. He couldn't step without hearing the crunch of their hard carapace. While the sight was shocking to see, a grin formed across his face. All the molopyr leaves were gone, and none of the beetles moved. He turned his attention to the plants, and a short laugh escaped.

"What is it? What's funny?" Luciana asked. "What does this mean?"

He beamed. "I'm sorry. It's not funny, my lady. It's great! The beetles ate the leaves, as I expected, and now they're all dead. They won't be able to infect the plant anymore. Even after only two days, you can see the impact." He held one of the verquash and angled it to the ladies. They leaned in closer as a yellow drop of liquid fell from the end. "You see that yellow bead? That's the infection leaching out. See how the yellow streaks from the top half of the fruit have mostly faded? In a few more days, the whole thing will be a healthy green. It's on all of them. See?"

Veron motioned to the other stalks. Yellow beads clung to the bottom of each fruit, waiting to fall. "And look at this," Veron said, pointing to the stalk where small flowers began to bloom. "New blossoms are already forming. Each of these will be a new, healthy verquash soon. You'll probably have double the production by the end of the growing season."

Luciana looked at Tessa as each lady raised her eyebrows. "Where's that gardener?" Tessa asked.

Veron looked to the house in time to see Tristan's head duck behind the gardening shed.

"Tristan! Come here!" Tessa yelled toward the shed.

In a moment, the gardener rounded the corner and pointed at his own chest. "Me? Did you want me?"

The two ladies scowled as the gardener trudged across the field, dragging his shovel behind. His shoulders slumped as he looked at the ground. Each step seemingly added more weight to his shoulders.

"Have you seen this?" Tessa asked when he arrived. He nodded. "And what is your conclusion?"

Tristan's eyes darted around. He held the shovel in front of him as if he tried to hide behind the blade. "Yes, my lady. I saw it. It seems that . . . um . . . I guess the boy was right."

Luciana snatched the shovel away, and the gardener flinched. "Yes, it seems he was. You accused him of poisoning the plants and trying to ruin you. It appears he was trying to help." He stared at the ground and didn't reply. "Tristan, how long have you been gardening here?" she asked.

He straightened. "Twenty years, my lady."

"And in all of that time, you never learned about these—" she turned to Veron. "What beetles were these?"

"Borticle," Veron said.

"Lady Luciana, please," Tristan said. "I—"

She held up her hand to cut him off. "Not only did you not learn about this garden pest, but you delivered rotten food to us for over a year. And when a *boy* comes along who knows more than you, rather than learn from his wisdom, you heap baseless accusations on him!" Her jaw was tight as she stared down at the gardener, who shrank under her glare.

"You . . . Ash. What else do you know about gardening?"

Veron blinked, unprepared for the question. "I . . . um . . . I know a lot, my lady. I worked in a garden for several years and am familiar with all the plants you have."

Luciana tossed the shovel to Veron who caught it firmly. "You've been promoted. You're taking Tristan's place."

Veron's breath caught as Tristan exploded. "What?" he yelled. "You can't do that! He's just a boy!"

"A boy who knows more about gardening than you do," Luciana said.

"I am *not* going to work for him!"

"You don't have to worry about that. You're dismissed. If you're interested in a housemaid position, we now have one available. You can speak to Tessa about it." Tristan's mouth hung open as the lady of the house turned away from him. "Ash, I want to see a good harvest."

"Yes, my lady. You can count on me!" he said, smiling as Luciana walked away with Tessa close behind.

When Tristan overcame his shock, his lips turned in a snarl, and he glared at Veron for a long moment. "You're gonna regret this, Ankler. You better watch your back," he uttered before staggering after the ladies, hurrying to flag Tessa down.

Anxiety rushed through Veron. *And I was on his bad side before?* He swallowed hard and shook away the feeling, looking at the shovel in his hand. He gripped the wooden handle and breathed in deeply. The smell of dirt caused his spirit to soar while he gazed over the vegetable garden plot. It was much larger than Artimus', but it was nothing he couldn't handle. He looked forward to it.

10

Market Adjustment

Brixton turned off Gate Street into Prinvestor, the area he'd avoided the previous two weeks. Twice, Morgan Fenster had come by the Department of Commerce, but Brixton hid in his back office to avoid speaking. His legs felt heavy as he walked. He could avoid the market no longer.

It was around noon on Finday when he arrived at the rolling, wooden gate of North Karad Market. When he stepped inside the courtyard, Morgan was the first to notice.

"Brixton!" the grocer shouted, setting down some food and running over. "I'm sorry . . . Lord Fiero . . . Congratulations. Do you know what happened to Veron?"

The other workers quickly gathered. Chloe, who had been dipping candles, wiped her hands on an apron. Henry held Greta's arm as they shuffled over. Jacob and Brock set down their tools. Everyone leaned in with hushed anticipation.

Brixton's collar felt hot. He had prepared a statement, but the words escaped him as he stared at their faces. *I betrayed him and sold him into slavery,* was his only thought, and he had to fight to keep it from escaping. "Bale attacked," he said, finally.

"We heard," Danyel, the baker, said. "Was Veron taken?"

Brixton glanced down and kicked the dirt. "When the soldiers arrived and started killing, Veron fought bravely. He rescued a woman and child before he was struck down by a Norshewan soldier."

The crowd audibly gasped. Chloe covered her mouth and held onto Mary. Morgan stepped in closer. "What do you mean . . . struck down?" the grocer asked.

"He was injured . . . mortally," Brixton said, his mouth twitching at the lie. "I held his hand as he died."

Tears sprung from the crowd's eyes. The women sobbed while the men wiped their eyes. Morgan fell to his knees and hung his head.

"I'm sorry it took me so long to come here," Brixton said. "I should have come sooner, but . . . I couldn't."

"What happened to his body? Can we bury him?" Danyel asked.

Brixton shook his head. "He—They buried all the ones killed in a mass grave outside the east gate." He shuffled his feet. As the crowd rested in their grief, Brixton's heart pounded as he prepared to deliver the ultimate deception. "The city solicitor came to me yesterday with another piece of news." The grieving faces looked at him. "Sometime before his death, Veron filed a will to pass ownership of the market to me if something were to happen to him, so now I hold the license under my name," he said as he waved a piece of paper in the air.

Morgan's eyes narrowed, and Danyel's head tilted to the side. "But . . . why would . . ." Morgan's question trailed off.

Brixton quickly replied, "I assure you, I was as surprised as all of you." He lowered his head in a false show of mourning. "His friendship was as dear to me as one could hope for. I promise you all, we will make Veron proud and honor his memory by running a thriving market. It's what he would have wanted."

Brixton leaned back in the wooden chair and stretched his neck. He sat in the market's office after poring over the financial ledgers for hours, trying to figure out how he would run things. As Lord of Commerce, he couldn't work in a dirty market every day. It wouldn't be fitting of his position, but he could come in once a month to collect his money. He grinned, realizing how well things were working out.

A knock rapped on the door before it opened.

"Morgan," Brixton said, suddenly nervous. "What is it?"

The grocer sat in a free chair. "I wanted to see if you needed anything."

"Actually, I do have some questions," Brixton said, relaxing. "What all did Veron do at the market?"

"A little of everything." A half-smile formed on Morgan's face. "He collected money from customers and helped me stock food. He ran errands to pick up supplies when someone needed something. He swept the courtyard whenever it got dirty."

"As a city lord, clearly I won't be able to do all of that. I assume you can take care of those things on your own?"

Morgan paused for a moment then nodded. "I'm sure we can make do."

"Good. So, Veron has been paying all of you one argen per week? Is that right?"

"Yes, sir."

"What about Chloe and this cheesemaker, Matteo? I've been reviewing the reports, and we don't make one argen in profit off candles or cheese most weeks. We can't pay them more than they bring in."

Morgan adjusted in his chair and opened his mouth, but no words came out.

"And this carpenter, Jacob? What's he been working on recently?"

"Well, the construction and repairs are mostly finished in the market. He has some jobs he handles now and then. We advertise his work in the far stall, and sometimes people hire him for outside work."

"And since he's paid by us, the money he makes goes to the market, correct?" Brixton asked.

"Correct."

"Does it amount to one argen per week?"

Morgan fidgeted again and glanced out the window. "Sometimes."

Brixton fixed his gaze on Morgan. "So, Veron pays these people every week, but the money they bring in often doesn't even match what they're paid? Why are they still around?"

"They're part of our team!" Morgan spoke quickly, his face flushed. "We all work together and help each other. It's the diversity of our products and services that make the market what it is. You can't just evaluate individual items. Chloe, Matteo, and Jacob are part of our family here, and it's that family that makes us successful."

Brixton tapped his pen absently on the desk as he stared. "So, tell me about this . . . profit sharing thing."

A grin formed on Morgan's face as his eyes lit up. "It was one of Veron's brilliant ideas. He wanted the workers to all be invested in the market's success. He felt if success benefitted them, they'd be more likely to work hard and help each other out. Veron took fifty percent of the profits each season and divided them up amongst the workers based on their contribution."

"He gave away *half* of the profits?" Brixton said as the pen stopped tapping. "I knew he gave some back, but I thought it was . . . less."

"Again . . . it's motivating to the team," Morgan said.

Brixton sat in silence as he looked at the book resting open in front of him. "Thank you, Morgan. That will be it for now," he said as he waved his hand in the grocer's direction. The chair scraped, and the door opened and closed, yet Brixton only focused on the numbers in front of him.

Veron could have been making much more money than he did! His heart sped up as he started writing down numbers. He calculated how much Veron had cleared and estimated how much more he could make with a few changes.

He looked out the window. The market workers milled about, smiles on their faces. A handful of customers walked between the displays with baskets full of goods. A hearty laugh sounded across the yard where Danyel spoke with a man, patting him on the back. His eyes drifted up the steps to the row of rooms looking out over the courtyard. Potted flowers decorated several of the windows, and a sign reading "Welcome to Our Home" hung above one of the doors.

Brixton continued writing on the paper, adding and multiplying various numbers. When he circled a number at the bottom of the page, a wicked grin crept over his face. *Veron, you really were such a fool.*

At the end of the day, Brixton shut the office door, glancing to the gate where Danyel slid the wooden door along its track. The workers bustled around the market, crating up their goods to move them under the protected stalls. The market would be closed the following day on Weekterm.

Brixton stood in the middle of the courtyard, but no one looked at him. He jingled coins in his pocket and bounced on the balls of his feet. When he cleared his throat, heads turned.

"Could I . . . Could I have everyone gather around for a moment?" His voice initially faltered, but he compensated by increasing the volume. "I know we'll all miss Veron greatly. He was a good friend to each of us. As I've gone through the ledgers, I confirmed what I always suspected . . . Veron was not a man of business." Heads stopped nodding, and a tight knot formed in the pit of Brixton's stomach. "The market has done well, but there are several decisions he's made which have resulted in much weaker profits than what's possible. Because of this, and for the good of the market, I will make three changes."

Several people began talking at once, but Brixton couldn't make it out. He held up his hand to get them to listen, but they continued to talk as they pressed in closer. "Please! Quiet down, please!" he shouted. The rumbling slowly lessened, giving him a chance to continue. "First, the wages you're making of one argen per week are much higher than any similar business."

Danyel spoke up. "Veron's been paying us that for two years, and—"

"I'm not cutting your wages," Brixton said as he raised his hand again. "But you will need to pay rent for your rooms." He gestured toward the rooms around the balcony above them while several heads followed. "Two tid per week is a great bargain."

"You're going to charge us two tid per week to remain in the homes we've lived in the last two years for free?" Henry asked, holding his wife's hand.

"As I said, the rate is very reasonable," Brixton said. The crowd settled but continued to grumble. "Second, outside of this market, profit sharing is unheard of in Karad. In some circles, it is seen as unethical and dangerous."

"How could sharing profit with workers be dangerous?" Morgan asked, folding his arms over his chest.

Brixton stood tall as he answered. "If the practice catches on and the people of Karad come to expect profit sharing everywhere, good businesses could close. We can't have uneducated people banding together to force change like that in this city."

"You think because we don't have a formal education, we don't deserve to earn a fair wage for our work?" Danyel asked.

Brixton swallowed to clear the dryness from his mouth but ignored the baker's question. "Furthermore, business licenses are granted based on the character and credentials of the business owner. By sharing profit amongst workers, all workers are essentially co-owners, which was not approved by the Department of Commerce. Subsequently, this makes the practice potentially unethical. As the Lord of Commerce, I must make sure any businesses I am involved in are above reproach. I need to set a good example for the rest of the city. As a result, I will, unfortunately, have to halt the profit-sharing effective immediately."

"No! That's not fair," Danyel yelled as Morgan held him back. "Veron always rewarded us for the hard work we put in. Now you want to slash our pay, and you expect us to be okay with that?"

"I expect you to accept what is appropriate for your position," Brixton said, the biting words silencing the rest of the crowd. "I'm very sorry for these changes, but I must do what's *right* and *fair*." Brixton glanced at the crowd of workers. Their faces were dark, and several crossed their arms as they stared back.

"You said you had three changes?" Morgan said through his clenched jaw, without inflection.

"Um . . . yes. I've been looking over what makes the market successful, and some departments aren't contributing to our profitability. It wouldn't be fair to the rest of you if I ignored this. To ensure the market is doing as well as it can, Chloe, Matteo, and Jacob must leave."

Chaos erupted. Matteo froze in place, Jacob's face fell, and Chloe knelt to the ground, crying while an older woman comforted her. The rest of the crowd yelled at Brixton and slowly closed in around him. He stepped back, his eyes widening. Icy fear rushed through his body as his back hit the gate. He had nowhere to go.

Brixton held up the license. "Don't forget, this is my market! You may not like the changes, but they are for the good of everyone, trust me." The crowd stopped advancing, and he breathed a sigh of relief. He shuffled to the side, where the gate's handle awaited him, representing his freedom. "I won't bother you all during the week. You'll be free to work as you normally do. I'll be back from time to time to check on the ledgers."

He exited the gate, the image of their angry, hurt faces imprinted in his mind. Shaking off the memory as he walked through Prinvestor, Brixton smiled to himself. While the market workers may not have approved of the changes, he knew one person who would have done the same thing—his father.

Back at the castle, Brixton glanced into his father's office. It was empty. He walked down the hall until he found his mother resting on a chaise in the sunroom. She faced the windows, the reddish-orange remnants of daylight hovering over the castle walls.

"Mother, do you know where Father is?"

"Hello, Brixton. Yes, he went to the hobbilade court."

Brixton glanced out the window. "But, it's nearly dark."

Elenor shook her head. "Tell that to your father. Maybe he'll listen to you."

Brixton left the room and made his way to the outdoor courtyard where he followed the path along the side of the castle. The wind had picked up, and the tree-shaped fountain misted him as he passed. He pulled his cloak tighter to stay warm as he walked through a portico into the back courtyard. On the far side, next to the city wall, his father stood with a soldier at the hobbilade court. Each of the men held a handful of knives in one hand and a mug in the other. Torches hung along both sides of the court, illuminating two servants holding targets at the end of poles.

Across the courtyard, his father laughed before setting his drink down and turning toward the targets. He took a knife in his right hand, stepped forward, and slung the sharp dagger down the court. A solid thud echoed off the stone wall as it sank into the larger of the two targets. His father cheered. Brixton crossed the courtyard while the other man took his turn. His flying knife glanced off the side of the same target and clattered into the wall.

"Hello, Father," Brixton exclaimed.

"Brixton," his father said as he selected his next knife. "You know Captain Gannon, I presume?" He launched the knife down the court where it missed the smaller target and stuck into the grass beyond.

Brixton turned to the soldier and nodded. Gannon's light-brown hair fell to his shoulders in a greasy, tangled mess. His nose hooked to the side, and pock marks dotted his face. "Yes, we've met. Captain? Congratulations on the promotion."

Gannon smirked. "Yes, Lord Billings promoted me after Mortinson's death."

"I've been filling Gannon here in on the finer details of being a baron," Raynor said before turning to the soldier. "It's your turn." The captain's knife landed solidly in the larger of the two targets. "We're going to need some loyal soldiers if we're to clean up the mess Rycroft left behind."

Gannon turned to Brixton. "I've assured your father he can trust me to do what needs to be done. There's nothing I'm unwilling to do in service of our city."

"So, Brixton, where have you been all day?" his father asked as he prepared to throw. "I know you weren't at the office."

Brixton grinned. "I've been at North Karad Market since noon. I thought things were good there, but it seems Veron left a mess behind. He was paying his workers way too much, and I've made some changes that are going to greatly increase profits!"

A solid thud sounded before his father turned to him. "The reason I know you weren't at the Department of Commerce is because I came by today. Do you know what I found?" Raynor asked as he stared with a hard gaze.

Brixton was taken aback. He ceased explaining his brilliant market changes and thought back to his other job. "I . . . um . . . I'm not sure. What did you find?"

"Tucker Waystone working as head clerk. Please tell me . . . why would a man convicted of stealing from the Department of Commerce, who spent a year in prison for his crimes, be the highest-ranking associate remaining in the office he stole from while you are nowhere to be found?"

Brixton froze. "He . . . uh . . . He served his time, so I thought he'd learned his lesson. I needed a good head clerk, and Tucker knows how to do the job."

"You're a fool, Brixton," Raynor said. "I worked for years to get that department into shape, and you're going to bring it down in weeks with your mindless trust of criminals."

Captain Gannon chuckled as he positioned himself for his final throw.

"The reason I came to the office to begin with is I received a complaint from my son-in-law, Magnus," Raynor said as a knife clattered off stone.

Brixton's stomach turned. The two downrange servants jogged quickly to them. They handed the knives to the men and promptly returned to where they had left the targets.

"Magnus says you've denied a license extension to Karad Lenders. He said it has nothing to do with business. It was simply because you don't like him." His father held a knife by the blade and turned his body to face the court.

"I don't like him because he's a jerk, and he stole my project at school," Brixton said as a flush crept up his neck.

His father froze with the knife in his hand and turned back to Brixton. "You are putting one of our city's most respected institutions at risk and potentially ruining the lives of several people—including your own sister—all because you're sore about something he did years ago when you were children?"

Raynor stared, waiting for an answer, but Brixton had nothing to say. He lowered his head and looked at the grass. A thump sounded, followed by the dismissive voice of his father. "Get out of my sight."

The words chilled Brixton as shame and anger raced through him. He walked away, shoulders slumped and head down. Another thunk sounded behind him, followed by a cheer. The laughter of his father and the captain faded as he walked back through the courtyard into the darkness.

11

City Needs

Chelci's lean arms were taut as she lifted the end of the one-wheeled cart and pushed it down the street. The effort was nothing compared to what she went through in Nasco, but it wasn't typical of upper-class women in Felting. She drew plenty of funny looks as she made her way through the city. Her warm cloak kept her comfortable on the brisk day.

"I don't know about this, Chelci," Emma said as she followed behind. "Who's going to want this trash?"

"This isn't trash," Chelci said. "There are full legs of chicken, several halves of potatoes, and look…" she stopped rolling it long enough to hold up a loaf of bread. "This full loaf isn't even touched. There's enough food in here to feed a half-dozen families for several days."

Chelci had instructed the servants to set aside any salvageable food that would be thrown out. After a couple of days, she convinced Emma to join her, and the two were on their way to the Red Quarter to give it away.

"Would you rather this be thrown away?" Chelci said as the cart bounced over a bump in the road.

"I don't know. I guess not," Emma replied. "I just think you could have your servants take it instead. Anyone but us," she said as she glanced around.

Passing a large, red column on either side of the road marked their crossing into the Red Quarter, and the scenery immediately changed. Dingy buildings in disrepair lined the road filled with trash. People in rags dotted the street, where they sat and stared vacantly. The smell of rot permeated the air, and Emma covered her nose with the end of her sleeve as Chelci sat down the end of the cart to rest for a moment.

"I don't think this is a good idea, Chelci," Emma said. "Our parents would kill us if they knew we were here."

"You know, I've never been here before," Chelci said, looking around at the despair on people's faces. Several rubbed their hands together around a fire in an alley to stay warm.

"I've only come once, but it was with my mother and two guards a long time ago. It was much nicer back then," Emma said.

"Come on," Chelci said as she picked the end of the cart back up. "I want to find Wesley."

Emma exhaled loudly. "I can't believe you want to go through all this trouble for some street beggar."

"It's not just him. It's all of them. Look around you, Emma," Chelci said as she continued pushing the cart. "We can't make all of their problems go away, but we can give them some food."

At the crossroad in the middle of the quarter, Chelci set the cart down and pulled her cloak tighter as the wind picked up. She scanned the street until she found Welsley and waved to catch his eye. He stood with a smile and shuffled over, holding a woman's hand. The woman looked in similar shape to Wesley, skin loose and face gaunt. The bit of hair she had was thin and stringy, but her crooked smile showed a joy Chelci did not expect.

"This is the girl I's telling ya about," Wesley said to the woman.

Chelci extended her hand to the woman. "I'm Chelci, and this is my friend Emma." Emma waved slightly but hesitantly stayed a few steps behind.

"Dolores," the woman said as she shook her hand. Chelci felt the scrapes and calluses of a hard life, but it wasn't a deterrent. She had plenty of scrapes and calluses of her own.

"Wesley and Dolores, we've brought food if you'd like some," Chelci said. "I know it's only leftovers, which seems insensitive, but it was all going to be thrown away, so I started saving it."

"Looks like a feast ta me!" Wesley said. "But we can't eat all this. Are you okay givin' ta some others, too?"

"Of course," Chelci said. "I figured it could feed several people, but I don't know how to decide who to—"

Wesley waved back across the street, where a dozen other men and women stood and walked their way.

"Well . . . okay. I guess that works," Chelci added.

"This here's Chelci, and she's brought us some food," Wesley said to the group.

Smiles dotted the crowd, and words of thanks filled the air as they took turns selecting food. The men and women hungrily devoured the contents until nothing remained but the cart's bare, wooden slats.

A young woman around Chelci's age shivered as she nodded in thanks before turning to leave.

"Wait," Chelci said without thinking, causing the woman to turn back toward her. She wore a thin dress with tears at the bottom and sleeves that stopped well short of her wrists. "You must be freezing. Do you not have anything warmer?"

The woman shook her head but kept her eyes down.

"Chelci, come on," Emma said. "You've given out all the food. Let's head back."

"Here, you can take my cloak," Chelci said as she sloughed off the expensive piece of clothing she had just bought a few days before. A bitter wind chilled her the moment the cloak came off, confirming the young woman's need.

The woman's eyes grew wide as she tentatively accepted the gift. She put it on slowly and seemed to melt with joy as she wrapped it around her. "Thank you, miss," she said quietly.

"I'll come back when I'm able," Chelci said to Wesley and Dolores as they thanked her profusely.

Chelci lifted the end of the cart and spun it around to head back toward her home. Emma silently fell in step as they made their way up the street. "I know . . . I know. You don't have to say anything," Chelci said.

"What?" Emma replied. "I wasn't going to say anything."

"I know I can't give away my cloak every time I see someone cold. I just felt sorry for that woman."

"I think it was really kind of you. Just don't expect me to give away all my clothes, too, and have to walk home in my underwear."

The laughter warmed Chelci, and the fact she could provide food and warmth to people comforted her. *I'm beginning to find my purpose.*

Chelci wheeled the cart through the side door to the basement while Emma held it open. Dodging bustling servants and tables, she set it in the storage room from where it came.

"I was there. I saw the cuts. That guard wasn't takin' it easy, I promise you that," a server said to another as they polished silverware at the side of the kitchen.

"They must've made it look worse than it was," the other argued. "No one walks around the next day after a whippin' like that, but he's out working in the garden, now! I say they took it easy on him."

"I heard somethin' about a magic elixir he took that heals overnight."

Chelci's ears perked up. "Who is this?" she asked as she angled past the servants. "Are you talking about Veron?"

The servants froze as they glanced between each other. "Ash . . . The new guy. I'm not sure his real name," one replied.

"Was he whipped recently?"

"Yeah . . . three days ago, now. He dumped a bucket of ash onto Lady Luciana while she was bathing," the servant said with a laugh. "He was really beaten up. I saw it."

Chelci raised her eyebrows. "This is the new housekeeper? Tall . . . bushy, brown hair . . . young?"

"Yeah, that's him. They promoted him to gardener—lucky kid."

Chelci stared wordlessly. *Those wounds couldn't have been from three days ago.* After a moment of silence, the servant cleared his throat, jarring Chelci back to the present. She nodded quickly before turning to leave.

"Ah, there you are," Luciana said as Chelci and Emma exited the stairwell on the second floor. "Where have you been?"

Chelci glanced at Emma. "We've been . . . walking through the city."

Luciana narrowed her eyes. "Walking . . . in this cold? What have you been doing?" They couldn't dodge her sharp-edged words.

Chelci brought her shoulders back and looked fully into her mother's face. "I was taking food to give to people who didn't have any."

"*Our* food? We *pay* for our—"

"The leftovers, Mother. I gathered what was being thrown out and took it to people who would appreciate it. Surely, you don't object to me taking our trash to give to others?"

Luciana sniffed as she stared back. "Where's your cloak?" she snapped.

Chelci's hands and face were still red from the walk back. "I . . . uh

. . . I left it by mistake while we were out."

"I don't want you doing that anymore. It's not safe out there. Let those people learn to take care of themselves. And *now* . . . you need to clean up. We have someone joining us for dinner tonight, and you need to look your best."

Chelci groaned. *I hate dressing up for stuck-up dinner guests.* "Who is it this time?"

"His name is Caspian, and he's a potential suitor," Luciana replied.

"What? No!" Chelci shouted, but her mother didn't flinch. "You can't parade me in front of people to try and marry me off!"

"I'm not parading you anywhere," her mother said evenly as she stared down her nose. "Besides . . . you agreed to meet with suitors."

Chelci clenched her jaw and exhaled through her nose. She looked to Emma—who was wisely silent—before staring back at her mother. "Fine. But you should have asked me first."

Luciana stared as she breathed in a long breath. Finally, her eyes softened, and she sighed. "You're right."

Chelci jerked her head back. *What did she say?*

"I probably should have asked you," her mother continued. "But you *do* need to find someone to marry, and it's not going to happen without meeting people. Meet with him. Please."

Chelci clenched her jaw, unsure whether to remain indignant or embrace her mother's softer side. Without responding, she turned and stomped to her room with Emma on her heels.

"Maybe he'll be okay?" Emma said as she sat cross-legged on Chelci's bed.

"Maybe he'll be pretentious and mean like all of them," Chelci said as she tore herself from the mirror to glance outside. The sun was close to setting, and it was nearly dinner time.

"If they're all mean, who do you think you'll marry?"

Chelci fiddled with her brush as she turned to her friend and shrugged. "I don't know. There are so many things I want to do first. I loved passing out food today. That felt amazing . . . helping those people. I want to do things that make a difference, somehow."

"You know, you don't have to stop just because you get married. I'm sure I'll help Matthew at the bakery after we're wed, but you don't have to stop being who you are."

"Yeah, I guess so."

Emma nodded toward the door. "What do you think that was with your Mother?"

Chelci raised an eyebrow. "You mean her saying a few words that weren't awful? She's probably trying to manipulate me into doing what she wants." She looked at the door and continued to think. "Or maybe she's growing a softer side. Who knows?"

Emma jumped up off the bed, walked to the window, and pressed her face against the chilly pane. "Your *man* should arrive any time now!" Emma said with a giggle.

Chelci tried to hit her friend with the brush, but Emma leaned just out of range.

"Whoever I marry, they won't be named *Caspian*, that's for sure," Chelci said as she turned back to the mirror and inspected herself.

"I believe the High Lord of Justice has a son named Caspian. I wonder if it could be him?" Emma said, continuing to stare out the window.

"Mother still thinks she can order me around however she likes," Chelci said.

"I always wished the son of a high lord would've been interested in me."

"Well, she's got another thing coming."

"Here he comes!" Emma shouted.

Chelci heard the rolling of wheels and the trotting of horses' hooves, but she didn't move to look out of the window. Her stomach twisted, and she took a deep breath.

"Don't you want to look?" Emma asked. "So you can see what he's like?"

Chelci issued a short, harsh laugh. "I'm sure I already know. Let me guess . . . His carriage is trimmed with either gold or silver, and his driver probably wears a brightly colored uniform with a hat far too large with some sort of feather on top." She looked at Emma, who shuffled her feet but didn't reply. Outside, the horses stopped and a door opened.

"And Caspian is tall, with dark hair and a full beard. His shoulders are broad, and there's not a crease in his expensive outfit. I'd guess he didn't even acknowledge whoever opened the door for him. As he walks up to the front door, his back is straight, allowing him to look down on the others." Chelci stood from her chair to approach the window. "How am I doing so far?"

Emma turned around. She pulled the curtains' edges together and blocked the window with her body. "Those things don't matter," she said.

"So I was right?" Chelci asked.

A pout appeared on Emma's face as she released the curtains and crossed her arms.

"Chelci!" her mother's voice called from outside the closed door. "Our guest is here! Come down!"

Chelci sighed.

"You sure you want to do this?" Emma asked as she put her hands on Chelci's arms.

"I don't have a choice," Chelci said.

"No, I mean . . . *this,*" she emphasized, motioning with her hand toward Chelci's body.

A grin grew at the corner of Chelci's mouth. She knew exactly what her friend referred to. "Absolutely."

12

Unwanted Dinner

Emma left out the front door with a wave as Chelci turned toward the dining room, where Jensen stood patiently by the doors.

"They're waiting on y—" Jensen's words stopped as he froze, reaching to open the doors. His eyes steadily widened as Chelci approached.

"They're waiting through here?" she asked.

The choreman nodded.

"Would you be so kind as to open the doors for me?"

"Uh, yes . . . Of course." Flustered, Jensen opened the doors leading to the dining room, allowing Chelci to enter.

Her parents sat at the table. Luciana wore an elegant dress with a string of gems around her neck. Darcius' pressed, gray suit was spotless. Next to her mother sat a broad-shouldered man with thick, black hair. The scruff of a large beard was visible, even from behind. As she stepped into the room, the man turned and began to stand. When his eyes found her, his smile faltered, and he hesitated.

"Chelci!" Her mother shouted. "What is this?" Luciana's eyebrows narrowed sharply as a dark cloud hovered over her.

"What do you mean?" Chelci replied with mock confusion, bringing her hand to her chest and cocking her head. She wore a plain, white shirt and her favorite brown pants—the outfit she wore when sword fighting. Her hair was pulled back, but she had refused to brush out the tangles. She had applied no make-up, leaving all her blemishes on display.

Her father's eyes were wide. He didn't speak but glanced nervously at his wife, whose look of horror was enough for both of them.

"You . . . uh . . . must be Chelci," the dark-haired man said, finally standing. He glanced furtively at her mother to confirm he was not mistaken, but Luciana's jaw was still agape. The man bowed slightly and continued. "I am Caspian Weatherbee, son of Edgar Weatherbee, the High Lord of Justice for Felting."

Chelci stifled a laugh. *Emma was right.* She nodded to him before walking around the table to sit next to her father.

Having recovered from her shock, Luciana spoke without opening her teeth. "Chelci, I told you to clean up."

Chelci examined her arms and hands before turning toward their guest. "Caspian, are there smudges of dirt on my face that I missed?"

The visitor fidgeted. "Um . . . No, I see nothing of the sort."

"What's the matter then, Mother?" Chelci asked. "You asked me to clean up, which I've done. Now, I'm here for dinner."

"Your outfit! It's—" Luciana said before Chelci interrupted.

"It's what? Is it indecent? Have I left my behind exposed?" Chelci made a show of trying to glance at her backside, resulting in a stifled laugh from her father.

"Darcius!" Luciana scolded. He cleared his throat and resumed a stoic expression before she turned back to Chelci. "You haven't done your hair or put on makeup."

"I'm sure our guest can look past frivolous things like hair and makeup. I'd expect he would rather get to know someone based on who they are rather than how artfully they apply rouge to their face."

Caspian swallowed hard and stared blankly. His shoulders relaxed when servers entered the room, delivering platters of nuts and cheese and filling up glasses of wine. The four of them turned their attention to the food and drink as awkward tension filled the room.

Eventually, Caspian broke the silence. "So, Chelci, what sort of activities do you enjoy?"

"I enjoy the outdoors," Chelci replied. "I like being in the woods and climbing trees, well . . . I used to enjoy trees." Her thoughts drifted to her experience fighting the valcor a few weeks prior. "And sword fighting!"

She chanced a glance at her mother, whose jaw clenched and eyes stared like daggers. Caspian appeared unsure how to respond to her revelations.

"Also, I've recently enjoyed helping others. I've started—"

"She used to take etiquette lessons regularly, and she'll be resuming them soon," Luciana said, interrupting.

"No, I believe I'm finished with those," Chelci countered with a harsh look.

Her mother wore a false smile and changed the subject. "How about you, Caspian? What do you enjoy?"

Their guest's shoulders relaxed, and his face softened. "I love hunting. I go most every Weekterm with bows and hawks."

"What do you hunt?" Darcius asked.

"Fox, deer, boar . . . anything that moves, really. Darcius, you know the boar on the wall of the billiard room at the Turba Club?" Darcius nodded. "That was me. Arrow right through the heart, dead in two steps."

Chelci groaned at the boasting. "Have you ever hunted anything truly dangerous like . . . a valcor," she asked, resisting the smug look she wanted to give.

The three others laughed politely. "If one ever shows itself around here, I'll be the first to go after it," Caspian said, puffing out his chest.

He wouldn't say that if he'd seen what I have.

"I've recently taken an interest in fashion as well," Caspian said.

Luciana perked up at the comment. "I noticed how exquisite your tunic is. Who made it?"

Chelci took notice of the tunic. Silver buttons and sharp black accents trimmed the rich, burgundy fabric. The collar was tight as it wrestled against his thick neck.

"Humberto designed it in Searis."

"Oh!" Luciana exclaimed. "Did you travel there?"

"No, my father sends out for them at the beginning of each season."

"We also would like to import our clothing from Searis, but . . ." Luciana glanced at Darcius, who was picking nuts out of a bowl. "We try to support the local shops here in Felting."

Caspian turned to Chelci. "Your outfit is . . . interesting. I've not seen others wearing anything of the sort."

Chelci didn't expect him to approve. She smiled pleasantly and replied, "A lady in a small village in the woods made the shirt, and I sewed the pants myself."

Caspian coughed while drinking his wine, and it dribbled down his beard onto his shirt.

"Your shirt!" Luciana exclaimed as she motioned toward a servant standing against the wall. The servant arrived in moments with a cloth and a glass of water.

"It's okay," Caspian said, motioning to the servant as he blotted the stain, which was the same color as the fabric. "You *made* them yourself?"

"Yes. Is that such a bad thing?" Chelci asked.

"Not at all. It's just—" he chuckled and glanced at Luciana. "I would think a family such as yours could afford to have clothes made."

"Of course we do," Luciana said quickly, with a false smile on her face. "Chelci simply enjoys . . ." She looked to Darcius for help, but he only shrugged. Rather than finish her thought, she changed the subject. "So, Caspian, how large a family do you intend to have?"

"I'd like four or five boys," he said before turning to Chelci. "What about you?"

"I'm not sure yet," she replied as her eyes narrowed. "I'll have that discussion with my future husband once I find the right person. I'll want to make sure we both have a say in however many children we raise, whether they be boys *or* girls."

"Have you thought about what you'll do after you marry, when you can no longer . . . play with swords in trees?" Caspian asked with a smirk. "Do you see yourself as the sort that entertains guests, or will you be the knitting type?"

Chelci cocked her head and stared back. "Why do you assume those are my only options? Is that all you expect a wife to do?" she asked, causing Caspian's brow to furrow. After a moment of silence, she leaned forward and raised her eyebrows. "Is the question confusing?" The tension was thick as she stared across the table at her guest.

Finally, her father broke the silence, changing the subject. "As a city judge and the son of the High Lord of Justice, I'm sure you must know a great deal about the current criminal climate in Felting?"

"Yes, High Lord Marlow. We've seen a rapid growth in crime the last few years. My father aims to release some new decrees soon to deal with it."

"Really?" Chelci said. "What decrees?"

"For starters, he's going to outlaw handouts to beggars. Anyone begging or giving out food to those who do will be thrown in prison."

"What? How is that good or helpful?" Chelci asked, leaning forward with her face pinched. Her mother's smug look made her blood boil.

"Our city is rife with beggars," Caspian said. "When people

help them, it only encourages the activity and de-incentivizes productivity."

"I've been saying the same thing for years," Luciana said. "Haven't I, Darcius?"

Chelci's father nodded silently, but Chelci's face reddened.

Caspian continued, "We need rigid laws and a show of force to start a change. Take the Red Quarter for instance. It's filled with thieves, street gangs, and women who sell themselves at night. It's immoral for us to allow this to continue any longer. We need something strict and decisive."

"There are people out there who are starving and freezing!" Chelci blurted, unable to contain herself. "It's a kindness to help them. Wouldn't you want someone to do the same for you if you were in their position?"

"No, I wouldn't. I would work and earn a living, legally. I wouldn't want anyone else to take care of me. If I didn't do that, I would be the only one to blame," Caspian said.

"Sometimes, it's not that simple," Chelci said. "There are plenty of people living on the streets who *want* to work, but can't find anything. I would think a better solution may be to help those people find work rather than throw them in prison."

The rest of the table fell silent. Chelci looked to her father, who picked at his food.

"I guess that's why we don't allow women to become lords. Am I right?" Caspian said with a chuckle echoed by both her parents.

Chelci clenched her jaw and breathed heavily through her nose. This son of a high lord was clearly not the man for her. She stood and threw her napkin down on her plate before walking toward the door. "I'm not hungry anymore. Caspian, thank you for visiting," she said as she left.

Her mother's protests muffled as the door closed. Chelci didn't look back. She stomped upstairs to her room, where she sat in a huff at the seat by her window.

I knew it. I knew that's what he would be like. Chelci thought back to her time in Nasco and missed the simplicity of life there: time with friends, having a purpose, joining the village guard. *Did I make the wrong choice in coming home?*

A door closed somewhere in the house, and her attention was drawn outside the window. Caspian walked to his carriage, her mother trailing behind. Through the closed window, she heard her mother's plea, "Please, don't go! She's having a difficult day today, but she's normally not like that."

"I appreciate the invitation to come tonight, but I have no desire to marry a young woman such as her," Caspian's muffled voice said as he grabbed the bar on the side of his carriage. "She is ugly, opinionated, and coarse. I would never marry someone as unrefined as her." He slammed the door to the coach, and the carriage took off down the long drive.

Chelci clenched her jaw. She leaned against the wall while the sting of his words worked its way through her body. *Am I really ugly and coarse? Maybe no one will want to marry me as I am?* A tear formed at the corner of her eye, and she wiped it away. The thoughts remained, unable to be wiped so easily.

Chelci's sword struck hard and fast, pushing Veron against the wall of the training room as their swords clanged together. Letting him recover, she walked back to the center of the space while Veron followed. After setting her feet, she roared in attack once more. Veron fended off the blows, wide-eyed.

Chelci panted as her sword sang through the air. A sheen of sweat glistened on her skin, and her hair stuck to the side of her face. She channeled the anger into her strikes, fueling her power and speed.

Finally exhausted, she lowered her sword and sat on the bench by the wall.

"Is everything okay?" Veron asked as he slowly approached.

Chelci inhaled deeply and shook her head as she tried to settle her breath. "It's my parents. They still don't care about what I want."

"What do you mean? What did they do?" Veron took Chelci's sword and hung both up on the wall.

"They tried to set me up with some awful son of a lord. They want to marry me off to someone . . . like them, I guess. I don't want someone like them." She sighed. "I don't know what I want."

"You've only been home, what, a week?" Veron asked. "I'm sure you have time to figure it out."

"I'm just worried I'm too different," Chelci said. "No one will want me because I'm too . . . opinionated . . . and ugly." An abrupt laugh escaped Veron's mouth, and Chelci harshly glared at him. "What?"

Veron looked to the floor. "No . . . I'm sorry. I wasn't laughing." He glanced at the clock on the wall before edging to the door. "I should head to my room."

"No, you don't. You have something to say. What is it?"

"It's really not my place."

Chelci glared as her face reddened. "Tell me," she said harsher than intended.

Veron held his head down and paused at the door, fingering the wooden frame. "I like that you share your opinions. I think it makes you interesting."

Chelci had braced herself for something much worse. The words softened her anger, letting her shoulders relax and a smile form.

Veron brought his gaze up and locked eyes with her. "And . . . you're more beautiful than any girl I've ever known."

Chelci stopped breathing, standing in her pants and plain shirt. She pushed back a sweaty string of hair that rested on her cheek as Veron bowed slightly and walked into the night. A warm feeling swelled in her body, pushing away all traces of hurt and doubt.

13

Night Meeting

Bale rested his hand against the stone column. The cold surface was smooth, worn down by hundreds of years of weather. The surrounding night was thick with heavy clouds that blocked out the stars and moon. His hair, black as night, rustled in the wind, while his thick beard and warm cloak protected against the frigid weather. He waited with five of his men at the offerdom south of Karad. Down the hill, two torches slowly emerged from the darkness, and a sneer formed on his face, tugging at his long scar. Taking his cue, Bale walked to the center of the stone ruins with Commander Ryker by his side.

Over the sound of the wind, the clinking of metal drifted up the hill as the torches neared. Soon, five men mounted the offerdom's eroded steps. Winded, they hesitated when they looked up. Raynor Fiero was the first to step forward.

"What happened?" Raynor asked with a tinge of anger. "We fulfilled our side of the deal, and you disappeared."

"It seems you've done well for yourself in the aftermath, *Baron Fiero*," Bale said with a low, even voice. "How am I to believe this was not your plan all along?"

"I didn't aspire to be Baron of Karad. I expected to be Regent of Feldor," Raynor replied, narrowing his eyes.

Bale turned to the man next to Fiero holding a cane. "Was he one of your men, Lord Billings?"

Gareth Billings' face screwed in question. "What do you mean?"

Bale's voice grew in volume. "We were supposed to have your support. After I killed Rycroft, your men were to pledge allegiance to me." Bale stepped in menacingly, his hand resting on his sword. "Instead, you sent a shadow knight."

The three soldiers behind Raynor and Gareth immediately stepped up and began pulling out their weapons. "Whoa, whoa. Hold on," Gareth said. "What do you mean by a shadow knight?"

Bale stared at the Lord of Defense and studied his face. "You know what I mean." Billings and Fiero exchanged glances of genuine confusion, and Bale second-guessed his accusation. "As soon as you were safely out of the room, a shadow knight arrived and killed my men. I barely escaped. You're saying you had nothing to do with it?"

"Honestly, Your Majesty, we know nothing of this," Raynor said.

"The shadow knights were dismantled years ago. I heard it from King Wesley myself," Gareth added.

"Apparently, they weren't." Bale released his sword hilt and relaxed. A quiet sigh surrounded him from several men.

"How can you be sure he was a shadow knight?" Raynor asked. "Anyone could claim that."

"He *was* one," Bale said, staring toward the city hiding behind the darkness. He clenched his fist to keep from trembling. "This . . . boy did things no one could do. He fought twenty-five of my best men and defeated them with barely any effort. My men didn't have a chance. It was terrifying." *Terrifying . . .* Bale cringed, immediately regretting his choice of words.

"Are you afraid of the prophecy?" Raynor asked.

Bale glared at the baron with quick, forceful breaths. *No one can see my fear,* he thought as he remembered the woman's Dream that predicted a shadow knight would kill him. Still wanting to partner with the man, he restrained himself from exploding at the question. "I'm eager to continue the plan we made to capture Felting. Both of you will receive the money and positions I promised, provided you supply your army and support."

Billings and Fiero looked at each other and nodded. "We are ready to do so," Billings confirmed.

"Good," Bale said. After standing up to his father's abuse as a boy, he resolved nothing would stop him from building his legacy, but the promise of death threatened to undermine his plan. "Before we can act, this shadow knight must be killed."

Raynor looked to Gareth, who shrugged. "We don't know who it is," the baron said.

"Does the name Veron Stormbridge mean anything to you?" Bale asked.

The shocked expression on Raynor's face was plain. "Veron? Yes, I know Veron, but he's not—" he turned to Gareth, who shook his head.

"Veron's good with a staff, but he's no shadow knight," Gareth said.

"Veron is the last shadow knight. I saw it with my own eyes. Where is he?" Bale asked.

"He murdered my son's fiancé the night of the banquet," Raynor said. "He was caught and thrown into prison." A wicked grin crept onto Bale's face until Raynor continued. "Unfortunately, he escaped some time ago. We don't know where he is now."

Bale's face hardened. He ground his teeth as a gust of wind cut through the silence. The Karad group pulled their cloaks tighter, but the men from Norshewa did not move. Finally, Bale turned and walked to the edge of the stone ruins, staring at the darkened city.

"How do we find him? Who knows him well?" Bale asked.

"Well . . . my son does. They used to be close friends," Raynor replied.

Bale turned to the baron with narrowed eyes as the corner of his mouth turned up slightly. "Get him."

A faint, scraping noise drew Brixton out of his sleep, turning him on his side. The groggy weight of his eyelids and the pitch-black room informed him it was still the middle of the night. Before he drifted back to sleep, a hand covered his mouth, causing his heart to race and his body to tense. His eyes bolted open. The outline of a soldier held a finger to his lips.

"Shhh. Quiet," the soldier said. "Your father needs you."

Brixton knew better than to question his father's orders, so he stumbled out of bed and hurriedly dressed as the soldier instructed. In the castle's courtyard, two horses waited, saddled and ready.

After departing the city through the south gate, they continued along the road for a few minutes before pivoting right and heading uphill. As the hill grew steeper, they dismounted and left their horses lashed to a log. Brixton yawned as he followed behind, watching his step as he trudged up the steep slope. Soon, the grass interwove with crumbling, stone steps reclaimed by the wild many years before.

Brixton wasn't sure what to expect, but it certainly wasn't the sight greeting him as he arrived at the top. A group of men stood in the middle of the stone slab. Two soldiers had torches, but their light barely penetrated the ring of columns bordering the ruins. He recognized Gareth Billings, who nodded in his direction. His insides churned when he saw his father.

Brixton was used to his father's pride and confidence, but his pinched expression and slumped shoulders were new. *Why does Father look so worried?*

Past them, a second group stood at the far end of the ruins, facing the river, but Brixton couldn't make out who they were.

"Where's Veron?" his father asked.

"Veron?" Brixton replied, glancing between the men to see if any indicated it was a joke. "You called me here out of bed to ask where Veron is?"

"Yes, what do you know?"

"Veron . . . He was—" Brixton stopped as he thought over the last few weeks. "I—I know as much as you, Father. He was in prison last I saw. I visited him once, but I heard he since disappeared."

Raynor stared at him. Brixton shifted his weight under the uncomfortable scrutiny. A man in the other group turned and walked toward them. As he approached, his tall, muscular frame and black beard grew visible in the flickering torchlight. Brixton's eyes widened as the long scar running down the left side of the man's face came into view. Brixton's muscles clenched when he made the connection. He stood face-to-face with King Edmund Bale.

"Do you know who I am, Brixton?" Bale asked.

Brixton swallowed and cleared his throat before speaking. "Yes, Your Majesty."

"Are you sure you don't know where Veron Stormbridge is?"

Brixton's throat ran dry. *I don't know where he is, but I'm sure I could track him down.* Brixton remembered the look of betrayal on Veron's face as they talked in the prison—after Brixton turned on him. The feeling didn't sit well, and he tried to push the memory away. "Yes, I'm sure. I don't know."

"You are the Lord of Commerce for Karad now, correct?" Bale's tone felt casual, and Brixton relaxed and nodded in response. "You seem young to hold such a distinguished position. You must be a man of drive and ambition."

"Thank you, Your Majesty," Brixton replied. "I try to do my best."

"Soon, I'll be in control of all of Terrenor and will need good people I can count on. I'll need leaders I can trust to place in positions of power. They'll receive lands and titles and will never want for anything. Are you interested in being someone I can trust, Brixton?"

Brixton couldn't move. He was twenty years old and had only been a lord for a few weeks, but the most powerful man in the land wanted to give him more prestige. He swallowed to clear his dry throat then nodded in response.

"That's good," Bale said. "Veron Stormbridge is the most dangerous person in Terrenor right now, and everything depends on him being found."

A laugh escaped Brixton's mouth, but Bale's harsh look quickly stopped it. "Veron? He's a common merchant who was a thief living on the street only a few years ago. How's he dangerous?"

"Veron is a shadow knight and is more threatening to me than an army of a thousand soldiers."

"A shadow knight?" Brixton exclaimed with another laugh. "No, you've got it—"

"That's enough!" Bale roared, immediately silencing Brixton. "I need to know where Veron is." He stepped so close Brixton felt heat from his breath. In a smooth motion, the king pulled a knife from his belt and held it to Brixton's neck, causing him to inhale sharply. "And I think you're lying to me."

The men at the ruins froze while tension filled the air. Brixton's legs trembled as he stared at the king. In his mind, he pictured the man he sold Veron to and knew where he could find him. He also remembered the look on Veron's face when they spoke in prison. *I can't do that to him again.* His jaw locked tight as he internally battled his desires. "I would like to help in any way I can . . . but I truly don't know where he is."

Bale narrowed his eyes and stared at Brixton for a long moment until he finally backed off. "In that case, tell me all you know about him."

14

The Red Quarter

"I f you're so afraid, you don't have to be here," Chelci told Emma
as she rolled the cart down the street. The sun shone brightly,
projecting an unseasonable mid-wiether warmth.

"It's not that I'm afraid. It's that . . . they made this law for a reason."
Emma said. "Why would you violate it only a few days after it was
decreed?"

"It's an immoral law, and it's not fair to the people in need."

"So, you're going to take them food, flagrantly violating the rule. Is
it worth getting thrown in prison?"

"They won't throw me in prison," Chelci said with a laugh. "Can
you imagine the uproar my parents would cause? No one wants to
be on the other end of Mother's wrath."

"Didn't your mother just tell you not to do this anymore?"

"Yeah, but she still wouldn't let them do anything to me. It'd be too
embarrassing for her."

"I don't know, Chelci. I think this is a bad idea, and I won't help
you."

"Why are you here then?" Chelci asked. The food in the cart jostled
as it hit a bump in the road. "If you don't approve and you won't help,

why are you coming?"

Emma was momentarily quiet until she finally spoke, "I worry about you going alone. The Red Quarter isn't a safe place. And why would you wear that necklace? It's like you're asking for trouble."

Chelci glanced down at the golden necklace her father gave her. She no longer enjoyed fancy clothing and jewelry to the extent she had when she was young, but the necklace reminded her of his kindness. "It's not like I'm wearing Mother's jeweled Barnaby Necklace—not that she would ever allow me. I'll be fine."

Emma groaned. "Chelci, you can be so bull-headed sometimes."

The two girls arrived in the center of the Red Quarter, and Chelci parked the cart by the side of the road. Wesley and Dolores weren't visible, but plenty of desperate, hungry faces glanced in their direction.

Emma haphazardly looked around. "I'm sorry, Chelci," she said, taking a step away. "I can't do this. I can't afford to get in trouble." As Emma walked away, Chelci remembered the disappointment and loneliness six years before when her friend refused to run away with her.

The hungry people gathering around snapped her back to the present. She smiled as she offered the fare to the thankful men, women, and children. The food ran out quickly, but a warm joy remained.

As she picked up the end of the empty cart and turned it toward home, something down the street caught her eye. Two soldiers in full uniform purposefully walked down the road. The crowd parted before them as they moved quickly, walking in her direction and staring.

Chelci's stomach jumped. *They're coming for me!* Instead of traveling the way she came, Chelci veered right toward an alley. At the end of the narrow street, she left the cart and ran.

Veron stepped under the shop's rickety covering and glanced at the supplies and tools. He had been head gardener at the Marlows' estate for over a week, and his spirits rose every day. The time he spent turning dirt, weeding, and harvesting reminded him of working with Artimus back in Karad. The other servants' respect gradually increased—except for Tristan, who still glared at Veron whenever they passed. Tessa had even complimented him on how nice the garden looked.

"Is there anythin' I kin help ya with?" the shopkeeper asked after the previous customer left.

"Possibly," Veron replied, holding a shovel, a sack with some short wooden stakes, and a new whetstone. "Do you have any paleno seeds?"

The man wrinkled his forehead. "Don't git much call fir them. Lemme see . . ." the man walked to the back of his shop where he rummaged through a large bin. "What need ya have fir them?"

"I thought they'd be fun to grow. Have you ever had them before?" Veron asked.

"No, I kent say that'a have. Ah! Here ya are!" The man held up a packet with a flourish.

Veron smiled as he remembered his time at Morgan's shop where he was first introduced to the spiny fruit. He relished the idea of growing some and showing them to Chelci.

"Thanks," Veron said as he took the package. "This should do it."

After paying the man for his supplies with coins he received from Tessa, Veron walked out into the street. The center of the Red Quarter greeted him. The area felt familiar. The sights and smells reminded him of the Bottoms back in Karad.

Before turning up the street to head back toward the Marlow house, a flurry of movement caught his eye. A young lady hurried as she pushed a wooden cart across the street and disappeared into an alley.

Chelci panted as she twisted and turned through the narrow streets. Residents sitting outside of dilapidated homes turned their heads slowly as she careened by. Before long, she was hopelessly lost in the depths of the Red Quarter.

Content she had left her pursuers far behind, she finally stopped and bent over to catch her breath, resting her hands on her knees. As she willed her heart to slow, Chelci noticed her surroundings.

The buildings were dark and dingy. Doors hung crooked on their hinges with paint peeling from the frames. Waste and rusted metal littered the alleys, and a sickly stench filled the air. She covered her nose with her sleeve.

Ahead, the path narrowed where a group of unsavory-looking men congregated. One man tapped another and motioned in her direction, causing Chelci's breath to catch. She took a hesitant step back before turning and moving in the opposite direction as she absently fingered her necklace. She turned down a side alley and picked up her pace.

After making a few more turns down unfamiliar corridors and passing underneath an arch, she emerged into a small, stone courtyard bordered on all sides by tall walls. *Dead end,* she thought dreadfully.

When she turned to head back the way she came, she froze. Six men entered the courtyard, walking slowly and fanning out. They were tall and appeared stronger than the others she'd seen. Their clothes were dirty, and their faces turned down in a grim display of want.

Two doors lined the stone walls behind Chelci. She ran quickly to try each, but they were locked. Her heart sank. She turned around as wicked grins formed on the men's faces. Her eyes darted as she anxiously thought of options. She tried to run past a large man with a beard down to his chest, but he grabbed her by the arm and threw her to the ground. Her face and hands scraped against pebbles on the ground, and her knee banged into stone, sending spasms of pain shooting through her body.

"Where do you think you're going?" the large man asked, prompting a laugh from the rest.

"Someone wearin' her dress with that necklace . . . I bet her parents'll pay a king's ransom," another sneered.

As she struggled to her feet, a broom leaning against the wall caught her eye. She scurried to grab it, spun, and held it in front of her. The men's violent laughter bounced off the courtyard walls as she brandished the miserable excuse for a weapon.

"Here, girl. Why don't you give that to me," a man said as he stepped forward, arm outstretched.

Chelci struck him sharply in the arm, then spun and hit him again in the stomach. The man doubled over, and a fresh round of laughter issued from the other five.

"Let me go!" Chelci shouted.

"First, I'd like to have a closer look at that necklace," one man said.

Chelci touched the necklace with one of her hands, picturing the smile on her father's face as he gave it to her. Unwilling to hand over the memento, she jabbed the man in the chest. Another approached from the side, and she hit him in the back, eliciting a groan.

"Enough!" the man shouted as he rubbed his chest. "Grab her!"

Chelci's eyes narrowed as she half-crouched, holding the broom out and preparing to strike. For a moment, none of the six moved. They glanced between each other as if waiting for someone else. *Maybe they're giving up?* Chelci thought for a fleeting moment. Suddenly, all six men moved at once, dashing her hopes.

She sprung into action. One man fell to the ground after a blow to the side of the head, and another backed up as her weapon stung him in the arm. To her dismay, the skirmish ended abruptly when two men grabbed her arms from behind and relieved her of the broomstick.

The one she hit in the head stepped forward as he held his ear. His red face and stony jaw glowered at her. "You're going to regret that," he growled as he slapped her across the face.

Chelci's cheek exploded in pain. She blinked to drive away the blinding white light. Before she could refocus, a fist hammered her stomach, knocking the breath out of her. She wanted to bend over and collapse, but the arms propping her up wouldn't allow it.

"Leave her alone!" a voice shouted from the other side of the courtyard.

Chelci barely heard the words at first due to the ringing in her ear. The arms holding her loosened a bit as the men turned. Through the mass of bodies, a sight filled her with hope. A young man with a shovel stood underneath the arch to the courtyard. Dirt stained his clothes, and he carried a sack in his other hand. *Veron!*

Veron burned inside as he took in the scene. Six men surrounded Chelci, holding her in place. After searching the maze of alleyways to find her, he arrived as a man punched her. He wouldn't wait to see what came next.

"Leave her alone," he said again with decidedly more force. The men holding Chelci dropped her to the ground, and all six turned their attention to him.

"Or what?" one man asked. "What are you gonna do about it?"

Veron tossed the sack to the side but held onto the shovel. He bent his knees and held its metal end toward the men. As they continued their slow approach, Veron cleared his mind and searched inside to find the origine. It almost worked after his whipping, but something suppressed his ability to use it. He gripped the shovel's rough handle tightly as his body strained. The faintest hint of a tingle built deep inside of him as sweat beaded on his forehead. *This isn't going to work.*

While distracted by his thoughts, the first man ran at him. Veron gave up his attempt to use the origine, stepped to the side, and struck the attacker with his shovel, sending the man crashing into the stone wall. He hit the next man with the blade's flat end on the side of the head, dropping him to the ground. Another man received a blow to the stomach with the wooden handle and reeled over.

"Veron, look out!" Chelci yelled from across the courtyard.

Veron turned to her as a man landed on his back and fumbled to grab the shovel handle. Keeping it just out of reach of the flailing hands, Veron backed into the wall, drawing an "Oof!" from the man as his grip loosened. Veron spun, throwing the man to the ground and following with a shovel blow to the chest.

Two men remained. The taller one held a broom like a sword and glared at Veron as he swung. Veron glanced the broom away with the shovel, stepped forward, and swept the man's legs out from under him with the other end. He fell onto the hard ground and groaned.

Veron looked to the last attacker, daring him to approach, but the man inched sideways toward the arch. A feint sent the man running. The other five—in various states of crawling or stumbling—moved quickly after him.

Veron tossed down the shovel and hurried to Chelci's side. "Are you alright?"

The side of her face was bright red. She nodded and grimaced, struggling to stand. Veron held Chelci's arm to steady her, but her knee buckled.

"Here, let me carry you."

Chelci put her arm around his shoulder as he picked her up. After years of running with stones, her light body was easy to manage.

"Is that okay?" Veron asked. "Does it hurt?"

She shook her head and looked into his eyes. "Thank you for finding me."

Veron sensed her body's tension evaporate. The softness in her eyes and her half-smile gave him all the thanks he needed. She wrapped her arms around his neck as Veron made his way out of the courtyard and headed back to the Marlow house.

After Veron carried Chelci home, a swarm of attendants swooped in and promptly whisked her away to her room along with her parents. He followed along, but they stopped him at the door. While waiting, he paced the hallway outside her room. After seemingly forever, his head jerked up as the door opened. Jensen waved at him to enter.

Chelci lay on her bed as he entered the room. A nurse sat beside her bed and dabbed her face with a cloth. The scrapes looked much better already. Chelci's mother and father stood next to the bed, but both stared at him. Veron wasn't sure what to do or say, so he stood some distance away. He held his hands together in front of his body, then behind his back—neither position felt natural.

"It seems you've been busy today, Ash," Luciana said, staring down at him. Veron shrank at the nickname.

Darcius chimed in, "You've done our family a great service. Thank you for your bravery and action, which was far beyond what we would expect from a housekeeper or gardener."

The words bolstered Veron, and he stood up straight. He glanced at Chelci, eyes glowing with gratitude.

High Lord Marlow continued. "Recently, Luciana and I discussed getting Chelci an attendant. But our daughter seems to have a way of finding trouble, and today's events suggest she may need a guard more than she needs a wardess."

Veron tilted his head as Luciana chimed in. "Chelci said you were amazing—that you fought off six men with nothing but a shovel. She insisted we appoint *you* as her wardman, to serve as both her guard and attendant."

Veron's eyes grew. He glanced at Chelci, who held a reserved grin on her face. "Other than your first-day mishap, your work has been exemplary," Luciana said. "However, we're hesitant to appoint a guard without any formal training."

"I've been trained!" Veron blurted. "I spent four years in Karad training under . . . um . . . a highly ranked veteran from their army. I learned how to fight with the sword, the staff, an axe, and lots of other weapons. I'm happy to demonstrate my skills in your sparring room if you like."

"He's more skilled than any of our other guards, Mother," Chelci added.

Luciana and Darcius looked at each other with raised eyebrows. After a long moment, Darcius shrugged his shoulders, and Luciana sighed as she nodded her head. "Very well," Darcius said. "We would like you to be her wardman. You will wait on her and provide anything she needs. Whenever she leaves the house, you will be with her and make sure she is protected."

Chelci grinned at Veron while his jaw slowly dropped. Her parents waited for his response, which came in a jumbled mess. "Yes—um—I . . . Of course! I gladly accept!"

Luciana raised a finger. "I've not forgotten the incident with the ashes. Any hint of impropriety will be met with harsh punishment. Make sure you don't step out of line, and know we'll be watching."

Veron nodded vigorously. He'd only been at the Marlow house a couple of weeks, and they already promoted him twice. His stomach fluttered at the thought of spending every day with Chelci. Things were definitely looking up.

15

The Search Begins

Morgan walked up Elderberry Street with a crate of cabbage he picked up from a local garden. The crate was light—not nearly as full as normal. In the week since Brixton fired Chloe, Matteo, and Jacob, he had already seen the market's sales drop. To his supplier's dismay, he couldn't afford as much as he had in the past.

The market was closed to customers on Weekterm, but as Morgan entered the courtyard, his feet slowed to a halt. The baker, Danyel, stood beside Henry and Greta. Morgan's wife, Catherine, and their kids continued in a line. Catherine stared at him while she wrung her hands out. The kids shook as they held onto each other. A Karad soldier in full uniform stood at either end of the line. "What's going on?" Morgan asked.

The wooden gate rolled to a close behind him, causing Morgan to spin around. Two more soldiers guarded the exit.

"What's the meaning of this?" Morgan insisted.

"Morgan Fenster," a voice said as a soldier with a captain's insignia exited the office to the side of the courtyard. The man offered a syrupy smile and gestured toward the office. "Would you please join me?"

Morgan glanced back to Catherine, her arm wrapped tightly around their youngest son, Will. Tears fell from his kids' faces, but they didn't make a sound. Morgan set the crate of cabbage down on a stand and slowly walked to the office.

Inside the stuffy room, two other soldiers stood in the corners, hoods obscuring their faces. "Won't you sit, please?" the man said, prompting Morgan to comply. "I'm Captain Gannon. Baron Fiero asked me to get some information, so I need to ask you some questions. Is that alright?"

The captain's smile did not fool Morgan. The fear on his family's faces and the other soldiers' severe looks told him all he needed to know. Still, he nodded.

"What do you know about the whereabouts of Veron Stormbridge?" the captain asked as he leaned on the side of the desk.

Morgan's forehead wrinkled as he stared at the man. "Veron died several weeks ago. Norshewan soldiers killed him when Bale attacked."

"We both know that isn't true." The captain's face didn't change as he spoke. "What else do you know?"

Morgan lifted an eyebrow. "I heard Veron died the night of the banquet. Ask Brixton Fiero. He was with him. Honestly, that's all I know."

"When was the last time you saw him?"

"That night, before he left for the banquet. He was supposed to receive the Gold Crown License Award."

Gannon narrowed his eyes as his smile faded. "How did Veron acquire his abilities?"

Morgan leaned forward in his chair. "I'm sorry . . . What? What do you mean?"

"How did he become a shadow knight?"

Morgan laughed. "A shadow knight?" He glanced at the other two soldiers, their posture indicating the captain was serious. "Veron wasn't a shadow knight. They don't even exist—that I know of."

"This isn't a laughing matter!" Gannon yelled as he slammed his fist on the table and leaned in. "Veron Stormbridge is a shadow knight. He murdered Baron Rycroft and escaped from the castle."

"What? No, he didn't—"

"You have been his closest friend for years, and I believe you know where he is."

Morgan stared at the captain while the room's silence grew. "Well, I don't!" he said finally, holding the captain's gaze without blinking.

The captain clenched his jaw as his eyes bore a hole into Morgan. A flick of the soldier's eyes to the corner told Morgan there was more going on than they led him to believe. A moment later, the scrape of armor and footsteps approached. The man in the corner lowered his hood to reveal a black beard and a scar on the side of his face. He stood menacingly as Captain Gannon shrank back to the wall.

"Your words are that of a loyal friend," the bearded man said. "I commend you."

Morgan's heart quickened. Something about the deep, resonant voice chilled him.

"Do you know who I am, Morgan?" the man asked. Morgan shook his head. "Over years, I recruited men, trained them, and gathered supplies. I marched for weeks and climbed over mountains to arrive at your city, where we entered with no resistance." The man took a dagger out and waved it in Morgan's face. "And I killed your baron with this knife as he looked into my eyes."

Blood drained from Morgan's face as he stared wide-eyed. He knew the imposing man.

"I am Edmund Bale, King of Norshewa and soon to be ruler of all of Terrenor. You would be wise to tell me what you know about Veron

Stormbridge."

Morgan's breath was steady. He set his jaw and didn't blink. Even if he knew where Veron was, he could never give up his friend—no matter what Bale did.

Bale continued, "I could ramble on about how it's your duty to tell me what you know. I could make empty promises about the great things I would give you in my new kingdom, but we both know it would be a lie. What I *can* tell you is you'll regret not telling me."

After a moment of icy silence, Bale stood abruptly and exited the office. Gannon and the other soldier pulled swords and ushered Morgan to follow.

In the courtyard, Morgan made eye contact with Catherine, appearing in no better shape than before. He followed Bale to the furnace, which already held a roaring fire. The Norshewan king grabbed the end of a poker sitting in the coals. He stirred the metal tool, and sparks shot out of the brick opening.

"I'm going to ask you again, Morgan," Bale said as he pulled the poker out. The end glowed red, smoke spiraling off it. "Where is Stormbridge?"

Morgan stared back defiantly as he stood tall. "I told you already—I don't know, and if I did, I wouldn't say a word. Do whatever you want to me."

The corner of Bale's mouth turned up slightly, and a soft laugh built. "Oh, Morgan. I don't intend to do anything to *you*." An evil grin spread fully across his face as he looked past the grocer.

A sinking feeling grew in Morgan's stomach, and his breath became ragged. Slowly, he turned. His heart stopped when his eyes found the target of the king's evil gaze. Just over his shoulder, Catherine stood clutching their kids. Tears streamed as two soldiers stood behind her with swords drawn.

* * *

His head covered by a hood, Bale lifted the remains of charred timber, searching for anything that might help. He imagined the large house that stood there years before. Fire reduced the structure to nothing, but the outline was easy to imagine. A high, stone wall surrounded the yard, containing a small shed and a garden's remains.

"What are we looking for, exactly?" Captain Gannon asked with a hint of impatience.

"Veron lived here for years," Bale said. "We're looking for anything that might give a clue of how he trained or where he may be now."

"Sir! Here!" a voice said from the other side of the ruin.

Bale approached two soldiers lifting a large beam of wood. It fell with an enormous crash as they pushed it over. One soldier dropped into the shallow depression and pulled a charred sword out of the rubble.

The king inspected the weapon. Although scorched and bent, it was in good shape. Two more swords, two daggers, and a battle axe were eventually uncovered amongst the debris.

"What was this place?" Gannon asked.

Bale took a deep breath and exhaled. His voice was low and reverent. "This is where he trained to be a shadow knight. He would have been young, so he must have had a teacher."

Rocks crunched as another soldier walked up to the group. "What'd you find, Lamont?" Captain Gannon asked.

"We talked to all the homes around," Lamont reported. "It burned down two years ago, and no one's lived here since."

"What about before that?" Bale asked.

"There was an old man in his mid-sixties who lived here for ten to fifteen years. The last four years were with a young boy."

Bale's heart sped up. "Stormbridge."

The soldier continued, "No one knew either of them. They kept to themselves and never offered more than a greeting when passing in the street."

"The man is the key," Bale said. "He must be the boy's teacher. Round up all men in their sixties and question them. I don't care what you have to do to get them to talk. If we can find him, we will find the knight."

"Sir," Gannon said. "I need to run that by Baron Fiero first, to make sure he—"

"Fiero answers to me!" Bale shouted. "I want the man found!" Lamont raised a wavering hand. "Yes?"

"He . . . died in the fire." The soldier said, pointing toward the remains of a garden. "They say the boy buried him there."

Bale exhaled loudly as he began to pace. *Where are you, Veron?* He felt so close but was out of leads. A cry of frustration bellowed from his lungs, causing the soldiers to jump.

"I want posters on every city corner," Bale said. ". . . in Karondir, Felting, Tienn, and every farmhouse crossroads throughout Feldor. I want you to go door-to-door and search every building in Karad."

"Your Majesty," Gannon said in a quiet voice. "That would—"

"Do it!" Bale roared. "Tell them it's on Baron Fiero's orders. Then search outside of the city. Scour the forest. Turn over rocks. Search the river. I want this boy found! Threaten anyone who could be protecting him, and make sure they're afraid! String up a body in Karad Square as a warning."

Gannon glanced furtively at his soldiers before turning back to Bale. "Who do we string up?"

"I don't care. Find someone. Kill someone—anyone. Him, for all I care," Bale said as he pointed at Lamont, who stepped backward. "Make sure the people of Karad know that Veron Stormbridge must be caught, and if they suffer, it will be because of him."

16

The Wardman

Veron stood in the head attendant's office while Jensen sized him up. As the most senior of the family's attendants, Jensen kept the serving staff in line, and he took the role very seriously. He scowled while Veron bounced on the balls of his feet, hands crossed in front of him.

"Wardman is not a position to be taken lightly," Jensen said sternly. "It will be your responsibility to make sure Miss Chelci wants for nothing. If errands need to be run, see them done. Make sure she has the food and clothes she needs. When she desires a bath, make sure it's prepared."

"Isn't it typical for a wardess to handle these duties for a lady?" Veron asked. "I'm happy to serve in any way . . . I just thought it seemed unusual."

"No, it's not unusual. You're not *bathing* her or *dressing* her. You're getting what she needs. In the homes of lords, men or women fill the roles. Lady Luciana's attendant before Violetta was a male servant. Are you uncomfortable with it?"

"Oh, no! It's fine. I was only curious."

"Your most important responsibility is her safety. When she goes out, you are to be with her. Make sure you have a weapon—we'll supply you with what you need. If something happens to her, you will be liable, and trust me . . . you don't want to be responsible for that."

Veron nodded. Even though he had impressed Lady Luciana on multiple occasions and she had begun to warm to him, he still worried one wrong move would cost him his collateral and endanger his friends in Karad. His new responsibility was important, and he aimed to do it well.

"Hurry along now," Jensen said. "She'll wake soon, and it's important you're there for whatever she needs."

With a smile plastered on his face, Veron scurried through the downstairs and took the spiral stairs two at a time. Arriving at Chelci's door, he extended his hand to knock but immediately doubted himself. *Do I knock? What if I wake her up? Do I stand here?* He glanced around the hall. Neither Elliot, Lord Marlow's wardman, nor Violetta, Lady Luciana's wardess, waited in the hallway outside the closed doors to their chambers. He turned the handle and quietly entered Chelci's room.

The curtains were drawn, so the room remained dark. The morning light sneaking through revealed Chelci sound asleep under the covers. *Do I wake her? Should I wait?* Feeling creepy watching her, he poked around the room.

A desk with a mirror and chair sat opposite the bed, and an enormous wardrobe rested against the opposite wall with a dressing screen beside it. Veron peeked out from behind a curtain to find a view of the house's long drive.

"I'm getting up. I'm getting up," Chelci said as her blankets rustled.

Veron turned and winced. He had allowed a sliver of sunlight from the edge of the curtain to fall directly across her face. "I'm so sorry! I tried not to wake you!"

"Oh! Veron!" she said as she grasped the ends of her covers and pulled them back up to her chest. "I forgot."

Veron averted his eyes. "I'm sorry, Chelci. I can leave while you get ready. I—I'm new at this and wasn't sure what to do."

"No, it's fine," she said quickly, lowering the covers. "I was just surprised. It's new to me, too. I've never had a wardman before." She swung her legs over the side of the bed and bounced onto the wooden floor. "We can figure it out together."

Veron nodded, his eyes focused on the wall while she walked in his direction. A flush crept up his face. He looked to the coffered ceiling as if trying to locate a bug hidden in the pattern of boxes.

"Veron, if you're going to be my wardman, you can't just watch the ceiling."

Veron dropped his gaze. Chelci's hair bunched against her head, rogue strands falling across her cheek. Her face contained no makeup—not unusual, but he was *not* used to seeing her in a silk nightgown. He lifted his chin, refusing to allow his eyes to drop below her neck and eliciting a laugh from Chelci. "What?" Veron asked.

"I've never met someone who's as . . ." she paused, appearing to search for the right word.

Awkward? Veron thought.

"Polite as you are," she finished.

The side of Veron's mouth turned up. "How can I help?"

"First, let me get dressed."

"You don't need me to lay out clothes or anything, do you?"

Chelci laughed and crossed the room to the wardrobe. "No, I think I can manage." She opened the doors and stared at the dozens of dresses lining the rack. "I'm curious, though. What would you choose?"

"Me?" Veron swallowed as he joined her. He thought he heard

a giggle, muffled by a hand. After looking through the dresses, he selected one with a green fabric edged in white lace. *This would probably look good.* He extended it toward her, shrugging in question.

Chelci cocked her head. "Why that one?"

"I don't know. I think you'd look pretty in it," Veron said. Chelci raised her eyebrows. "I'm sure you'd look pretty without it on, too," he added, causing her eyes to widen. "I mean . . . I'm sure you'd look pretty in anything you wore or didn't wear . . . I mean—" Veron lowered his head into his hand and groaned.

"Thank you." Chelci smirked as she took the dress from Veron's hand. "But I think I might freeze to death in this one."

Taking a second look, Veron noted the thin fabric and short sleeves. He flushed as she set the dress back and selected a blue one with long sleeves and several layers. "This will do for today."

Veron nodded. "Yeah, that's a better choice."

Chelci stepped behind the dressing screen as Veron moved to the other side of the room. He watched the opposite wall, wondering what to do next when he heard teeth chattering behind him. "Are you okay?" he asked over his shoulder.

"Yeah, it's just cold."

"Would you like me to make a fire?" Veron asked, glancing at the darkened hearth where a stack of wood sat ready to be lit.

"No, don't worry about it, I don't intend to stay here long."

After a moment, Chelci's footsteps indicated it was safe to turn around, so he did. She nearly took his breath away. The striking blue color perfectly complimented her skin tone. He marveled at the simplicity of her beauty. "You do your own hair, right? Or do you need my help with it?" he asked.

"What do you mean?" she said in a playful tone as she tossed the wild strands back and forth. "Is something wrong with it?" She laughed, sat in the chair in front of the mirror, and picked up a brush.

"I can manage fine . . . but, if you want to give it a shot . . . ?"

Veron gulped as he took the brush from her extended hand and studied her hair. Unsure where to begin, he gingerly held some of her hair in one hand and ran the brush through it with the other. After a few strokes, the tangles melted away, leaving it straight and glossy.

"Have you ever brushed a girl's hair before?" Chelci asked.

Veron's heart jumped. "Is this wrong? How should I do it?"

Chelci laughed. "Oh, no. You're fine. I was just curious."

Veron's face warmed when he noticed her watching him through the mirror. He forced himself to focus on her hair.

"How do you feel about your goal so far?" Chelci asked.

"What do you mean?" Veron replied as he brushed out a tangle.

"Doing the best wherever you're at and making something of your life."

"Oh, yeah. Good, I guess. Who would've thought I'd go from floor-scrubber to wardman in only a couple of weeks?"

Chelci watched him for a moment before adding in a quiet voice, "I would have." Veron's mouth tweaked with a grin as he continued his work.

When he finished the job, Veron lowered the brush and stepped back to evaluate. The earlier tufts had disappeared, and he smiled at his work. "What's next?"

"Would you mind letting the kitchen know I'll be down soon for breakfast?"

"Of course." Veron set down the brush and walked to the door.

"Veron," Chelci said, causing him to turn with his hand on the doorknob. Her eyes sparkled with friendly creases at the corners. "I'm glad you're my wardman."

A warm feeling flooded him as he returned her smile. He felt stuck as he held her gaze, unable to tear himself away. His heart quickened, and his hand grew clammy on the knob. With much effort, he nodded and left through the door.

* * *

Veron lightly descended the stairs. He'd served as Chelci's wardman for three weeks, and every day felt like a gift. He'd grown comfortable waiting on her and taking care of her needs. Some days, they went on long walks just to get out of the house and talk. Even though they were together during the day, they continued their sparring sessions at night.

The day before, she instructed him to wake up extra early but wouldn't say why. He was long used to rising before the sun, but his body still complained when he rolled out of bed.

Where is she? he thought after opening her door to find an empty bedroom. He looked under the bed and behind the dressing screen, but Chelci wasn't there. As he was about to leave, a note on the desk caught his eye. "Meet me in the kitchen." The strange request didn't faze Veron. He left her room and bounded down two flights of stairs to the basement.

As he walked into the kitchen, the sight greeting him was the last thing he expected. Chelci carried a large bowl with a heavy-looking sack across the room. The burden thudded when she dropped it onto the long worktable.

"Veron," she said upon seeing him gawk at her. "Come here. I need your help."

"Chelci, what are you doing?"

A broad grin covered her face. "I'm making breakfast for the servants."

"What?" Veron's jaw dropped as he stared at her. "What are you making?"

"Nothing fancy, just some Nasco Rolls with butter. The servants all get up so early to make food for my family. I figure they're probably hungry in the morning, so I thought it would be nice to make something for them."

Veron chuckled and shook his head. "Yeah, I bet they would like it. What do you need help with?"

"Can you get a bucket of water while I gather the ingredients?"

Veron didn't know how to bake rolls, but he could certainly gather water. By the time he returned, Chelci had gathered the rest of her ingredients and utensils.

"How do you know how to bake? I doubt your mother taught you."

"Did you forget that I lived in the woods for six years? I learned all sorts of things. I've baked plenty of bread before—just never for this many people. Can you help me with the rye flour?"

Chelci lifted a large sack and leaned it toward the empty bowl, straining to pour just the right amount. Veron helped hold the heavy bag while she lowered the opening.

"A little more," she said as Veron lifted it higher. "A little more."

Suddenly, the weight of the flour shifted, and a massive heap dumped into the bowl. The fine grain billowed into the air, dusting both Chelci and Veron with a light-gray powder. After a moment of shock, laughter filled the room as they looked at each other.

"That's one way to do it, I guess," Veron said.

"You look like a ghost!" Chelci said between laughs as they tried to dust themselves off.

After measuring out the proper amount, they did the same with an identical sack of wheat flour. Next, she added salt, molasses, water, and yeast, then finally tossed in chopped turnfoil root and some carrington seeds. She worked and kneaded the mixture. Soon, a sticky dough covered her hands.

Veron watched as she labored, leaning in slightly, entranced by her movements. She pushed the dough with the heel of her hand, turned it, and slapped it onto the table.

"What?" Chelci asked.

Veron sat up straight, caught by the question. "What? I didn't say anything."

"That grin on your face. What are you smiling about?"

"Oh. I didn't realize I was smiling. I'm sorry."

"It's okay. You're allowed to smile," she said with a laugh.

"I don't know. It's just . . . You. You make me smile." A blush swept over Chelci's face as she looked down at the dough. "Here you are . . . this daughter of a high lord. And you're out giving food to poor people and waking up early to bake rolls for servants. You're different . . . in a good way."

Chelci cleared her throat and looked around, wanting to change the subject. "Can you grab that cloth? We need to let it sit awhile," she said as she put the worked dough back into the bowl. Veron covered it with the cloth. "I sure am a mess," she said, holding out her doughy hands and inspecting herself with a chuckle.

"You've still got some . . ." Veron pointed to the flour in her hair. She scanned around, as if trying to figure out how to clean up. "Here, let me," Veron said as he stepped closer.

Chelci stood still as Veron brushed the flour from her hair. Close up, he noticed more flour on her face. "Do you mind?" he asked. She extended her chin. With light fingers, he dusted flour from her jaw, her cheek, and finally a bit off her forehead. His heart beat loudly as he brushed her soft skin. After cleaning the flour, he tucked a loose strand of hair behind her ear, earning a smile in return.

Their eyes held each other for a long moment until Veron finally cleared his throat and stepped away. "So, what's next?"

Chelci deeply exhaled. "Now, we need to get things ready to bake. Can you start a fire in the furnace while I clean my hands?"

Veron looked to the wall where a large brick oven sat. Danyel at the market taught him well how to start a furnace. Before long, the oven was hot with the fiery coals evenly spread.

By the time the fire was ready, the dough had rested long enough. After dividing it into balls and setting them on sheets, Chelci placed them in the furnace.

The rolls finally baking, Veron and Chelci sighed and leaned back against the worktable. Sweat dripped down both their faces, and flour dusted their clothes.

"Wow, that's a lot of work," Veron said.

"I can't believe there's a staff of people who do this for us every day," Chelci said as she walked to the side door, briefly opening it to look outside toward the sky. The chill of wiether rushed in and provided relief from the intense heat filling the room. "They'll be up soon."

While the delicious smell of bread filled the basement, Veron and Chelci rummaged through the storage rooms. They returned with containers of butter and jam, which they set out on the table. It didn't take the rolls long to bake. When she gave the word, Veron removed the sheets from the oven. Finally, Chelci popped the rolls into a basket and covered them with a cloth.

While finishing the last sheet, footsteps and voices sounded on the stairs. Soon, the head chef, Corbus, emerged into the kitchen with Paloma and three other cooks.

"What is this?" Corbus yelled, glaring at Veron.

"It was my idea," Chelci said quickly. "I wanted to make you breakfast."

"Miss Chelci! I beg your pardon. I didn't notice you," the chef said as he bowed. When he straightened, a puzzled look covered his face. "You made us breakfast?"

"It's not much," Chelci said, gesturing to the table. "Just some rolls with butter and jam. Please, take some if you like."

All five cooks froze, staring wide-eyed. "I've been a cook here for thirty years. No one has ever made breakfast for me before," Paloma said.

Her eyes glistened, and Veron realized how unique this gesture was. The cooks eagerly took the rolls, which were still warm. They slathered them with jam and butter and laughed as they took a moment to sit and eat before beginning their daily work.

Corbus was the only one who looked skeptical. He took small bites, as if he judged the baking quality. Ultimately, he seemed to approve and stuffed the rest into his mouth. "Okay, it's time to work. No more sitting around, you four," the head chef said with a frown before ordering the others to their tasks.

"Paloma, would you tell the rest of the servants these are for them when they come down?" Chelci asked.

"Of course. I'll make sure they know," said the cook as she took a second roll. "Thank you, miss."

Chelci turned to Veron, and they both exhaled as the cooks busied themselves. "What should we do now?" she asked, followed by a yawn. "Go back to bed and get some more sleep?"

Veron nodded his head. "We could do that," he said. "Or . . . I don't suppose you'd want to go for a morning run through the city to wake up, would you?"

"I couldn't run in this," she said, looking down at her dress.

Veron shrugged. "You could change."

Chelci tilted her head and raised an eyebrow. "My wardman would have to run with me to keep me safe from all the danger out there. Do you think he'd be up for that?"

"I think he could handle it," Veron said with a grin.

"The real question is . . . Would he be able to keep up?" Chelci said before turning with a laugh and running toward the stairs. Veron was two steps behind as he raced after her.

Late that night, Veron walked up the stairs with heavy steps. He had just wrapped the long day with a sword fighting session with Chelci. While he enjoyed the time together, as they grew more familiar, the sessions reminded him of his Dream. The vision of being stabbed haunted him, and whenever he saw Chelci's mother, he wondered if that was the day she would die.

It was his first Dream, so he wasn't sure if it would come true, though people said they always did. The ability of Dreams to predict the future drove Bale to seek the Shadow Knights. It was why Veron's father died. *But how am I supposed to fight those men from the Dream if I still can't use the origine?*

As he and Chelci grew closer, Veron wrestled with saying something to her about it all—her mother, his Dream, the Shadow Knights. He paused at the top of the stairs, resting his hand on the wall. As he stared down the dark hallway, his heart pounded at the thought of spilling his secrets. *I could at least warn her about her mother.* Veron turned and descended back to the second floor.

They had returned separately to the house to avoid questions about being out so late together. Chelci would likely be in bed but not asleep yet. Veron quietly turned her doorknob.

Padding through the dark room, Veron whispered her name, not wanting to startle her. Suddenly, he halted, and the hair on his neck stood on end. Chelci lay in bed, but a tall, dark shape hovered next to her, frozen in position with a club raised and ready to strike.

Veron's eyes shot open wide. "Who are—" He abandoned his question mid-sentence and charged. The figure, clothed in black and wearing a hood, quickly backed away from the bed and pointed the club at Veron. The threat didn't stop him. Veron barreled into the dark figure, grabbing around his waist, and crushing him against the stone wall. The person groaned with a deep voice. The club beat against Veron's back as the attacker tried to break free, his thick beard pressing into the side of Veron's face. Veron flung the body to the floor.

"What's going on?" a suddenly alert Chelci asked from bed.

Veron didn't take the time to reply. The man scrambled to his feet. The shadow of a club swung toward Veron, but his instinct took over. He stepped forward and caught the attacker's arm with his own, knocking the club to the side. Veron kneed him in the gut and followed with a blow to his chest. A loud pop sounded as Veron struck the figure across the jaw.

The man moaned as he stumbled away. Veron glanced at Chelci to make sure she was okay. By the time he looked back, the shadowy figure was out the door.

Veron ran after him, but when he passed through the doorway, the assailant was gone. His pulse thundered in his ears. His chest rose and fell rapidly as he quickly checked down the hall before returning to Chelci's room.

"Are you alright?" Veron asked as he approached the bed.

"I'm fine," Chelci replied. "He didn't touch me. Who was that? What happened?"

Veron shook his head. "I have no idea. I came here to—" He paused, deciding it wasn't the time to discuss his originally intended topic. "—to make sure you were okay, and I found him here . . . just standing there, about to attack you."

Chelci breathed in sharply. "But why would someone attack me? That doesn't make any sense."

"I have no idea," Veron said, massaging his aching hand. He moved to the door. "I'll alert the guards."

"Veron, wait. Don't alert anyone."

Veron's face contorted as he paused. "Why not?"

"Well . . . I'm fine, and whoever it was is scared off. Alerting people won't do anything."

"Yeah, but what if he comes back? What if he's still waiting out there?"

"I doubt that's the case," Chelci said. "I worry about Mother and Father. What would they say if they knew someone attacked me? What would they think about you?"

Veron jerked his head back as he furrowed his eyebrows. "Me? Well, I'd like to think they might be pleased that I stopped another attack."

"But, how did that man get here in the first place? Why didn't you inspect my room first when I came to bed? Why were both of us out so late?"

Veron walked back to the side of the bed. "Are these questions *you* have? Do you think I should have—"

"No! Not at all! But I know my mother. If there is any reason for criticism, she'll grab onto it. And I'd hate if she were to find a reason to . . ." Chelci paused before her voice softened. "I don't want her to take you away from me."

Veron breathed in deeply before nodding his head. "Okay. I won't alert them. But I am going to inspect your room every night."

"Deal," Chelci said.

"Now try to get back to sleep," Veron said as he patted her bed and moved toward the door. "I'll be standing outside in the hall."

"You can't stand out there all night!"

"I won't stay all night, but I'll give it a few hours . . . just to make sure."

＃ 17

Dress Fitting

Veron set down his porridge, yawned, and slid onto the bench next to Nathaniel.

"You okay?" Nathaniel asked. "You look . . . tired or beat up. I can't tell which."

Veron flexed his hand. The ache had faded since the night before, but the lack of sleep hadn't helped. "Yeah, I'm fine. I had a tiring day yesterday."

"I feel like I never see you anymore," Nathaniel said. "Do you miss the floor scrubbing and water hauling yet?"

Veron laughed as he filled his spoon with the steaming boiled oats. "No, I can't say I do. How's it been?" He put the spoon in his mouth, enjoying the feeling as it warmed his belly.

Nathaniel shrugged. "About the same as usual. The new girl, Carin, is having a rough time, though. She can barely carry anything, and she keeps spouting off to everyone how unjust her life has been and what has happened to her. I haven't seen Tessa that mad in a while. If she were an ankler, I bet they would whip her or threaten to invoke her collateral. Instead, she's on chamber pot duty for a week."

Veron swallowed to clear his suddenly dry throat at the mention of collateral. "Housekeeping duties weren't that bad. I enjoy waiting on Chelci much more though."

"What's she like?"

"Not like you'd expect. She's not her mother. She cares about people and doesn't act like she's better than everyone. Talking with her is . . . refreshing—like talking with a friend."

Nathaniel stared. He narrowed his eyes as his mouth curled up. "You like her, don't you?"

"Pfff—" Veron stopped before denying it. "Of course, I do. Who wouldn't?"

"Oh, wow!" Nathaniel hit the table playfully. "Just be careful. That's all I'll say. Someone like you can't be with someone like her. If you try to make it happen, you're going to end up in a world of hurt."

Veron focused on his food as he considered his friend's warning.

"Tomorrow's her friend's wedding, right?" Nathaniel asked.

"Emma's? Yeah. I'm going with Chelci to pick up her dress today."

"And you get to go?" Nathaniel asked.

Veron nodded as he swallowed another mouthful.

"Lucky. I bet the food will be amazing!"

"I don't know if I'll get to eat. I'll probably have to wait with the rest of the servants in a holding chamber or something."

"Still . . . I wish I could go." Nathaniel scraped his bowl's dregs with his spoon. "Don't let your mind get carried away with hopes about Chelci. Every time I see her parents, her mother talks of setting her up. If you keep this up, you're preparing yourself for disappointment."

Shuffling feet drew Veron's attention as Tristan and James rounded the corner, carrying bowls. Veron tensed. Tristan received his position back in the garden after Veron was promoted, but the ugly looks the gardener always gave him indicated he still held a grudge.

Veron was about to turn back to his bowl when something caught his eye. A blueish-yellow bruise marked Tristan's jaw and right cheek.

Veron breathed in quickly. *The beard. The size. It was Tristan!* Veron jumped from his seat and grabbed the gardener, bunching his tunic in a fist.

"Hey, what are you—" Tristan protested, dropping his bowl of porridge to the floor with a crash.

Veron pulled the man through the doorway by his shirt and pushed him down the basement hall, away from the other servants. "It was you!" Veron growled as he pushed Tristan against the stone wall.

Tristan glanced around with wide eyes as if looking for help, but no one was there. "What are you talking about!" he shouted back.

Veron narrowed his eyes. "You know."

"Know what?"

"You attacked Chelci, and I gave you that bruise," Veron growled just above a whisper.

Tristan made as if to laugh. "That's ridiculous!" he shouted as James and Nathaniel both appeared in the hall.

"Veron, what are you doing?" Nathaniel asked.

"I got this bruise when James accidentally smacked me with a hoe yesterday," Tristan said. "Didn't I, James?"

The landscaper nodded. "He's right. You can ask Montgomery, too. He was there."

Veron pulled Tristan close. "You're lying."

"You're crazy!" Tristan said.

"Why did you do it? What would you gain?"

"I still don't know what you're talking about. Did someone attack Chelci last night?" Veron didn't reply as Tristan looked at the other two servants. "I thought you were her protector? She was attacked on your watch? Wow! That won't look good."

Veron gasped, and his eyes slowly widened. *He did it to make me look bad!*

"Poor job you're doing letting people attack her in her bedroom,"

Tristan said.

Veron tightened the grip on his tunic. "I never said it was in her bedroom," he said in a low voice.

Tristan's eyes betrayed a moment of fear before hardening again. He spoke in a measured cadence. "As I said . . . I was with James . . . and Montgomery."

Veron clenched his jaw and stared for a long moment. "Gah!" he exclaimed finally as he released the gardener's tunic. James and Nathaniel walked back into the servants' dining room, and Veron followed.

"Maybe next time, I'll take more than a club," Tristan muttered to his back.

Veron's blood boiled as he turned around. The smirk on Tristan's face instantly faded. He held up his hands and began protesting when Veron pounded him in the jaw with all his strength. The gardener collapsed to the floor, holding his mouth and groaning.

Standing over the man, Veron pointed at his face. "Try to set me up like this again, and you'll regret it. And if you go near her . . ." He bent down to make sure he was heard. "I will kill you."

Chelci knocked on the Bartons' door, causing a solid thump to echo inside the house. The temperature was mild. Her long-sleeved, yellow dress kept her comfortable as she stood on the stoop. Behind her, Veron waited in the street, sword dangling from his hip.

"I promise, Mother, I'll be back soon," Emma's voice said from behind the door just before it opened. Chelci's friend hurried out with a radiant smile.

"What's going on?" Chelci said as she put her arm around Emma's, and they began up the street. "Why are you so happy?"

"I'm happy to spend time with my friend," Emma replied, earning a glare from Chelci. "Okay . . . Matthew's coming by soon. He's taking over for his father at the bakery, and he has some brilliant ideas he wants to share with my father. I promised I'd be back to support him, so I can't stay out long."

"Well, I'm glad to have you with me while I can."

"You know, I still feel awful . . . for the Red Quarter," Emma said. "I just left you there, and you could have been—"

"I told you, forget about it. You were doing what you thought was right, and I'm fine. Stop beating yourself up."

Emma nodded as she kicked a rock mid-stride. "So, what's it been like having your own wardman?"

Chelci half-glanced toward Veron, walking several paces back. "It's really nice. I always have someone there to help when I need it. I can go anywhere in the city and feel safe."

"What's he like?" Emma said before leaning forward to whisper. "He's kind of cute."

Chelci smacked Emma's arm playfully. "He's sweet. He's . . . not like anyone I've been around before. We talk together. We even sword fight."

Emma's eyes widened before leaning in even closer. "Is this the servant you fell in love—"

"Shhh," Chelci whispered back. "I told you, I'm not in love with him. But . . . Yes, he's the one I told you about."

Both girls glanced back at Veron, gazing obliviously around at the city as they walked. When Emma turned back to Chelci, she raised her eyebrows and knowingly grinned.

"Stop that," Chelci said, hitting her again. The two girls continued arm in arm down the street.

When they reached Turba Square, Chelci and Emma made their way to the opposite side and opened the door to Rosalie's Dress Shop. A bell announced their entrance, but it did little good. The shop owner was busy measuring another woman.

"Hello, Rosalie," Chelci said, waving across the shop.

"Welcome, ye dears," Rosalie replied. "I've got yer dress all ready, Chelci. Make yerselves comfortable. I'll be with ye as soon as I can."

Veron glanced around the shop and motioned toward the door. "I'll be just outside," he said.

Emma flared her eyebrows toward Chelci with a smirk.

"Stop it," Chelci muttered through her teeth.

The girls busied themselves, browsing the various dresses hanging around the shop. Chelci breathed in deeply, savoring the smell of clean fabric then rubbed her arms to fend off the shop's early-morning chill.

"I'm glad you got your dress from here. Rosalie's the best," Emma said. "Did you know she came from Tarphan?"

"No, I didn't."

"Yeah, she can be a little . . . odd, but Tarphans make the best clothes. I got my dress from her, too."

Chelci brushed her hand along a red, silk dress, admiring the color.

"So, has your mother said anything about your visit with that Caspian fellow?" Emma asked.

"Ugh, don't remind me," Chelci replied. "No, she didn't say anything. I know she really wants me to marry someone soon, but she's seemed . . . more understanding. I think."

"That's a change."

"Yes, it is. It's odd, but . . . it gives me hope for our relationship."

"What does she think about Veron?"

Chelci glanced out the window where her wardman waited and watched the square. "She's been impressed with him. Well, besides his whipping on his first day."

"What? What for?" Emma said.

Chelci chuckled. "Something about him stumbling in while she bathed and dumping ash on her. I'm not totally sure. I think she had the guards take it easy on him because he was back on his feet in no time. Since then, his work's been great. She promoted him to head gardener and then wardman in only a few weeks."

"Does she know about you two?"

"What? No!" Chelci yelled, drawing a look from the others in the store. She continued in a quieter voice. "There is no 'us two.' He's my wardman. There's nothing else to know."

Emma smirked but didn't reply.

"I'm so sorry ta keep ye waitin'," Rosalie said as she approached the girls.

"It was no trouble," Chelci said. "Seems busy here today."

"Yes, it is. Are ye ready ta see the dress?"

"Yes, please," Emma chimed in. "I have to leave in a moment, but I can't go before I see it."

Rosalie stepped into a back room and emerged in a moment with a dark-blue silk dress draped across her arm.

"Oh, I love the color!" Emma said. "Hold it up!"

Chelci took the dress and held it up to her shoulders, allowing the fabric to drape down her body. The sleeve length and hem looked right. She smiled, pleased with the design.

"It's gorgeous. I love it!" Emma said, squeezing her arm.

"How's yer dress treating ye, dear?" Rosalie said to Emma.

Emma's shoulders relaxed as she seemed to melt. "Oh, it's perfect. Thank you."

"Ooohhahahaha," Rosalie said, laughing and clapping her hands with wide eyes. "I'm so glad."

Emma flared her eyes furtively toward Chelci, who covered her mouth, stifling a laugh at the shop owner's odd display.

"Are you alright if I go, now?" Emma said. "I need to get back home before Matthew arrives."

"Sure," Chelci said. "I'll see you later."

"Just make sure you don't end up looking better than me. Remember, it's my wedding." Emma smiled then left the shop, ringing the bell as two more ladies entered.

"Well . . . now we need ta make sure I got the measurements right," Rosalie said as she took the dress and led Chelci to the back corner, where a large divider provided privacy.

"Rosalie, do you have a moment?" one of the other ladies called across the store.

The shopkeeper frowned. "I need ta help these ladies. Ye need help dressin' though, I expect?"

"Yes, I don't believe I could manage this on my own," Chelci replied.

Rosalie nodded and turned to go before pivoting back quickly. "What's yer wardman's name?"

"Who? Veron?"

Rosalie walked away, and in a moment, Chelci heard the shopkeeper's voice. "Veron! Chelci needs yer help."

A flush crept up Chelci's neck. *Veron can't help me dress.*

A moment later, Veron leaned around the privacy screen. "You need . . . help?" His hesitation was obvious as he stood awkwardly, half hiding behind the barrier.

Chelci looked at the dress then back to him. "Yes . . . um. I need to try this on, but . . ." She glanced over the divider to where Rosalie helped the other two ladies. She sighed. "I guess customs are different in Tarphan. Um . . . can you hold this?"

Chelci handed the new dress to Veron, who held it out straight. She untied the ribbon holding her current dress around her neck. "If you don't mind, could you—" She stopped and glanced up. His eyes were closed with his head turned as far around as possible.

"Just let me know what you need," Veron said.

"You're fine like that." Chelci lifted her dress over her head and hung it over the top of the divider. The chill in the shop prickled her bare skin. She felt exposed, standing in front of Veron in nothing but her underclothes, but the edges of her mouth curled. She fought back a laugh as she looked at him, straining to give her as much privacy as possible. "Can you lift it higher?"

Veron lifted the dress a bit, and Chelci brought the hem over her head and slid in. The fabric was silky smooth. It felt cool to the touch but also warmed her. The sleeves came to her wrists, and the hem fell just above the floor. She reached around to fasten the hooks in the back, but she couldn't manage it.

"Um . . . Veron, I could use some help with the back."

He opened his eyes, which flared suddenly. "Wow! You look beautiful!"

Her cheeks warmed as she glanced down at her feet. Her tousled hair fell in front of her face, hiding her embarrassment. Chelci turned around, the movement chilling her exposed back. "Can you help me fasten these?"

Chelci held her breath as Veron stepped closer. He didn't speak as his hands worked on the fasteners. Occasionally, his callused fingers brushed her bare skin, sending a warm shiver through her body. *Are his hands trembling?*

"There you go," he said after a moment.

She examined herself in the mirror hanging on the wall. The dark blue fabric looked regal and made her skin shine. Light blue embroidered swirls decorated the upper part of the dress and sleeves, and the front was respectably high, falling just below her neck. It was nearly a perfect fit. It hugged her waist and chest without being too constricting.

"How is it?" Rosalie asked as she poked her head around the divider.

"It's perfect," Chelci said. "I love it."

Rosalie pinched in the fabric and inspected the waist. She took out a measuring device, holding it up to Chelci's body. "I need ta take in the sleeves a bit. Other'n that, I think it looks right. When's the event?"

"The wedding? It's tomorrow."

"No problem. I'll finish it up then bring it by yer house tonight. Can I help ye change back?"

Chelci nodded, and Veron ducked back behind the divider. A feeling of disappointment crept in while Rosalie helped unfasten the back of the dress.

18

The Barnaby Necklace

After returning from the market, Veron climbed the stairs to the third floor. He walked down the hall, unfastening his sword when some movement ahead caught his eye. Tristan emerged from one of the rooms and walked toward the stairs. When their eyes met, Tristan flinched subtly. The yellow bruise on his cheek was even more prominent than before. Both men stared as they passed each other in silence.

When Veron arrived at his room, he paused, staring through the doorway. *Is this the room he came from?* He looked back down the hall, catching Tristan looking his way before descending into the stairwell. Veron entered but nothing looked awry. *Why would he have been in my room?* After leaning his sword against the wall, he looked around some more. He had no possessions, so there was nothing for Tristan to take. An uneasy feeling remained, but he shrugged it off.

Later that night, after the servants ate, Veron stood in line to clean his dishes in the kitchen. When it was his turn, he dunked his plate in the sudsy water and scrubbed it with a brush. As he worked, Lady Luciana exited the stairwell.

"Tessa," she said, flagging down the house steward. The petite lady joined Luciana by the stairs, and they spoke in restrained voices. "Have you seen the Barnaby Necklace?"

Veron glanced over as he continued scrubbing. Tessa's forehead wrinkled. "No, my lady, not recently. Is it not in the safe?"

Luciana inhaled deeply. "No, it's not. And I haven't used it since the Binghamton Ball last season."

"Did you lose your jewels, Lady Luciana?" a rough voice said from farther back in the line.

Veron cringed as he pictured the large beard and bruised cheek of the gardener. Luciana looked toward the voice and stared without response.

"Come on, Ash," Drevyn, the mason, said over his shoulder.

Veron jumped and realized the plate was long clean. He moved out of the way and grabbed a rag to dry it.

"Well, I think that necklace is incredible. I sure hope none of the servants stole it," Tristan added.

Veron jerked his head to the back of the line and froze with the rag covering his plate.

"How would one of the . . ." Luciana's voice trailed off. She stood frozen for a moment then eventually turned and hurried up the steps.

Tristan's eyes angled to meet Veron's while the trace of a smirk formed. *Oh no!* Veron thought as his stomach dropped. He immediately felt dizzy.

"What's wrong?" Nathaniel said, standing behind Drevyn.

"Uh . . . um—nothing," Veron said quickly, putting his clean plate down on the counter. "I've gotta go."

Veron moved quickly to the stairs. As he passed the ground floor, Luciana's voice called to the house guards, "Rupert! Dorrick! Come here!" Veron picked up his pace as he continued to ascend. On the servants' level, Veron hurried to his room.

He must have hidden it somewhere in here, though there weren't many hiding places. The light was dim with the sun recently setting, but visibility was just enough to search. He looked in the wardrobe—bare except for the few clothes he owned. The drawer of the table next to his bed was empty. He dropped to the floor and checked under the table as well as his bed.

Down the hall, footsteps arrived, drawing his attention. "Search them one by one," Luciana said in a husky voice. "If one of them took it, they're going to regret the day they ever started working here. Come find me when you're done, and don't let anyone come or go from this floor!"

Veron's heart pounded even faster. *I've got to find it!* He gently closed and locked the door before turning back to search. It was clean behind the wardrobe and bed. The mattress creaked in a familiar way as he pressed down along its length. Nothing seemed out of place. When he lifted the edge of his mattress, an object tucked under it at the far corner clinked. Veron gasped. His arm trembled as he pulled out the unfamiliar item.

The heavy necklace draped in his hand, covered in gems. It was too dark to make out what the gems were, but he could see enough to know he was in trouble. Veron ground his teeth as he pictured the gardener somewhere in the house, waiting for its discovery. *Well, I'm not gonna get caught.* Veron breathed quickly and paced the room. They wouldn't believe him if he told the truth, and they'd stop him if he tried to leave. The window caught his eye. *That's it!*

Veron opened the window and looked over the garden far below. He cocked his arm to throw the necklace away but stopped when he noticed two people sitting on a bench. *Argh! They would hear if I threw it.*

Knock, knock. "Open up!" Rupert's muffled voice shouted a few doors down, and Veron turned around. *They're not here yet, but they will be soon.*

Veron took a deep breath then exhaled slowly as he paced again, racking his brain for options. *I need to somehow get it back in the safe.* He stopped suddenly then poked his head back out the window. *Can I make it?*

Cautious to not alert the people far below in the garden, Veron stepped out his window onto the slanted roof. The slope was slight enough for him to keep traction as he padded toward the circular, tower-like structure where the spiral staircase rose from the basement to the third floor. He pressed an arm against the outside wall of the stairs and leaned cautiously over the corner at the edge of the roof.

The height surprised him. It had been a while since he'd been so precariously far above the ground, and the stone patio two floors below made him hesitate. When he spied the office window just below him, his hope surged.

Veron turned and inspected the circular wall. The stones on the outside were rough and uneven. Many stuck out, creating plenty of hand and footholds. After tucking the necklace in his pocket, he breathed slowly to steady himself. *Come on, Veron. You can do this.*

He found a foothold just below the roof's edge and two solid placements for his hands. He gripped tightly as he swung his body off the slate tiles, putting all of his weight onto the wall. The stone's grit rubbed under his fingers as he glanced around. Crouching, he extended his free leg to another ledge below. As he reached to find new handholds, a gust of wind picked up. Stone pressed against his face as he pulled his body close to the wall. Sweat dripped down his nose, and his arms trembled. His tunic snapped in the breeze, threatening to pull him off, but thankfully, the wind died as quickly as it arrived. Veron exhaled in relief.

After a few more movements downward, the window lay opposite the corner from him. Inside, the office was dark. Veron held tight onto a sturdy ledge with his left hand while he extended his right leg across the gap, placing it against the windowsill. Both feet secure, he leaned his body fully toward the window. Veron's pulse raced as he prepared himself for the one thing he had no control over. He dug his fingernails into the edge of the window opposite the hinge. After taking a deep breath and holding it, he pulled firmly on the frame. His heart leaped as the window smoothly opened.

Veron ducked through the window and landed softly on the office's rug. He walked through the dim light around the desk and dug the necklace out of his pocket. Before he even had a moment to consider what to do about the safe, footsteps approached out in the hall and the knob jiggled. Veron dropped to the floor, cradling the necklace in his hand to keep it from making a sound. As the door opened, he scooted underneath the desk, pushing his body as far back as he could, careful not to kick anything.

The room lit up with the warm glow of a lantern. Darcius Marlow's deep voice mumbled something about the window before Veron heard it close with a faint creak. Veron cringed as the light made its way around the back of the desk, and a clunk sounded on the wood as if something metal were set on it. He adjusted his head and fought away a gasp. Darcius stood a mere hand's width away from Veron's curled-up legs. *Please don't sit down. Please don't sit down.* Veron covered his mouth with his hand to stifle his heavy breathing while the missing necklace dangled across his face. *Maybe this wasn't such a great idea after all.*

"You're going to be fine, Emma," Chelci said as she and her friend entered the house from the back door where they'd sat talking in the garden for over an hour.

"I know, and I'm sorry for burdening you with my crazy worries," Emma said. She tucked her chin to her neck and spoke to reassure herself. "Tomorrow, I will get married, and everything will be great."

Chelci smiled and squeezed her friend's hand as they reached the front door. "I'll see you tomorrow."

After Emma left, Chelci climbed the main staircase from the entrance hall. As she neared the top, a commotion grew amidst a scuffling of feet. "Ouch! Take it easy," Veron said.

Chelci rushed up the last few steps and turned the corner to see guards Rupert and Dorrick dragging Veron by the shoulders. Dorrick rapped on the door to Luciana's room.

"Veron?" Chelci asked as she approached. "What is this?"

"Chelci!" Veron replied, straining his neck against the guards' grips to look behind him. The door opened before he could say more.

"We found your thief, Lady Luciana," Rupert said. A smirk grew on Luciana's face as she stepped closer. "At least, we believe so," the guard added.

"What do you mean?" she said. "Did you find the necklace?"

"The Barnaby Necklace is missing?" Chelci asked.

"Well . . . no," Rupert said to the lady of the house. "But we think he took it and did something with it."

"This is my wardman," Chelci said boldly. "How dare you accuse him of stealing."

Darcius emerged from his room, the next one down the hall. "What's going on here?" he asked.

"Why do you think he took it?" her mother asked, ignoring her husband.

"We figured it would be on the servants' level," Dorrick said. "We blocked off the floor, so no one could have left. Then we searched every room, but the necklace was nowhere to be found."

"But Ash wouldn't open his door," Rupert said. "We pounded on it for minutes, but he didn't even reply. We were about to break it down when he finally let us in."

"What were you doing, Ash?" Luciana asked with narrowed eyes.

"I wasn't feeling well! I told these guys. I was lying down, trying to rest away the ache in my head. Their pounding sure didn't help. I tried to ignore them, but finally, I gave up and opened the door."

"That's rubbish," Rupert said. "He wasn't even responding. I'm telling you, he was up to something."

Luciana stepped even closer. "Did you swallow them?"

Veron's face screwed up. "What? No! I—I don't even know what you're talking about!"

"Did you throw them out your window in the garden?" She turned quickly to the guards. "Did you check the garden?"

"Not yet, but we will," Dorrick replied.

"I was just in the garden with Emma," Chelci said. "I can assure you we would have heard something tossed from the third floor."

"Look, I promise you, I didn't take your necklace."

"Do we need to take you to the whipping post again?" Luciana asked.

"No!" Chelci yelled. "Mother, this is crazy! He didn't take your necklace."

"Oh, really," she said, turning to her. "And how do you know?"

"I—I just . . ." She faded out, realizing she didn't truly know and couldn't prove his innocence. "You probably just missed it in the safe," Chelci said before stomping down the hall and opening the office door.

As the crowd followed, Darcius sighed. "I was in the office only a few minutes ago, checking again, Chelci."

She held out her hand. "Give me the key. I want to look."

Her father took off the leather cord around his neck and handed it over. Chelci walked around the desk, her mother following. The key fit snugly into the lock. After a metallic click, the heavy door swung open, but Chelci's heart sank as she looked inside. The large, bejeweled necklace was nowhere to be seen. A hefty sack of coins rested against the back, and a short stack of legal documents sat on the bottom.

Luciana leaned over to peek in as Chelci sighed and sat on the floor. "Oh, Chelci," Luciana said with a chuckle. "Do you think we'd simply—" Her voice stopped suddenly. All heads turned in her direction as she bent down and tilted her head. She reached into the short slit underneath the safe and touched an item peeking out—a small gem. As she pulled, the rest of the necklace emerged. "Oh."

Chelci stood and crossed her arms. Luciana straightened and looked around the room, blinking rapidly. Finally, she turned to Veron, whose chest rose and fell with even breaths. The guards released their hold on him after her subdued nod.

"How much did you drink at the Binghamton Ball?" Darcius asked as she blushed.

"Come on," Chelci said, looking at Veron and nodding toward the door. As they walked out of the office, heading to her room, Tristan caught her eye at the end of the hall, lurking and staring in their direction. She glanced at Veron, wearing a smirk as he looked back at the man. When she glanced back at the gardener, he had already sulked away.

"What's that about?" Chelci asked as she held the door open to her room.

Veron chuckled. "You want to hear what *really* happened with the necklace?"

Chelci's eyebrows lifted, and she closed the door behind them.

19

Wedding Party

Veron's wool coat soaked with sweat as he watched the reception from the back of the room. It was mid-wiether's day, but the unseasonable warm spell that blew in overnight made it feel like early suether. While the windows were open, guests dripped with sweat as they talked, laughed, and danced their way around the room to the tune of a lively Tarphic band.

The High Lord of Civility spoke at the brief ceremony, officially joining Matthew and Emma in a lawful union. Each family's patriarch signed documents of approval, and finally, the guests enjoyed the main reason any of them attended.

The sumptuous buffet's tantalizing smells taunted Veron. Roasted meat, steamed vegetables, and exquisite pastries filled tables around the edges of the large hall. Forbidden from joining, he watched as the guests gorged themselves on the delicacies.

Veron couldn't help but admire the room with its tall windows and ornate chandeliers. The city's wealthy citizens used the Felting Common Hall for weddings and parties. A typical baker would not have been able to host such an event, so Emma's parents shouldered the financial burden—a fact her already inebriated father proclaimed to anyone in earshot.

As he scanned the room, Luciana Marlow's familiar necklace caught his eye, and his thoughts drifted to Tristan's attempted set-up. He promised he would make the gardener pay but had no interest in actually retaliating. He simply wanted the man to leave him alone so he could do his job.

His gaze wandered to Chelci, who stood arm in arm with Emma, talking. She would not be in danger at the party, but it was still his job to monitor her whereabouts. He silently grumbled as another young man approached her for small talk. It would only be a moment before he led her by the hand to the dance floor. *I need a drink,* Veron thought as he turned and ducked through the nearest doorway to the kitchen.

To his dismay, the kitchen was louder and hotter than the hall. Cooks and servers scurried around, filling platters and cleaning dishes. *At least I don't have to watch suitors fawning over Chelci.*

He spotted Elliot, Darcius' wardman, filling a cup with water. Elliot nodded and offered it to Veron before filling up a second. "Thanks," Veron said. While the other two household attendants hadn't immediately warmed to the new group member, they were at least polite despite his anklet. Veron followed Elliot back to the main hall where they joined Violetta standing by the wall.

"What do you usually do at these events?" Veron asked after gulping down the drink.

"Wait," Elliot said.

"Eventually, Luciana will need her hair fixed or decide she wants me to run back home to fetch a hat or bracelet or something," Violetta added.

"Sounds fun," Veron said dryly.

"It's a good chance to talk with other servants. You can hear news from all over the city," Elliot said. "Apparently, most of Felting is on edge right now."

"Why?"

"Bale's recent attack on Karad," Elliot answered. Veron's breath left, and his throat nervously dried up. "Everyone seems excited about the new baron, Fiero, and how he stopped the Norshewan king, but no one knows Bale's whereabouts. Some insist he went back over the mountains to retreat home, but some worry he'll turn up at the walls of Felting or Karondir. Some say he's even been seen inside Karad."

"What would—" Veron cleared his throat to fix the croaking. "What would happen if Bale attacked Felting?"

Elliot inhaled deeply. "They'd stop him at the walls. Then Karad's army would come from behind and Karondir's would arrive from the east. Bale would be pinned in from all sides and defeated."

"It looks like your charge has been popular tonight," Violeta said.

Veron turned to her with a quizzical expression. "Who? Chelci?"

"Yeah, it seems an endless line of men clamor for her attention."

"Ever since she returned, she's been one of the most sought-after young ladies in Felting," Elliot added. "It's a pity she doesn't act like a lady. She could have made a fine catch."

Veron ground his teeth but held back his words. He scanned the room until he found Chelci dancing with another man. He looked twenty years her senior, well dressed in a sharp suit despite the askew collar. His flushed face told of his drinking that night. One hand rested low on her hip, and the other held her hand and a glass of wine at the same time. Chelci's lips pressed together tightly, and her eyes rolled at each trip of his feet. *He could at least put his drink down for a moment.*

A sudden, bawdy laugh erupted from the man as his hand slid to her rear. Chelci's body stiffened. When he leaned in to whisper something in her ear, she took his hand holding the glass and flung the red wine in his face. Yelling curses and mumbling nonsense, the man stumbled away.

Chelci left the dance floor and stormed to the side of the room, but no one else in the crowd noticed. Veron immediately grabbed some white napkins from a table as he went to her, arriving the same moment as her mother.

"I saw that," Luciana said in a strained voice covered by the music and dull thrum of conversation. "What on earth were you thinking?"

Veron dabbed Chelci's face, dripping with wine.

"I stood up for myself!" Chelci shot back, glaring at her mother. "You didn't hear what he said to me."

"I don't *care* what he said to you. Do you know who that was?"

"Lord Bottom-Grabber from Drunkington, I believe?" Chelci said with a sneer.

"That was Gilbert Leal, one of the most prominent lawyers in the city. His wife recently passed away, and he's a very eligible catch. He would have made a fine suitor . . . until you flung wine in his face like a spoiled girl!"

Veron finished dabbing Chelci's face but hesitated at the purple spots staining her chest. Chelci noticed his reticence and took the cloth, handling the job herself.

"If you like him so much, maybe *you* should marry him, Mother," Chelci said.

Luciana glared. "You promised to be agreeable and find a husband."

"I never agreed to anything of the sort," Chelci said. "I agreed to meet with suitors. I never said I would be agreeable."

"Well, now you've shown how ugly you can be to half the city."

Chelci gestured to the people in the hall. "No one even noticed. No one cared. *You* never care about *me*!"

Tension filled their corner of the room. Chelci and her mother locked eyes in a long stare until, finally, Luciana lowered her head and heavily sighed. "I'm sorry, Chelci." Veron and Chelci perked up at the uncharacteristic apology. "I *do* care about you. I push hard sometimes, but it's not because I want to control you. It's because . . . I want something good for you. I know I can get carried away though."

Chelci nodded after a moment. "Thank you for saying that. It means a lot."

While the Marlow ladies exchanged words of understanding, Veron looked around. The party continued as normal. People talked, and the music played, but suddenly, he felt uncomfortable. *Something is wrong,* he thought, but couldn't figure out what. The dull hum of hundreds of conversations all blended together. Chelci and her mother talked, but their voices sounded as if they were underwater while Veron's eyes scanned the room.

There! Directly across the hall, a familiar-looking man stared—not at Chelci, but at Veron. The man wore a green, loose tunic tied in front with a pair of brown pants. A large, brownish-red beard with streaks of gray rounded out the man's face. His hair was a darker shade of brown and fell partially over his eyes. The piece of bread hanging out of the man's mouth hid half his face, but his eyes clearly gaped in Veron's direction. Slowly, the man lowered the food, and Veron gasped. *Danyel!* He hadn't seen the baker from North Karad Market in nearly half a season, ever since he was thrown into prison and forced into servitude.

"Ash, is something wrong?"

Veron snapped out of his frozen stance and turned to Chelci and Luciana. "I'm sorry, Lady Luciana. There's no problem," he blurted. Chelci's mother raised an eyebrow but soon turned back to her daughter.

Veron found Danyel again, and the two stared at each other, unmoving. He nodded his head toward the side door before turning back to Chelci. "I'll dispose of these," he said as he took the stained cloths from her.

Arriving at the door first, Veron stepped outside. His heart pounded as he waited. In a moment, his friend emerged, and Veron attacked him with a hug and an enormous smile before the baker even had the chance to make it down the steps.

"Danyel, what are you doing here?" Veron asked during the tight embrace.

"Me? What about you!" Danyel yelled as he pulled away. "How are you alive? We heard you were dead! Well . . . Brixton told us you were dead, then Bale said you were alive!"

"Wait . . . What?"

"What happened to you? How'd you get here?" Danyel asked, grinning broadly.

"Brixton betrayed me. He tried to blackmail me, then sold me. I ended up as a slave here in Felting."

Danyel inhaled through clenched teeth, and a whistling sound filled the alley. "I should have known. That selfish piece of—"

"What happened with Bale? You saw him?"

"Yeah, we saw him. He claimed you were a shadow knight. Is that true?"

Veron stiffened before glancing around to make sure no one else watched or listened. Other than Artimus, Bale was the only person he'd ever told. One piece of the Shadow Knights' code was never tell others about your abilities. *But that code is mostly to protect me from people like Bale.*

Veron breathed in deeply. After exhaling, he bobbed his head in a tight nod.

"Whoa!" Danyel said as his eyes opened wide.

"But I can't do much of anything with it," Veron said quickly. "I could do these amazing things for a couple of days, but then it disappeared. I don't know what happened."

"We assumed he made it up. That's amazing!"

"It hasn't helped me much here, and it didn't help me do anything about Brixton."

"I can't believe Brixton told us you were dead."

"I can. That way, he could steal my market. How is it, by the way? How are the rest of the workers?"

Danyel's smile disappeared, and he closed his mouth. He took in a deep breath, then exhaled. "It's not good."

Veron's heart thumped loudly. "What happened?" he asked, leaning in and growing wide-eyed.

"Brixton sent Chloe, Jacob, and Mateo away."

"No! Why?"

"He didn't think they brought in enough profit," Danyel said as Veron issued a cry of disgust. "He may have been right, but still . . . They were part of our family. After that, he started charging us rent to live in the rooms above the shops."

Veron shook his head. "The thought crossed my mind a while ago, but . . . It just wasn't necessary."

"Also, he ceased the profit-sharing bonuses."

"No!" Veron bunched his hands into a fist.

"Yeah. Morale was low after that. Francis quit a short while later. After half of the market died, customers thinned out. There weren't as many items to buy, so the interest wasn't the same."

Veron groaned. "Why didn't Brixton change it back and rehire them all?"

Danyel shook his head. "We tried to tell him, but he's rarely there. He's too stubborn. But the worst was when—" he stopped and lowered his chin. He blinked rapidly and wiped at the corner of his eye.

"What happened?" Veron asked as his friend composed himself. The longer the silence continued, the harder his stomach churned.

"Three or four weeks ago, Bale wanted information about you—where you were—anything. He thought Morgan was holding back, so he—" Danyel's voice wavered as his lips trembled. "He killed the kids."

"No!" Veron's heart twisted, and a sick feeling filled his gut. He struggled to breathe.

"Catherine lost it, attacking the soldiers in a fit of hysteria." He looked to the ground. "They killed her too."

Veron's legs grew weak, and he held onto Danyel's shoulder to keep from falling. His vision blurred. *It's all my fault!* A trickle of tears turned into sobs. His breath came in ragged bursts. Danyel put his arm around him as Veron mourned.

Eventually, the tears slowed, and Danyel helped him stand up straight. "The Mallours left soon after," he said. "Now it's just Morgan and I left."

Veron wiped his nose and eyes. "Tell Morgan I'm so sorry. If I had known, I would never have—"

"Hey," Danyel said sharply. He held Veron by the shoulders and looked him straight in the eyes. "You have nothing to be sorry for, Veron. This was *not* your fault." He raised his eyebrows, and Veron eventually nodded in acceptance. "Now . . . How can we get you out of this place?"

"I can't," Veron said as he hung his head. "I'm a servant of justice. The Marlows have a collateral sheet listing Morgan, Chloe, and you." Danyel breathed in sharply. His eyes widened as Veron continued, "I *want* to run. I *want* to fight my way out of there, but if I did, she could have all of you killed!"

"We have to do *something*. What do you need?" Danyel asked.

"I'm actually alright . . . really, I am." Veron sniffed and wiped his nose again. "It hasn't been so bad. I'm a wardman for this girl who's incredible and kind. She's the daughter of a high lord." Veron glanced briefly toward the door. "Speaking of which, I need to get back in soon, but . . . How about you? How are you handling all of the uh . . . everything?"

Danyel shrugged. "I'm doing okay . . . considering. I *have* met a girl."

"Really?"

"Yeah. Lynette. She's the one bright spot recently. She lives with her parents in the Docks and launders clothes. She's sweet."

Veron nodded with a reluctant smile. "That's great, Danyel. So . . . you never said why you're here."

"Oh, sorry. Emma Barton is my cousin. I haven't seen their family in years. They generally don't like to be seen with the poor carriage driver turned baker from Karad, but . . . you know . . . family."

The two smiled as they stared at each other. "It's so good to see you, Danyel," Veron said.

"You, too."

"Veron, there you are," Chelci said as she popped her head out the door.

"Uh . . . yes, I came out to get some fresh air," Veron said quickly. "I was just coming inside." He nodded to Danyel before following Chelci back into the hall.

20

Nighttime in the Garden

After much drinking and dancing, the Marlows decided it was time to leave. It was a short walk back to their house, so Luciana dismissed their carriage, declaring it was good for them all to use their feet. Darcius and Luciana walked along the stone street while Chelci and Veron followed behind. Elliot and Violeta had retired earlier when the Marlows allowed it, but Veron stayed.

"Who was that man you talked with, Veron?" Chelci asked, quiet enough her parents couldn't hear.

Veron hesitated in his stride, giving away any semblance of nonchalance. "What man? Who do you mean?"

"The one you met outside. You seemed . . . familiar."

Veron swallowed hard. "Oh, he was no one. Just wanted to talk." Veron kept looking forward but felt Chelci turn to stare. His neck grew hotter as he continued to ignore her.

"I don't believe you," she said. "The way you looked at him. It was as if you had known each other a long time."

Veron's heart beat quickly. He longed to tell Chelci everything about who he was and where he came from, but he didn't want to be whipped . . . or have his friends killed. "We're not supposed to talk

184

about our past."

Chelci sighed. "I'm sorry. I don't mean to test you. I just . . . want to know more about you." Veron kept his mouth closed and faced forward.

"You know what, Chelci?" Darcius said, interrupting the silence as he glanced back over his shoulder. "When you get married, the party will be at least . . . eight times this." Not normally prone to excess, the high lord's cheeks flushed from the drink, and his words slurred. "We'll have . . . music and exquisite food and . . . acrobats. It'll be the talk of the city."

"What if I don't want acrobats, Father?" Chelci said.

"Don't be silly," Luciana said. "Who wouldn't want acrobats?"

Chelci rolled her eyes as she glanced at Veron, and he stifled a laugh.

Lanterns lit the street at regular intervals along the wide lane, providing a warm path of light to follow. Thankfully, the temperature felt much nicer after the sun had set. The information from Danyel rested heavily on Veron's heart and consumed his mind, but the peaceful moment of walking with Chelci helped lighten the load.

"What do you want your wedding celebration to be like?" Veron asked softly.

She gazed toward him, backlit by the lantern on the wall behind her. "I don't really care that much. I think it's silly to spend that much on some huge celebration. It seems like it's more an excessive show for the family than a celebration of the bride and groom. Did you see Emma?"

"Yeah, she looked exhausted," Veron replied.

"She wanted to leave hours ago, but they had to stay. Neither she nor Matthew wanted that enormous event, but her father insisted. I think she would have rather had something small instead of being around a bunch of people she doesn't know."

"Yeah, that would be my preference, too. If we ever get married, we should make sure to have a nice, small ceremony. Haha!" Veron cringed. *Too much,* he thought. He had tried to keep the tone light but immediately realized the comment was out of line.

When he glanced at Chelci to see her reaction, his stomach lurched. She had stopped walking and stared at him with wide eyes, her hand covering her mouth. Her chest rose and fell rapidly. *I shouldn't have said anything.*

"I was just kidding," he said quickly. "I didn't mean anything—"

Chelci stepped toward Veron, but didn't look at him. She stared just over his shoulder. Veron turned to see what held her attention and the blood drained from his face. While seeing Danyel was a shock, nothing could have prepared him for this.

A lantern illuminated a sign in the middle of the stone wall. Veron took a hesitant step forward, hoping a clearer view would change the view, but it didn't help. The image of a young man with bushy hair stared back at him from the paper. The crude sketch wouldn't help anyone identify the person, but the sign's words stole his breath.

Veron Stormbridge - Murderer - Wanted - Living or Dead
Five gold sol for info leading to his capture

Veron spun toward Chelci, who took a step away. "Chelci, no. This isn't true. I can explain—"

"What's this?" Luciana said as she and Darcius stumbled toward them. Veron froze. "Oooh, five gold sol. That's quite the reward . . . for a murderer. Ash, keep a close eye on Chelci. Who knows where this Stormbridge fellow or any other criminals may be lurking." She hiccuped as she turned back up the street.

She doesn't remember my name! Veron thought with a sigh of relief. He snapped his attention back to Chelci as she fixed her jaw and walked up the street. "Chelci . . . Let me explain—"

She stopped walking and stared at him, hands on her hips. The edge in her quiet words pierced him. "Tell me, Veron. Tell me about your past and how you got here."

Veron opened his mouth to speak, but nothing came. He thought of Danyel, enjoying the time with his family. He thought of Chloe, wherever she was—hopefully reunited with her husband. Finally, he pictured Morgan, grieving the loss of his family. "I can't, Chelci," he said. "I really want to, but there are reasons—"

"Stop!" Chelci said, holding up her hand as she stared at him. Thunder rumbled in the distance, emphasizing her harsh rebuke. Veron quieted, at a loss for what to do next. Chelci turned to catch up with her parents, and Veron followed a few steps behind. During the silence, the joy of their previous conversation was long gone, replaced by the pain of fear and regret.

Veron paced his small room, the image of the sign fixed in his mind. *Who wouldn't turn me in for a reward of five sol?* Clearly, Chelci had mixed feelings about it. She didn't even allow him to check her room before she retired. She hadn't spoken to him since they saw the sign. At least her parents didn't make the connection, but most anyone else in Felting wouldn't hesitate to turn him in if they knew.

Who would post something like that? And why would they care so much about finding me? Brixton could likely track him down, so it wouldn't be him. *Maybe Raynor Fiero? He may want justice if he thinks I killed Brixton's fiancé and got away. But five sol?* Bale's name kept popping into his mind. He was the one person who would care most about finding and killing him. It had to be him. *Could Bale be working with Fiero to track me down? I've got to talk with Chelci. I need her to understand.*

Veron opened his door and poked his head out to make sure no one else was around. After descending one flight, he stopped before exiting the stairwell. Darcius and Luciana stood in the second-floor hallway just down from Chelci's door. They talked loudly and swayed drunkenly. Rather than raise questions from her parents, he decided to get her attention another way.

Light rain fell as he stepped outside. He found several small pebbles and threw them at Chelci's window with a soft *tap*. After a few rocks found their target, Veron's breath caught as her window opened and she poked her head out. Veron couldn't see her face in the darkness, but he imagined its glare.

"Chelci, I need to talk with you. Please! That sign is wrong. You need to know the truth." Veron whispered as loudly as he could manage, but Chelci didn't reply. She moved to close the window, and desperation filled him. "I'll tell you!" he said. She froze with the window half-closed. "I'll tell you everything. Meet me in the garden."

Veron took her lack of movement as a good sign. He slowly stepped toward the garden and noticed she only fully closed the window once he was nearly out of sight.

Veron raced around the house and paced along the garden path, wringing his hands as he glanced toward the house's back door every few seconds. The excitement quickly waned as the minutes ticked on. Soon, a steady rain fell.

Shoulders slumped and hopes dashed, Veron stepped into a side alcove. He sat on a bench where a tree above kept off most of the rain. As he leaned forward, elbows on his knees and head in his hands, tears of disappointment welled up in his eyes.

After a moment, the crunch of rock drew his attention, and he snapped his head up. Chelci stood on the path at the entrance to the trees. She wore a cloak with the hood pulled up to keep off the rain. Her brown hair cascaded out from the sides of the hood, and he could barely make out the lines of her face in the dim light.

"You came," Veron said as he wiped his eyes.

Chelci didn't step any closer, though. "I'm afraid, Veron."

The words were a blow. Chelci, the brave girl who lived in the woods for years, who could wield a sword and take on a bunch of dangerous men, was afraid of him. Veron didn't know what to say. "I'm afraid too, Chelci. You have to know I would never hurt you . . . ever." His eyes pleaded for her trust.

Her shoulders loosened. As they stared at each other, listening to the sound of raindrops fall, Chelci took slow steps in his direction. "What are you afraid of?"

Veron laughed softly. "You mean, besides someone turning me in for a five sol reward?" He slid over on the bench to give her room. When she finally sat under the cover of the tree, she removed her hood and turned to him. His throat dried as he forced his thoughts into words. "Tristan keeps trying to ruin me at every turn, and I'm afraid of your mother. I'm worried if I get in trouble, she'll have me whipped, or she'll have my friends—my list of collateral—killed."

"I know you're not supposed to talk about yourself, but I won't tell her you said anything."

Veron nodded. "I know you wouldn't. Still . . ." Veron's mind turned to the prophecy referring to the Shadow Knights and Bale. "I'm also afraid of my future. I know there are . . . things I'll need to do I'm not looking forward to. Things I can't avoid."

"Secrecy shrouds so much about you, Veron. Tell me what happened." Her eyes pleaded, softening his resolve.

Veron swallowed hard. He took several breaths as he built up courage. "I grew up in Karad . . . living on the streets. I stole, begged, and did whatever I needed to live." Shame rushed into Veron as he said the words, causing him to look at his feet. "I met a man who took me in. He was the last of the—" Veron stopped himself. There was only so much he wanted to share. "He taught me everything: how to read and write, how to garden, how to fight. He even got me a job working with a grocer. I owe him everything. Then he died . . . because of me." Chelci's hand rested on his upper arm, comforting him a bit.

"With the skills I learned, I started a market. I made new friends—a family, really. I had a place to live, food to eat, a business I owned." An edge crept into his voice. "Then, it was gone. A supposed friend was jealous of what I had. He framed me for murder and threw me in prison."

"I'm so sorry, Veron."

"My friend felt guilty, at least some. Instead of killing me, he sold me into slavery, and I ended up here—the same day you came back."

"Oh Veron, I had no idea." Chelci's words were soft, wrapping him in kindness. He leaned into her while she put her arm around him, rubbing his arm. "We need to do something about it."

"There's nothing to do," Veron said.

"I could tell Father. I could explain—"

"Explain how I broke the servant's rule to not speak about my past? Why do you think there are rules like that to begin with?" Veron said, causing Chelci to quiet while he sat back up. "That would only result in killing my friends from the market. I told you, there's nothing to do. We just need to hope no one recognizes me."

"Who knows your real name?"

"Everyone here calls me Ash. Nathaniel's the only one who knows me by Veron, but I don't think he'd turn me in."

"Should I call you Ash, too?"

Veron laughed softly. "It wouldn't hurt." He exhaled slowly as he stared out at the garden. The rain had strengthened, and splatters from the surrounding stone path grew.

"But, why would they offer a five-sol reward?" Chelci asked.

Veron's stomach turned as he adjusted his body. He wanted to share but hoped to leave out anything about the Shadow Knights or

Bale.

"If your friend sold you into slavery, and he was the one who had the issue with you, why would someone still be looking for you and want you dead?" Chelci asked.

Veron gazed into the puddles forming on the stone path.

"What are you still not telling me?" Chelci took her hand off of his back and folded her arms across her chest.

"Everything I said was true," Veron said as he turned back to her. "But there are some things I can't tell you."

Chelci stood and left the bench to walk toward the house.

"Chelci, wait!"

She didn't wait, so Veron ran after her. The rain turned into a downpour as he emerged from the tree's protection. By the time he caught up with her at the entrance to the alcove, his clothes were drenched.

"Chelci, please." Veron placed his hand on her shoulder to halt her progress.

Chelci spun around. Although it was dark, Veron saw the anger in her eyes and felt her passion. "You ask me to trust you and say that things aren't as they seem. You tell me pieces of your life, but won't fully open up." Her hair was soaked, but she didn't bother putting up her hood. "How am I supposed to believe anything you say when you keep hiding things?"

"Yes, I keep things from you!" Veron shouted, trying to be heard over the rain's tumult. "You want to know why? It's because I'm a *slave* who has had the few things I've ever loved taken from me. My teacher, my market, my friends, my parents that I never even knew, my freedom—all of it . . . gone."

"What are you hiding, Veron?" Chelci shouted as she stepped closer.

Veron's heart raced as his mind screamed to tell her the truth. His inhibitions faded as the rain drummed steadily on his body. "You want to know what I'm hiding? I hide my feelings. I hide my hopes and wishes. I'm a lowly slave who has everything dictated to him about what he can do and say. It doesn't matter what I want because I can't have it. It doesn't matter that I wake up every morning, and all I can think about is you, Chelci. It doesn't matter that every moment of the day, I wonder what I could do to make you happy. Someone like me doesn't have that luxury. You are everything I could ever want in a girl! I love your spirit and your heart for others. I love that you're not above cooking and sewing, and how you look when you wake up with messy hair and no makeup. But none of this matters because you're the daughter of a high lord and I'm a slave! I'm a hopeless fool! I know we can never be together, but I can't help—"

Chelci reached out, grabbed his soggy tunic, and pulled him to her. The shock silenced him, and when she pressed her lips into his, his mind went blank. One of her arms wrapped around him, and the other found the back of his neck. When he returned the embrace, he pulled her body impossibly close, melting into her arms as they kissed, hard and fierce. Electricity jolted through his body as their lips remained locked. The pelting rain only heightened the moment.

His heart pounding, Veron reluctantly pulled away but refused to loosen his arms. He panted as he looked at Chelci with a huge grin. The sweet smile she returned soothed his immediate fear about her regretting the intimate moment.

Wordlessly, the two held hands as they walked slowly through the downpour back to the house. Veron's mind whirled as it tried to keep up with the soaring of his heart. He didn't know what would come next, but at least he wasn't alone.

Two stories above the garden, a pair of eyes watched, hidden in the darkness. Tristan grasped the windowsill with his dirt-stained hands and slowly lowered it. Now that the two figures below had walked off, there was nothing left to hold his attention. Safe from the splatters of rain, he stroked his chin as his face sprouted a despicable grin.

21

Consequences

Chelci closed her door and leaned against it, reliving the previous moments in her mind. A sigh escaped her lips as she waited for her pounding heart to slow. Puddles formed from the water dripping off her clothes and body, but she didn't care. She was oblivious to everything except the memory of the kiss.

I should tell Emma, now! She quickly laughed away the idea. It was the middle of the night on Emma's wedding night. Interruptions were the last thing she wanted.

Chelci paced her room, leaving a trail of water along the path. The smile on her face was a permanent addition, and her cheeks ached. Beginning to shiver, Chelci fumbled through her wardrobe to find something dry. After tugging and pulling on the wet fabric, she removed her soaked clothing then dried with a spare cloth. Afterwards, she put on a nightgown, leaving the wet clothes in a pile on the floor. She wasn't sure what to do with them and figured Veron could help with them in the morning.

Veron. I can't believe I just did that! Her smile returned as she thought of him. She wanted to be with him. *I still don't understand the reward. There's something he has yet to tell me.* She brushed the concern out of her mind, preferring to focus on what just happened. They would have to keep their feelings secret. Her parents wouldn't let him remain her wardman if they knew.

Chelci got under her covers and stared at the ceiling. Her mind was alive with ideas, and butterflies filled her stomach. Eventually, the late hour caught up with her, quieting her mind as she fell into a deep sleep.

The sound of the door opening brought Chelci gradually out of her rest. Her heart leaped with excitement at seeing Veron again, but the weight of her eyelids fought back. She hoped he would let her sleep longer, given how late they were up. She stretched her arms and yawned as he bustled about the room, opening curtains.

"*Ash*," she said, emphasizing his alias. "I'm eager to see you too, but don't you think we could use a little more sleep after such a late night?"

She opened her eyes and sat up, expecting to find the morning sun's blinding light, but the windows were dark. Something was wrong. She blinked her eyes and looked to the end of her bed. Her stomach dropped at the sight. Her mother and father stood, fully dressed, with scowls on their faces.

"Mother, Father, good morning," Chelci said in as friendly a voice as she could manage. The pleasant greeting wasn't returned.

"What did you do last night?" her mother asked in an icy tone.

Chelci looked between her parents as she racked her brain. "You mean the wedding? I . . . uh . . . went to Emma's wedding. We got back late. I know you had some to drink, but do you not remember how late we got home?"

"Don't disrespect me, you fool!" Luciana snapped. "I remember when we got home. What happened after that?"

"Ver—" she caught herself. "My wardman helped me settle, and I went to sleep."

Her father leaned over and picked up the pile of clothes laying on the floor. A trace amount of water remained. "What are these from?" Darcius asked in a sharp voice. His forehead pinched—a sight she was not used to seeing from him.

"My clothes? Oh, yes, I went for a walk outside before retiring. I wasn't tired after the wedding excitement, and I got caught in a sudden rainstorm."

"Was *he* there?" her mother asked.

Chelci angled her head as if she wasn't sure who her mother was talking about. "Who? Ash? Yes, I asked him to come along just to make sure I was safe . . . it being so late. I sat on the bench to think, and he watched from afar."

"From afar?" her mother said, words thick with disbelief.

"Yes," Chelci said. Inside, her stomach turned.

"Nothing else happened?" Luciana asked.

Chelci shook her head.

"That's not what we heard," Darcius said as Chelci's pulse quickened.

"We heard you kissed that servant," her mother said in a biting tone.

Chelci paled. Her legs tingled, as if cold water flowed through her veins. Her breath came quickly, and panic filled her mind. "What?" she said feebly. "Where did you hear that?"

"It doesn't matter!" Luciana roared. "Is it true?"

Chelci couldn't breathe. She tried to respond, but her body wouldn't work. *What will they do to me? What will they do to him?* She wanted to refute the claim. She opened her mouth but couldn't make out the words. Finally, she lowered her head, resigning to the guilt and consequences to follow.

Veron jumped as his door slammed against the opposite wall. The rude awakening disoriented him. The window was still dark, and after the late night, his body ached from lack of sleep. Rough hands pulled him out of bed and put him in shackles.

"Hey, what's going on?" he yelled. The men who woke him were two house guards. "Rupert, Dorrick, what is this? What's going on?" At the far end of the hall, illuminated by a lone lantern, a bearded man stood with arms crossed. A wicked grin played across Tristan's face as he stared him down. Veron's stomach churned as the men pulled him in the opposite direction.

The guards didn't speak as they dragged him down three flights of stairs. At the end of the basement corridor, Rupert opened the last door to a rarely used storage room. He pushed Veron in and closed the door behind him.

"Rupert!" Veron cried through the door as he pounded on it. Muffled footsteps faded, and the storage room's darkness pressed in on him. The musty smell reminded him of Artimus' garden shed after a rain. He searched and found the small room only contained a few boxes. Veron leaned against the back wall and allowed his body to slide to the floor. *What did Tristan do? Did he see the poster?* As he sat, waiting for answers, the sound of footsteps returned. Veron shuffled to his feet, hoping for the best.

When the door opened, Veron's hands shot to his eyes. The lantern's harsh light blinded him after the pitch blackness. He slowly dropped his hands to see Tessa holding a lantern aloft and Lady Luciana's glare. Behind them, Rupert, the guard who whipped him weeks before, stood with crossed arms. Veron felt the color drain from his face.

"What gives you, an ankler—a servant of justice, the right to think you can defile my daughter?" Lady Luciana asked.

"What? I didn't—" Veron stopped, remembering the kiss in the garden. *Did someone see us? Did Chelci tell?* A terrifying thought caused his legs to shake. *Is Chelci turning me in for five sol?* "I . . . uh—"

"Don't deny it!" she roared and stepped in closer. Veron shrank against the wall. "You kissed in the garden last night. You . . . a mere servant! I trusted you! I promoted you, and you betrayed that trust!" Luciana fumed as she paced the small room. "In what world do you think you're worthy of my daughter—the daughter of a high lord?"

"I'm sorry, Lady Luciana," Veron said, holding his head up. "I didn't intend to upset you, but I do think Chelci has the right to make her own choice."

She stopped pacing and glared at him. Her eyes danced with fire from the lantern as her chest heaved from the rapid breaths. "You forget your place."

"I may be a servant in your house, but I'm a person, just like Chelci, and just like you."

"You're nothing like me . . . or her."

"Sure, I didn't grow up the son of a lord, but it's not the station someone is born into or the amount of money they make that decides a man's worth."

"You fool," Luciana said. "You think you can corrupt my daughter with your radical ideas? I knew we never should have promoted you to wardman. Now, you'll pay for your errors." She turned and nodded to Rupert.

"Go ahead! Whip me!" Veron shouted. "Do your worst! Let everyone see. I don't care."

Luciana's face twisted into a sneer. "Trust me . . . you'll care."

Veron's stomach turned as Rupert stepped forward. One hand held a short whip, different from the one Veron experienced upon his arrival. It contained several strands, each topped with a blade. His other hand held a thick bludgeon. Veron cringed.

"I don't want everyone to see your punishment," Luciana said. "I don't want them feeling sorry for you. But I also don't want anyone else getting any ideas about the liberties they can take with my daughter." She stepped so close Veron could feel the warmth of her breath. "Maybe they'll hear you scream?" She nodded to Rupert as she and Tessa stepped outside, leaving the lantern behind and closing the door.

Chelci paced her room and wrung her hands. After her parents stomped out, she tried to follow, but found the door locked from the outside. Her tiredness was long gone as the adrenaline ran through her. *What are they going to do to me . . . or to Veron?*

Twice, footsteps sounded in the hall outside. She watched the doorknob but didn't hear a key, and the knob never turned. She considered using the secret passageway through her wardrobe's back panel to escape and warn Veron. Her parents had likely forgotten about its existence, but it would be too late to get to him.

Chelci's head jerked up as she heard a faint, muffled yell. She couldn't pinpoint the source, but someone was in a great deal of pain. Her pulse and breathing grew rapid as the screams continued. Deep inside, she knew where they came from. Chelci plopped on her bed and covered her ears with a pillow to block out the sound of agony. When the yelling finally stopped, she sat up and wiped her eyes. She wrestled with her internal guilt, measured by the anger toward her parents.

Unable to wait any longer, Chelci stood and walked to the wardrobe. She flung the door open and pushed her clothing aside to reveal the panel with the small knob she could slide at the back.

Suddenly, a key worked at the door, and Chelci jumped. She quickly closed the wardrobe as the doorknob to her room turned and her mother entered.

"What did you do?" Chelci yelled as she crossed her arms.

"It's not your concern," Luciana said. "He will have no part in your life anymore."

"Was that him screaming?" Her mother didn't answer the question. "Was it? What are you going to do to him?"

Luciana glared at her daughter as she took a deep breath. "First, we will invoke his collateral. I believe he had three people listed on his sheet. We must kill them to let other servants know the consequences of such actions."

"No! You can't do that!"

"Then, what's left of his body—now that Rupert is finished with him—will die slowly in the Felting dungeon, never again seeing the light of day."

"No!" Chelci screamed as she fell to her knees.

"Chelci, we can't have our servants thinking they can have their way with you. We must take strong action."

"Mother, please don't do this! It was my fault. Take it out on me, instead! I was the one who kissed him! He did nothing wrong. He's been nothing but polite and helpful and a great person . . ."

Luciana stood silently for a moment as Chelci's voice faded away. "Yes, we definitely must eliminate him," her mother said as she walked to the door.

Chelci stood and quickly closed the distance, resting her hand on her mother's shoulder. "Mother, please spare him. What do you want? I'll do anything!" she pleaded.

Luciana sloughed off the hand and went to open the door but stopped with her hand on the knob. Slowly, she turned around and looked at her daughter as a wicked grin formed. "Anything, you say?"

Chelci's throat went dry. The two stared at each other until finally, Chelci gave a short, slow nod.

After the whipping and beating, Rupert closed the door, leaving Veron in darkness again. Collapsed on the cold, stone floor, pain throbbed through his body to the beat of his pulse. His tattered shirt fell loosely against his body. His back was mostly numb, but he still felt the tenderized bruises on his arms and legs where the club made its mark.

Veron heaved in ragged breaths. He fought to bring his mind to the present, but the pain pushed it away. *I have to find the origine.* He pushed against the floor, digging his fingers into the cracks between the stones as he flexed his muscles. Pain valiantly fought against his efforts, and he cried out anew. Panting again, Veron ceased his effort as he rested. *I can't let them beat me. I must find a way!*

Veron pushed the thought of Chelci and her mother from his mind and focused on himself. He heard his heartbeat. He felt his lungs expand. Soon, he sensed what he sought—the tingling informing him the origine was ready. He groaned as he pulled the energy with all his strength. It felt more difficult than ever, but he soon prickled all over his body as the cuts and bruises healed. The effort was immense. His groan turned into a yell as he fought to control the power. Far too soon, the source depleted, and Veron collapsed his body onto the floor. He was empty.

* * *

Veron quickly lost track of the days in the darkness. During the daytime, a slight light shone through the crack in the bottom of the door, but his room was pitch black at night. Servants came by once per day to bring him water and stale bread, but they never spoke. His wounds healed well after the origine struggle. Scars remained, and soreness lingered where his bruises were. He was happy to only deal with those small reminders.

After several days of waiting in the locked room, a whisper roused him from sleep. His eyes shot open.

"Veron," the whisper said again.

Veron shuffled toward the door. "Hello?" he whispered back.

"Hey, it's me, Nathaniel." Veron smiled, relieved to hear his friend's voice. "I'm sorry I haven't been by. No one's allowed to see or talk with you."

"That's alright," Veron said. "I figured as much."

"It's the middle of the night. I snuck down because I had to check on you."

"Thanks. It's good to hear someone's voice."

"Are you okay?" Nathaniel asked. "We all heard when they—you know . . . that night. I know you're tough, but . . ."

"I'm okay," Veron said. "It probably sounded worse than it was."

"I wonder if you're trying to set a record for the most whippings in the shortest amount of time? Did you really kiss Chelci?"

Veron chuckled. "Yeah. She kissed me, actually."

"Man, you've got some guts! That's all any of the servants are talking about. There are a few who think you deserved it for going too far, but most believe it's amazing. You've got quite the group of supporters out here."

"What happened to Chelci? Is she okay? Did they punish her?"

"I don't know. She's been in her room a lot. The few times I've seen her, she seems alright . . . not physically hurt, at least."

Veron sighed as he leaned against the wall. Chelci's safety was number one on his mind, but he also worried about those on his collateral list. "What else is going on? I'd love to have something to think about other than my injuries."

"Not much is different," Nathaniel said. "High Lord Weatherbee's law prohibiting feeding the poor ruffled some feathers in the city. Many of the servants have friends and family affected by it."

I wonder how Chelci's taking it? Veron thought.

"There's a lot of talk about Bale from Norshewa," Nathaniel said, causing Veron's body to stiffen. "Some people say he'll attack Felting, but it sounds like it's a rumor. I think people just like to make up stories."

Veron shuddered as he thought of Bale attacking. "Thanks for coming to visit me, Nathaniel."

"No problem. I probably should get back. I'll try to visit again soon."

After his friend silently disappeared, Veron lay back down on the hard ground. Encouraged by Nathaniel's kindness and the small amount of news, Veron closed his eyes again. He would sleep sounder with the hope that Chelci may be alright.

* * *

Several pairs of footsteps paraded down the hall on the other side of the door. Veron sat up straight, unsure if they came to visit him or not. It had been a couple of weeks since his whipping, and the days blended together.

A key worked the lock, and the door opened a moment later. Sunlight flooded the room, and Veron covered his eyes.

"Stand up!" Luciana Marlow yelled harshly, bringing him to his feet.

As Veron stood, he gradually lowered his hand to find the lady of the house with Tessa and Rupert. The guard stepped toward him, and Veron inhaled sharply. His body flinched, anticipating another beating. Rupert fumbled for Veron's hands and unlatched his restraints.

The tension in his body relaxed, and he rubbed his hands. When he looked up again, Tessa held out something to him—a fresh pair of clothes. *What is this?* He took the clothes as he turned to Luciana.

"Against my better judgment, I am not sending you to prison, and I will not be invoking your collateral," Luciana said. Veron's eyes grew as he held his breath. "You will—" She cut herself off. Her eyes flit to the ceiling while she took in a deep breath then sighed. "You will remain a servant in our house, but you will be a housekeeper again. You *will not* speak to my daughter or even make eye contact with her. If you cannot follow this, there will be no leniency next time. Do you understand?"

Veron relaxed his shoulders and nodded his head enthusiastically.

Luciana stepped closer, narrowing her eyes and sneering. "Of course, if you're physically unable to work, we'll be forced to terminate your work agreement." She roughly grabbed Veron by the shoulder and shook him.

With the origine's help and a couple weeks recovery, his wounds had healed nicely. He felt strong. As she shook him, he flexed his muscles and stood still as a statue. Luciana's eyes flared for a moment before narrowing as she released her hold.

"Don't worry about me, Lady Luciana. I'm fully fit to work."

From down the hall, an unseen voice called out, "Lady Luciana! They're arriving!"

Luciana stared fixedly at Veron for a long moment. Suddenly, she turned and left the small room with Tessa and Rupert. This time, they did not close the door.

As Veron stepped through the doorway, he looked cautiously around, half-expecting a trap or attack. Nothing happened. After putting on the clothes, he walked the length of the basement hall. The eerie quiet unsettled him. *Where is everyone?*

Veron shrugged as he plodded up the spiral stone stairs. With no one to tell him what to do, he wanted to return to his room. While passing the second-floor landing, the hum of conversation and crowd of bodies drew his attention. House servants either craned their necks out one of the front windows at the far end or gathered around the balcony overlooking the entry hall. Veron found his way to an empty spot along the balcony.

Down below, Darcius and Luciana stood with straight backs and smiles on their faces, dressed in their best outfits. Many of the people-facing servants flanked the large entry room: Elliot and Violeta, Corbus, Hugar, and the house guards. Tatiana was the only member of the housekeeping crew allowed in the prominent reception position. Of course, Tessa waited dutifully beside Luciana, stretching her neck to appear taller.

Chelci stood in front of her parents while her mother rested her hands on her shoulders. In contrast to their erect postures and looks of pride, Chelci was not pleased to be there. Her mouth fixed in a hard line. Her shoulders slumped, and her head drooped slightly toward the floor. Her sour expression didn't hide her beauty, amplified by her dark red dress.

The other servants surrounding the second-floor balcony whispered to each other. "It's not every day you meet a baron," a server said to another at Veron's left.

"I bet he's rich," another voice said.

A baron? A baron's coming here?

"There you are!" a voice nearly lost in the hubbub called from behind as a hand landed on his shoulder.

"Nathaniel! They let me out!"

"Yeah, that's great," the other servant said before his face darkened. "Have you heard, though?"

Veron raised an eyebrow. "Heard what?"

Nathaniel took a deep breath and exhaled while Veron waited. "You're not going to like it. Chelci—"

The doors below suddenly opened, and the crowd hushed as head attendant Jensen entered the hall. He announced in a clear voice, "High Lord and Lady Marlow, Baron Raynor Fiero of Karad has arrived."

Veron gasped aloud, drawing sharp looks from those standing close. The blood drained from his face. He held his breath as a tall man with blond hair and a sharp-looking tunic entered.

A small contingent of people walked in with him, but Raynor held himself singularly. His heavy footsteps echoed on the stone and bounced off the room's walls as he approached the Marlows.

"What about Chelci? What'd she do?" Veron whispered, keeping his attention on Raynor below, hoping he didn't look up.

Nathaniel whispered back, "From what I hear, *she* convinced her mother to spare your life." The words stunned Veron, and his heart swelled with gratitude.

"Baron Fiero, we're so honored to have you," Lady Luciana said. Her words were fast and high-pitched.

"Indeed, the honor is mine," Fiero said as he kissed her offered hand before turning to Chelci. "And you must be the daughter. Let me look at you."

Veron ground his teeth, seething while the baron inspected her as if she were a cut of meat. An uneasy feeling churned in his stomach. "What are you not telling me?" he whispered to Nathaniel. "How did she convince her?"

Nathaniel paused before replying. "You know how her parents keep trying to set her up with a suitor? To save your life and let you remain here, she agreed to marry one of them."

Veron's stomach lurched as if someone had kicked him in the gut. He reached his hand out to steady himself against the railing.

"Yes, I think she'll do," Fiero said below as he took a step away from the Marlows. "Chelci, allow me to introduce you to . . . a successful businessman, a champion swordsman, the Lord of Commerce for Karad, and of course, my son . . . your future husband, Brixton Fiero."

Veron's mind blanked. His breath became ragged, and he had to grip the railing tightly to keep from falling. A boy with short, straight blond hair and a brightly colored tunic stepped forward. Brixton.

No! Anyone but him! Veron backed away from the railing. Nathaniel glanced at him, but he kept moving away. Once he was out of sight, he turned and ran.

II

Encounters

22

Arrival

The carriage bumped over holes in the city street, jostling Brixton as he leaned against the side. He and his father had arrived in Felting minutes before, after a full day's journey. It was difficult to sleep in the rolling vehicle. He rubbed his eyes and yawned, even though it was nearly midday.

His stuffy clothing didn't help his attempts to sleep. The colorful linen vest and matching wool coat Father insisted he wear looked nice but wasn't comfortable. His hat rested on the seat next to him.

"I'm ready to be there," Brixton said as he slid the curtain to peer outside. His father merely grunted as he watched out his own window. "I don't remember the ride being this long and uncomfortable."

Outside the window, people walked about carrying food and visiting stores. The streets were clean and wide, a fact that always impressed Brixton when he traveled from the smaller city of Karad.

"Father, why do I have to marry this girl?"

Raynor's eyes narrowed as he turned. "Because I said so."

"Yes, but why now? Why her? I've never even met her!"

"Now, because you seem to bring failure to everything you touch. Only you could take a successful market and run it into the ground in weeks. I want you to be married before your personal defeats compound and no one in Terrenor will deign to consider you. Her, because she's the daughter of a High Lord. Even with my elevated station, it's the best you can hope for. And I don't care that you've never met her."

Brixton breathed in deeply as he pushed away his father's ever-present insults. "Have you met her before?"

His father paused a moment. "I saw her when she was young. On my visits to discuss Department of Commerce business."

"What do you remember of her?"

"I remember her playing with dolls and climbing trees in the garden."

"What?" Brixton yelled. "When was this?"

"It was a long time ago. Apparently, she's been living in the woods for the last six years."

"Wait . . . you're marrying me off to some wild girl who's been living in the woods?"

"She's a regular girl. Her parents assured me she'll be a compliant, dutiful wife."

Brixton huffed as he leaned back in his seat. "She'd better," he mumbled.

"Keep in mind, there's an expectation of you in this marriage," his father said. "The Marlows are a very influential family. Both Darcius and Luciana have a lot of information about what goes on in this city." He leaned forward and lowered his voice. "You know what's coming soon." Brixton swallowed the lump in his throat and nodded as his father continued, "It may be useful for you to have access to their information and influence, so don't miss an opportunity to ingratiate yourself with all of them."

Brixton sat up straight as he furrowed his brows. "But if Bale is—"

"Hush!" Raynor slammed his foot into the carriage's wooden

floorboard. Brixton shrank back against the wall. "Don't say that name, you fool."

"I'm sorry, Father. If . . . things are going to happen as you have been planning with . . . *him*, why does it even matter? You're going to be . . . you know, and then you can do whatever you want."

Raynor spoke softly again. "It matters because I don't trust . . . *him*. We're working with him to get what we want, but ultimately . . . *he* is not what we want. After we take the city and I'm in control, Billings and I should be the ones in power. Once the king is gone, we'll deal with *him*."

The carriage hit a large bump, and Brixton pressed against the wall to steady himself. *I was never excited about working with Bale, but I'm surprised Father already plans to betray him.*

"When we arrive at the Marlows' house, be on your best behavior," Raynor said. "You need to make them like you. Who knows, maybe you'll be able to do something right for once."

Brixton followed his father as they stepped out of the carriage. The house was impressive. The Fieros' old house was one of the nicest in Karad, but the Marlows' put it to shame. Dozens of windows lined the front facade of the stone exterior. Two fountains spouting water high in the air decorated the middle of the circular drive and the stairs to the front door. Father's wardman stepped down from where he had ridden with the carriagemaster, and all three of them walked up the front stairs.

At the top of the stairs, an attendant bowed and ushered them inside a grandiose entry hall. Polished marble floors reflected like mirrors. Gold and silver designs on the walls made it feel like a small palace. A balcony ringed the second floor, filled with gawking servants. *It's like they think I'm royalty,* Brixton thought with a smirk.

After his father introduced him, he took off his hat and stepped forward to be presented to Chelci. *She looks okay, I guess.* Her hair was full and straight. Her face was . . . fine, but nothing spectacular. Her slumped posture and scowling expression didn't help. Brixton frowned as he noticed her muscular arms. *What is she, a blacksmith? What woman has arms like that? She's not nearly as pretty as Hailey.* His thoughts drifted momentarily to his ex-fiance. *At least she won't fall for my best friend.*

Chelci lifted her cold, dead eyes to meet his. She spoke with little inflection. "Brixton, thank you for coming. I look forward to getting to know you."

"As do I," Brixton added, smiling broadly despite her lack of warmth.

Silence filled the courtyard. Servants watched from around and above. Brixton's neck reddened as the parents stared, waiting for him to do something.

"Well, I'm sure you've had a long journey," Luciana said, her extra-bright expression masking the awkward moment. "Baron Fiero, if you'd like, we can show you to your rooms. Chelci, why don't you show Brixton our gardens?" Her pointed look indicated it wasn't a suggestion.

"Yes, Mother," Chelci said. "Brixton? Would you care to join me?"

"Of course," he replied as the servants disbanded. Brixton followed Chelci through two more rooms to the back of the house, where a door led them outside. Planted rows of vegetables filled the yard to the right. Meandering paths of stone led through trees and bushes on the left. Chelci led them slowly along the wooded path.

"So . . . marrying someone you've never met. How about that, huh?" Brixton said.

Chelci's mouth fixed in a hard line as she stared ahead. "I'll admit, I'm not happy about it."

"I was furious when they told me," Brixton said. Chelci glanced at him with raised eyebrows. "Marriage isn't something to take lightly, and for my parents to tell me I had to . . . ? I didn't like it, but I understand. Our parents want us to keep up the family tradition of success and wealth. People like us can't fall in love with just anyone, so I guess it makes sense . . . still . . ."

Chelci's body tensed the longer he spoke. "Tell me about your family," she said.

"My father is . . . powerful. As the Baron of Karad, he's the most influential man in the region, and before that, he was the Lord of Commerce. Success seems to follow him. And my sister recently married into the Hampton family. You know High Lord Hampton, I'm sure."

"I've heard of him."

"Their family has a lot of prestige."

"Hmm," Chelci mumbled.

Brixton caught an eye roll as her disinterested gaze wandered the garden. *This isn't working,* he thought as he racked his brain. "To tell you the truth," he continued. "It's not always easy being in the Fiero family."

Chelci snapped her head toward him, eyebrows pinched together. "What do you mean?"

"There's a lot of pressure."

Half of Chelci's mouth turned up. "I know what that's like," she said, the tension in her body fading.

"My father can be . . . demanding."

"Sounds like my mother," she said. "What's it like, living with him?"

Brixton hesitated at the question and took a deep breath.

"You don't *have* to talk about it if you don't want," Chelci added.

He glanced toward the house to make sure no one was around, then took a deep breath, feeling an unexpected twinge of emotion. "He's not a kind man. He's angry most of the time, and all he cares about is money and power. He hits my mother as well as me and my sister."

Chelci raised her hand to her mouth. "I'm so sorry."

"Thanks. I've learned to live with it, but I've also learned I don't want to be anything like it."

"What *do* you want to be?" she asked.

"You mean as a father . . . a person . . . for a job?"

"Anything," Chelci said. "If you weren't the . . . Lord of Commerce, what would you want to do?"

A smile crept over Brixton's face. "You know, it's silly, but when I was younger, I wanted to be a baker."

"Really?" Chelci's expressive eyebrows revealed a genuine interest. "That's not silly."

"Yeah, I thought it would be fun . . . you know? Baking bread every morning, waking up and smelling the warm yeast and delicious pastries. It would be simple . . . yet satisfying."

"You should know I make a mean Nasco Roll," Chelci said.

"What's that? Nasco Roll?"

Chelci smiled. "That's what we call them. It's a roll I learned to make when I lived in Nasco."

"That's right, you lived in another village for a while." Brixton stopped at the entrance to a ring of trees and nodded to a bench on the far side of an alcove. "Do you want to sit for a bit?"

Chelci fidgeted as she stared into the alcove. "Why here?"

"I just thought you might like to sit, but we don't have to if you don't want to."

"No, it's okay. This is fine," Chelci said as she hesitantly walked to the bench.

Brixton followed and sat next to her. "So, enough talk about me. Tell me about yourself, Chelci."

She turned and looked at him, eyes wide. "You want to know about me?"

"Is that okay?"

Her mouth opened partially, and her eyes seemed lit like a spark. "Of course! It's just . . . People rarely ask about me."

"Tell me about that village thing. Why'd you go there?"

She shrugged. "I don't know. I just wanted to."

"Come on. I'm sure there's more than that. I bared my soul about my family."

Chelci exhaled as she sat up straight. Placing her hands in her lap, she looked straight ahead. "Well . . . I was twelve. My mother and I didn't get along well, and I concluded anywhere was better than here. So, I ran away. I know . . . it's ridiculous and irresponsible—"

"I think it sounds amazing!" Brixton interrupted. "I thought about running away plenty when I was younger, but I was never brave enough."

"I did feel brave, but—to be honest—it was pretty foolish. My time there was purposeful. I learned a lot, and I grew as a person. But, eventually, it was time to come home."

"I think it's incredible, Chelci." Brixton stared at her, and she blushed. "So . . . what do you like to do?"

"I like adventure," she answered. "I like traveling and exploring. I don't want to sit all day gossiping with other women or stitching designs to hang on a wall. I want to do something!"

"I understand that."

"I don't like to dress to impress people. If I *want* to put on makeup and do my hair, I'll do it. I hate the expectation and the judgment when I don't. Basically, I loathe being told what to do."

"Noted," Brixton said with a laugh. "What's something you're passionate about?"

Chelci looked toward the trees as she cocked her head. "Helping others," she said after a moment. "I hate when people are mistreated, and I want everyone to have an equal chance to be taken care of."

Brixton leaned forward, listening intently. "What sort of people?"

"Like . . . the servants in our house. I want to help them. Their jobs are to make my life easier, but if I can do something that makes them smile, or takes work away from them, I love it. Some servants here are . . ." Her gaze drifted back toward the house as she looked toward the roof. ". . . are really great. I want to make sure they're treated well."

"You remind me of a friend I used to have," Brixton said. "I never had his brains or skills, but he always challenged me to be a better person." They sat in silence for a moment while Brixton's thoughts drifted to Veron.

"While you're here, maybe we can find our way to the kitchen, and you can teach me some Karad recipes?" Chelci said, breaking the silence.

"Oh no," Brixton said, shaking his hand and chuckling. "I said I had an *interest* in being a baker, but my knowledge is nonexistent."

A thoughtful smile crossed her face. "Maybe I can teach you something, then."

"That sounds good," Brixton said as they stood to leave the alcove of trees. "So, in recap . . . I'm going to be a nicer husband than my father, and I'm never going to tell you what to do. Got it!"

Chelci's hearty laugh encouraged him he was on the right track. Brixton extended his elbow but noticed an odd, contemplative look on her face. "What is it?"

"Oh, nothing. It's just . . ." The lines of thought on her face formed into a smile. "I expected this meeting to go differently," she said, slightly laughing at the end. She gently linked her arm through his as they followed the path back to the house.

As Brixton unpacked clothes from a trunk, the side door to his room opened, and his father entered without warning. *I wish he would at least knock.*

"What do you think? Will we have any problems with her?" Raynor asked.

Brixton tossed a shirt down on his bed. "No, I don't think so. She should be fine. She does have a lot of . . . ideas though."

"What do you mean?"

"I don't know . . . things she does and doesn't like to do. The way she likes to help people. It could be difficult to deal with."

"Deal with it," Raynor snapped. "Don't scare her off. Connect with what she likes, and make her think you like it, too."

Brixton sighed. "I would rather just be myself and see if she likes me as I am."

"No! She won't want that. We need this family's support—her parents, too." Raynor stepped closer and stood in Brixton's face. "I'm leaving in the morning to return to Karad. Can you do this?"

"Yes, I already am."

Raynor narrowed his eyes and stared at his son. "Good, I'll see you in a week," he turned and left, closing the door hard behind him.

23

Avoiding the Past

Veron ran through the halls, twisting and turning down corridors, trying to get as far away from the entry hall as possible. His chest hurt, not from running, but from the feelings of betrayal bubbling up in him. At the end of the house, Veron opened the door to the library's upper balcony. He hurried to the end of the walkway. Books surrounded him on three sides as he sank to the floor behind a chair.

How is he here? Did he track me down? Is he here to turn me in for a reward? Fighting his initial instinct, he soon considered Brixton may have no idea he was at the Marlow house. *Maybe he's truly just here to marry Chelci?*

The thought of the marriage sent shudders through his body. Before he knew it, tears fell freely as he considered his loss over the last couple weeks and Chelci's fate. Soon, the sadness turned to anger and rage. He took the closest book off the shelf and threw it against the opposite shelf, where it thumped uselessly to the floor.

"Veron?" Nathaniel's voice called from the doorway. Veron didn't reply. Moments later, his friend emerged around the side of the leather chair. "Hey, are you okay?"

Veron shook his head and wiped his eyes.

"I know it's got to be tough seeing Chelci with someone else, but . . . you and she were never an option. You know that, right? It could never have worked with you two. This was bound to happen." Nathaniel's voice was kind, but it did not soothe the anger and fear.

Veron shook his head. "It's not that. Well . . . it's not *just* that. It's Brixton."

"Lord Fiero? Do you know him?"

He nodded. "Yes, I know him . . . very well. He's the reason I'm here as a servant. He's the one who threw me in prison." Nathaniel's eyes widened as Veron continued, "He's not good for Chelci. She can't marry him, and . . . he can't see me while he's here."

"Why does that matter? If he's the reason you're here, wouldn't he know you're here?"

"It's not like that. He just can't know. It's vital he never sees me."

"So, what are you gonna do?"

Veron sighed as he leaned his head against the bookshelf. "I don't know. I can't talk with Chelci, or they'll throw me in prison. I can't talk to Brixton because . . . I can't." His head jerked to Nathaniel. "*You* can talk to her!"

"Uh . . . no. That's not gonna work."

"Yes, please! I need you to do it!"

"Veron, think about it. I go up to Chelci—who I don't know at all—and tell her the servant she kissed, who still likes her but can't look at her, doesn't want her to be with the new, rich, prestigious fiancé?"

"Perfect!"

"How do you think that's gonna go?"

Veron exhaled in frustration. "I know. You're right. I've got to talk to her."

"How are you gonna do that, though? How can you get her alone?"

Veron pursed his lips. "I'm not sure. Are you willing to help?"

A skeptical look crossed Nathaniel's face. "What do you have in mind?"

Veron pressed against the sewing room door, ear flush against it. He had waited for what seemed like hours, alternating between pacing and listening. Finally, he heard what he listened for and moved against the wall.

"We need to clean them, but I want to make sure you don't need any alterations first," Nathaniel said as the door opened. He walked across the room to a table strewn with fabric while Chelci followed behind.

"Chelci," Veron said softly as he stepped off the wall. She jumped and turned toward his voice.

"I'll be leaving," Nathaniel said quickly as he ducked out the door and closed it behind.

"Veron! You can't be here! Mother will kill you!" Chelci closed the distance between them quickly and rested her hands on his upper arms. "I mean it, she will literally have you killed!"

"I know, but I had to risk it. I have to talk to you."

"Are you alright?" she asked as she looked him over. "You don't look too bad. I heard you screaming. I assumed you were . . ."

"It wasn't as bad as it sounded," Veron said quickly, trying to avoid speaking of his unusual healing abilities. "Listen, I have to talk to you about Brixton."

"Brixton?" Chelci's face screwed up. "What about him? Be quick though, you really can't be here with me."

"You can't marry him, Chelci!"

She tenderly rested her hand against the side of his face. "Veron . . . I know what you're feeling. I care about you, too, and I wish it could work between us. It can't though."

"I—I know . . . but not Brixton."

"Veron, I had to make a deal with my mother."

"I know you did, but you shouldn't have! Saving my life isn't worth throwing yours away!"

"I'm not throwing mine away. Brixton is . . . he seems sweet . . . enough."

"What? No! Chelci, you don't know him."

Chelci stepped back and put her hands on her hips. Her kind face had turned angry. "Oh, and *you* do?"

"Yes, Chelci, I do!"

Chelci paused and wrinkled up her forehead. "How do you know him?"

"Do you remember what I told you about my past? About how a friend of mine betrayed me? Brixton was that friend!"

Chelci narrowed her eyes. "You knew Brixton in Karad?"

"Yes!"

"And he's the one who was jealous of you, then framed you for murder, and threw you in prison?"

"Yes!"

She stared in silence for a long moment. "Are you sure you just don't want to see me with someone else?"

"That's not it! I owned the market he stole from me. He blackmailed me into giving him money then kidnapped a girl I liked."

"A girl you liked?" Chelci asked, tilting her head.

"That's irrelevant. Chelci, Brixton murdered his fiancé! He stabbed her in the stomach in front of my eyes. All because he thought I stole her from him!"

Chelci intently stared at Veron as he panted from the explosion of words. "I'm not sure what to make of this. I trust you, but . . . Either way, I have to do what I have to do, and at this time, it's marrying Brixton. Not because he's the man I choose, but because I made an agreement. I'm doing this for you, Veron."

"No, Chelci. You have to believe me!"

"Veron, stop! You're not making this any easier." Tears fell down Chelci's cheeks. "I'm sorry. I have to go."

Chelci fled through the door, wiping her eyes. Veron was too stunned to follow. He slumped to the sewing room floor and leaned his head against the wall. *What am I supposed to do now?*

24

House Tour

Bundled in a thick cloak, Chelci breathed in deeply and exhaled, creating a cloud of breath that obscured her vision. Fog hovered over the Felavorre River, the morning sun yet to chase it away. She loved to explore the packed, dirt path along the river as a young girl. She and Emma used to run along the banks, chasing frogs into the water and finding turtles on logs.

"So, what's he like?" Emma asked, snapping Chelci out of her thoughts. "Brixton. You haven't said a word about him."

Chelci sighed. "I'm not sure. I *think* I like him."

"Yeah?" Emma said with a half-smile.

Chelci began to stroll along the path as she talked. "He seems alright . . . I believe. Apparently, his father is a piece of work. Brixton doesn't want to be anything like him, so I guess that's a good sign. He has this . . . politeness to him and a humble side—unlike any other suitors I've met. He actually wanted to be a baker at one point."

"Really?"

"Yeah, and he wanted to know about me. Can you believe it?"

Emma laughed. "Well, that's a pleasant change."

Chelci tucked a loose strand of hair behind her ear and smiled. "He asked me about my passions and interests. I was so shocked I spilled everything. I told him everything I like—stuff I would *never* have told the average person for fear of scaring them off. But he . . . seemed to like me more after it."

"Well, that's good," Emma said.

"Yeah, I think so."

"So, you're going to go through with it? You're going to marry him?" Emma asked. "This engagement seemed to come out of nowhere."

Chelci exhaled, then slowly nodded her head. "Yeah, I have to. For Veron's sake."

Emma snapped to attention. "What do you mean, 'for Veron's sake?'"

Chelci rubbed her chin as a flush crept over her face. "I kissed Veron."

Her jaw dropping, Emma grabbed Chelci's arm. "What! How have we not talked about this? You kissed Veron! What were you thinking?"

Chelci laughed and shook her head. "I know! I know! You've been busy being married and all. I haven't been able to tell you about it. It was the night of your wedding. We were talking in the garden late that night about . . . a lot. He's had a hard life, but he still has a great spirit I love. We were soaked from the rain, and he was going on about how much he cared for me. I guess I got caught up in the moment, and I kissed him."

"Wow," Emma said with wide, unblinking eyes.

"It was amazing. I had it in my mind we could make it work—that we could have this secret relationship. Apparently, another servant saw us and told Mother, and that was the end of it."

"And you agreed to marry whoever your parents picked if they spared Veron?"

Chelci nodded. "They beat him, but she didn't send him to prison to die. I made her keep him on as a servant, too, but he's not allowed to talk to me."

"Are you getting a new attendant?"

"No. They said I could do without until I'm married."

"That's too bad," Emma said. "Do you think you would have married Veron if this hadn't happened?"

"Ha! I don't know," Chelci said as she turned back to the path and continued walking. "I definitely wouldn't have agreed to let my parents pick someone for me."

"But, Brixton isn't a terrible option, I take it?"

Chelci hesitated for a moment. "I think he'll be fine."

Emma stared hard, making Chelci fidget with her hands. "What is it?" Emma asked. "You're not telling me something."

Chelci looked at her feet as she walked, internally debating how much to say. "Veron told me some things."

"Veron . . . who's not allowed to talk with you?"

"Yeah, I know. He risked getting caught and killed to tell me things about Brixton. He says he knew him before he came to our house."

"How? That's crazy!"

"I know! What are the chances? But he claims he knew him, and he said some things . . . awful things about him. I've never doubted Veron before, but they couldn't possibly be true."

"What'd he say?"

Chelci shook her head. "I don't even want to repeat them. They're so far out there."

"So, you think he's lying . . . because . . . he wants you for himself?" Emma asked.

"Maybe? But I don't see how he could expect that to happen."

"He must be jealous."

Chelci frowned as she walked, dragging her feet in the dirt. "So, how's married life been?" She asked after a moment, eager for a change of topic.

Emma blushed as she smiled and looked toward the ground. "It's been . . . nice," she said, giving a small laugh.

"What about at night? Is everything okay in the—"

Emma smacked Chelci's arm. "Chelci!" she shouted as her face turned strawberry red. "Yes, everything's good there. Matthew's been great in every way. He even made dinner yesterday, after a long day at the bakery."

"Have you been working there, too?" Chelci asked.

"Not every day, but most of them. It's nice. We get to be together and talk all day. He's kind to his customers. I love seeing it. I enjoy the job, too. It's simple . . . but rewarding."

A pang of jealousy filled Chelci. *Brixton seems like the type who could enjoy that, but I don't think our lives will ever look like it—not with his position.*

Chelci tapped her friend on the arm. "Look, Emma . . . a turtle." A turtle sat motionless on a log that extended from the shore into the water. "What a life that would be, huh? No worries about marriage. You just get to sit on logs and enjoy the sun all day."

"I don't know," Emma said. "I think it might get old."

Chelci laughed. "You're right. I don't think sitting on logs is for me. There's too much I want to do."

Later in the day, Chelci walked down the stairs into the foyer. She had spent extra time doing her hair and makeup and wore one of her favorite dresses. As she entered the sitting room, Brixton stood with a smile on his face.

"How was your time with your friend?" he asked.

"It was nice," Chelci replied. "I love a cool morning along the river. We'll have to take a walk there this week."

"I would love that."

"Are you ready for the promised house tour?" Chelci asked.

Brixton gave a comical bow as he mimed removing a hat. "Whenever my lady is ready."

Chelci walked through the house, showing him the multitude of rooms at a leisurely pace. He inquired about the furniture's history. He paused to admire the paintings and tapestries, commenting on the quality.

"I must say . . . I thought our old house in Karad was large, but yours is much more impressive," Brixton said.

"I don't know that I find it impressive, but it is large," Chelci said. "Personally, I'd rather have something smaller and easier to manage."

"Yes, I agree," Brixton said after a pause.

Chelci searched his face. His look was genuine. "I think large houses are a silly waste of resources meant solely to impress others."

"It's settled then," Brixton said, slapping his leg. "I noticed a nice hollow on the ride down here, halfway from Karad to Felting. It's the perfect place for an exquisite mud hut for us. I can ride my horse to Karad for work, and you can visit your friends and family in Felting whenever you like. We can host dinner parties for the squirrels and garronts in the nearby forest."

Chelci laughed. "I assume we'll need to live in Karad?"

"How do you feel about that?"

"That's fine," Chelci said after a slight pause. "I've only been once, but it seems like a pleasant city."

"I haven't spoken to Father about it, but we may be able to live in my family's old house. Now that they've moved into the castle, it sits empty. It's no mud hovel, but it's a nice place."

"I'm sure it would be great," Chelci said as she opened the door leading to her favorite room. "And this is our family's library. When I have nothing else going on, this is where I usually am."

"Amazing!" Brixton said, turning in a circle and staring at the two-story room filled on all sides with packed bookshelves. "Have you read all of them?"

"Ha! I wish!" Chelci said. "I do love to read, but I haven't even scratched the surface. Father likes to buy every new book he sees. No one's touched the large majority of them."

Brixton walked to a nearby shelf to look closer.

Chelci grew more comfortable with Brixton the more time they spent together, but Veron's words continued to gnaw. "Did I hear correctly? Were you engaged once before?" she asked.

Brixton's body stiffened at the question as his hand paused on a book. "Yes," he replied coolly. "Her name was Hailey. She was the daughter of the Lord of Defense of Karad."

"It didn't work out, huh?" Chelci asked, trying to appear casual.

Brixton was quiet for a long moment. "A friend of mine was jealous of us. He tried to seduce her, but when she turned him down, he killed her."

Chelci inhaled sharply. She narrowed her eyes and swallowed to clear her dry throat. "I'm so sorry. That must have been awful." *Is he talking about Veron? Who's telling the truth, Brixton or Veron?*

Brixton nodded. "Thank you. Yes, it was tough, but I got through it."

"What happened to your friend?"

Brixton's face froze, as if he weren't ready for the question. "My friend? He . . . um . . . He received what he deserved. Enough about all of that, though. I prefer not to dwell on it."

"Of course. I'm sorry. So . . . your father said you were a successful businessman. What businesses have you run?"

"Oh, besides running the Department of Commerce, I also own North Karad Market. It's a market where we sell . . . well . . . we sell groceries and bread."

Chelci's breath quickened. *I bet that was Veron's business.* "Hmm, that sounds nice," Chelci said flatly. "Has it done well?"

"It *has* been good . . . over the last couple of years. Recently, things have been slower though."

"Why did you start a market?"

"Well, I . . ." Brixton paused. "I love helping people . . . and everyone needs groceries, right?"

"Yes, I guess they do."

"A while ago, I started this thing where, each Weekterm, when the market closed, I took food close to spoiling and handed it out to the city's needy."

"Really?" Chelci asked, her face perking up.

Brixton nodded. "Overall, Karad is nice, but there are a lot of poor people who need help. The market is a great way to use my resources to help them."

Chelci stared. *Everything he says sounds good, but is any of it true? If I could get him and Veron to meet, maybe I could figure it out.* "Would you like to meet some of our servants?" she asked.

"Um . . . Sure." Brixton's response did not carry his usual enthusiasm.

They left the library, and Chelci led Brixton down the stairs to the kitchen. The room was busy. Stoves roared with flames, and cooks chopped vegetables as they prepared dinner.

"Hello, everyone!" Chelci called over the room's noise. "I want to introduce you all to my fiancé, Brixton. I'm sure you've seen him but maybe haven't had the chance to meet him."

Everyone greeted them with waves. Chelci walked him around to each person and introduced the servants by name. Most were friendly, although Corbus barely acknowledged the Lord from Karad, insisting his work needed his attention. Paloma, the eldest of the cooks, made up for his inattentiveness by wrapping Brixton in her arms and squeezing him in a big hug.

"Thank you," he said. "What an amazing welcome."

"I've been looking out for Chelci since she was a little girl," Paloma said. "I'm happy to see her finally have a man who can look out for her."

Nathaniel entered the kitchen with a yoke of buckets as he headed toward the side door. Chelci had only spoken with the servant occasionally but knew he was close with Veron. The two were always together.

"Nathaniel!" she exclaimed as she waved to flag his attention. Down the hallway behind him, a loud clattering sound echoed through the kitchen.

He stood rigidly. "Yes, Lady Chelci," he said with a curt bow.

"Have you met my fiancé, Brixton?"

"I saw him when he arrived, but we haven't met," Nathaniel said as he turned to Brixton. His gaze was hard as he offered an almost imperceptible nod.

"It's nice to meet you, Nathaniel," Brixton said. His wary smile faltered under the servant's glare.

"I was hoping to introduce him to my old wardman," she said. "I know you're often together. Do you know where he is?"

Nathaniel's eyes flared. "Um . . . He, uh . . ." He turned back down the hallway and a frown quickly appeared. "I'm not sure where he went. We've been making water runs. He must have been called away."

"It's no matter. Another time, perhaps," Chelci said, dismissing Nathaniel to continue his work. With no more servants to introduce, Chelci turned back to Brixton. "Come on. I have one more thing to show you."

"Impressive!" Brixton said as he stepped into the sparring room at the end of the garden path. "We had nothing like this. Well, we do now in the castle, but not growing up. I had to visit my training master's workshop to practice."

Chelci's ears perked up. "You had a training master?"

"Yeah. Father thought it important I learn."

"Really? You want to . . . see what you've got? Try out your moves on me?" Chelci nodded toward the wall of swords.

Brixton laughed. "What . . . now? With you? I don't think so."

"Why not?" Chelci said, feeling indignant.

"First off, I will not fight my bride-to-be. And secondly . . . you're wearing a dress."

"So . . . you're worried about being beaten by someone in a dress. Got it."

"Wait! Hold on!" Brixton said. "Fine! Let's go."

He walked to the wall of weapons and skimmed them. Chelci watched him as she chose hers without looking—the light sword given to her by Aleks in Nasco. Brixton chose a longer, heavier sword. He walked to the middle of the room with the natural gait of someone who knew their way around a blade.

Holding their swords aloft, the two circled. "Honestly, I don't want to hurt you, Chelci," Brixton said.

"That's kind of you," Chelci said as she stepped in and swung at him three times in succession. Brixton parried the swings away before stepping to the side.

"Wow," Brixton said, flaring his eyes. "You seem like you know what you're doing."

"You surprised? You think because I'm a girl, I don't know how to sword fight?" She moved again, quicker this time.

Brixton jumped out of the way, barely moving his sword in place. The playful look on his face twisted into a serious expression. "If I did before, I don't now."

Brixton attempted a strike, but Chelci could tell it was half-hearted.

She didn't even bother glancing it away. Instead, she spun to the side and hit his back with the flat part of her blade. Brixton staggered. Chelci seized the opportunity and kicked, striking his hand where he held his sword. He cried out as his weapon flew into the air. Quickly snatching it, Chelci held both swords to Brixton's chest as she cocked her head, declaring victory.

"Okay . . . That was impressive," Brixton said, puffing.

A grin formed on Chelci's face. "You'll have to do better than that if you're going to impress me," she said. She handed the heavier sword back and returned to the center of the room. "Again!"

25

Unavoidable Dinner

"I know you say he's awful, but he didn't seem that bad to me," Nathaniel said to Veron as they ate dinner in the servants' dining room in the basement.

"Believe nothing he says. It doesn't matter how great of a person he tries to make everyone believe he is. It's all a lie," Veron replied.

"You talked to her, right?"

"Yes!" Veron said in a hushed tone, glancing around to make sure no one listened in. "I told her everything, but she doesn't believe me. She keeps parading him around like he's the greatest guy ever."

"He did seem pretty nice," Nathaniel said, prompting a glare from Veron. "But . . . of course, he's awful."

Veron sighed. "There's nothing else I can do."

"Do you think you can keep hiding from him the rest of the week? Luckily, you ran when they came down into the basement."

"I only have two more days. As long as I can stay out of sight, I think I'll make it."

"Hey, Ash!" a rough voice called from the other side of the room. "How are those housekeeping duties treating you?" Tristan's laugh was joined by a couple others, but Veron didn't turn.

"Ignore them," Nathaniel said.

Veron's fist bunched up. "Tristan turned me in."

"Really?"

Veron nodded. "I'm pretty sure. I think he saw us when we kissed in the garden."

"Well . . . that's all done now. Just leave him alone." Nathaniel grabbed his plate and tilted his head toward the door. "Come on. Let's go."

Finished with their food, the young men cleared their dishes into the kitchen, setting them on the counter. Tatiana had just finished eating and was about to leave the kitchen.

"Tatiana!" Veron called.

She stopped just short of the stairs while Nathaniel continued up.

"I've been feeling a little under the weather today. I'd rather not be around the family or our guest if I'm sneezing or coughing. Would it be alright if I worked on chores either down in the basement or up on the servants' level until the lord from Karad leaves?"

"Sure, I think that's fine. Remind me in the morning, and I can make sure of it."

Veron grinned after she returned to the stairs.

Behind him, an argument cropped up, drawing his attention. Tessa held a large, open ledger and yelled at Osmund, the pantrymaster. "It doesn't add up, Osmund! Our household has not increased, yet we're paying double what we did for food last year! You need to figure out where that money is going, and you need to do it now!"

"I'm sorry, Steward," Osmund replied. "Food prices have risen, and people seem to eat more. Plus, garden production is down. But, I'll redouble my efforts. You're right . . . we need to figure this out." His eye caught Veron standing to the side and motioned to him. "Ash, you know!"

Veron didn't want to draw attention to himself, but now he had to join the conversation. "What's that, Osmund?" he asked as he stepped closer, prompting a glare from Tessa.

"Garden production was abysmal before you came here, wasn't it?"

"It was in bad shape, yes," Veron agreed.

Osmund turned back to Tessa. "When production is low, we have to spend more to supplement our stores."

To their side, Oliver emptied a pile of wasted food into a trash bin. Much of the food looked unused. "Wasn't lady Chelci taking food like that to the needy?" Veron asked the server.

"Not since that new law," Oliver said. "No one can hand out food, so we have to toss it."

Veron turned back to Osmund and Tessa. "Is that part of the problem? Are we throwing away so much food our costs are running up?"

"There's a cost," Osmund said, "but it's hardly new. We've always dealt with wasted food."

"Osmund, can you help me?" someone called from a nearby storage room. Osmund nodded to Veron and Tessa before leaving.

"If you'd like, I could look through the books to see if I notice anything to save money?" Veron said. "I wouldn't mind. Before I came here, I ran a business for several years."

Tessa shrugged. "Sure. I keep the ledger down here on the shelf. You're welcome to look through it."

A clattering noise and a yell found their way down the stairs just before a server with an armload of dishes arrived. "We need help!" Veron and Tessa both turned their heads, but the rest in the kitchen were buried in their work. "Steward Tessa, there's a wine spill in the dining room. We need to clean it up."

Tessa turned sharply to Veron. "Go! Take some damp towels with you."

Veron froze. *The dining room! That's where Brixton would be!* "I . . .

uh . . . I can't."

The house steward's glare returned. "You're a housekeeper, aren't you? This is your job! Go, now!"

Veron hesitated. He looked around the kitchen, hoping another housekeeper was around and available. He was alone. "I'm, um . . . I'm not feeling well," he said, resting his hand on his stomach.

Tessa's hands were on her hips as her eyes shot daggers at Veron. "I don't care how you're feeling. If you're not up there in ten seconds, Lady Luciana is going to hear about your refusal."

Veron snapped into action. He grabbed some rags and dunked them in the basin before quickly wringing them out. As he ascended the stairs, his plodding footsteps reminded him of the drumbeats preceding prisoner execution. He exited the staircase on the ground floor and walked through the sitting room, pausing at the door to the dining chamber. Talking and laughing radiated through the door. His heart pounded. His mind raced to think of a way out. *I could hide or track down Nathaniel and ask him to do it?* His friend was probably up on the third floor, but it would surely get back to Tessa. Unable to find a way out, Veron pushed the door with his shoulder and walked into the room.

Once inside the dining room, Veron immediately looked to the floor. An inkling of hope teased him as he saw the seating arrangement from the corner of his eye. Brixton sat next to Luciana near the door and faced away toward Chelci and her father.

With Brixton unable to see him, Veron risked a glance at Chelci. His breath caught as he found her eyes focused fixedly on his. A sorrowful grimace crinkled her forehead, and sympathy tugged at her eyes.

Luciana noticed Chelci's gaze and turned her body. Veron immediately averted his eyes to the floor. "Ah yes, Ash. The spill's over here." She gestured while holding a full glass of wine, almost spilling it as well. Appearing content in her directions, Luciana turned back to the table and laughed as she made a comment Veron didn't hear.

His hope increased as he walked to the puddle of wine on the opposite side of Brixton. With all the dinner guests engrossed in food and conversation, Veron worked on the floor. The spill was large, but it only took a moment to wipe it up using the damp and dry rags he brought. When all was clean, he slunk back toward the wall and slowly stood. He didn't risk glancing at Chelci as he crept toward the exit.

"Brixton, would you like some more food? You seem to have quite the appetite," Luciana said.

Veron didn't glance to see the response. The pulse thumping in his ear muffled Brixton's answer. Every step he took sounded like a bell announcing his presence. As he extended his hand to open the door and leave, his heart sank. The words that reached him, heard clearly over the pounding, were horrible.

"Ash, before you leave, would you clear Brixton's plate?" Luciana said.

Veron froze. His fingers felt the wood on the door. Another few steps would grant him freedom. *Can I run? Where would I go?* Running would do nothing. Against every instinct in his body, Veron turned and walked toward Brixton.

He stopped just behind his old friend and leaned forward, extending his hand as far as he could. After setting his used utensils on his plate, Brixton lifted it to Veron. Just before Veron could grasp it, Brixton turned slightly. Their eyes met. Brixton's friendly smile instantly turned, and his eyes widened. He gasped as his body flinched. The plate—just out of Veron's reach—fell from Brixton's hand, knocking the table's edge and shattering on the floor.

"Oh, dear!" Luciana cried as she stood. "Ash, what did you do?"

Veron immediately kneeled to the ground, head down. He frantically worked to pick up the fragments of Brixton's dishes.

Brixton spoke in a shaky voice. "It was my fault, Lady Luciana. I—The plate slipped from my hand. My apologies."

The dishes collected, Veron turned toward the exit without speaking or looking at the others. He pushed the door and left the room as fast as he could.

Downstairs, he set the broken dishes and soiled rags on the counter for others to clean up.

"What happened up there?" Oliver asked.

Veron didn't reply or even look in the server's direction. Instead, he ran to the stairs and continued up three flights. He didn't stop running until he had returned to his room and closed the door behind him.

He breathed in ragged gulps of air. His mind raced, trying to think of the ways it could play out. *What am I going to do now?*

26

Under the Surface

Brixton paced his room.   He had retired immediately following dinner, despite repeated protests from Chelci's mother. While he wanted to know the family and make a good impression, finding Veron was a wrinkle he had not expected.

How did he end up here? he asked himself despite knowing the answer. *What if Chelci or her parents find out what I did to him?*

He breathed in deeply, remembering Bale's request. *Bale is our ticket to Father ruling Feldor, but he needs Veron dead. And I'm the only one who knows where he is.* Surely, turning him in would mean a substantial reward—more than the five sol listed on the posters. He would probably receive a prominent position in the new country's leadership. If his father became Regent of Felting, maybe Brixton could take his place as Baron of Karad?

An image of Veron's face from the dungeon in Karad flashed into Brixton's mind. It was the look of pain—of betrayal. Veron was always good to him . . . even if he attracted the attention of his father and his fiancé. *I wonder if that shadow knight thing is real? Could he really have special abilities he never told me about? Could he be some hidden warrior capable of taking on a thousand soldiers?* Brixton laughed

241

to himself. Veron . . . from the streets of Karad. There was no way that was him.

∗ ∗ ∗

Breakfast was quiet the following day. Brixton barely spoke more than a few words to Chelci or even made eye contact.

"So, what do you two think of roasted rydanor for the wedding reception?" Luciana asked bright-eyed as she delicately picked at the food on her plate. "I know it would be expensive to import from Tarphan, but many people here have never eaten it. It would be quite the delicacy. I hear the meat is deliciously tender."

"Sure," Chelci said, staring at her plate, looking deep in thought.

"And I've already spoken with Vintner Felavorre. Demarcus says he has some special new batches of wine they're saving for the wedding. Isn't that great?"

"That's great, Mother."

"Brixton, do you know what color your parents will wear at the ceremony? I was going to wear blue, but I wonder if your mother will have the same. I should probably make other plans just in case. Do you know?"

Brixton rapidly blinked his eyes. *Why would I know what my mother is going to wear? Who even cares?* "No, Lady Luciana. I'm afraid I don't know, but I'll inquire."

After breakfast, Brixton and Chelci went for a walk in the city. During Brixton's schooling years, he rarely ventured past the school grounds, so Chelci promised to show him Turba Square and the surrounding shops.

"That building houses the Department of Trade," Chelci said, pointing as they walked side-by-side down the street. "And Father works just past it at the Department of Commerce."

Brixton grunted in response. His office in Karad paled in comparison. Twice as tall and wide, it gave off a stately impression that left him feeling inadequate. As Chelci continued to talk about the city, his mind drifted, thinking about what Veron might have said and what he should do about it.

"Would you like to see my friend's shop?" Chelci asked as they stopped in front of a store with 'Westscott Bakery' written across the front. Large, glass windows displayed rows of bread and pastries. "I thought it may interest you because of . . . you know—the bakery thing."

"Sure."

A bell rang as Chelci opened the door, and immediately, a warm greeting called out from behind a counter. "Chelci! Good morning!"

Chelci walked around the counter and gave an enormous hug to a young lady and man working there, both of whom wore aprons covered in flour. "This is my fiancé, Brixton," she said as she gestured to him with traces of white freshly dotting her dress. "He's leaving tomorrow to head back to Karad. Brixton, this is my best friend, Emma, and her husband, Matthew."

"It's good to meet you," Brixton said with a slight wave. "I've heard so much about you both."

"Brixton, I hear you're quite the baker!" Matthew said enthusiastically.

"Oh, no," Brixton replied. "I've never actually baked anything. When I was a kid, I once had a silly thought that it would be fun."

"It's not silly," Matthew said. "It's a good job—" he turned to Emma and extended his hand "—especially when you have a treasure like this working next to you. People need bread, and I enjoy making it for them."

"Yes, of course," Brixton said quickly. "It's not silly for someone like you, but . . . for me . . ." He held his hands with palms up. "The money . . . You know?" He laughed, and his unfinished comment hung in the air. Chelci, Matthew, and Emma looked at each other, and Brixton wished one of them would say something.

"Would you two like a pastry?" Emma asked as she lifted a tray she had arranged as they arrived. "I finished them a moment ago."

"All by herself," Matthew chimed in, drawing a smile from Emma.

"That's right. He let me do the whole thing," she added, beaming with pride.

"Sure, I'd love to try one," Chelci said, looking at Brixton as he walked closer.

He selected one of the small, puffed items. Sugar sprinkled at the top of the pastry stacked in flaky layers. His eyes widened as he took the first bite. The sweet flavor and the crisp, buttery texture were perfectly balanced.

"This is incredible," Chelci said through a partially swallowed mouthful, bringing her hand to her chin, ensuring no crumbs fell.

"It really is!" Brixton added as his eyes grew. "I wish I knew how to bake. I would make these every day! Emma, this is impressive!"

Her face reddened as her smile increased its size.

Chelci and Brixton stepped out of the bakery as Brixton finished his second pastry. He liked them so much he asked for another, which Emma was proud to offer.

"Your friends seem nice," Brixton said.

"Yes, they're kind," she replied.

"When they come and visit us in Karad, maybe we can persuade them to bring some of those pastries," Brixton said with a laugh. The visit to the bakery perked him up, but his concerns about Chelci and Veron quickly returned.

A short distance down the street, the narrow path opened into a wide square. Its size reminded Brixton of Karad Square, but with five or six times as many shops. Food vendors in carts dotting the center sold nuts, fruit, vegetables, fish, grains—any fare one may want. Vendors called out and waved food and wares to get his attention. Colorful signs and flags dotted the storefronts and carts. Spiced meats tempted his nose. A band of musicians played stringed instruments and sang a lively tune in front of a tall statue in the square's center. A throng of people milled around, shopping, talking, and watching.

He followed Chelci as she meandered through the carts. She didn't seem to want anything specific. She took it all in, looking at everything. Although the variety of shops distracted him, Brixton couldn't shake the questions he wrestled with. "So . . . Chelci, your family seems to have a lot of servants. Where do they come from, and how long have they been there?"

"I'm not sure, exactly," she replied. "Mother or Tessa hires them. I think most of them are from somewhere in Felting, but I don't know for sure. Paloma, Jensen, and Violetta have all been here since before I was born . . . I believe. There are plenty of others, and some have only been here a short time."

"What about the servant at dinner last night?" Brixton asked. Chelci's arm tensed as she reached to pick up a decorative bowl from a vendor's stand. "The one who cleaned up the spill."

Chelci turned to him, eyebrows knitted together. "Servant from dinner? I'm . . . not sure who you mean."

"You know, the tall one with the brown hair. Around our age. He cleaned up my plate after I dropped it."

"Oh, yes . . . that one," she said. Her eyes did not appear to register a moment of recognition. "You're talking about Ash. I don't think he's been here long."

"What's his story?"

Chelci cocked her head. "Why do you want to know? He's just a servant."

"I—I was curious. I like knowing about people, that's all." He let his eyes wander the square, trying to appear casual. "What do you know about him?"

"Not much. He's a housekeeper—cleans floors and clothes and stuff. I think he worked in the garden for a bit before he was a wardman." She near-imperceptibly flinched and looked to the ground.

"Wardman? For . . . ?"

"Oh, um . . . for me, actually. But only for a few weeks. He didn't work out."

"Really?" Brixton asked. "He was your wardman? This . . . Ash fellow?"

"Yeah, just briefly." Chelci resumed meandering through the square.

"What did he do for you?"

"You know . . . just normal stuff. He was my guard when I went into the city with Emma, and he made sure I had things I needed around the house. Sometimes he'd spar with me."

"Spar? As in . . . sword fighting? Is that typical of a wardman?"

Chelci shrugged. "I think it's different for everyone."

"What did you talk to him about?"

Chelci stopped and put her hands on her hips. "What is this? Why are you interrogating me about some servant I hardly know? Did he look familiar to you or something?" Her eyes shot daggers.

Brixton fought to keep from audibly gasping. *Does she know?* He raised his hands. "Wha—No! I'm sorry! I was just curious." Brixton stared back for a long moment. Chelci seemed to squirm under his gaze. "What is it?" he asked.

"What do you mean?"

"What are you not telling me?"

Chelci shifted her weight as her eyes flitted around again. "Nothing," she replied as she turned to walk away.

"Don't you walk away from me!" Brixton yelled as he grabbed her arm. Chelci froze and slowly turned to look him in the eye. A few nearby vendors glanced their way.

"Let go of me," Chelci said slowly in a low voice.

Brixton stepped closer and spoke forcibly. "You'll be my wife soon. Don't you *ever* think you can disrespect me!"

Chelci didn't back down from his icy glare. She grew stronger from it. After a moment, she yanked her arm free and leaned in. "Don't forget . . . I'm not your wife yet. And if that's how you're going to treat me, 'not yet' will become 'not ever.'" She turned away from him. "I'm going to spend some more time around the shops. Don't bother following."

Brixton stood in place, stunned as he watched her walk away. He clenched his jaw when Chelci disappeared around a corner. *Veron told her.*

Chelci stormed out of the square, passing shops filled with colorful dresses and carts piled with delicacies. She barely noticed them. Her hands hurt from how tightly she clenched them. Away from the crowd, she released a pent-up yell of frustration, prompting two birds sitting on the edge of a building to take flight.

At least some of what Veron told me must be true, or Brixton wouldn't be so interested in him. But that doesn't necessarily mean everything was accurate. Chelci sighed as she paced back and forth in front of a cistern, water flowing into a basin below. She pulled her hands to her chest to stop their shaking.

If it all is true, I can't marry someone like him, can I? She swallowed hard as she pictured Veron's face. *What would happen to him if I refused to marry Brixton? Or what if Brixton refuses me?* She hadn't considered the possibility he may want to back out himself. *Mother would accuse me of sabotaging the arrangement, and she'd be just as mad.*

Chelci sat on an empty bench. Tears welled up. She felt trapped. All options seemed impossible to accept. Her face in her hands, she cried freely. The fountain's trickle covered her sobs but did nothing to ease her heart.

Brixton nodded as Jensen let him in the front door. The house was quiet. Returning alone, he hoped to avoid questions about Chelci's whereabouts. He padded to the stairs of the entry hall, hoping to make it to his room unseen.

"Chelci, is that you?" the voice of Luciana Marlow called from an adjacent room. Brixton cringed as he paused with his hand on the marble railing. Hesitantly, he placed his foot on the bottom step when the voice returned. "Brixton? Who's there?"

Brixton sighed as his shoulders slumped. "Yes, Lady Marlow, it's me." Retreating down the steps, Brixton went to find her.

"Brixton! How did you like the city? Where's Chelci?" Luciana asked as he entered the sitting room where she and Darcius lounged. Chelci's father nodded to a servant standing in the corner, who moved to pour a cup of tea for Brixton.

"Um . . . Chelci met a friend of hers . . . Emma. They wanted to talk, so I gave them some privacy."

"Please sit, Brixton," Darcius said, pointing to an open chair, which Brixton took as a servant handed him a steaming cup. "What did you think of Turba Square?"

"I enjoyed it," Brixton said, leaving out the public argument. "It's colorful and lively. I'm actually thankful for the chance to talk with you both, though."

Brixton sipped his tea while the Marlows sat straighter. "I am too," Darcius said. "Chelci means a lot to us, and we've had little chance to talk with you."

"First of all, thank you both for giving me the honor to join your family," Brixton said. "I feel humbled to have this opportunity. Although my father is a baron, and I am a lord, I sometimes feel like I'm just a young man trying to make his way in the world. Never did I imagine I could unite with a family like yours."

"The honor is ours, Brixton, but I appreciate your words," Luciana said.

"I want you to know that I will make sure your daughter has everything she could ever want. She will live in the nicest house and wear the finest clothing. The Fiero-Marlow bond will be the most powerful in all of Feldor!"

Luciana beamed as she glanced at her husband. Darcius spoke up. "Of course, that sounds wonderful. But, know that Chelci can be . . . headstrong. It's important to the success of your marriage that you listen to her and understand what *she* wants."

"Oh, of course!" Brixton replied, setting down his cup. "She doesn't know yet, but I'm already developing plans to build a library in our home. I'm sure it could never be as impressive as yours, but I know she loves to read."

Darcius nodded. "Yes, she does."

Brixton leaned forward. His hands sweat as he held them together in front of him. "What I really want you two to understand is I hope to expand the greatness your family has built over the years. I want all our accomplishments to be a reflection on you." A smile curled at the corners of Luciana's mouth while Brixton continued. "I'd like to support anything you have going on. If you have commercial goals for Feldor, I will be your greatest supporter. If there are . . . political situations or problems, you have my word, I will be behind you fully. All you need to do is keep me informed of what's going on." He stared emphatically. "I want you to know you can trust me with anything."

Brixton flashed a grin, hoping it set the Marlows at ease. Thankfully, they nodded their heads. "We're thankful to receive you as a son-in-law," Luciana said. "We know you will grow to do great things."

After tea with Chelci's parents, Brixton stepped outside to think in the garden. The conversation with the Marlows encouraged him, but it didn't change his situation with Chelci. He walked circles around the meandering path, anger and frustration building.

If she were to try and back out, Father would kill me. Why did I have to lose my cool with her? Brixton groaned as he ran his hand through his hair, pulling at the ends. If Veron hadn't turned up at the Marlows' house, everything would be fine.

"Excuse me!" a voice called through the trees.

Brixton stopped his march as he peered through the trees toward the voice's source. In a moment, a bulky, bearded man shuffled through the trees carrying a hoe. Dirt stained his clothes, but he bore a broad smile as he waved.

"You must be Brixton," the man said. "It's good to meet you. I'm Tristan, the gardener."

Brixton raised his chin as he looked down his nose at the man. "Can I help you, Tristan?"

"I wanted to congratulate you on your engagement. Chelci's a fine catch . . . a fine one indeed. You're a lucky man. If you ever need anything while you're here, let me know, and I'll be happy to help."

"Thank you." Brixton turned to leave.

"I mean that! I can find anything you want in the city, and I know everything going on here. You just let me know how I can help."

Brixton turned back around slowly. "You know everything? What about the housekeeper, Ash? I think he used to be a wardman. Do you know anything about him?"

The gardener's face turned grim. "Yes, I know quite a bit about him. What would you like to hear?"

27

In the Open

Veron sat on the bench in the sparring room as midnight approached. He constantly glanced at the door, hoping Chelci would arrive. Earlier that day, he'd left a note in her room—the same one she had written to him his first night, but he wasn't sure she would come.

He felt hopeless about the situation. More specifically, he felt it about *her* situation. He said his piece about Brixton, but she didn't seem to believe him. Now that Brixton saw him, he was unsure about everything. He didn't know how Brixton would react. Regardless of what happened to him, he wanted another chance to get through to her.

The crunching of rocks sounded outside the door, and Veron quickly stood, feeling light with anticipation. When the door opened, Veron's hopes crashed, and his mouth fell slack. Brixton glared as he sauntered across the room.

"What are you doing here?" Veron asked in a shaky voice.

Brixton held up a small piece of paper. "I went to Chelci's room and found a note . . . 'Practice Midnight?' It may not have been for me, but I figured I might see what was going on."

251

Veron warily watched, half-expecting Brixton to run at him, but his old friend appeared unsure of his next move. "What do you want?" Veron asked.

Brixton's shoulders eased. "Honestly, I'm not sure. I didn't expect to find you here at the Marlows' house."

"Where'd you expect to find me?" Veron spat. "Chained in a quarry, hauling stones?"

"Veron, I'm sorry about it all—about what I did," Brixton said, causing Veron to narrow his eyes. "Did you know Bale is looking for you?"

Veron's throat went dry. He hoped to avoid the subject. "Yeah, I saw a poster."

"No one's turned you in?"

"Most people forgot my real name. They call me Ash." Brixton raised an eyebrow. "I spilled an ashbox on Chelci's mother my first day here, and the name stuck," Veron said, and Brixton laughed. "So, what are you going to do . . . about Bale?"

Brixton pursed his lips. "Bale asked where you were several weeks ago. I could have tracked you down before this if I wanted to."

"What about now? Now that you know where I am, are you going to tell him?"

Brixton slowly looked to the floor and shook his head. "What about you? Are you going to say anything . . . about me?"

"I already told Chelci."

"Yeah, I gathered as much. Are you planning to tell her parents?"

I would if they wouldn't have me beaten and killed, Veron thought. "I *will* tell them. I'll tell them everything you did . . . unless you leave Chelci alone."

Brixton laughed, his confidence seeming to grow. "No, you won't, Veron. You won't because they won't care." He circled the room as he continued. "I've learned a lot since I've been here. For example,

I learned that *you*, a servant, have fallen for the daughter of a high lord."

Veron inhaled quickly. He tried to hide his expression, but it was futile.

"Don't get me wrong. I applaud your ambition. Instead of going after a lowly candle maker, you're setting your sights on someone loftier. Bravo! The problem is . . . you can't have her. Now, your foolish love is clouding your judgment. From what I hear, if you talk with her or even make eye contact—which it seems you've already done—you'll be sent off to prison to die."

"Chelci deserves better than you! That's why I told her!" Veron said, fighting to keep his voice down.

"Also, I've learned if Chelci refuses to marry me, her mother will have you killed. How's that for irony? It doesn't matter that she may like you. It's *because* she likes you that she'll end up marrying me."

"You're despicable, Brixton."

"Would you like to know what else I've learned? I found out Chelci's parents care more about prestige and connections than their daughter's welfare. So, be my guest—tell the Marlows everything you know. Just don't blame me when they ignore and kill you."

Veron stepped in close to Brixton. Although he talked bravely, Veron smelled his ex-friend's fear. "I heard about the market," Veron said. "You got greedy and tried to take profit back from the workers, but the plan backfired." Brixton shifted his feet as Veron continued, "Even the workers you didn't fire left on their own. Also—" He leaned in closer and spoke in a hushed growl. "I know about Morgan's family."

Brixton's face went pale. "That wasn't my fault. I had nothing to do with—"

"Of course it was your fault!" Veron hissed in a strained whisper. "It's *all* your fault!"

"Veron . . . I feel awful about Morgan's family. Really, I do. But, I can't do anything now."

"I don't care if her parents have me killed. I *will* tell them everything." Veron said, quaking with fury.

"Bale still wants to know where you are. I think maybe I *will* pay him a visit!" Brixton replied through clenched teeth.

The two young men panted and held stares at each other. They were so close Veron smelled Brixton's breath.

"I don't want to fight with you, Veron," Brixton said at last. "If you leave me alone, I promise I'll do the same."

"Oh, you'll let me enjoy my slave life in peace and happiness?" Veron said, his voice dripping with sarcasm. "How generous a gift!"

"Tell me about the Shadow Knights," Brixton said, suddenly.

Silence blanketed the sparring room. Veron took a step backward as his face screwed up quizzically. *How does he know? Bale . . . of course. That's why he's offered a reward to find me.*

"Are you a shadow knight, Veron?"

Veron stood tall and held Brixton's gaze. "Yes, I am."

It was Brixton's turn to be shocked. His eyes grew and his mouth hung agape. "How? What does that mean?"

Veron sighed before speaking. "I trained with someone, but . . . the abilities lasted barely a day—the day I met Bale."

"What is it?" Brixton asked. "What can you do?"

"It doesn't matter anymore. I'm just a regular person again."

Brixton's gaze hardened. "A regular person, huh? Sounds convenient, but I don't believe you. I think you still have it." He walked directly to the wall and selected two swords before turning back to Veron. "You're going to prove I'm right, or you're going to die."

"You want to fight?" Veron's pulse raced as he considered fleeing.

"Brixton?" a soft voice called from outside.

Chelci! As Brixton looked to the front door, Veron turned and ran out the side exit. He continued running past the path into the thick trees surrounding the garden. After a moment, he stopped, listening over the sound of his heaving breaths. *He's not following.*

Veron crept carefully back to the sparring room. Both the front and side doors were closed, and he immediately worried for Chelci. He climbed the tree next to the building, stepped onto the roof, and pushed open the loft window. After soundlessly entering, he observed the scene below.

"I felt bad about how things went at the market," Chelci said, standing a distance away from Brixton. "You were out of line, but I realize I could have responded more kindly. For that, I'm sorry."

What happened at the market? Veron wondered.

Chelci continued, "If we're going to get married, as I've committed to my parents, we need to work on communicating better when we get upset, rather than yelling."

Brixton nodded. "Yeah, you're right."

"I went to your room to apologize, but you weren't there or anywhere else in the house. So, I came to check out here. What are you doing here, by the way?"

"I . . . uh . . . wanted to come and check out the swords." He raised his hands with the two weapons. "They're impressive."

Chelci tilted her head to the side. "Why would you do that in the middle of the night?" Brixton stared back without responding. "Actually, why would you do that at all? We were just looking at them yesterday."

"Why do I need a reason?" Brixton sounded irritated as he placed the swords back on the wall. "I don't have to explain myself to you."

"Watch your tone, Brixton."

"I'll use whatever tone I like. Also, would you like to know what I found out today?" Brixton said as he walked closer to her and got in her face. "I found out my fiancé has been kissing a servant—*Veron.*"

The sound of Chelci inhaling reached Veron in the loft. "You like him, don't you? Admit it!"

Tension filled the room during the long pause. "So what if I do?" Chelci yelled in reply. "He's three times the man you are on your best day!"

"I'm warning you, Chelci. You'll be mine alone, and you'll do what I say!"

"If you have any hope of being my husband, you'll take that back and speak differently to me!"

A loud smack sounded as Brixton's hand struck Chelci's face, sending her reeling toward the ground. Veron's blood was ablaze. His muscles twitched, and he instinctively hurdled over the railing of the loft.

He pushed panic away as he focused, pulling from deep within to summon the origine and strengthen his legs. The source fought against him, so he pulled even harder. When his feet hit the floor, he landed solidly with a loud crash, slightly crouching. The wooden floor beneath his feet splintered and cracked, sending small shards in all directions. He slowly lifted his head to stare at Brixton, standing directly in front of him. The young man's face was white, and his eyes bulged.

"How did you do that?" Brixton asked. "Is that a shadow knight ability?"

After a moment of silence, they both glanced at the wall of swords before running to them. Veron pulled his sword off the wall and immediately moved to a defensive position to deflect an overhead strike from Brixton.

"Get out of my life, Veron!" Brixton roared as he attacked with three successive blows. Veron parried each as he moved and ducked around his opponent's nimble sword.

"You first," Veron replied, adding a strike from the side that Brixton blocked before spinning away.

"Chelci, are you okay?" Veron looked toward the corner where she lay curled on the floor. He almost missed Brixton's lunging attack. After knocking the blade away, he followed with a kick to Brixton's back, sending him stumbling into the wall.

"You always have to be the best, don't you, Veron?" Brixton shouted, pushing off the wall to reorient.

Chelci stirred and rose to her feet. "Both of you, stop this!" she yelled.

"I don't want to fight," Veron said. "I'll quit if you will, Brixton."

Brixton nodded, and Veron tossed his sword to the ground. Veron blanched as Brixton's mouth turned up in a sneer and he ran at him, swinging his weapon. Unarmed, Veron dropped to the ground and narrowly rolled underneath the blade, retrieving his own sword. Emerging from the maneuver, he lifted his weapon in time to block Brixton's next strike.

"Come on, Veron. Use your ability to stop me!" Brixton taunted as the two circled each other.

"What does he mean, Veron?" Chelci asked.

Brixton laughed. "Oh, Veron. She doesn't know?" Veron swallowed hard as Brixton continued. "You pride yourself on being honest, yet you lie about your true identity!"

"Brixton, I'm serious! Stop this!" Chelci pulled on his shoulder.

"Leave me be!" Brixton yelled as he forcefully shoved her away. She careened into the wall, hitting her head directly on the wood and falling to the floor.

"Chelci!" Veron yelled and ran to her, leaning over her body. Her chest moved. Her eyes fluttered as they tried to open. Suddenly, a sharp sting radiated through his right arm. "Argh!" He spun. Brixton stood next to him, blood dripping from his sword. "That's enough! This has gone too far."

"I told you, use your power to stop me, or you will die!" Brixton shouted as he brought his sword down toward Veron's head.

Veron rolled away and shifted his sword to his left hand before standing. Brixton came at him hard. He struck from the right then the left. Veron parried and shuffled his feet backward, but his skill with his left hand was lacking. His movements were slow, and Brixton seemed only to speed up. After deflecting two strikes from the left side, Brixton spun quickly and struck Veron's extended sword. The weapon flew from Veron's hand, clattering uselessly against the far wall.

Sucking in a ragged breath, Veron's back pressed against the wall as sweat dripped down his face. He stared at the sharp tip held to his chest, pressed delicately into his shirt.

"Use your power. Escape from this, or you will die," Brixton said.

Veron breathed in and out as he stared at Brixton, pleading with his eyes. "I can't do it." Finally, he lifted his chin as his breath evened out. "Do what you must," he said as he closed his eyes. Veron waited, bracing himself for the sharp pain. The wait was excruciating until, finally, he opened his eyes.

Brixton stood in front of him, but his look had softened. The sword tip dropped. "I *think* you're telling the truth." Brixton's voice was softer, too. His shoulders relaxed. He nodded as he dropped his sword. After glancing at Chelci's unmoving body, Brixton walked to the door and left into the night.

"Here you go," Veron whispered as he lay Chelci onto her bed. "Oh, Chelci, your face. Does it hurt?" Dark red spots covered her forehead where minor scrapes had clotted.

Chelci tenderly touched her forehead and winced.

"I need to get some supplies to clean the wound," Veron said as he turned to leave.

Chelci grabbed his arm tenderly. "Don't go, Veron. Please don't leave me."

"I'll be back shortly."

"I can't be alone. Will you stay with me tonight?"

Her eyes swam with pain and fear. He swallowed to moisten his dry throat, thinking of the dire consequences if they were discovered. "I'll be back in a few minutes. I need to grab some things from the kitchen, okay?"

After she nodded, Veron left her room and tiptoed down the hall to the stairs, lighting the way with a small lantern. In the empty kitchen, Veron scoured the storerooms, looking for the ingredients Artimus taught him to use years before. He heated water and ground up herbs as he brewed Chelci's elixir. Before he left the kitchen, he stopped to add the household ledger to his pile.

Back in Chelci's room, Veron set the tray down. "Drink this first," he said, handing her a cup of tea.

"Ugh, what is this? It tastes awful," she said after sipping down half.

"It will help you sleep. You'll start to feel it soon."

After she finished the herbal tea, Veron dipped a rag into the bowl he had brought. Chelci recoiled as he touched it to her forehead. "Argh, that stings!"

Veron smirked, remembering the sensation well. "Yes, it does. It will help though. It's called magic water."

"You just made that up," Chelci said between winces.

"Actually, I didn't. That's its name." Veron spent a few minutes cleaning her face and the cut on her hand. "Feeling any better yet?"

"Mm-hmm," Chelci mumbled as her eyelids drooped.

"I see the tea is working already." He placed his hand tenderly on the uninjured side of her face. "You rest. I'll be here all night, watching over you." She patted his hand as she lolled her head to the side to smile at him.

Veron moved across the room, setting the tray on an end table next to a high-backed chair. He sat down, rolled up his right sleeve, and groaned as the fabric stuck to the bloody mess underneath.

Veron closed his eyes and cleared his mind, preparing to wrestle with the origine to heal. *No!* he realized suddenly. *It'll drain my energy too much, and I need to stay alert.* He sighed as he took the rag from the water and wrung it out. He clenched his teeth as he dabbed it against the cut, breathing slowly through his nose and grimacing.

"Veron," Chelci said in a childlike voice. "What'd Brixton mean about your special ability?" Her words slurred and slowed considerably toward the end of the sentence.

"Well . . ." Veron said before giving it some thought. As he was about to continue, Chelci's breath became rhythmic. Veron laughed. She was asleep.

After a few minutes of dabbing his arm, the pain lessened to a dull throb, and he breathed evenly again. Using a needle and thread he found in the kitchen, he clenched his jaw as he went to work sewing it up. The magic water had already numbed the area, so the job was easy. Once finished, he set the rag and bowl aside and took up the house ledger. *Let's see what we can find here.*

28

Financial Discovery

nock, knock. The sound slowly registered in Veron's mind. The second time it came, his mind understood its significance, and his eyes shot open, confirming his fear. He had fallen asleep in Chelci's room with the house ledger open on his lap. Sunlight shone through the window, and Chelci remained sleeping in her bed.

The doorknob clicked as the door rattled in its frame. "Chelci, are you in there? Why is the door locked?" her mother's voice called.

Veron closed the ledger and jumped to his feet, wincing as he grabbed his injured arm. Chelci sat bolt upright in her bed and stared at Veron with wide eyes from across the room.

"I meant to leave in the early morning," Veron whispered.

"Yes, I'm here, Mother," Chelci said loudly. "She can't find you here. She'll kill you," she whispered to Veron.

"Unlock the door this instant," Luciana said.

"I'm sorry, I'll get the door for you," Chelci called.

"Should I hide somewhere?" Veron whispered.

"Quick, get in here," Chelci whispered and ushered him to the wardrobe. She removed the back panel, and a dark passageway revealed itself. "Follow it around to the hallway. Listen to make sure it's empty before you exit."

Carrying the ledger, Veron didn't hesitate to step past the dresses and enter the passageway. In an instant, the light from her room disappeared as the panel slid back into place.

Feeling in the dark with his good arm and clutching the ledger with his other, Veron slowly made his way through the narrow passage. Through the wall, he heard the muffled sounds of Luciana entering Chelci's room. He couldn't make it out, but he imagined Chelci fabricating some story about the origin of her forehead scrapes. After a moment of shuffling, the passage ended at a soft covering of fabric that allowed a faint bit of light through—the tapestry in the hallway. He listened through the barrier but heard nothing. Veron pushed the fabric aside and exited the passageway into the empty hall next to Chelci's room.

Veron yawned and rubbed his eyes, staring at the roll and fruit in front of him.

"Hey, wake up," Nathaniel said, snapping his fingers in front of Veron's face as he set down a plate and sat next to him.

Veron shook his head and picked up the roll. "I know. I'm so tired though."

Nathaniel leaned in close. "Did you get to talk with her?"

Veron pursed his lips as his eyes looked to the ceiling. "Well . . . kind of."

"What do you mean?"

"Brixton showed up instead," Veron said, chewing on the roll as Nathaniel's eyes widened. "Chelci did, too."

"What happened?"

"There was a lot of yelling. Brixton and I fought."

"With swords?"

Veron nodded, then surreptitiously lifted his sleeve where only Nathaniel could see the stitched-up wound extending across his arm.

"Whoa! Are you okay?" Nathaniel asked quietly.

"Yeah, I'll be fine."

"So, uh . . ." Nathaniel leaned in closer, keeping his voice down. "What happened with Chelci? Did you convince her of anything?"

Veron sighed. "It doesn't sound like it. She still plans to marry him."

"What?"

"It's because of me. Her parents will kill me if she doesn't, and she cares too much about me to let it happen. But, I care too much about her to let it happen, so . . . I'm not sure where that leaves us."

"What are you gonna do?"

Veron shook his head. "I don't know. We have time, though. The wedding's not for six weeks. Maybe I can get through to Chelci in that time. Or maybe I can figure out a way to get her parents to release their threat over me . . . somehow." Veron went to work on his fruit. "Brixton is leaving today, right?"

"Yeah, after breakfast, I hear."

"Good. It couldn't be soon enough."

"I hear next week, something big is happening," Nathaniel said, adopting a conversational tone.

"What do you mean? What's happening?"

"Some big event. I don't know the details. Luciana's been talking with Tessa, Tatiana, and Corbus about it. They're hosting some sort of gathering."

"Great," Veron said with a heavy inflection. "You know what that means for us?"

"Yep . . . lots of cleaning," Nathaniel answered, lifting his cup of water.

"Lots of cleaning." He hit his glass to Nathaniel's. "Hey . . . at least we're good at it!"

"That we are," Nathaniel said with a laugh.

The young men finished their food and cleared their plates into the kitchen. Veron noticed the house steward walking in his direction.

"Miss Tessa!" Veron called, drawing her attention and pulling out the house ledger. "I went through the ledger and noticed some things. Do you have a moment? I believe they could save the household some money."

Tessa glanced at the clock hanging over the entrance to the stairs. "Sure, I have a few moments. What did you find?"

Veron glanced around the room, observing the other servants either working in the kitchen or eating in the dining room. "Is there somewhere we could talk that's more private?"

Tessa raised an eyebrow as she inhaled slowly. "Sure. Follow me." Tessa led the way up the stairs and they emerged on the ground floor. She proceeded to the entrance hall and gestured to two chairs, where they sat.

"Last night, I spent some time reviewing it and found several areas of note, or possibly . . . discrepancies," Veron began. "First off, I believe you're right about the food. Our garden production has been down—which I believe is preventable . . . with a more qualified gardener—but that's not the main issue."

Veron flipped through the pages. "See here? Garden production and food purchases are tracked every week. Yes, purchases are higher than necessary, but the *real* problem is this . . ." Veron flipped to another page and pointed to a line.

"What am I looking at?" Tessa asked.

"This is food cost per head."

"I don't remember this."

"I . . . uh . . . took the liberty to calculate it. Starting almost a year ago, the cost per head rose significantly, and now it's nearly double what it used to be."

"I don't understand," Tessa said. "People are eating double what they used to?"

"Not at all. I wasn't here, but I heard about an accident a year ago involving garden fertilizers in the storerooms. There was an explosion that damaged some rooms and the outer basement wall, correct?"

"Yes. We lost some food, but that doesn't explain all this."

"True, but have you inspected those storage rooms abutting the wall recently?" Veron asked. Tessa stared back silently. "When it rains, moisture dampens the wall and fills the room with humidity that ruins food. I bet that late wiether and early suether, when the rains came and the temperature rose, there was more rotten food. As the temperatures dropped this wiether, the dampness combined with occasional freezing temperatures expanded the cracks in that wall. Once the temperature changes in the next few weeks, the food cost per head will climb even higher as conditions worsen and more spoils."

Tessa nodded her head. "What do you suggest we do?"

"First, you need to move the food. Use the storage rooms on the opposite side of the basement. Then, get Drevyn to reseal the entire wall."

"Why wouldn't he have done that last year after the accident?" Tessa asked.

Veron chuckled. "I don't know. I wasn't here. So, the wall should be the priority, but there are also other changes that could help decrease food costs." Tessa raised an eyebrow, which Veron saw as approval to continue. "We seem to do a poor job of rotating the stores."

"What do you mean?"

"When the gardeners bring in fresh food or the cooks go to town to buy supplies, they simply pile it in the storerooms. As a result, the older food, in the back of the pile, sits there too long and goes bad."

"Wouldn't Osmund be doing that?" Tessa asked. "Making sure items are rotated?"

"He doesn't get the food. He probably doesn't know what's new and what's old."

"How would you solve that?"

"Well . . . I would suggest having people bring food to Osmund and let him put it up. That way, he knows when it arrives and can make sure the right items are being moved around as needed."

"Okay, that sounds reasonable," Tessa said.

"Another thing," Veron said. "I noticed a lot is thrown out every meal."

"Yes, well, it's difficult to know exactly how much to cook," Tessa argued. "We need to make sure the family has whatever they want."

"True, but rather than throw away leftover food, why don't the cooks use it?" Veron asked.

Tessa leaned back. "What do you mean?"

"It won't keep long, but there's no reason they can't recycle cooked vegetables or meat into the next day's soup or meat pie."

"I guess that's true," Tessa said.

"It would significantly cut down on waste. I bet if you did all this, the food cost per head would drop to a quarter of where it is today."

Tessa nodded her head as she stood. "This is good. Nice work. I appreciate you taking the time to—"

Veron cleared his throat, halting Tessa mid-sentence. "Um . . . actually, I found some other things, too."

Tessa narrowed her eyes and tilted her head back. After a moment, she took her seat again. "Go on."

Veron grinned as he flipped back through the ledger. "According to this sheet, this is the total household account, correct?"

"Yes, that's correct."

"Where is this kept?" he asked, causing Tessa to raise her eyebrows and incline her head forward. "Oh no, I'm not trying to find it," Veron said quickly. "My point is . . . I assume it's kept somewhere in the house, hidden and locked up . . . right?"

Tessa stared at him but didn't refute his assumption.

"That's what I figured," Veron said. He pointed to the number at the bottom of the page. "This is *a lot* of money."

"I'm well aware of the family's money," Tessa said.

"What I'm saying is . . . there are better uses for this money than keeping it locked up and hidden."

"What do you mean?" Tessa asked.

"All over this city, there are businessmen, bankers, investors, and lords looking for ways to use money," Veron said.

"So, we should become a charity ward and give it away?"

"Well, that would be great too, but . . . no. You should help fund lending houses. Not to cheat the people, but to give them opportunities to borrow money at a reasonable rate to do something good with it."

"You're saying we could lend the money out and collect interest?"

"Yes!"

"It sounds risky," Tessa said.

"If you put it all in one place, yes. But not if you spread it around." Tessa stared at him, apparently displeased with the idea. Veron continued, "Look . . . if it were my money, I would keep a quarter of it here, locked in the secret vault. Then, I would take the rest and work with various, *established* Felting lenders to fund their existing practices. They're already doing the work. Most would be happy to take on new investors. It allows them to do more, and the Marlows would get a steady stream of money in return."

Tessa stared again. Veron imagined the wheels turning in her brain as she thought through what he said. "Anything else?" she asked, finally.

Veron cleared his throat. His hands were immediately clammy as he looked back at the ledger and slowly turned the pages. "Yes, there is one more thing." When he stopped flipping, he pointed to a page and looked back at Tessa. "Gardening costs are not this high."

Her eyes narrowed again. "What do you mean?"

"I mean . . . look here. Five argen for tools? Eight argen for fertilizer?" Veron expected Tessa to respond, but she only proffered a confused look.

"Are you saying they don't cost that much?"

An abrupt laugh escaped Veron's mouth. "For the third week of wiether? No one is fertilizing anything then! Maybe in the weeks leading up to the premweek, but even then, it should be half that! And tools? Tristan never buys tools. When I worked the garden, everything was at least five years old. I had to buy a new shovel because the old one was falling apart. And that only cost me two tid!"

"So what do you think is happening?"

"I think Tristan is scamming the family. I bet he's got a huge stash of money hiding up in his room because he's probably been doing this for years. Now, I don't have proof, but I'd look into it." Veron closed the ledger and handed it back to Tessa. "Anyway, that's what I've noticed so far. I hope they're helpful. There's probably more, but I was falling asleep while skimming through it."

Tessa nodded. "Thanks for checking it out. I'll look into these."

Veron plunged his scrubbing brush into the bucket then gave it a moment to drip. "What about now?" he asked Nathaniel, who stood next to the third-floor window, looking down to the drive in the front of the house.

"Nothing new," Nathaniel said. "Just talking. I still think we should be down there. Half the household is lining the drive to see Brixton off."

"That's the last place I want to be right now," Veron said as he took the brush and resumed scrubbing the wood floor. "Plus, they usually want the housekeepers out of sight whenever possible . . . especially me."

"Ohhh!" Nathaniel said, still looking out the window and partially covering a huge grin with his hand.

"What?"

"Brixton moved in to kiss her cheek, and she leaned away!"

"Yes!" Veron said. "Way to go, Chelci!"

"Okay . . . he's in the carriage now . . . and is driving away." Nathaniel left the window and joined Veron next to the bucket. "What are you gonna do, now that the source of all your drama is gone?"

"Don't forget about Tristan," Veron said with a laugh. "I'm sure I'll still find some way to get in trouble."

The young men worked on the floors as they moved the bucket down the hall. When the water grew dirty, they took turns hauling it downstairs, emptying it, and refilling it with fresh well water.

"Why are we cleaning the third floor?" Nathaniel asked. "We never clean this. No one cares if the servant's floor is dirty! No one important ever comes up here!"

"I think it's *because* no one ever cleans it. Look . . ." Veron gestured to the brown sludgy water in the bucket. "It's filthy."

"I wish I knew what this big event was."

"My big event just happened—Brixton leaving," Veron said with a grin. "I'll scrub the entire house on my knees if it gets rid of him."

"You do realize he'll be back in six weeks for the wedding, don't you?"

"Don't remind me," Veron groaned.

Rapid footsteps ascended the steps. Veron glanced up as Luciana Marlow emerged into the hallway, followed by Tessa and Rupert. His breath caught as they hastened down the hall. Luciana locked eyes with him but didn't slow as she stepped past the two young men scrubbing on their knees.

"What do you think's up?" Nathaniel whispered as they both turned to watch. Near the end of the hall, the group disappeared into a room. "That's the gardener's room."

Veron nodded his head, held his breath, and swallowed hard. After a moment, he turned back to the bucket and dunked his brush again.

"What are you not telling me, Veron?"

Veron leaned closer. "I talked with Tessa earlier this morning. I said some things about Tristan."

Nathaniel's eyes widened. "What'd you say?"

Veron turned his attention to the floors and continued scrubbing. "That I think he's stealing money from the Marlows."

"What? Why would you say that?"

"Because I think he's stealing from the Marlows."

"Oh, man! If that's true . . . they wouldn't whip him because he's not an ankler, but they could send him to prison."

The footsteps returned, and the group made the return trip up the hall as intensely as they had upon arriving. As they passed, Tessa made eye contact with Veron, but her grim look revealed nothing.

With the excitement gone, the boys continued their work. They scrubbed their way down the hall as the light from the windows rolled across the wall in time to the sun's movements.

As they neared the end, footsteps came up the stairs. This time Rupert alone emerged into the hall. "Ash! Lady Luciana wants to see you."

Veron's stomach twisted. He looked to Nathaniel, who wished him good luck. After dropping his brush into the bucket and standing, he wiped off his knees and walked down the hall to follow the guard.

Lady Luciana stood at the window, looking outside as Veron entered the downstairs study. "It is dangerous and above your station to accuse someone else of stealing without proof," she said.

"My lady, I'm sorry, but I thought—"

Luciana held up her hand, stopping his protest. "But you were right."

"He was stashing money?"

"Seven sol, six argen."

Veron whistled in amazement.

She pivoted, gesturing to the doorway behind him. "See for yourself."

Veron turned as Tristan walked by, hands clasped behind his back and head hanging limply. Two Felting soldiers walked alongside, holding his shoulders while Rupert and Dorrick followed closely behind. Just before they passed out of sight, Tristan looked up. His eyes widened, and his body stiffened. "Ash! This is your doing!" he yelled. He wrestled away from the soldiers' hold. With rage in his eyes and his arms restrained, Tristan ran at Veron.

Veron deflected the hurtling body with his arm, sending the gardener's momentum into the arm of the high-backed chair that hit him in the groin. Tristan doubled over with a groan. As he tried to turn around, a soldier's thick club hit him on the head. His eyes rolled, head went limp, and his body slumped to the floor.

"Sorry about that," one of the soldiers said as they quickly picked up the unconscious body and carried him out.

"What will happen to him?" Veron asked as the soldiers disappeared.

Luciana moved to sit at the desk then motioned to the opposite chair. "He's sentenced to spend twenty years in the city dungeon . . . which means he'll likely die in two."

Veron pursed his lips as he sat. He was thankful the gardener was gone but unsure how he felt about him dying for his actions.

"I inspected the storage rooms next to the kitchen," Luciana said. "We found cracks in the walls—large ones where moisture seeps through, even though it hasn't rained for two weeks. And when I looked at the storage areas, I found food, purchased just yesterday from the market, covering nearly rotten food under it." Luciana leaned across the desk as a grin gradually formed on Veron's face. "Do you really think we could use our money and collect interest by investing with lenders in the city?"

"Of course I do!"

"Do you know how to do that?"

"I know where to begin," he said confidently. "First, you'd need to speak with—"

Luciana held up her hand to stop him. She joined her hands together on the desk and looked down at them in silence for a moment. "I want to apologize to you." Veron's eyes widened as she looked at him and continued. "I heard how you stopped the gardener from attacking Chelci in her bedroom, and I learned the real story behind the missing necklace."

Veron gasped. "Chelci told you?"

Luciana nodded. ". . . while she pleaded for your life. I'm starting to believe your first-day ashbox incident was the gardener's fault as well—like you said."

Veron wanted to reply but was too shocked.

"Your work as a servant has been outstanding—" She held up a finger. "—except for your actions with Chelci. Her falling for you is not acceptable, and you need to know your place." She took a deep breath as she paused. "With all this said, I'm willing to give you another chance with more responsibility. Can you handle it?"

"Yes, my lady, of course. I'm willing to do anything!"

"We find ourselves in need of a new gardener, again. I need someone who knows what they're doing and isn't stealing from us. I would like you to fill this role."

"Of course. I'd be happy to!"

"Additionally, it seems those who manage our household ledgers do not fully understand what to look for. Besides working the garden, I would like you to advise Tessa on finances. You are not in charge, but I would like your insight."

Veron couldn't believe what he heard. His mouth fell slack as he stared back at her.

"However, the rules around my daughter remain," she added with a raised voice. Veron nodded. "You may not talk to or even look at her. This marriage with the Fiero family is important to her and us. If you ruin it, you will be through. Do you understand?"

"Yes," Veron said weakly, before clearing his throat. "I'm happy to accept these roles, and I understand about Chelci."

Luciana turned her attention back to some papers on the desk as she waved her hand toward Veron. "That will be all."

"Yes, my lady. I appreciate that." He stood and backed toward the door. "I won't let you down."

Veron felt light that night as he ascended the stairs to his room. With all his recent ups and downs, this was possibly the most surprising. Helping with the family's finances made him sweat. It was much larger than anything he'd dealt with, but he was confident he could handle it.

He admired the servant level's clean floors as he walked down the hall. It felt good to work hard at a task and see the result. When he closed the door to his room, a small note on the floor caught his eye. It was crumpled and worn, but the writing was clear. "Practice Midnight?" A grin formed on Veron's face, but it wasn't from the message. It thrilled him to meet with Chelci regardless of her mother's threat. The note's new addition made him grin. Drawn in the bottom corner was a small red heart.

29

Planning

"This had better be something good," Bale muttered as he followed Raynor Fiero and several guards through the dark corridor of Karad Castle. He raised his hood as they emerged into a room where a man and woman in their mid-thirties stood with a motionless body on the floor. Their heads jerked up as the crowd entered.

The arms and faces of the man and woman were thick with a layer of dirt and grime, and they both stood with a slight stoop. Their clothes were thin, threads dangling loosely from the ends.

"Lord Baron," the man said toward Fiero with a half bow. "I've somethin' for ya." He kicked the lifeless body with a look of triumph on his face.

"What's this?" Raynor asked.

"This is the body of Veron Stormbridge," the woman said, leaning in.

Bale inhaled sharply. He knelt toward the body with Fiero, who bent down to turn the lifeless head up. The deceased young man appeared similar to the shadow knight he met. The brown hair and face were close, and his height was about the same. Bale narrowed his eyes. *He doesn't look quite right.*

"This is not Veron Stormbridge," Baron Fiero said as he stood. "Who is this young man?"

"I swear, it's him!" the man said with a glance to his wife.

After a moment of silence, Fiero turned to Bale. "It's not him. What should we do with these two?"

The man and woman's eyes drifted to Bale as their necks retreated slightly. His piercing stare made them look away.

"I told ya, it's a bad idea," the woman muttered as she nudged the man with her elbow.

Bale lowered his hood and inspected the woman, holding her by the chin. Her clothes' putrid smell turned his nose. "Take them away," he said to one of the guards as he backed away. "Discard their bodies outside the walls."

"What? No!" the woman shrieked.

"Please, we—we thought it was him!" added the man.

The guard roughly grabbed them. While they shrieked and howled, he pulled them toward the door as another guard picked up the body.

Bale left the room, heading back the way they came with Raynor and guards in tow. The wailing behind faded as the distance increased.

At the end of a long hallway, Bale pushed open a heavy door, allowing it to slam against the wall. The men inside jumped. On the chamber's far side, a torch rested on the wall, illuminating Billings, Captain Gannon, Ryker, and Cyrus—one of Bale's lead captains. The men huddled around the crude map on the table. Without saying a word, Bale returned to a dark corner of the room where he resumed pacing.

"Well?" Billings asked. "Anything good?"

"False alarm," Fiero said as he entered. "Just a pair of reward seekers." A chorus of frustrated sighs bounced off the walls.

"Sir," Ryker said, looking at Bale as the king continued wearing a path into the stone floor. "We've been waiting for weeks doing nothing. I think we need to at least begin planning."

"Agreed!" Cyrus added.

The King of Norshewa stopped and stared. He tried to calm his breathing so he didn't explode at the men. "Did you find the shadow knight?"

Ryker glanced at the others. "No . . . not yet."

"Have I not been clear?" Bale growled, stepping in their direction. "I believe I have. We can't do anything until he's found!"

"Your Majesty, I must agree with them here," Raynor Fiero said, half-raising a wavering hand. "If we wait to plan until we kill Veron, we'll be behind. I believe we can at least consider our strategy . . . even if we delay taking action."

Bale looked between his men then down at the map. "Fine, but we take no action until I say."

"Of course," Fiero said with a nod as the men around the table breathed a collective sigh of relief.

"I think we should discuss how to get into the city," Ryker said.

"Agreed," Billings said. "The question is, will we do it against a heavily fortified Felting or one that is off guard?"

"Is there a way to approach the city without them knowing?" Ryker asked, pointing to the map. "Can we come down the river and attack from this South Dock?"

Billings shook his head. "That's what everyone does. All the waterfronts are inaccessible except at that point. Most attacks over the last several hundred years have come from there, and the city is ready for it. They'll completely abandon the walls around the city before they take one person off the landing around that dock. That path is out."

"But, they'll see us coming down the road if we march straight to them," Fiero chimed in. "Could we bring the army through the forest?"

"It'd take longer to get there, but we could arrive nearly undetected on their doorstep," Gannon replied. "I think that's a solid option."

"What do we do when we get there?" Ryker asked. "It's not smart to blindly charge the castle from out of the tree cover."

The other men didn't have an answer. Bale spoke up from the side. "What about allies inside the city? Do we have any?"

"Wesley still believes Karad pledges fealty to him, I imagine," Fiero said. "I wonder if we can use that?"

"You imagine?" Ryker said. "We can't plan based on that."

"I know a few leaders in the Felting army who'll support whatever we plan," Billings added. "I'm confident they'll help."

"Good," Bale said. "What else?"

Fiero cleared his throat. "We *should* have another connection soon. Not one who will align with our goals, but one who may be a source of information."

"You don't sound very confident," Bale said as he walked closer to the baron.

"My son returns tonight. He's engaged to the daughter of a Felting high lord, and I'm hoping he's earned their confidence."

Bale raised an eyebrow. "You doubt him?"

Fiero fidgeted at the question. "Let's just say I'll wait until he returns before staking my life on it."

Bale chuckled and returned to the map. He leaned over the table, bracing with his hands and staring intently. "Is there a secret entrance, like the grate in the wall we used to get in here? Or maybe a tunnel opening somewhere outside of the city?"

Billings shrugged as he looked at Fiero. "Probably, but nothing I'm aware of."

Silence followed while the men stared at the map. Bale's irritation grew at their lack of ideas.

Cyrus stepped closer and raised a hand. "You know . . . if we *did* move some men into position now, we could—"

Bale's gloved hand moved like lightning, and his fist collided with Cyrus's nose, drawing a cry of pain from the captain. "I said, we take no action!" Bale roared as he leaned over the cowering man, groaning on the floor, holding his face and dripping blood from his hands. Bale ground his teeth as he turned to the map. The flickering torch's light danced over the drawing of the city as he seethed.

In the proceeding quiet, a pair of footsteps approached outside. When the door opened, Brixton Fiero entered slowly, looking around like a fly afraid of being squashed.

The elder Fiero lifted his chin and stiffened. "Brixton, I hope you have good news to share?" he asked.

"I do, Father."

"Did everything go as planned with the Marlow family? Is our alignment solid?"

Brixton nodded his head. "More or less. The wedding is on . . . six weeks from now in Felting."

Raynor nodded slowly. "Good. It seems you can do something right after all."

Brixton looked to the ground as he shifted his weight. "Um . . . That's not even the good news." His jaw fixed in a hard line as his chest puffed up. The rest of the room looked at him, waiting. Finally, after a long moment of silence, he turned and looked Bale straight in the eyes. "I . . . I know where Veron Stormbridge is."

Bale's mouth turned up into a wicked grin as he slowly nodded his head. "That is good news," he said before turning back to others. "*Now* . . . we can begin."

30

Collin

Veron closed his eyes and faced the sun that had recently risen over the city. The warmth hugged him, and he smiled. Inhaling deeply, the smell of freshly turned dirt tickled his nose and reminded him of Artimus. The flat end of a hoe punched his rear, startling him from the moment of peace.

"Am I gonna clear all of this myself, or are you gonna help?" Nathaniel asked as he struck the hoe back into the ground.

"Actually, I just remembered I need to look at some finance stuff. I'll let you finish," Veron said as he feigned putting his tool down and walking away. Nathaniel's glare made him laugh. "Only joking!" he added quickly.

"You're gonna use that as an excuse for everything, aren't you?" Nathaniel adopted a squeaky voice as he waved his hands in the air and said with a mock impersonation, "Oh, there's an emergency that needs my financial wizardry, immediately!"

Veron's mouth turned down. "That is *not* how my voice sounds."

Nathaniel burst into laughter and dug back into the ground. "How is it, by the way? Advising the Marlows on their money?"

"It's not hard," Veron said as he dug through the dirt, pulling on the hoe. "For the last week, I've been auditing how they spend things. It's crazy how much waste there's been."

"Do you think you'll be able to do that lending stuff you talked about?"

Veron shrugged. "Yeah, I'm sure I can. I'm going to look into it next week."

Nathaniel leaned against the wooden handle. "How do you know all this? It's like you went to King's Academy or something."

Veron chuckled. "No, not me. I've had some excellent teachers over the years though."

As he pulled the hoe through the dirt, a young boy walked along the path from the house to the well. Disheveled hair obscured his face as he walked with his head down. Empty water buckets waved at either end of the yoke, carried awkwardly over one shoulder.

"Who's the new guy?" Veron asked Nathaniel as he pointed in the boy's direction.

"Collin? He started yesterday . . . new housekeeper."

"He looks young," Veron said.

"He's probably your age."

"He won't make it back to the house with any water if he carries it like that." Veron stared, remembering his first day. He bit the side of his cheek as he watched. "I'll be back in a minute."

Veron set down his hoe and bounded across the field to meet the new servant along the path. "First time carrying water, huh?" Veron asked as the smaller boy stopped suddenly and stared at him, wide-eyed. After a moment, he nodded his head. "I'm Veron. You're Collin, right?" Another nod. "You going to draw water?" Again, no response except for a nod. "You know you can talk, right? I won't eat you or anything."

Collin laughed and appeared to relax. "Sorry, everything's been a little overwhelming." His accented voice was soft, like a boy afraid to speak too loudly lest he wake his parents. His arms and legs were thin—though surprisingly muscular.

"Try bringing the yoke in the other direction," Veron said as he gestured with his hands. "Rest it around your neck on both shoulders."

Collin repositioned the burden, almost dropping a bucket in the process. "Oh, that's much better, thanks!" he exclaimed.

"Do you know how to draw from the well?" Veron asked, receiving a blank stare in return. "Here, I'll show you."

Veron led the way down the path to the well. He showed him how to set the buckets down at the same time so they didn't lose their delicate balance.

"Here's the handle. Turn it to drop the bucket," Veron said. "The other way," he corrected as the bucket on the rope raised.

After a moment, the draw bucket made it to the water in the darkness below. "Can you feel weight on it yet?" Veron asked. Collin tested the handle in the other direction and nodded. "Now, bring it up."

The smaller boy continued turning. He struggled as the bucket of water neared the top. Soon, he used his other hand to help turn. When the bucket finally arrived, Veron showed how to pour it into one of the empty ones Collin brought.

"Now, do it all again," Veron said. "Three more will fill both of them." Collin shook out his arm before he resumed. As he reeled in his second haul, Veron glimpsed a metal anklet peeking out from the bottom of his pant legs. "Hey! You're an ankler!"

Collin looked quickly at him before adjusting his pant leg lower, dropping the partially raised bucket in the process.

"It's okay," Veron said as he pulled up his own pant leg, revealing his metal band. "You're in good company. Nathaniel, over there in the field, is one, too."

"Wow, I thought I was the only one!" Collin said, visibly relieved.

"There are a few more of us, too. It's not fun. Some servants pick on us. I think they're just jealous. They wish they could have such cool ankle decorations."

A smile crept over Collin's face as he grabbed the handle to reel the bucket in again. "What'd ya do to get it?" Before Veron could answer, Collin's eyes grew large. "Oh no! I forgot there's a rule, right? Forget I asked."

Veron laughed as he leaned in closer. "You know what? It's a stupid rule." The boy's face relaxed until Veron said, "They accused me of murder."

Collin gasped as his hand slipped on the well crank. He caught it with his other before it unraveled.

Veron laughed. "Don't worry. Being accused doesn't mean I did it."

"So, ya didn't kill someone?"

Veron was about to deny it when he thought of the old mill where he left the bodies of Mortinson, Slash, and Bruiser. "Well . . . It's a long story. The gist of it is . . . A friend of mine was jealous of me. He set me up to take the fall for some stuff I didn't do, then sold me into slavery. I ended up here." Collin poured the water into one of his buckets. "What about you?" Veron asked. "Where do you come from? Your accent . . . It doesn't sound from Felting."

"I've spent much of my life hopping carts, moving between different farming villages and cities, looking for work. The last few years, I lived in Karad."

"No way!" Veron shouted. "I'm from Karad!"

Collin's eyes lit up. "My older brother and I lived in the Docks, just on the south side of Kulling Square."

"That's crazy," Veron said. "I lived in the Bottoms and Upper Sherry for most of my life. I came through that square all the time."

"Wow," Collin said, looking out into the distance. "Devon and I arrived on a farmer's cart two years ago, looking for work. The docks wouldn't hire me 'cause I was too small, but Devon got to work a half-wage. I begged in the square during the day, and Devon worked. We got by on his small wage, living in a tiny, one-room dump that smelled like mold and cat urine."

Collin lowered his head as his cranking slowed. "A bit ago, Devon got sick. He couldn't work for weeks. We ate other people's trash for days before I found someone willing to check on him. The old man said Devon needed bortleberry elixir, or he was going to die. It terrified me. I couldn't lose my brother, but I couldn't afford the medicine."

"What did you do? Did he get better?"

Collin looked at Veron as he continued reeling in his next bucket. "I went to Fielding's Apothecary. Ya know how he has that large glass window where he displays all those bottles?" Veron nodded. "What do ya think sat right up front?"

"Bortleberry elixir?"

Collin nodded. "The old man had written what the letters looked like. There it was, right in front of me. The only thing separating it from me was a thin pane of glass. I went in and asked the apothecary if I could have some. I resorted to begging, telling him about my brother. He was nice enough but said he couldn't give it away."

"How much did it cost?" Veron asked.

"One argen two tid. I only had two pintid."

Veron whistled. "So what happened?"

Collin exhaled with a sigh. "The next day, when the apothecary showed up to his shop, he found the glass shattered and most of the medicine stolen. Of course, he knew it was me. He pointed me out to a constable when he spotted me in Kulling Square, and they threw me in prison."

Veron grimaced. "That stinks. Did your brother at least get better?"

"I don't know. I haven't seen him since, but I'm sure he's dead by now. That was weeks ago."

"Maybe the medicine worked? He could've recovered?" Veron tried to give the boy hope.

Collin shook his head and looked at Veron with doleful eyes. "I didn't take it."

Veron's forehead wrinkled. "Who was it?"

"I've no idea. Believe me, I thought about it. I wish I had, looking back, since either way I'd have ended up here. At least Devon would've had a chance. They assumed it was me, and I couldn't prove it wasn't."

Veron's heart ached for the poor boy. "I'm sorry, Collin. A word of advice, though . . . don't go around talking about it with the rest of the house. Depending on who you talk to, it could get you in trouble."

After Collin filled up the last bucket, Veron showed him how to get them balanced again and back on his shoulders. He staggered with the extra weight. "Take smooth steps. If you jostle the water, it's more difficult," Veron said.

"Yeah. Thanks for the help, Veron!" Collin called over his shoulder as he proceeded down the path.

"How'd that go?" Nathaniel asked when Veron arrived back in the field.

"Good." Veron watched the boy disappear around the side of the house to take the water inside. "Seems like a good kid. He's an ankler, too."

"Nice. We'll have to keep an eye out for him."

A few moments after Collin disappeared, Hugar lumbered around the corner, heading for the garden. Although officially in charge of all craftsmen and outside workers, Hugar rarely interacted with the gardening crew. "Hey! You two! Meeting in the kitchen!"

Veron and Nathaniel glanced between each other, dropped their tools, and walked toward the house. "What do you think this is about?" Nathaniel asked.

Veron shrugged. *I hope I'm not in trouble for something else.*

When the young men entered the kitchen through the side door, the place was packed. All housekeepers, cooks, servers, attendants, and every job in between were gathered. A dull roar of conversation filled the room as Veron sidestepped others to stand by the back wall.

After a few more servants trickled in, Tessa stood on a stool by the stairs and motioned with her hands for everyone to quiet. "I'm sure you've all heard we've been preparing for a special event. Tomorrow, we will host King Wesley, his wife, his advisors, and several other guests here at the Marlow house for dinner."

Chatter immediately filled the room, prompting Tessa to hold up her hands and raise her voice. "This will be the first visit our king has paid to this home, and it's our job to make sure the place is perfect! Tatiana has been heading up cleaning efforts, which are nearly done. Corbus has a special meal planned, so cooks and servers, look to him for instructions. Jensen will speak with all attendants and guards. Make no mistake . . . anyone acting outside of proper decorum will be punished. Anyone who doesn't perform perfectly with spotless presentation will regret it! Do you understand?"

Veron nodded along with the others as Tessa scanned the room. *Wow! The king! I wonder what he's like?* Veron thought. Wesley was king for as long as Veron had been alive. The image of an elderly man with a cane, tottering his way up the steps to the Marlow house came to mind. Veron's face turned grim as he thought of the injustice that flourished under King Wesley. Many of Veron's problems came from people in positions empowered by the king.

"You will prepare for this event all day," Tessa said. "Remember . . . there is no room for mistakes!"

31

A Royal Visit

Raucous laughter bled through the ceiling, and Veron looked up. He sat around a table in the servants' dining room, reading through the household ledger while other servants played cards.

"What do ya think they're doin' up there?" Collin asked as he drew a card from the deck.

Nathaniel glared at the ceiling. "Probably telling stories about all the crooked ways they've earned money, and the people they've stomped out to get where they are."

"Sounds about right." Drevyn nudged Nathaniel with his elbow. "Your turn."

Nathaniel drew a card, smiled, and promptly laid down three star jesters and two diamond princes. "And with that, I am out!" he said triumphantly. Collin and Drevyn threw down their cards, groaning in defeat. "Come on, Veron! Play a round with us!"

Veron shook his head. "Not now. I'm in the middle of something."

"You're always working," Nathaniel said. "They're partying upstairs. We should take it easy down here."

"The guests are partying, but all the servants up there are working,"

Veron noted. "The only reason we're here is because they want us out of sight."

"All the more reason for us to party. Am I right?" Drevyn said with a grin.

"Why do they have some servants with them while others remain out of sight?" Collin asked as Drevyn dealt another round.

"Some servants are more visible than others," Nathaniel said. "Whenever there are important visitors, the family has all the attendants—choremen, wardmen, carriagemasters, and guards—along with servers and stewards visible and ready to help. Their roles are refined. They keep the dirty-fingered outdoor workers and chamber-pot-smelling housekeepers tucked away unless needed."

"That doesn't quite seem fair," Collin said. "I'd like to meet the king."

"Again," Veron added. "They're working, and you're not. Do you really want fair?"

Collin picked up his cards. "I would've liked more *fair* back in Karad," he grumbled. "Did you know they wrongfully imprisoned me? They accused me of stealing, but I didn't do it. Stupid justice system. I'll draw two," he said, taking two cards from the pile.

Veron glanced warily at Nathaniel and Drevyn, who all had the same look. "Um . . . Collin," he said. "You've got to be careful talking like that. None of us mind, but you could get in trouble spouting off about injustice."

"I don't care," Collin muttered while he arranged his cards. "They can all hear it if they like."

"Trust me, you would care. I've had my fair share of trouble." Veron nodded down the hall. "Last time, they beat me and locked me in that storage room at the end of the hall for weeks."

Through the open doorway to the kitchen, Tessa caught Veron's eye as she came down the stairs. She barked instructions at Corbus while the other cooks shrank away. Veron jumped from his seat.

"Steward Tessa, do you have a moment?" he asked as she turned to head back to the stairs.

"Be quick!" she replied, resting her foot on the bottom step. "I'm needed upstairs."

"I'm looking for some financial books on investments and loans to help me with some ideas. Would the Marlows have anything like that in the library?"

"Yes, they have an entire shelf on the second floor for . . . number books and such," she replied before scurrying up the steps.

After nervously biting the side of his cheek, Veron followed, continuing along to the second floor. The hall was quiet, devoid of visitors. He walked to the library's upper entrance without encountering anyone and cracked open the door. The din of conversation met him from the open space below, but the balcony railing prevented anyone from seeing him.

Wanting to avoid disturbing the guests below—and the trouble that would surely follow—he tiptoed into the room. He faced the back wall as he walked along the balcony, scouring the shelves. After a moment, he found a shelf loaded with what he sought—economics, finance, advanced mathematics. Veron selected three finance books. Stacking them in his arms, he turned to leave.

"What are you reading there?" a voice asked. Veron jumped and spun toward the source, dropping two of his books.

He was so focused on the shelves he hadn't noticed the man sitting in the old leather chair, reading a book of his own. The well-built man was middle-aged—possibly just older than Morgan. His thick, light-brown hair was neatly trimmed, matching his beard. The creases around his eyes gave the impression of kindness while his smile helped Veron relax.

"I'm sorry. I didn't mean to startle you," the man added.

"It's alright," Veron said as he scooped up the dropped books. "I should have been more aware. Are you visiting with the king's party?"

"Ha!" the man laughed as he glanced toward the railing. "I'd hardly call it a party, but . . . yes, I came in their company, unfortunately."

"Unfortunately? What do you mean?"

"People think everything the king does is exciting," the man said as he leaned forward in the chair and whispered. "Let me tell you, he's not that exciting. So . . ." he leaned back and gestured toward the books. "What brings you up here?"

"I, uh . . ." Veron glanced back at the shelf. "I needed some books. I'll leave you alone though." Wanting to depart before anyone else saw, he took a few steps toward the door, but the man held up his hand.

"You don't need to run off on my account. What are the books for?"

Veron hesitantly stepped back toward the man while staying close to the back wall. "Um . . . I've got some ideas about how to manage the Marlows' money. They keep it locked up, but I think there's a better use."

"Like what?"

"They could work with lenders to fund other city businesses, possibly investing in promising companies that need start-up help. If they put their money to work, they can gain a lot more."

The man tilted his head, knitting his brows together. "You're a servant here?"

Veron nodded. "Yes. I'm the head gardener and financial advisor for the Marlows."

The man chuckled. "That's quite the combination. Have you been here long?"

"No, only a half-season, actually. I used to live—" Veron stopped himself from oversharing. "I'm sorry. We're not supposed to talk about our pasts." The man nodded, as if he understood. "I used to live in a nearby city," Veron said.

"Interesting. What's that like, living in the city?" he asked. Veron fidgeted as his eyes danced around. The man quickly added, "You don't need to talk about yourself, but I'd love to know what your impression of city life is. I'm close to the king, so it's important to know such things."

Veron nodded as he shifted his weight. "Things are . . . good. I've seen what life is like on the streets, and it's . . . nice." He cringed at the lies but wasn't comfortable saying more.

The man leaned forward again. "Oh, come now. Living on the streets is *nice?* Tell me how you really feel."

Veron took a deep breath. "How I really feel?" His heart pounded at the idea of being honest with the unknown man. *Maybe the truth can help make things better?* He nodded as he pursed his lips and glanced at the floor. "Please forgive me for being blunt, but . . . from what I've seen, the king's rule has led to widespread corruption and a growing gap between the rich and poor in both justice and living conditions."

The man's eyes widened, but he nodded eagerly, as if he wanted to hear more.

"I know of city lords who stole coins from the king's treasury to line their pockets. I've seen soldiers use their position to steal from the city's people. I've seen the word of a rich man believed while a poor man's was ignored. When someone works hard all day to earn a few tid, such injustice is hard to swallow. Unfortunately, it's expected and even accepted, so no one does anything about it. Ultimately, I think the responsibility lies with the king."

"Wow," the man said. "I wasn't sure what to expect, but it certainly wasn't that."

Veron's stomach immediately turned as he realized what he said. "I'm so sorry! I didn't intend to badmouth the king. I shouldn't have said anything. I should go."

"No, don't go," the man said. "I'm surprised but intrigued. I imagine you're right, and I may say something to the king about it."

Momentary fear shuddered through Veron, but pride quickly replaced it. He remembered Artimus telling him years before that he should do something about things he finds wrong with the world. *Maybe this is my chance?* Veron thought.

"If the soldiers are leveraging their position to steal . . . what would you do about it?" the man asked.

Excited by the chance to make a difference, Veron set his stack of books down and stepped closer. "I think it goes back to accountability," he replied. "Right now, the soldiers do whatever they want with no consequences. Once, I saw two soldiers use force to steal money from a woman."

"How do you know she hadn't stolen it from someone else and they weren't simply righting the wrong?" the man asked.

Veron shook his head. "I saw the whole thing. She did nothing. They came upon her, beat her, took her money, and walked away. The woman would never report them because no one would believe her. Even if they believed her, the justice system is run by the thieves, so it won't do anything."

"But if citizens could bring any complaints against soldiers, what's to stop them making up fabrications?"

"I'm not saying every complaint would be valid, but they should all be heard from an unbiased person with the power to do something. It's not just soldiers. I knew a carpenter once who had a lord cheat him out of his livelihood. He tried to do something, but he was laughed at and ended up on the streets with his family."

"Why was he laughed at? Maybe his claims weren't valid?" the man said.

"They laughed at him because the lord who had committed the injustice was the same man who dispenses justice in the city. They laughed because no one would support bringing a claim against the same person who decides the claim's validity."

"Yes, I believe I see what you mean."

Encouraged by the man's attentiveness and implied understanding, Veron's inhibitions faded. "There's injustice happening all over Feldor, but the people who feel the brunt of it are afraid to act. They know nothing will be done, plus it's likely if they raise an issue, they'll rot in prison to be silenced. A rich or powerful person shouldn't be trusted more than someone without station or money in our kingdom. They're no less of a person and deserve fair treatment."

"You've mentioned the difference between rich and poor a few times. Are you suggesting the king should distribute money equally to all?" the man asked.

"Hardly," Veron replied. "Then no one would work. But there are good people living on the streets—ones that are bright and hardworking. They just need something to help them get started."

"The large cities have food dispensaries for that reason—to help the poor with what they need."

"Ha!" Veron scoffed. "What they need . . . Pfff. Have you ever lived off the food from a dispensary?" The man was silent. "Yeah, I thought not. They do nothing more than allow the barons and lords to pat each other on the back. It doesn't meet the people's needs. What if the city had a system where it listened to its people and learned their true needs?" Veron's eyes lit up while the man leaned in attentively. "One person might be too sick to work and simply need medical attention, which they can't afford. Another might be perfectly capable but just needs a job to get started where he can earn a meager wage to bring home food. Someone else may need to build a skillset. Why can't the city teach its people some basic skills, so they're able to hold down a job? Also, some people *are* ready, skilled, and healthy, but they need a small loan to get started. What if the city came along and gave them financial help to begin as well as guidance on how to do it?"

Veron's heart pounded like a drum, rising in volume with his voice. "And *that* is exactly what King Bag-of-Bones is missing. He doesn't realize his kingdom has overlooked its people only to benefit the rich and privileged he spends his time with!"

Suddenly realizing how loud he'd grown, Veron shrank and glanced warily toward the balcony. Thankfully, the crowd below was undisturbed by his outburst. "I'm sorry," Veron said. "I actually hear King Wesley is a good man. I just get carried away when I think of all I've seen."

A hard line formed on the man's face. His eyes pierced Veron as he mulled on a complicated thought. In a moment, his eyes flicked past Veron's shoulder.

"Your Majesty! There you are!"

The approaching words froze Veron where he stood. *Luciana!* He hadn't escaped the balcony without being seen. Even more frightening than being noticed was where she directed her words—at the man in the leather chair.

"We've been looking all over for—" Luciana's voice cut off suddenly. "Ash! What are you doing here? Why are you bothering King Wesley?"

He's . . . the king? "I . . . I'm sorry, my lady," Veron stuttered without taking eyes off the man. "I was looking for a few—"

"I asked him to stay, Lady Marlow," the king said in a gentle, warm voice. "He was quietly going about his work and was trying to leave until I asked him some questions. I hope that's alright?"

"Yes . . . um . . . of course!" she replied.

"You're . . . the king?" Veron said, his voice shaking as he mentally replayed his harsh statements.

King Wesley chuckled. "Yes, I'm afraid so."

Veron bowed his head, still fighting to control his voice. "I'm so sorry. I thought you were . . . old?"

The king let out a hearty laugh. "I feel old most days. I've been king for twenty-seven years, but they chose me when I was seventeen."

Veron snapped his head up. "Seventeen? Why would the high lords choose someone so young?"

Wesley shrugged. "You'd have to ask them, although most are dead now. I like to think they saw who I was apart from my age. I venture to say you may be familiar with that idea . . . Sir Financial Advisor."

A small grin curled at the corner of Veron's mouth as he caught the glint in Wesley's eye. *Is he complimenting me?* With horror, Veron remembered the awful things he'd uttered. "I'm so sorry about what I said, Your Majesty. I . . . I—"

"Think nothing of it," the king said with a voice like a soothing blanket. "Many of the ideas you shared are oversimplified and somewhat naïve." Veron's eyebrows knit together as his face fell slightly. The king continued, "You fail to account for the chaos that would ensue from levying charges against soldiers and lords. You also dismiss the natural human aspect of greed and laziness that arrives when handouts are plentiful."

"But, what about—"

The king held up his hand. "Still, you bring up excellent ideas that have potential, and I'm thankful you shared them. Now, I must return to the party. I've been hiding away in this corner for too long." Wesley walked to Luciana, who stood by the balcony railing, glaring at Veron throughout the conversation. Before he descended the wooden spiral staircase leading to the main floor, he stopped and turned back to Veron. "It was great to meet you . . . Ash . . . was it? Is that your actual name?"

A knot formed in Veron's throat. His eye flitted to Luciana, who continued to hold her fixed glare. Veron thought of the wanted poster, and his heart pounded as he shook his head. "My name is . . . Veron," he finally said. The king nodded but inclined his head, as if waiting for more. "Stormbridge," Veron added with a slight croak.

A twinkle gleamed in the king's eye. "I enjoyed meeting you, Veron Stormbridge," he said.

Fear surged through Veron as the king and Lady Marlow descended the stairs, leaving him alone. After gathering his books, he walked to the second-floor door. As he was about to leave, a commotion sounded below. He returned to the balcony's edge and leaned over the railing. His breath left him when he saw the disturbance's source—Collin walking through the crowd.

"King Wesley!" the young servant shouted, drawing the attention of all the men and women. "It's not fair! They convicted me of theft, but I didn't do it. I shouldn't be here!" Before he could get close, the other servants grabbed him and dragged him out of the room, kicking and screaming. The door closed behind, muffling his yells, but the damage was done. A furious Luciana Marlow stomped out after him.

32

Further Consequences

Veron woke early the next day, jolted awake by the fear of both his own discovery and what would happen to Collin. After dressing, he walked down the hallway to Collin's room and rapped softly on the door. There was no response, so he tried again. "Collin?" Nothing. Veron's stomach turned as he realized where the boy likely was.

He made his way to the basement and along the long hallway to the old, familiar storeroom. No lanterns were on in the house. The cooks weren't even up to begin their morning routines.

"Collin," Veron whispered as he knocked softly on the solid door. "You there?"

A weak voice replied, "Veron? Is that you?"

"Yeah, I'm here. Are you okay?"

A groan followed a light shuffling sound. "I hurt everywhere. It kept me up all night."

"What'd they do?" Veron asked.

"They beat me. I'm sure some of my bones are broken."

Veron winced. He knew the feeling, although he could mostly heal himself. "I'm sorry, Collin. I know what that's like. What were you thinking, approaching the king like that?"

"I thought maybe he could do something. You know? If he heard my story, maybe he could free me or something."

"I know what you mean. But if Karad's justice system has sentenced you, the king won't overrule them based on a servant's ravings. Plus, I'm sure you embarrassed the Marlows in front of him. They would never let that slide."

A light sigh escaped the door. "Yeah, you're right. I wasn't thinking. My mother always warned me about thinking things through."

"You have a mother?" Veron asked, caught off guard, having assumed the boy an orphan like him. He slid to the ground, sat on the cold stone, and leaned against the door.

"Liliyana . . . she died when I was eight. When she got sick, my brother and I tried to take care of her, but it was no use. I held her hand the night she took her last breath. Then we were on our own."

A sniff sounded through the door after a moment of silence, and Veron wiped his own eyes. "I'm sorry, Collin."

Collin cleared his throat and continued. "Thanks. It was lonely after that, but I was thankful to have Devon."

"Did you ever know your father?"

"No, it was only the three of us since I could remember," Collin said.

"Do you know who he was?"

"Mother told us—" The break caused Veron to lean toward the door. "No, it's silly," Collin finished.

"It's okay. What did she say?"

"She said . . . he was a shadow knight."

Veron's heart stopped beating and chills ran through his body. He opened his mouth but froze. Soon, his breath grew ragged and pulse raced as he placed his hand against the door.

"I know, it's ridiculous," Collin said. "She probably made it up to give us a fun story. I know the Shadow Knights aren't real."

Veron swallowed hard. He ignored the blood thumping in his ears as he tried to calmly speak. "What was his name?"

"John. That's what she told us, at least."

Veron pictured the book, trying to remember the names at the end. *I think there was a John not far above Father's name!*

"We'd often ask about him—if he died or was still alive somewhere. She always grew cagey and would try to change the subject. Like I said . . . she probably made it up."

Veron breathed in deeply, fighting between the desire to share and the pressure to keep his past hidden. *If he's the son of a shadow knight, I wonder if he would have the same abilities?* After a long, silent moment listening to his pulse, Veron spoke up. "She may not have made it up."

"What do you mean?" Collin asked after a beat.

Veron exhaled. "The Shadow Knights are real."

Collin shuffled around and his voice grew closer. "How do you know?"

Veron's words caught in his throat. When he managed to speak, he trembled. "I know . . . because my father was one, too. And . . . so am I."

"What?" Collin gasped, sending him into a coughing fit.

"My father was William Stormbridge. He died when I was five, but I found another knight, Artimus, years later. He trained me and taught me what they can do. I spent four years with him before he died."

"That's amazing!" Collin said. "I wonder if my father is out there somewhere?"

Veron grimaced, imagining the dead knights' bodies after Bale's men attacked and killed them. He couldn't hurt Collin more—at least not yet. "Yeah, I wonder, too."

"So, what can you do? What are these awesome powers?"

"Well . . . I used to have super-speed, strength, and healing powers, but I lost the ability. For the last half-season, I haven't been able to do anything. I'm a regular person again."

"What do you mean, you lost it? You can't bust down this door and get me out?" Collin asked with a laugh.

"No. I used to be able to do anything I wanted. Now, there's only a trickle of the special power left—nothing like what it used to be. I wonder . . ."

"You wonder what?"

"If your father was really a shadow knight, could you learn it, too?"

"Do you think it's possible?" Collin said, his voice sounding lighter, with a dose of excitement.

"Maybe," Veron replied. "I don't know a lot about it, but . . . maybe when you get out and heal, we can try some things."

"Yeah, that would be great!"

Veron heard rustling down the hall as other servants filled the kitchen. "I should go," he said as he stood. "You take it easy, Collin. It might take you a while to heal."

The younger servant coughed again. "I don't think I have a choice," he said with a laugh. "Thanks for being a friend, Veron."

The words warmed Veron's heart as he left.

Veron leaned against his shovel and wiped the sweat off his brow with his sleeve while Nathaniel approached the middle of the field with an armload of supplies. They sorted through sacks of seeds and decided the best approach was to divide up the planting. The weather was warming, so it was time to plant crops for the new season.

"Did you learn anything useful from those books?" Nathaniel asked, crouched in the dirt a row from Veron.

"Yeah, I was up late reading last night," Veron replied. "Did you know that when Felting re-established their kingdom after driving off the Norshand occupiers, they didn't base the currency system on copper, silver, or gold? It was all wooden."

"Huh . . . No, I didn't."

"Also, if you track inflation based on average taxes paid per citizen over the last hundred years, people have paid roughly two percent more every year!"

"That's . . ."

"Fascinating, right?"

"The most boring thing I've ever heard."

Veron playfully mocked a hurt look before throwing a chunk of dirt at Nathaniel, who laughed.

"Did anyone give you trouble about your chat with the king?" Nathaniel asked.

Veron shook his head, turned back to his row, and grabbed more seeds. "Thankfully, no. If he hadn't spoken up for me, I don't know what would have happened."

"Do you think someone will make the connection between you and those wanted signs around the city?"

Veron breathed deeply and exhaled. "I hope not. I only saw it once, but I don't get out into the city much. I'm not sure how prevalent they are." Nathaniel turned his head away and fumbled with his bag of seeds. "What?" Veron asked. "You're hiding something."

Nathaniel turned back and exhaled. "When I went out to the shop this morning, I saw three signs."

Veron groaned. "I'm doomed. Luciana knows my name. The king knows my name. Someone will put them together."

Nathaniel bobbed his head and focused on the dirt in front of him. "I feel bad for Collin," he said after a moment.

"Yeah, I went and visited him this morning. They beat him up pretty badly."

"What was he thinking?"

Veron shook his head. "He was desperate, I guess. He doesn't realize life here can be okay. I mean . . . Luciana is no joy, but . . . overall, it's alright."

Movement caught his eye in the garden path, where Tatiana determinedly walked. Seizing the moment, Veron crossed the dirt patch and flagged her down. "Tatiana, what's going to happen with Collin?" he asked.

The head housekeeper stopped. Her unfriendly look didn't spark confidence. "Because of his outburst last night?" she asked. "Lady Marlow and Tessa wanted to fire him, but I encouraged them to give him another chance. He's only been with us a few days, so he may be still figuring out how things work. Plus, we've gone through a lot of housekeepers recently."

"I didn't think people fired servants of justice? How would that work . . . sell him to someone else? Can you send someone back to prison and get a refund?"

Tatiana tilted her head and furrowed her brows. "Servant of justice?"

"Yeah, you know . . . the metal anklet."

A look of recognition washed over the housekeeper. "Oh, right . . . I forgot about that. He wasn't a servant of justice. He was a regular servant, hired here in Felting. He said he liked to wear the anklet, and I didn't see the harm in letting him."

"No, that's not—" Veron stopped, thinking through it all. "Didn't he say he was convicted of theft to the king? That he shouldn't be here?"

"I don't know what that was about. Maybe something in his past? I'm not sure. Either way . . . he's not a servant of justice. I should know. I hired him."

Why would he tell me he was a— Veron stopped mid-thought as he realized something. *He never actually said he was . . . just that he was thrown in prison at some point. That's odd though.* "So if he's a regular servant, why was he beaten?"

"What do you mean?"

"Last night? Why would they beat him? Was Luciana trying to get him to quit or something?"

"I didn't hear about a beating."

"Yeah, I spoke with him this morning," Veron said. "He's locked in the storeroom."

"Hmm . . . I'm not sure. That would explain why I couldn't find him today. I'll look into it. Right now, I'm late."

Veron's unfocused eyes looked to the blurry ground as Tatiana left. With his brows pinched, he strolled back to where Nathaniel planted seeds.

"You look puzzled," Nathaniel said when Veron arrived and took a small sack of seeds.

"Did you know Collin wasn't an ankler?"

"What do you mean? I thought you saw it?"

"I did," Veron said as he crouched down to put seeds into the prepared holes. "He has a metal anklet, but he's just a regular servant. He wore it because he wanted to."

"That's odd. Why would they beat him?"

"That's what I'm wondering. Maybe Luciana was trying to drive him out?"

"Because of what he did?"

Veron nodded. He covered a seed with dirt and patted it down before glancing back toward the house. When he stood, he dusted off his pant legs. "You alright working here? I need to check something."

"Collin," Veron whispered as he knocked on the storage room door. No one answered. "Collin, are you okay?" He knocked louder.

"What are you doing there?"

The house steward's harsh voice met Veron from behind. He turned to see Tessa with her hands on her hips, looking at him. "I was just—" he glanced back to the door before turning to Tessa. "Why was Collin beaten? I know what he did with King Wesley, but . . . if he's a regular servant, wouldn't you just dismiss him?"

Tessa's face screwed up in confusion. "What are you talking about?"

Why doesn't anyone know what I'm talking about today? "His beating? Last night?" Her face showed no signs of understanding. "Last night, Collin was thrown into this storeroom and beaten." No response. "Were you not aware of this? I spoke with him about it this morning."

"This morning? You spoke with Collin today?" Tessa asked.

"Yes."

"In that storeroom?"

"Yes! Why is that so hard to understand?" Veron's tone dripped with frustration.

Tessa grabbed a lantern from the hall and stepped quickly past Veron. When she turned the door handle, it didn't resist, and the door swung open. They entered the room. His own, painful memories of the place flooded him, yet the room was empty.

"Are you sure Collin was here?" she asked, holding the lantern up as she looked back at Veron.

"Yeah, I heard him behind the door. He was—" Veron looked at the floor as he knelt. "He said he was beaten."

Tessa crouched, running her hand over the spotless stone floor, free of any blood or stain. "And you're sure it was this room?"

"Yes, I'm positive."

Tessa stood and scrunched up her face. It looked like she was about to speak, but instead she left the room and walked away.

"What is it? What's going on?" Veron asked.

Tessa stopped and turned. "I don't know. But I know Collin wasn't beaten last night, and he wasn't locked in this room."

This doesn't make sense, Veron thought. "Then where is he?"

"No one knows," Tessa answered. "He didn't show up for work, and no one has seen him all day."

Veron reeled. *Either Tessa is lying or Luciana is up to something.* He shuffled down the hall as his stomach turned. *I hope he's okay.* Either way, the garden needed to be planted, and Veron had work to do.

33

Unmasked

Veron's muscles ached as he yawned and walked down the steps for breakfast. Yesterday's full day of planting left his legs, back, and shoulders sore in ways he hadn't felt in some time. Exhausted, he slept past his normal time and dressed in a hurry. When he exited the stairwell into the kitchen, he wanted to look for the servants' food, but three men in uniform, standing with Tessa, drew his eyes.

The men were tall and bulky. Their tunics were gray and blue with long white gloves extending nearly to the elbows. A metal breastplate covered their chests and wrapped around the back. Their creased pants were black and tight, disappearing into tall, spotless brown boots. Black berets with gray accents sat atop their heads. Each man rested his left hand casually on a gleaming silver sword with an elaborate golden handle.

The King's Royal Guard! What are they doing here? A sense of unease tingled inside. *Something's not right. Where is everyone?* Veron scanned the room, normally packed with people. Other than Tessa and the guards, it was empty.

"That's him," Tessa said, locking eyes with Veron. The guards moved in his direction.

Veron gasped. *No! They know!* He backpedaled and turned to sprint up the stairs. His flight was quickly stopped by Luciana Marlow, who had come down a moment after him.

"I'm sorry, Veron Stormbridge. There's no running from this," she said with her mouth fixed in a hard line.

Veron froze, unsure what to do. The guards soon stood on either side, giving him nowhere to go.

"Take him, quickly," Luciana said in a hushed voice. "Don't let anyone else see."

Veron felt sick. His pulse quickened as he frantically scanned for an escape route. A guard clutched him by the elbow, and the three of them ushered him out the side door.

Around the front of the house, the guards led Veron into a waiting carriage. He hesitated mid-step as he entered the vehicle. It wasn't the same hard, cold vehicle that brought him to Felting. It was comfortable and fancy. The cushions were thick and covered in red velvet. The fine fabric draping the windows matched the guards' uniforms.

As they rolled away, the guards looked casually out the windows. They didn't appear menacing or on alert. "Where are you taking me?" Veron asked.

The guards didn't speak, but the color drained from Veron's face when their destination quickly approached—the castle. *Luciana will get her reward, and I'll end up back in prison.*

The castle was only a few streets away from the Marlows' house. Veron watched out the window as they passed by the guards standing at the outer-wall gate and stopped in front of the castle's main entrance.

As Veron stepped out of the carriage, his jaw dropped. He'd seen the towering structure from a distance, but nothing prepared him for it up close. He craned his neck to take in the massive stone construction. Thick walls surrounded it, giving off an air of impenetrability. Turrets jutted into the sky so high it seemed they disappeared into the clouds.

"Come on," a guard said.

Inside, the castle was equally impressive. Gold and silver filigree pressed into the wooden doors and moulding. Large, open spaces with rich furniture filled each room. Lanterns and candles lined every passage, providing an inviting atmosphere.

Veron followed the guards up a grand staircase in the entrance hall then ascended several smaller staircases. He lost track of how many they climbed. *I thought they'd take me to a dungeon, but maybe they're locking me up in a tower?*

They exited another staircase and marched down a grand hall to an enormous meeting room. A large, oval table sat in the middle with chairs spread around. Three arched openings on one side of the room led outdoors to a balcony.

The guards ushered him through the first arch, and Veron's breath left him. Stone walls surrounded a large open balcony on three sides, but the fourth looked out to the north. The low wall barely prevented a reckless person from plunging to their death below. Veron stepped toward the edge.

In the early-morning haze, the castle's various ramparts jutted out around him, both below and above the balcony. Far below, Felting looked like a toy model. The walls of the city appeared brittle as twigs. Woods and fields, blanketed by a covering of ominous storm clouds, separated the Benevorre and Felavorre Rivers and surrounded the city to the north. A stiff breeze forced Veron to hug his arms.

"Stunning, isn't it?" a voice said to the side, and Veron jumped.

He turned to see King Wesley looking casually out over the view. The king wore a worn gray tunic with leggings and an old pair of boots.

"Yes, Your Majesty, it is," he said with a shaking bow.

"When I left the Marlows' house the other night, I had two thoughts. One was that I, the king of Feldor, had found the wanted criminal, Veron Stormbridge, who so many searched for."

Veron swallowed hard as his eyes flit around him, looking for ways to escape. The royal guards stood near the only doorway.

"Secondly, I'd met a young man whose ideas and experience could be useful, so I was torn about what to do with you." The king stepped closer. "Veron, were you in prison for murdering someone, and did you escape?"

"I was thrown into prison when a friend of mine killed his fiancé and blamed me for it," Veron replied in a calm but firm voice. "That same friend sold me as a slave. I never killed her though, and I never escaped."

The king held his gaze intently, causing Veron to fidget. "Why would Karad offer five sol for your capture?"

"I—" *How much do I say about what happened to me? Veron thought. Should I talk about the Shadow Knights? Surely, he'd understand. But what if he asks me to prove my ability? I can't do anything. He'll just think I'm a liar about everything.*

"I saw Edmund Bale while I was there, and I heard his plans," Veron said, and the king's eyes widened. "He was going to kill Baron Rycroft then align with Raynor Fiero and Gareth Billings. They promised they would support him along with Karad's army."

The king stepped toward the edge of the balcony as he stared into the distance. "What was the next part of their plan?"

"I'm not sure. Fiero would be in charge, but I don't know what that means."

"Hmm. They couldn't appoint him to be baron. Only I could do that. With Karad's army supporting Bale's, they could . . ." He turned suddenly to Veron. "Why haven't they attacked us here? Their combined armies would be a formidable force."

Veron imagined their combined armies marching to Felting. *Why would they wait? Maybe he's afraid of me?*

"What?" the king asked. "What is it?"

"I'm sorry?"

"That grin. You're thinking something."

"Oh . . . I was thinking . . . Maybe he's afraid of you?" Veron suggested, causing the king to relax. "I imagine the five sol reward is to keep me silent. I doubt Fiero would want me telling someone like you what I know."

The king stood tall and came close to Veron, narrowing his eyes. "So, you've been a servant at the Marlows' house since then?" the king asked, and Veron nodded. "And I'm supposed to believe the word of an accused murderer against Fiero, an established public servant of Feldor for many years?"

Veron had nothing left to say to defend himself. Around him, the guards pressed in closer. Veron's stomach twisted as the king nodded to the closest guard. The man approached, holding a long, thin awl and a hammer. Veron flinched. He tried to run, but two sets of arms held him still. The guard stood directly before him, holding up the metal instruments. Veron closed his eyes, blanking his mind to whatever came next. Someone grabbed his foot and held it in place. He jumped when the sound of metal on metal rang across the balcony and a sharp pressure pulled at his leg.

The action repeated itself several times until something happened. A weight lifted from him—a weight he didn't even know was there. Air seemed to flood his lungs, filling him with . . . *life, passion, hope? What is it?* Veron opened his eyes as the metal clasp around his ankle fell loose and clattered onto the stones along with the metal pin that held it together. He flexed his arms, which felt more alive than ever. The world around him appeared vibrant, colored in brighter hues and sharper focus. Veron gasped as he sensed a warm tingle in the pit of his stomach. He froze. *Is that it? Is it back?* He hesitantly pulled from inside, and a rush of energy swept through his body. *The origine! It's back!* A smile covered his face as he lifted his hands triumphantly in the air. Suddenly aware of where he was, Veron lowered his arms, but his grin remained. He glanced back to the fallen shackle then turned to King Wesley for an explanation.

"I believe you, Veron Stormbridge," the king said. "A man faced with death will often say anything to escape. It's rare for it to be genuine, yet you speak the truth. I can tell. From what I understand, you have served well in the Marlow house. In a short time, you progressed from a lowly housekeeper to finance manager. I believe your skills and abilities extend past that, though. The honest perspectives you shared with me the other night were refreshing. I rarely hear anything so bold and yet . . . filled with potential."

The king pulled a piece of paper from inside his tunic. Veron recognized it immediately—the list of his collateral names. "I bought you from the Marlows—at no small expense, given the bounty on your head." The king extended the paper, offering it to Veron. "And I give you your freedom."

Veron's jaw hung limp. His mind went blank as he stared at the king, unable to process the words. With a shaking hand, Veron accepted the paper and glanced at his bare ankle. "Thank you . . . Your Majesty. I—I don't know what to say."

"I do have something I require of you though." A lump formed in Veron's throat as he feared whatever came next. "I want you to be one of my advisors."

A laugh escaped Veron's lips. "Me?"

"I have plenty of people giving me advice and feedback, but they've all lived in the castle for years. Very few have worked a job requiring any effort for most of their lives or have any first-hand experience."

"Yeah, but—"

"Do you know what I think whenever I get advice from someone?" Veron stared dumbly while the king continued. "I ask myself what they want. Most people have an agenda. People advise me to enact laws 'for the good of the kingdom' when in reality, the advisor will actually benefit the most. I can taste the greed when they speak. Yet, here you are, a servant, wrongly accused of a crime, filled with insight and perspective no one around me has." The king stepped closer to Veron. "Do you know what I see when I look at you? Truth. I feel it pouring out of you. I believe what you say, and I need more people like that around me. Will you accept the position?"

Veron's neck was hot. He shuffled his feet and looked to the ground. *Is this my chance to make a difference?* He lifted his chin to stare the king in the eyes. "Thank you, Your Majesty. I accept."

Chelci picked at her food with her fork but hardly ate. Something gnawed at her, but she wasn't sure if she was being paranoid or not. Usually, Veron worked in the garden early in the morning, but she hadn't seen him there before breakfast. She asked Tessa about it, but the steward claimed she didn't know anything. Nathaniel said he'd been looking for him, too. It was like he disappeared. Chelci was sure he wouldn't run away, so she had a sinking feeling about his fate.

"Chelci, your father and I were thinking," Luciana began, cutting the silence. "Why don't you spend some time in Karad? Maybe a few weeks? I imagine it would be helpful to get to know the city before you move there."

Chelci wrinkled up her forehead. "Um . . . I don't know. I think I'd rather stay—"

"I sent a messenger bird to the Fieros this morning. I'm sure they would love to host you. After all, they do live in Karad Castle now," her mother said with a twinkle in her eyes.

"But this is my last chance to see Emma and . . . be here."

"You don't want to be rude to your future family, do you?" Luciana asked.

"No." Chelci sighed before giving in. "Sure, I guess that would be fine." Her mother smiled broadly and returned to her meal. After a moment to think, Chelci set her fork on the side of her plate and looked at her parents. "Mother, Father, what happened to Ash?"

Her mother had just put a baby tomato in her mouth and nearly choked. "Ash?" Luciana asked, after clearing her throat.

"You know, the servant . . ."

Chelci's father stared pointedly at his plate, avoiding her gaze. Her mother glanced at him for a moment before responding. "You're not supposed to speak with him."

"I know, and . . . I'm not. I just hadn't seen him and wondered if he was okay."

"He . . . uh . . . You know he's helping advise us on our finances," Luciana said.

"Yes, I know."

"He is traveling with High Lord Plummer, from the treasury. Ash had some ideas about money management and investments. Your father mentioned it to Ernest, and he jumped at the chance to spend some time with him. They're on a trip to Karondir and won't be back for several weeks. Isn't that right Darcius?" She nudged her husband.

"Yes . . . that's right," he said without inflection as he moved his food around his plate with a fork.

"For several weeks?" Chelci asked with a heavy tone of disbelief.

"Yes, five weeks I believe." Luciana glanced again to Darcius, who continued to stare at his plate. "Probably just after your wedding, I'd guess."

That's convenient, Chelci thought. *Why wouldn't the other servants know he left, though?* She resumed picking at her food.

"Speaking of the wedding, I reserved the Turba Pavillion!" Luciana said.

Chelci quickly tuned out her mother as she prattled on about flowers, dresses, and the like. *I wonder what Veron is doing right now? Traveling to Karondir with the High Lord of Treasury? That seems unlikely.* While the thought irked her, something else bothered her even more that she couldn't shake. *Why is Father lying to me?*

* * *

Bale's boots sank into the soft ground as he walked through the rain. The twisted canopy of leaves blocked out the heaviest drops, but a steady drizzle dripped to the earth even long after the rain stopped. Tents dotted the forest, hiding behind trees and large boulders, stretching far along the valley floor.

His army had hidden out of sight at the edge of Kyrd Forest for half a season, waiting to find and kill the shadow knight. While sentries stationed around the perimeter had to kill a few wandering woodsmen, their location was so far undiscovered.

Bale nodded to the guards stationed outside his tent before flinging the flap open. "Ryker, how fares our army?" Bale asked as the commander stood along with his advisor, Desmond.

"They grow restless, Your Majesty. They gathered and trained for years and marched for weeks. Now, many wonder what we're doing here, hiding outside of Karad in the woods."

Bale looked fixedly at Ryker, determining his motives. "And how about you? Do you wonder what we're doing here?"

Ryker looked to the ground and spoke in a wavering voice. "Of course not. Had I been in the castle and seen this warrior, I'm certain I would have responded as you have."

Desmond spoke up, "I believe your men, who weren't there and don't know you as we do, do not understand the wait."

"They don't have to understand!" Bale roared. "They only need to follow orders!"

"Of course, Your Majesty," Desmond said. "And they do know . . . and obey."

"Couldn't we just attack?" Ryker asked. "Twenty men are standing by, ready to go."

"Double the number, but don't send them yet. We must know about Veron's ability," Bale said. "Brixton wasn't sure, and I can't let him get away again."

Silence filled the tent as the men listened to the pit-pat of water on the roof. "I guess we wait then," Desmond finally said.

The slosh of wet boots approached the tent, and muffled voices conversed. Soon, the flap pulled back, and a guard poked his head in. "A visitor, Your Majesty," the guard said.

A boy with lean, muscular arms entered the tent. His clothes dripped, and his eyes flitted between the men. He bowed his head and turned his body toward Bale.

Bale's mouth twitched as he looked the boy over. "I hope you have good news for me, Collin."

"I do, Your Majesty," the boy said. "Veron Stormbridge *is* there, and he's lost his powers."

"You're sure?"

Collin nodded. "I am."

Bale's face twisted into an evil grin, fists clenched in celebration. "That is good news. And you thought he was too young to do the job," he said to Desmond, who slightly shrank back. "Thank you, Collin, for your work. You have done a great service for your king." He turned to Ryker and spoke in a low, even voice. "Send the men."

34

Advisors Council

Rejuvenated from a warm bath in the castle's bathhouse, fresh clothes, and a good night's sleep, Veron strode down the main hall. Ahead, guards flanked massive double doors, concealing a large chamber with a dozen men milling about in huddled groups, scattered around the oval-shaped table from the day before. The guards nodded to him as he approached.

Veron immediately felt out of place as he entered the chamber for the Advisors Council meeting. Various, huddled men shot him furtive glances and continued talking amongst themselves. They were the high lords of Felting and the king's advisors. Their faces were not friendly. Veron strolled through the room as shoulders boxed him out. He quickly noticed his youth, everyone in the room being over twice his age.

"Veron," a voice said as a familiar face approached.

"High Lord Marlow, hello," Veron replied, unsure what else to say to the man.

Darcius shook his head with a brief chuckle. "I see you've moved up in the world. Congratulations."

"Thank you, sir." Veron was glad to recognize someone but

remained on guard. The High Lord of Commerce had been friendly enough until he found out about Chelci and Veron's kiss.

"High Lords and advisors! Welcome!" King Wesley and his booming voice entered the room from the balcony. He walked directly to the end of the table while the rest of the crowd settled into their chairs. The king nodded in Veron's direction. The welcome gesture eased the nagging voice in his head telling him he didn't belong.

"Thank you all for coming today. I want to welcome our newest member, Veron Stormbridge," the king motioned toward him. All heads turned in his direction as a murmur grew. "I've added Veron to my advisor team. He comes highly qualified from his time spent in both Karad and Felting."

"Your Majesty," one of the men said in a shaking voice. "This . . . *boy* is wanted for murder. There are signs around the city."

"That matter is settled, and the signs have been taken down. There is no need for your concern," Wesley replied.

A few grumbles filled the room. The lone words of welcome came from Darcius Marlow, who nodded to him again.

"We have a few topics to discuss today," Wesley continued. "First, I'd like to check on our progress with the Fairness of Food Edict. We've run the trial for three weeks. Weatherbee, what results have you seen?"

Edgar Weatherbee, the High Lord of Justice, had an oily beard, broad shoulders, and faux grin. Veron had a sinking feeling as he spoke. "Incredibly, Your Majesty," he said, turning a gaudy gold ring on his finger. "The markets are practically devoid of beggars. Shoppers are no longer hassled. The streets are less crowded. It's a rousing success."

"I have to agree," a short, hunch-backed man exclaimed as his flat palm slapped the table. Eldon Crone was the older of the king's two other advisors. "Productivity is up across the city. It's been wonderful."

"Good, good. So, you propose we confirm it into law then?" the king asked.

"I do," said Weatherbee.

"It sounds to me like it's settled," the king said. "Unless anyone else—"

"I'm sorry . . ." Veron raised his hand. The heads all turned in his direction once more, and his stomach roiled. His hands felt clammy as he set them back on the table. "What do you mean by. . . 'productivity is up?'"

Eldon scoffed and glanced at the others. "I mean people are working harder and producing more." His words were deliberate and slow, as if spoken to a simpleton. The other men laughed, and a humiliating redness crept up Veron's neck.

"Yes, I realize that," Veron said, adjusting in his seat. He paused as he considered his words. "I'm not doubting your conclusion, but I'm curious how you determined it?"

Eldon leaned his head back and stared down his nose at Veron. His voice was low and stale. "It's clear to see. The people of Felting have simply been more productive since we enacted the edict. When you've served the city as long as I have, you can tell."

"Agreed," another voice said around the table, followed by several fists pounding in approval.

"But, how did you *see* it?" Veron asked, glancing between Crone and Weatherbee. "Did you walk the city and inspect food and textile production? Did you calculate it using reports of sales or taxes or something?" Veron leaned forward, waiting on a response, but the advisor only stared back with narrowed eyes. "If I were to increase productivity, I would need empirical progress measurements. You can't simply wander a market and put your finger in the wind to see how it's blowing."

"I'm sorry, but where did you come from?" High Lord Weatherbee said, the greasy smile gone.

"I agree," said Geoffrey Bilton, the High Lord of Defense. "Who is this *child?*"

"I . . . uh," Veron glanced around the table before pointing to his ex-master. "I was High Lord Marlow's gardener."

Cries of outrage erupted.

"This is preposterous!"

"He has no right to be here!"

"You have no idea what you're talking about!"

"Please!" King Wesley said, holding his hands up. The men quickly settled down. "I personally selected Veron to be here, and I don't appreciate your rudeness. I'm sure he doesn't, either. Veron . . . please continue sharing your thoughts."

Veron breathed evenly as the men turned back to him. Scowls covered their faces except for Darcius, who shrank in his seat with a hand partially covering his face. "As I was saying . . . I think you would want to measure some working output. It could be from a production factory or even surveys taken in the city."

"City surveys . . . Bah!" Edgar Weatherbee spat.

"I think the most accurate would be taxes collected over a certain period of time. Take two tax seasons and compare the productivity using sales, income, leases, and the like." Veron looked around the table, surprised to find the scowls gone. Most of the men looked elsewhere.

"That *is* the measure I had suggested," Bryon Hampton, the High Lord of Trade, said, earning a harsh glare from Weatherbee.

The king looked hard at the high lord. "Edgar, if you're claiming it's been a success, but have no evidence—"

"I can just tell! I don't need measures or surveys. That's such a pain and a waste of time." Weatherbee insisted, looking around at the other men. "You've all felt it too, right? People are all doing better, it's been great—"

"People are *not* all doing better," Veron said with increasing confidence. The rest of the men immediately quieted. "If you walk the streets on the other side of the city, you'll see it. People are malnourished. They can barely move. They're eating stale bread thrown in the street. I met a man named Dirk who lost both legs in battle fighting for you, High Lord Bilton. He lost work as a soldier, and no one will hire him because he can't walk. Is he any less of a man? Do you know what he does? He spends his days creating arrows for the army, but he's only paid a pittance because people know they can take advantage of him."

Veron breathed heavily and looked around the table. Some looked at him, jaws hanging limply, while others stared at the table to avoid eye contact.

After a moment, King Wesley cleared his throat. "I think it's prudent to further evaluate the edict's effectiveness before we confirm it. High Lord Weatherbee, I suggest you and your men spend some time in the city talking with the people. Find out how the law's affecting the city's workers." The king turned to another bearded man with a hooked nose wearing a brown cape. The man rested his hands on his bloated belly. "High Lord Plummer, can you work with High Lord Weatherbee and Eldon to build productivity measures? I want answers based on facts, not feelings."

"Of course, Your Majesty," Plummer said with a slow nod.

"Run the numbers by Veron. I'd like him to confirm the method is fair and accurate."

The color drained from Veron's face as the older men glared at him.

"Now, let's move on to the principal topic I want to discuss," the king said and folded his hands in front of him on the table. "Edmund

Bale."

Nearly every man spoke at once. At first, Veron couldn't distinguish one from another. Finally, High Lord Bilton's voice rose above the others, quieting them down. "It's preposterous! Bale doesn't have the men to attack us, and he wouldn't even consider laying siege to Karondir!"

"He's never listened to sense before," said Quincy Hilliard, the other advisor slightly closer in age to Veron. "He could still attack, even if it is preposterous."

"Then, we'll defeat him!" Bilton said, eliciting nods from around the table. "We can hold the docks along the river against an army three times their size. And our walls are strong. We'll know they're coming before they're even halfway here. We'll have plenty of time."

"They defeated him at Karad. There's no way he'll continue," said Byron Hampton. "More than likely, he's already headed back over the mountains."

Darcius Marlow raised a hand. "I've heard rumors of Bale walking around freely inside of Karad. But I don't know if they're anything but rumors."

"I heard them, too," Weatherbee chimed in. "But I also heard he was seen playing hobbilade with Baron Devenish in Karondir." Spots of laughter dotted the room. "I'm not sure how reliable either is."

"I say we flush him out," Quincy said. "If he's hiding somewhere in the forest, we should take our army, find him, and finish him once and for all."

"We should not underestimate the size of Bale's army," King Wesley said, and the rest of them hushed.

"We estimate he could have no more than eight or nine thousand," Bilton said. "It's a decent number, but we should be able to defend against them, especially with our walls. Karad only keeps five thousand men, and if *they* could stop them . . ." The conversation halted as the room sat deep in thought.

"The Norshewan army is the most brutal group of fighters in Terrenor," Byron Hampton said. "If they *were* to get inside the walls, it would devastate the city."

"True, but I'm telling you, they couldn't get in," Bilton replied.

"Veron?" the king said, nodding to the opposite end of the table.

Veron's face flushed again as all eyes fell on him. "Um . . . It's not just Bale's army we'd need to stop," he said. "It's Norshewa and Karad combined." The room fell silent while the men stared at him.

"Absurd!" the High Lord of Defense finally shouted.

"It's true," Veron insisted. "Raynor Fiero and Gareth Billings joined Karad's forces with Bale's."

Everyone at the table roared. Half of the men stood, fighting to be heard over the others.

"I can speak for the Fiero family," Marlow said when he could get a word in. "They are well-mannered and highly respected. Our daughter is engaged to Raynor's son, Brixton." Veron's stomach turned. "I do respect Veron, as I've seen the quality of his work, but I can't say I believe Fiero is a traitor."

"Gareth Billings is no traitor either," High Lord Bilton said. "I've known him since he was a young, eager army recruit."

"What does a *gardener* possibly know about this?" Eldon Crone said in a haughty voice. "Don't tell us you became an expert at military strategy between manure applications." Several laughed at the jab.

"No, I'm not a military strategy expert . . . although I *have* studied a great deal," Veron said, and the laughter doubled.

"Tell them, Veron," the king prompted when the laughing settled.

"I know because I heard Fiero and Bale talking," Veron said. "I was in Karad Castle when Bale arrived."

No one spoke for a long moment until Eldon interjected, "Of course you were. I'll bet you were hiding inside a large ceremonial vase when Fiero and Bale stopped next to you to reveal their secret plans." Laughter echoed once more.

"I'll wager he was also hiding behind the hobbilade targets in Karondir while Bale played with his friend, Devenish," Bilton shouted over the laughing.

"No, actually, I was . . ." Veron cleared his throat and gestured with his hands, mimicking pushing two opposing walls above him. "Above them . . . braced between two walls as they talked under me."

The laughter redoubled in intensity from all but High Lord Marlow and the king. "That's enough!" Wesley shouted, silencing the sniggers. "Veron, do you believe Bale will attack Felting?"

Silent faces turned to Veron, and he fidgeted in his seat. "I—I'm not sure. I don't know his plans." A general sigh issued from the men, and the tension faded.

King Wesley continued. "As far-fetched as it may sound, we would be wise to keep Veron's information in mind. If Fiero and Billings have joined forces with Bale, their army will be significant." None of the men disputed the idea. "Bilton, I would like you to draw up plans of defense considering any potential scenarios we might face. Then, send a messenger bird to Karondir. Let them know to be on guard, and see if they know anything else. Also, I suggest you send scouts into the woods. If they're out there somewhere, it would be good to know."

"It will be done," the High Lord of Defense replied as he scowled in Veron's direction.

"Does anyone have any other topics to discuss?" Wesley asked.

Veron's mind whirred, thinking through the changes he wanted to see. The justice system needed an overhaul. The taxation strategy could use improvement. He almost raised his hand to speak but had already felt the men's ire enough. *I'll wait until the next meeting.*

As the group dismissed, King Wesley waved Veron over, and a lump formed in his throat. He'd been in one meeting and irritated everyone there. It was far from the good impression he'd hoped to make.

"Thank you for speaking up," the king said. "These men have been here for a long time. Most of them are stuck in their ways and rarely look past their own desires. I need someone like you to voice the truth, even when it makes you a target. That was very brave."

Veron beamed. "Thank you, Your Majesty."

"Our next advisor meeting isn't for four days. Enjoy your freedom, Veron. I imagine you could use a bit of a break." The king winked before turning to go.

Four days of freedom! What should I do? A plan instantly formulated. He wanted to visit Morgan, and four days was enough time to make the trip to Karad and back—as long as he avoided running into Bale, Fiero, or anyone who may recognize him. Before leaving, he wanted one thing more than the others—to see Chelci.

Veron left the room at the back of the crowd, but Darcius Marlow waited for him by the door. "Those were some bold words today, Veron," he said as he fell in step and the two walked down the castle's main hall.

Veron laughed softly. "Bold . . . Stupid . . . Who's to say?"

"I think you're wrong about the Fieros."

"I hope so," Veron replied. "But I don't believe I am."

"I guess we'll see." Marlow breathed in as if to say more but paused instead. "Also, I wanted to apologize. I'm sorry for how cold I've been. When we learned about . . . you and Chelci, it shocked me. I didn't want her marrying a servant, and I think we overreacted. You showed a lot of wisdom in there, and I'm glad you said it. I think the king and the rest of the men needed to hear it."

Veron watched the man's face as they strolled. His repentance seemed genuine.

"I know Chelci's engaged to Brixton, and I know this changes nothing. But for what it's worth, I wanted to say I'm sorry."

A smile tugged at Veron's face. "Thank you, High Lord Marlow—"

"Please, call me Darcius."

"I appreciate it, Darcius. It's good to have someone on my side."

35

A Night Visit

Chelci turned in her bed and readjusted her pillow, unable to sleep. Elenor Fiero's message arrived earlier in the day, confirming their desire to host Chelci in Karad. The servants packed her things and she was to leave first thing in the morning. She wasn't looking forward to it but felt she couldn't decline.

A sound tugged at her attention. *What is that? A mouse? A bug?* She heard a soft, tinking sound, but wasn't sure if it was in her mind or real. A louder sound caused her to sit up in bed and look toward the window.

Chelci rose from her bed, crossed to the window, and looked outside. Shadowy shapes in the night would normally give her pause, but her heart leaped at the figure on the ground. She opened the window.

"Veron?" she said in a loud whisper.

"Chelci!" the dark shape replied. "Can you meet?"

Chelci nodded. "Yeah!"

"Meet me in the training room!"

Chelci closed the window and hurried to grab a robe. A grin

covered her face as she tied a sash around her waist and cautiously opened the door. The hall was quiet. Chelci stepped softly past both her parents' rooms and down the stairs. When she exited the house, the cool night air chilled her skin, but she barely noticed as she hurried along the winding path. A dim light grew inside the building as she opened the door to see Veron placing a lantern on the wall hook.

"Veron!" she yelled as she ran and wrapped him in her arms. He looked striking, wearing new clothes. He would get in trouble if someone caught them together, but she had to risk it. "I heard you went to Karondir. What happened?"

Veron pulled away at the suggestion. "No, I . . . um . . . They sold me to the king."

"What!" Chelci yelled, holding lightly onto his arms and prompting Veron to shush her. "You're a servant to the king, now?"

"Not exactly. I met him at the party the other night."

"Yeah, I heard about that. Mother said you were snooping around in the library."

"I wasn't—" Veron stopped himself and breathed before continuing. "It doesn't matter. I met the king, and apparently, he liked me. He bought me from your parents and freed me from my servant of justice sentence."

"He freed you?"

"Yeah, look . . ." Veron lifted the hem of his pant leg to show his anklet was gone.

"So you're free? What does that mean? What are you going to do?"

"Well, he actually uh . . . I'm one of his advisors." Veron grabbed at his collar while he tried to hide a blush.

Chelci started to speak, but her jaw froze. She shook her head to free up the words, "You're an advisor to the king? Veron, that's amazing!" Chelci released his arms and paced the room. "There's so much you can do! You can help him see the things that are wrong in Feldor." She froze and pointed at him. "Do you think you can overturn that stupid food restriction law for poor people?"

Veron laughed. "I . . . uh . . . actually already started on that earlier today."

Chelci beamed with pride. "I always knew you were more than a simple housekeeper. But, even then, you were an excellent housekeeper."

"I always wanted to do the best I could," he said with a grin.

Chelci froze as a thought struck her. Her eyes widened, and she stared at Veron.

"Is everything okay?" Veron asked. "What is it?"

"You're not a servant in our house anymore," she said, barely above a whisper, before swallowing a lump in her throat. "You're a free person. Mother can't threaten you." Every ounce of loyalty and family commitment raged against her, but she couldn't deny her feelings.

"What are you saying?" Veron asked, voice full of anticipation.

"That means . . . I don't have to marry Brixton." A warm feeling of joy and relief flooded over Chelci as she spoke, and a smile covered her face. "Mother can't hold your death over me anymore. They can't make me marry him!"

A broad grin grew on Veron's face. "Yeah, I was going to ask you about that."

"That means, I'm free to do what I want," Chelci said as she rested her hands on Veron's arms and looked into his eyes. "We're allowed to talk and be together." Her body surged with electricity. She stared freely at him, unafraid of getting caught. She ran her hands lightly up his arms. The muscles were lean but strong. She ached for him to wrap her up. Her heart pounded so loudly she was sure he'd be able to hear it.

Veron slowly tensed, and his eyes wandered as the moment of

silence between them grew. "We . . . uh . . . We could spar!" He backed away from her hands and took a few steps, grabbing their swords from the wall.

Chelci bit her lip until he returned. His eyes sparkled like a child with a sack of candy. His hair stuck up in awkward tufts, making Chelci smile. He extended her sword to her while raising his eyebrows. Chelci's smile turned into a shifty grin as she took the sword and leaned it against the wall.

"I don't want to sword fight," she said. Chelci lifted the lantern's side door and softly blew out the small flame, filling the room with a cozy darkness. The moonlight barely illuminated them. Chelci stepped closer and lowered his sword hand. Tenderly, she took the weapon from his grip and leaned it next to hers. Chelci rested her hand on his hip. It gradually traveled around to his back as he moved closer until their bodies pressed against each other. Chelci looked up into his eyes. They were soft and kind—yet afraid. He didn't pull away.

"What do you w—want to do then?" he asked waveringly.

Chelci's other hand found his cheek. It was soft, a crease confirming the smile she could barely see. "I want to kiss you."

The crease grew. His arms trembled as he wrapped them around her back, pulling her closer ever so slightly. Chin down, he leaned in. Chelci's pulse thumped as she raised her lips toward his. She moved slowly, anticipating the moment.

Suddenly, his entire body stiffened. His arms became like steel and his jaw set firm. To Chelci's disappointment, Veron moved his hands to the side of her hips and pushed her gently away. "What's wrong?" she whispered.

"Shhh," Veron replied with a finger to his lips. "Something's out there." He grabbed his sword from against the wall and tiptoed to the window set in the door.

Her heart sank as the electric moment faded, quickly replaced with a sense of alarm. She took up her own sword and followed. Standing beside him, she peered through the door into the darkness surrounding the house and gardens. "What'd you see?" she asked, setting her hand on his back.

"There were figures. Three or four of them."

Chelci racked her brain to think who would be out at this time of night. "Maybe it's the landscapers working late?"

Veron shook his head. "These people weren't supposed to be here."

"What do you mean?"

"They were ducking through the shadows. They didn't want anyone to see." Veron stared into the darkness. Suddenly, she felt his back tense before he spun toward her. "Stay here. Climb up into the loft and keep quiet."

"I don't think so," Chelci said, grabbing his hand on the doorknob. "I'm coming with you."

"Chelci, I'm serious!" he whispered harshly.

"So am I! This is my house. If you don't want me coming, you're gonna have to tie me up, so good luck." She shot daggers at him with her eyes. "If there's trouble in the house, you know I can help." Veron hesitated, allowing Chelci's impatience to build. "Come on, let's go!"

Veron gave up. He turned the knob and stepped cautiously onto the dark garden path. "Follow me," he whispered.

Veron skirted the garden on the far end, staying underneath overhanging tree limbs. They passed behind the well and approached the side of the house at the basement entrance. Veron's head was on a swivel as they moved furtively along, crouching and slinking to remain invisible. When they reached the side door, Veron peered into the window for a moment but didn't seem to gain any information. He turned to Chelci and held his finger to his lips. Veron turned the doorknob slowly. When the door was wide enough, they both entered.

The kitchen was dark. A faint light from outside shone through the window, but it was still difficult to see. Veron and Chelci crouched behind the closest worktable. She followed as he moved toward the stove against the wall. Suddenly, his hand grabbed her leg, forcing her to stop. Pressed up against his side, she could only hear her own breath for several seconds before another sound arrived.

It was faint, reminding her of bare feet on grass. Then she heard it from two directions. Her blood ran cold when voices whispered a barely audible salvo of words.

"Anything?"

"Nothing. The basement's empty."

"Don't worry, we'll find him. Kill anyone you see on sight."

Chelci stifled a gasp, covering her mouth with her free hand. Veron tensed next to her at the sudden movement.

"What was that?" a voice said.

Veron's grip on Chelci's leg tightened. Her heart pounded as she struggled to keep her breath under control. Her grip on the sword clenched so hard her hand hurt. The men were silent as the soft steps drew closer.

Chelci felt Veron's muscles grow taut like a bowstring about to be loosed. At the end of the aisle, a dark shape came into view, draining the blood from Chelci's face.

"Hey! There's—"

The next moments blurred in Chelci's head. Veron sprung into action, but it was so fast, it was like he disappeared. The man in her vision was cut off mid-phrase as his words contorted into shouts of pain. His body fell against the wall as a dark, wet substance sprayed against it. On the opposite side of the room, Chelci sensed a skirmish as men's voices shouted for a moment before twisting into anguished cries.

Unwilling to remain on the sidelines, Chelci stood quickly, gripping her sword. She turned to the voices' source and looked for the men. The only person there was Veron. He looked down and stood motionless. Chelci scurried around the table and came to his side. She inhaled sharply when she saw four more bodies lying on the ground.

Veron pushed one of the men with his boot. The body rolled back, devoid of life. "I was afraid of this. I knew it was coming," he said, staring down for a long moment.

"How did . . . But they . . . How did you do that?" Chelci asked finally.

"We don't have time," he said, snapping to attention. "Your mother's in danger."

"My . . . mother?" Chelci screwed up her face at the unexpected words. "What do you mean? Who are these people?"

"Come on. Be quiet and quick."

36

Battling Destiny

Veron led up the winding stairs, holding his sword ahead. Chelci followed on his heels, more confused than ever. The second-floor hallway was empty, and Veron waved them forward. Mother's room was the second door on the left, and Veron opened it without knocking. *Mother won't like this!* she thought. Inside her mother's room, moonlight streamed in through the windows, illuminating Luciana, asleep on the bed.

"Luciana!" Veron whispered loudly.

"Veron, what are you doing?" Chelci asked quietly.

"Luciana, wake up!" Veron moved to the side of the bed.

"She's not gonna like—" Chelci stopped mid-sentence as Veron reached out and covered her mother's mouth with one hand and shook her gently with the other.

"Luciana!" he called again.

Chelci's mother jerked awake. A mumble strained through Veron's hand, and Chelci cringed at the sight.

"Luciana, quiet!" Veron held a finger to his lips. "It's me, Veron. I need you to listen, *quietly.*" When her mother stopped thrashing, Veron removed his hand and spoke quickly. "There are men here.

Men that want to kill me."

"What is the meaning of this—"

"Quiet!" Veron repeated, silencing her. "Whatever happens, you *must* stay in your room. Do not come out. Do you understand?"

"What are you doing here?" Chelci's mother asked in a voice far too loud. Her eyes suddenly danced between the two of them before they grew large. "Wait! You can't be togeth—"

"Mother, be quiet!" Chelci whispered. "There are men here. Veron just killed five of them in the basement." Luciana quieted.

"I know we've had our issues, and you don't want me near your daughter," Veron said. "But I'm trying to protect you. I need to go out there, and *you* need to stay in your room. They will kill you if you don't. Do you understand?"

Luciana's eyes flit between the two. After a moment, she nodded. "What's going on?" she asked quietly.

Veron appeared satisfied and moved to leave. "We don't have time. Just stay here and be quiet. Chelci, stay and guard your mother."

"What? No, I'm not—" Chelci glanced back at her mother, who sat bewildered on her bed. With a huff, she left the room and closed the door behind her before hurrying to catch up with Veron.

"What are you doing?" he whispered. "You need to stay—"

She silenced him with raised eyebrows. "I'm staying with you." Her words left little room for discussion, and finally, he nodded. "Do we need to warn Father, too?" Veron shook his head. Questions spun through Chelci's mind. *Why are these men here? Why would we warn Mother but not Father? How did Veron kill the ones in the basement so fast?*

She followed him down the stairs into a dark corner of the sitting room below. Veron held up his hand. They stood still as statues, waiting. Soon, a lone shadow crossed through from the opposite hall. Veron moved out of the shadows and silently stalked the intruder. As they crossed into the large entry hall, the light grew from the large number of windows. Chelci felt exposed.

Gripping her sword, she and Veron were only a few paces behind the dark figure. Taking a few quick steps, Veron closed the gap and pushed his sword against the shadow's back. "Don't move," he whispered. "Turn around slowly." The intruder froze for only a moment. Instead of gradually turning, he spun quickly, raising his sword. Veron's weapon found its mark and sank into the figure's back.

The intruder let out a sharp cry, staggered against the nearby wall, and turned around. It was a young man, much younger than Chelci expected. He was thin, but his arm rippled with muscles as it clenched a sword. His face looked familiar, but she wasn't sure who it was.

Veron stiffened, and a gasp escaped his lips as he took a step backward. "Collin, what are you . . . What is this?" Veron asked in a shaky voice.

Collin? He's that servant! Chelci realized. *He was here for a few days. I don't understand!*

Collin set his jaw and winced as he struggled to sit up. "We're here for you, Veron," he said.

"I don't understand," Veron said. "Who sent you?"

The young man managed a painful-looking grimace as he held his back. "I think you know."

"Bale. You were with him all along, weren't you?" The color drained from Veron's face. "It was Brixton, wasn't it? He sold me out!"

"Brixton?" Chelci asked. "He did this?"

Collin nodded before entering a coughing fit. Blood spit onto his clothes. "There's no way out, Veron." Collin indicated with his head around him.

A sickening feeling filled Chelci's stomach as she turned. At both sides of the hall, ten men with swords and dark expressions blocked the escape. Above them, another fifteen lined the second-floor balcony. The men all held swords and looked hungry for blood.

"Stand to my back!" Veron shouted as he moved to the center of the room and turned away from Chelci, his back to hers.

She trembled and stared down the men. With a forced show of confidence, she yelled, "Back off all of you! You will not get to him!" Her lips curled back in a snarl. She held her sword, ready to strike. Veron moved behind her to engage the men on his end of the hall, but she didn't dare turn.

The closest man lunged at her, swinging his sword. Chelci spun to the side and knocked away the blade. She followed with a kick to his hip, and he flew into the wall. The next man attacked, but she was quick. She parried his sword, but it was forceful and almost knocked her over. She fought off two more strikes before landing a cut on the man's arm. He hissed and backed off. Immediately, two men replaced him, another six directly behind.

I can't do this, Chelci thought. *I can't fight all of them off.* She held her sword high and bared her teeth. They glanced between each other and hesitated for a moment. Suddenly, a body jumped in front of her. *Veron? What about—* Chelci glanced behind her and her jaw dropped. Ten bodies lay strewn across the floor of the entry hall. "How did you—" Chelci began, but stopped as Veron moved.

His body was a blur. She couldn't even see his sword from its rapid movement. The men fell one at a time—sometimes two at a time—dispatched by a force they couldn't possibly hope to defend against. One body flew into the air from where Veron punched him. Another crashed into the stone wall, leaving a dent in the stones that had stood solid for hundreds of years. He jumped and whirled in a flurry of steel and sweat. *What's going on? How is this possible?* Chelci's sword hung limply in her hand as she watched the carnage with wide eyes.

When the last man fell, Veron's movement slowed to a normal speed, but Chelci was shocked. While she stood frozen, a rough arm wrapped around her, and a knife's cool steel pressed against her throat. A cry escaped her lips, prompting Veron to turn.

"Drop your sword, or she dies!" the man yelled.

"Leave her alone!" Veron shouted back, panting.

Chelci pivoted her head. Half of the men from the balcony had descended the stairs and surrounded her while Veron fought.

"We won't leave her alone until you turn yourself over to us."

Veron stepped closer as he spoke, "If you kill her, there is nothing that will stop—"

Chelci cried out again as the blade bit into her neck. Veron stopped moving.

"What is this?" her mother's tentative voice called out from the top of the stairs, followed by a gasp. "Release her at once! Who are you all?"

"Luciana, leave! Now!" Veron shouted without taking his eyes off of Chelci.

"What are you all doing in my house?"

Luciana's voice wavered. Chelci didn't dare turn her head because of the knife, but she strained her eyes to the side. Her mother stood at the top of the stairs in her robe. Men slowly moved, surrounding her. Chelci heard inaudible mumbling as her mother disappeared behind the wall of bodies. Her mother's cries felt like a stab in the gut. Chelci heard her body crumble to the ground just before the men turned back in her direction.

"No!" she yelled, her throat straining against the metal blade. The arm around her tightened as tears welled in her eyes—tears of loss for a relationship never made right and a mother who never fully understood her.

Shouts and questions echoed from all corners of the house as other servants roused from the noise to investigate. "Stop this! It's me you want!" Veron yelled.

"Then put down your sword," the man behind her growled.

"How do I know you'll let her go?"

"She's not the one we're here for. Give up, and I promise we won't harm her."

Through blurry eyes, Chelci held Veron's gaze. *Don't do it, Veron! They're just going to kill you!* Slowly, Veron set his sword on the ground and stood straight before kicking the weapon away. *Veron, No!* Tears sprung anew inside her.

Men surrounded him. As if moving in a choreographed routine, they began at once. Several swung their swords, but Veron moved as fast as lightning. He ducked and whirled out of the path of the weapons, kicking a man and sending him flying. The men continued slashing at the air desperately but found nothing. One by one the men fell, even though Veron had no weapon.

Chelci began to hope. *Maybe he can beat them all?* As she sat, transfixed by the impossible display, the blade bit deeper into her neck, drawing a startled cry. Veron stopped and turned to her. His jaw was set like stone, and his body projected power and control. He stepped toward her with fire in his eyes.

Chelci saw the attack. She tried to call out, but couldn't form the words in time. As Veron moved toward her, a man sank his sword into his back. His body arched and eyes squinted as he cried out. Chelci paled as another man stabbed him in the gut, and one more ran his sword through Veron's chest, just left of his heart.

"NOOOOO!" Chelci screamed. Veron locked eyes with her as his knees sank to the ground. His fight was over. He looked helplessly at the swords sticking into his body before the men pulled them out. Veron slowly fell to his side. Lying on the hard stone, he maintained eye contact with Chelci for a moment until his lids finally closed.

The men seemed to disappear instantly. There was no more knife to Chelci's throat. A cacophony of yelling voices came from upstairs. The household had arrived to see the devastation, but she paid them no mind. Only one thing held her attention. She scurried across the floor to Veron and set her arm gingerly on his shoulder. "Veron! It's gonna be okay! We can . . ." she choked on the words. "We can fix you up."

Chelci glanced around, hoping something more inspiring would come. She only found dozens of dying bodies. There was nothing to do. House servants came quickly down the stairs, but she turned back to Veron.

Blood covered his chest and pooled on the ground around him. As tears streamed from her eyes, she wrapped her arms around him and held his body close. The faintest of breaths reached her neck, but she sensed it waning. His body was still warm, yet his life rapidly fled.

"Veron, I'm sorry I couldn't help more," she said through sobs. "Thank you for what you showed me . . . what people can be like. I'll never meet someone like you again." She leaned back to look at him, wiping her eyes with her sleeves. Blood stained her own clothes, but she didn't even notice. Chelci brushed his hair back as his chest lowered one last breath and his head fell limp. Tears sprang anew. Chelci held his body tightly and wailed, her cries echoing off the stone walls.

After a moment of grief, she laid his body gently on the floor and turned. Her father stood by the stairs with tears in his own eyes while servants gathered a respectful distance away. Chelci wiped her tears away again and stood. "Mother?" she said. Father shook his head. His jaw was tight. Chelci walked to him, and they hugged. "I'm sorry, Father."

She sensed his inner conflict similar to hers. *I should be sadder. She was my mother.* Emotion tugged at her, but her body no longer responded to it—overshadowed by the loss she felt for Veron.

"Who were they?" he asked after a moment.

"They were here for Veron."

"I'm sorry . . . about Veron. He was a good man. I'm sorry we pushed him away. You deserved—" Darcius choked up mid-sentence.

"It's alright, Father. I understand."

"I just wish that—" Darcius gasped as his body tensed.

Chelci stepped back to see what was wrong. His face looked white as he stared over her shoulder. When she turned around, her heart leaped while her legs trembled. Veron sat up, propped by an arm, looking at her. Sweat covered his brow. His face was pale, but a hint of a smile tugged at his mouth. He was alive.

"Are they gone?" he asked in a hoarse croak.

"Oh, Veron!" Chelci yelled as she ran to him. She knelt to the ground and threw her arms around him, eliciting a wince and a groan. "I'm sorry," she said as she gingerly loosened her hold.

"It's okay. I'll be alright," Veron said as he panted, clearly exhausted.

"How is this possible?" Chelci asked. "I saw them— I saw you—" Chelci couldn't finish as she fumbled, lifting the hem of his tunic to inspect his wounds. Blood covered his clothes and most of his chest, but he didn't recoil at her touch. The gashes where the swords cut him were dark with a tight scab. Chelci lightly touched the wound over his heart, but Veron didn't appear in pain. "It's already healed? How did you—" she stopped when she saw his sheepish grin.

Her father and various servants pressed around them, leaning in. Veron shrugged and glanced between those gathered. "I . . . uh . . . I guess there's something else about me I never told you."

37

Difficult Decisions

Brixton spun his sword absently with the tip down and pommel under his hand. As the days pressed on, he grew increasingly anxious. He wistfully thought back to earlier times when he was a clerk at the Department of Commerce. There were no plots to overthrow governments or schemes to blackmail friends. Life was simpler.

His father coughed across the room, drawing his attention from the spinning weapon. Men gathered in the large sunroom where he had killed Hailey a lifetime ago. Bale stood by the window, gazing outside into the night. His men, Ryker and Desmond, hovered around a map spread out on a table and argued between themselves quietly. Brixton's father stood in conversation with Lord Billings and Captain Gannon. They all waited. For two days, they looked for the return of the company of men sent to Felting—the men sent to kill Veron.

Two men entered the room, and all heads jerked in their direction. The man in front looked at Bale and nodded. "It's done. The shadow knight is dead."

Brixton's heart sank unexpectedly. The news of his one-time friend's death left him strangely empty and anxious.

341

"Are you sure?" Bale asked. His shoulders were suddenly alert, and his eyes gleamed. "Was there any trouble? Tell me what happened."

"He . . . uh . . . put up more of a fight than we expected. Those abilities you mentioned . . ." The man glanced around the room as he fiddled with his tunic's hem. "He still had them."

"What?" Brixton said. Fear instantly manifested itself as drops of sweat on his forehead. "As I said, I wasn't sure."

Bale glanced at Brixton, then ran his hand across his chin and was silent for a moment. "Collin *was* sure about it. Possibly, it's something that comes and goes." Brixton exhaled as Bale continued. "Where's Collin? I want to hear his thoughts."

"As I mentioned, he put up more of a fight than we were ready for," the man said. "Collin was killed."

"How many did you lose?" Bale asked, devoid of emotion.

The man cleared his throat. "Thirty-five, Your Majesty."

Sharp breaths and gasps sounded around the room. "One man killed thirty-five soldiers," Ryker said. "How is that possible?"

Bale turned to him. "Believe me, it's possible."

"A girl fought as well," the man said.

Brixton perked up. "A girl? Who? Is she okay?" he asked. His father's scoff traversed the room.

"Um . . . I'm not sure who she was, but I think she was still alive," the man said, and Brixton exhaled in relief.

Bale turned back to the men. "Thank you. And excellent work." He promptly crossed the room to the map on the table then clapped his hands together and rubbed them in spirited anticipation. "Now, we can attack!"

"Very good," Ryker said. "We're all agreed on approaching from the woods, correct?" Heads nodded around the room. "When we emerge a stone's throw from the city, we'll be able to block off reinforcements." Ryker turned to Billings. "You say there are no soldiers from Karondir yet, yes?"

"That's correct," the Lord of Defense replied. "According to my scouts, the army at Karondir is none the wiser."

"And we're all set on the false treaty?" Desmond asked, glancing between the men.

"I know that's what we planned, but I still don't like it," Gareth Billings grumbled. "It's not . . . proper."

Ryker scoffed. "Proper. Who cares? We say we want to negotiate a peace agreement with him. When Wesley meets with us, we kill him. They'll be without a leader and facing down an enemy twice their size. They'll swing open the gates and welcome us in. It's that simple."

"I'm fine with it," Captain Gannon added, earning a nod from Brixton's father.

"I don't care whether it's proper or not," Bale said, chiming in last. "If it wins the battle, it's justified. However, I've thought about it, and I want to consider another option."

"You want to try a direct assault on the gate or come from the river?" Desmond asked.

"Neither. I've got a better idea," Bale said, turning to Brixton. Brixton's stomach churned as the king's dark eyes pierced him. "You have a good relationship with one of Felting's High Lords, don't you?"

Brixton felt his hands turn clammy as all eyes in the room were on him. "Yes, Your Majesty. Marlow, the High Lord of Commerce."

A wicked grin crossed Bale's face. "Good. I think we can use that."

Brixton wrung out his hands as he paced his room in the castle. Whenever he looked into Bale's eyes, he crumbled under the expectation. The man was a force, and now he wanted Brixton to actively betray his own country.

Turning in Veron was one thing, but this is something else. Bale's promises were alluring. Brixton had worked for years to grow from an entry-level clerk to Karad's Lord of Commerce. With one more action, he could become Commercial Envoy of the Norshewan empire, in charge of all commerce in Terrenor, and part of Bale's inner circle. At least, that's what the king promised him. His heart leapt at the idea. Power, money, influence—it was all at his fingertips.

Despite the excitement, and even after his verbal confirmation, Brixton was hesitant to commit. Part of him longed for a simpler life. He thought about Matthew and Emma's smiling faces in the bakery. They were so happy doing something ordinary. Even on the cusp of becoming one of the greatest men in Terrenor, Brixton found himself jealous of a baker.

Maybe partnering with Bale is the wrong path to take? But what else is there? Chelci? He wasn't sure how Chelci fit into his plans. As much as she seemed to hate him, they were still to be married in a few weeks. *Betraying my country will jeopardize it. Maybe I should stick with her and forget all of this?* He shook his head. *Bale will still take over, even without my help. It makes sense to be on board. Unless . . .*

Brixton stopped pacing and looked at his desk. Blank paper and a pen waited for him. Slowly, he walked to the desk and sat. He picked up the pen and turned it in his hand. *Do I dare? Would it work? Or would it just get me killed?*

He turned his head to make sure the door was closed. He strained his ears and confirmed no one approached. His heart beating quickly, he put the pen to the paper and wrote. *"Dearest Chelci—"* He stopped as his hand shook. After tapping the pen against the desk a few times, he leaned back and groaned under his breath, unsure what to do.

* * *

Bensen patrolled the well-worn path, his eyes sweeping along the moonlit tree line for any sign of disturbance. A breeze blew, tickling his beard and chilling his left leg. His right—now made of wood and metal—felt nothing. Behind him, glowing in a ring of lantern light, the village of Nasco rested peacefully, trusting the night watch to keep them safe.

The Academy trainer's senses tingled as the wind brought something new to his nose. The odor was faint but distinct. His muscles tensed, and his heart quickened. A memory filled his mind as he spun around. *It's here . . . somewhere.*

Moving as best he could on one good leg, he loped to the next patrol section, using his staff to steady him as he dashed. He stopped after a short way when he arrived at Finley, who casually strolled along.

"Have you seen anything?" Bensen asked in a clipped voice.

Finley cocked his head and stared back. "I see *you* . . . in *my* section. Is something wrong?"

Bensen looked past the young man. "I smell it."

Finley raised his nose, testing the air. "My gas? My stomach was upset a while ago, but it shouldn't—"

"Not *you* . . . *it.*"

Finley's eyes bugged. "It?" He spun frantically, peering into the darkness. "I—uh . . . You—uh . . ."

"It's here . . . somewhere."

"Do—Do you want me to raise the village alert?"

Bensen ignored the question. "Come on," he said, racing farther along the path.

After turning a corner at the far east end of the village, Aleks came into view ahead, moving along the path. Bensen slowed to a walk. At a distance, Aleks tilted his head and raised his palms in a shrug.

"You okay?" Finley shouted over Bensen's shoulder.

"Hush!" Bensen whispered, holding out his hand.

Suddenly, the wind changed directions. *There!* Bensen snapped his nose toward the edge of the woods. It was strong and unmistakable. "Finley," he said in a calm voice. "Raise the alert."

Finley's eyes steadily grew as he nodded and walked backward. After several steps, he turned and ran.

Bensen unsheathed his sword and moved purposefully down the hill, balancing the staff in his other hand. By the time he arrived at the bottom, Aleks had joined him, puffing from his short run.

"I smell it," the younger guardsman said as he pulled out his sword and stood beside Bensen.

Without a word, the trainer walked into the dark forest. Shapes took form as the darkness created silhouettes in the moonlight—a log, a rock, a tree. The smell grew stronger with every step, but he heard nothing.

"There!" Aleks whispered and pointed to something metallic on the ground.

Bensen crouched to inspect. Blood dotted the sword's surface as if sprayed on, and a mangled mess of flesh lay beside it. Reaching out his hand, he touched the mutilated skin—*cold*.

"Jarvis?" Aleks asked in a wavering voice.

Bensen clenched his jaw as he nodded. "A third of him, at least." He stood and scanned the woods as the deep gong of the village alert bell filled the air. Nothing appeared while he surveyed the darkness. When the final bell faded, he beckoned to Aleks and turned back to the village.

By the time they summited the hill, a dozen members of the village guard had gathered, with more on the way.

"What is it?" Russell asked in a gruff voice.

"Is it back?" Royce asked. Aleks nodded.

Bensen waited without speaking as the men continued to arrive. After counting twenty guards, he held up his hand to grab their attention. "The valcor is back!" he shouted. The men grew silent.

The only sound remaining was the whistle of the wind cresting the hill. "It took Jarvis."

A general mutter filled the crowd as heads bowed. "Is it gone?" a man in the back of the crowd asked.

"I don't know. We need every one of you on guard tonight. Cut the patrol sections in half, and I want at least two men in every group. It's gonna be a long night."

The sky began to lighten as Bensen walked his section with guardsman Brannon following a few paces behind. Footsteps crunching the dirt path drew his attention toward the village from where Russell approached.

"Still quiet?" Russell asked.

Bensen nodded. "Nothing for hours."

"Good. The elders are gathered."

Bensen turned to the other guardsman. "Brannon, give it another half hour before retiring. Can you relay the message along the watch?"

"Of course," Brannon replied.

Bensen looked along the dirt path to the next pair of guardsmen. "Aleks!"

The young man in the distance looked in his direction as Bensen signaled to him with a wave. After a short run, Aleks arrived, and the three men walked briskly into the village.

The village meeting room sat in the village center, off the grassy center, and next to the school. The three village elders sat waiting on the wooden benches when Bensen, Russell, and Aleks entered. The room was plain, with two rows of benches formed in a circle and windows on all sides.

"How many attacks does this make?" Peter Bebbington asked as the men sat. Peter was the most senior of the elders. His thin whips of gray hair rested flat against his mostly bald head. His shoulders and neck hunched over, slumped with age.

"This is the third," Bensen confirmed as he propped his wooden leg out to the side, ". . . since the original when Elise injured it."

"Chelci," Russell corrected.

"Sorry . . . yes . . . when *Chelci* fought it and I lost my leg."

"How did it happen?" Norman Taurel asked, leaning forward on his bench. "Was there any warning? Did anyone hear Jarvis?"

Bensen looked at Aleks. "I didn't hear a thing," the young guardsman said. "He patrolled the area next to me. I saw him from time to time, but . . . I didn't hear a sound. I hadn't even noticed his absence."

"We found . . . *parts* of him a short way into the woods," Bensen said.

"Is this valcor the reason for our recent missing hunters?" Alfred, the third elder, asked.

Russell shook his head. "We don't think so. They left in the morning and were to return before night. So far, we don't think it's active during the daytime. Plus, the hunters were heading farther north than the area around the village."

"So, you think they had an accident or something?" Peter asked.

"It's possible," Bensen said, glancing at Russell. "But with two separate hunting parties disappearing two weeks apart . . . a simple accident seems unlikely."

"Then it could be this beast?" Peter said.

"Sure . . . It's possible," Bensen replied.

"Well, we have to protect the village, so what do we do? How can we stop this thing?" Norman asked.

Russell spoke up. "We've staked out the old nest several times, but we think it's abandoned. And we can't find any other nests or dens."

"We're planning to double the village watch each night, and I think it's time to issue a curfew—everyone in their homes by nightfall," Bensen said.

"What if we sent out hunting parties?" Aleks suggested.

Bensen's stomach turned. An imagined throbbing pain shot through his missing leg at the thought of wandering through the woods, searching for the animal. He glanced at Russell, whose mouth was fixed in a grim line.

"I think it may be time," Russell said.

Bensen nodded slowly as a sinking feeling settled in his gut. "Yes, I think you're right." He glanced at Aleks then back to Russell. "Let's make the plans."

38

A Visit Home

Veron rounded a bend in the road, and Karad's walls suddenly loomed before him. It felt like a lifetime since he'd seen them. It reminded him of his trip in chains to be sold as a slave. Underneath him, his horse—on loan from the king's stable—walked along at a steady pace. The strong, dark-brown animal seemed like he could go on for days without tiring.

A breeze picked up. It was late-wiether, so the days grew warmer. Veron closed his eyes and leaned his head back as the wind surrounded him, a smile covering his face. He felt pure joy for the first time in a while. He was free once again. No longer living on the streets or as a slave, he was now an advisor to the king! Yet, the person on the smaller horse next to him gave him the most delight.

Chelci's long hair blew behind her as she looked forward. The midday sun peeked from behind a cloud, giving her a warm glow. The brown pants and sword at her hip would have looked out of place on any other woman, but she made them look natural. When the wind shifted directions, Chelci's hair twirled and wrapped around her head. She turned to Veron, peering at him between a disheveled mess of strands. After giving a wry grin and shrugging her shoulders, she and Veron erupted in laughter.

"Thanks for coming with me, Chelci," Veron said.

She fought with her hair to push it back. "I wouldn't miss it. Ironically, I'm supposed to be traveling to Karad right now, anyway, although I have no desire to see the Fieros anymore."

Veron watched her while the breeze continued to blow. "I'm sorry about your mother," he said in a soft voice.

Chelci's mouth fell as she nodded. "Thanks. It's strange . . . I feel like I should be devastated, but I don't feel much. Does that make me a bad person?"

Veron shook his head. "No. You're one of the most caring people I know. Your relationship with your mother was . . . difficult."

"I am sad about her though—about the loss of . . . what could have been. I could see her trying. Since I'd been home, there were moments of softness, like she wanted to understand me but just couldn't get past her nature."

"Yeah, I saw some of that, too," Veron said. "You're sure your father will be okay?"

"He said he wanted to bury himself in work for a while. I'm not sure it's healthy, but I can give him some space for a few days."

Veron nodded. The clopping of horse-hooves filled the air as Veron thought about Luciana Marlow. She was a vile woman but didn't deserve such a death.

"How did you know about her?" Chelci asked.

"What do you mean?"

"Mother. It seemed almost like you knew they were going to kill her."

"I'm sure it sounds crazy, but . . . I had a Dream about it."

"Really?" Chelci leaned forward in her saddle, jaw agape. "That's incredible."

"Yeah . . . well, I wasn't sure if it would come true or not. I saw us fighting. I saw your mother . . . you know. But I woke up when they stabbed me." Veron glanced at Chelci, but she stared at the road silently.

"If you knew she would die . . . why didn't you say something?" Chelci asked softly.

Veron's throat grew dry. "I'm so sorry, Chelci! I wanted to, but I worried it would sound crazy. Plus, I didn't even believe it. I haven't been able to use the origine—the power I told you about—for a long time until a couple of days ago. I thought the Dream was impossible. Then, it all happened at once!"

"No, I get it," Chelci said, offering a weak smile. "That would have sounded crazy. So, did everything in your Dream come true?"

"Sort of. The events happened, but the details weren't exact. My sword was different. Some of the people were different."

"I've never had one before," Chelci said.

As the horses continued along, Veron's thoughts turned to another Dream—one he'd worried about for years. He took a deep breath as he rubbed the back of his neck. "There was another Dream from a long time ago that's been on my mind. Around fifteen years ago, a woman in Rynor had a Dream showing a shadow knight would kill Edmund Bale."

Chelci gasped. "Is that why his men were there to kill you?"

Veron nodded. "He tried to have them all killed many years ago and nearly succeeded. One survived, and he taught their ways to me. Now, I'm the last one."

"So, do you think you can kill him with your powers?"

Veron swallowed. He didn't share the part of the Dream that said he was supposed to die. "If he stops trying to kill me first, yeah, I guess I probably can—when the time is right."

Veron glanced off the road to the left. The steep embankment climbed up to the stone offerdom's ruins. The crumbling symbol of oppression reinforced Veron's determination. He had to fulfill his calling, no matter the cost.

Soon, they entered Karad through the South Gate, and Veron hiked up his hood to avoid being recognized by anyone he might know. The familiar sights of the Gate Street vendors and the buildings lining the road warmed Veron's heart. As they crossed Dock Street, Veron's thoughts turned to Artimus. *He didn't deserve to die as he did . . . killed by street thugs trying to steal money. I sure am thankful for everything he did for me.* They dismounted at Elderberry Street.

Veron cringed as they approached his market. Several wooden slats were broken, and garbage littered the street. It was midday, so the door was open, but the courtyard was almost empty. Goods only filled two of the seven wooden displays Jacob had built the last couple years.

"Excuse me. Do you have any ripe paleno fruit by chance?" Veron asked, causing the middle-aged man rearranging produce to turn.

Morgan Fenster had aged over the last season. He looked leaner, and his face lined with worry. He had been through a great deal. The weight of sorrow caused his shoulders to sag and mouth to droop. Despite the forlorn look, when Morgan recognized him, his body came alive. A broad grin grew on his face, and he seemed to grow taller. "Veron!" he shouted.

The man ran across the courtyard and wrapped Veron up in an enormous hug, causing him to melt in his friend's warm embrace. Both men cried tears of joy at their reunion.

"I told you he was alright!" Another voice shouted as Danyel emerged from the back corner by the oven. Danyel wiped his hands on his apron and walked to join them.

"I can't believe it's you," Morgan said, pulling himself back to look at Veron. "We heard you were dead, then you might be alive, then you *were* alive."

"Morgan," Veron said in a serious voice. "I heard about Catherine and the kids. I'm so sorry."

The grocer's face dropped as he nodded. He took in a deep breath then blinked rapidly. "Thanks." His voice choked with emotion.

"I feel awful about it all. If not for me, they never would have—"

"Stop it!" Morgan said, sniffing then shaking Veron firmly on the shoulder. "You didn't kill them."

"I know, but . . . If I hadn't—"

"No! I will never forget Catherine, Emma, Jack, and Will but—" Morgan's voice cracked, causing him to pause. A tear fell from one of his eyes. "We will mourn them, but you will not shoulder the burden. It wasn't your doing. I don't want to hear another word about it, Veron." He cleared his throat and wiped his eyes. "You understand?"

Veron stared long and hard at his friend until, finally, he bobbed his head and exhaled.

"So, are you going to introduce us to your friend?" Danyel asked.

Veron jumped as if coming out of a trance. "I'm so sorry, yes!" He turned to Chelci, who smiled warmly. "This is Chelci Marlow. She's my . . ." Veron froze. His eyes grew as he stared at her. *What do I call her?*

"I'm with him," Chelci said, winking toward Veron as she extended her hand to both men.

Veron felt a flutter inside as a grin grew on his face. *She's with me!* Snapping out of his trance again, he turned back to the men. "Yes, Chelci's with me."

"Well, we are thrilled to meet you, Chelci," Morgan said. He flashed his customary smile, but Veron sensed the hurt underneath.

"You were at the wedding," Danyel said, looking to Veron for confirmation. "I knew I recognized you."

"Chelci, you remember the man I was talking with? When I avoided your question about my past?" Veron said. "That was Danyel. He's the market's baker."

"So, what are you doing here? I thought you were a slave? How'd you get away?" Morgan asked.

"We don't need to watch our backs for someone coming to claim your collateral, will we?" Danyel added.

"No, you're safe now."

Danyel's shoulders relaxed. "Did you do such a magnificent job as a wardman that they let you go?"

"Um . . . Not exactly," Veron said, rubbing his neck and looking to the ground. "Chelci and I had a thing for each other, and . . . her parents didn't approve." He glanced at Chelci, who blushed.

Danyel gasped as he pointed at Chelci. "*You're* the high lord's daughter?"

"Yeah, like I said . . . it didn't go over well," Veron said. "Chelci saved my life by promising to marry Brixton, but—"

"Brixton!" Morgan yelled. "Brixton Fiero?"

"You know Brixton?" Chelci asked.

"I told you I knew him," Veron said to her. "This is the market he stole."

"Are you marrying Brixton?" Danyel asked.

"Not anymore. He doesn't know that yet, though," Chelci replied before turning to Veron. "You see . . ."

"The king bought my freedom from the Marlows," Veron said.

"King Wesley freed you?" Morgan said as his eyebrows raised.

"Yes," Veron confirmed. "He, uh . . . He asked if . . ." Veron turned to Chelci, looking for the right words. Finally, he turned his palms up and shrugged. "I'm one of the king's advisors."

The two men from the market were frozen silent. Slowly, Morgan's face seemed to thaw. His mouth turned up and his eyes filled with life as a great bellow erupted from his chest. Danyel followed suit.

"Oh, Veron. Why does that not surprise me?" Morgan said between laughs as he wiped the corners of his eyes. "So, you go to Felting as a slave, and less than a season later, you're promoted to the king's advisor?"

"Something like that, yeah," Veron said.

"And on top of it all . . . you're a shadow knight?" Morgan raised an eyebrow as he stared at Veron.

"Yeah, that, too," Veron confirmed, prompting a whistle from Morgan.

"But your abilities are gone?" Danyel asked.

Veron wore a mischievous smile. "They were, but . . . they're back!"

"You should watch him fight!" Chelci chimed in. "It's amazing how he moves. You can barely even see him! And how he heals himself? It's incredible!"

"I would love to see it," Morgan said.

Veron laughed. "Maybe I can give you a demonstration."

"And he's prophesied as the one who defeats Bale!" Chelci added.

"Well, that *is* something," Morgan said, rubbing his chin.

"Yeah . . . *something* is right," Veron said as he cringed. "So, anyway . . . I can't be away long. I need to be back for an Advisors Council meeting soon, but we were hoping to stay the night. Would you mind if we used two rooms?"

"Of course," Morgan replied. "Most of the rooms are empty now."

"My old stuff wouldn't happen to still be here?" Veron asked, bracing for the worst.

"Your chest?" Morgan said with a grin before nodding up toward the second floor. "Your old room hasn't been touched."

Veron glanced eagerly to Chelci. "Come on." They ascended the balcony stairs and entered Veron's old room. The sweet, woody smell was just as he remembered, and everything was in its place. He crouched in front of the chest against the wall and removed the key from around his neck that he kept.

When he opened the lid, a sigh of relief escaped his lips. *Chronology of the Shadow Knights* stared back. He lifted the book gingerly and ran his hand over the cover.

"That's the book?" Chelci asked.

Veron nodded. "It's the last remaining resource containing the knowledge of the Shadow Knights."

"Except for your head."

Veron laughed softly. "Yeah." After setting the book aside, Veron pulled out the black cloak.

"Whoa, that's nice," Chelci said.

"This is what they wore. When they went on missions or . . . whatever they did. I guess I don't really know much about them."

Veron pulled out the back scabbard, and his pulse sped up. *Where is it?* He looked behind the chest then glanced around the room.

"What are you looking for?" Chelci asked.

Bending down, Veron peered under the bed and exhaled. After leaning forward, he pulled the long sword out from under the bed and held it up. The clean metal shined bright as ever. The blade's scrolling remained just as he remembered. The inset ruby bathed in the sunlight, appearing on fire.

"This," Veron said. "This is Farrathan, the original sword of Talon Shadow, passed down through the knights over centuries."

"It's beautiful."

Veron put the sword into the scabbard. As he strapped it on his back, an outside voice made him freeze.

"Morgan!"

Veron locked eyes with Chelci, who looked equally alarmed. He knew that voice anywhere. Brixton Fiero had arrived. They crept to the window.

"Morgan, Danyel . . . We need to talk," Brixton said in the courtyard below. The two men gathered around and stood with their arms crossed. Brixton didn't have his usual confidence. He kicked at the dirt while staring at the ground. "I'm . . . uh . . . going to be leaving tomorrow, and . . . I won't be back for a while." Morgan tilted his head but didn't respond. "With the sales slowdown, and with my departure, I've decided not to renew the market's seasonal license for suether."

"You piece of—" Veron's mutters were cut off by a quick jab from Chelci as she held her finger to her lips.

"What?" Danyel said, puffing out his chest and standing aggressively. "You're closing us down? First, you come in and ruin everything, then you put us out of business!" Morgan held Danyel back.

"Where are you going?" Morgan asked.

Brixton glanced around as if he sought the answer on the stall's wooden slats. "I'm going to do something that . . . um . . ." He shook his head after a pause. "I'll be traveling . . . around." He made as if to add something, but his words seemed stuck. His body angled away as if he wanted to leave in a hurry. "For what it's worth . . . I'm sorry about the market."

Veron jerked his head back as he peered from his hiding place. That wasn't what he expected to hear.

"Veron built something great here. I wanted to do even better, but my ideas didn't pan out how I'd hoped. You all had something good, and I ruined it. I'm sorry."

Danyel's shoulders settled, and he and Morgan calmed.

Brixton continued. "Get what money you can from the rest of your supplies. You can keep it."

Morgan and Danyel stood stoically as Brixton walked away. When he was about to exit, his eye stopped on the two horses Veron and Chelci had tied to the side, and he walked to them. "These are fine horses," he said as he rubbed his hand along the taller one's flank.

"Are these yours?"

"He's going to find us," Chelci whispered.

Morgan promptly answered, "Travelers. They arrived from Felting earlier and will stay with us for the night. They're out in the square now, I believe."

Brixton nodded his head and looked over the animals again. After a moment of delay, he left.

Veron emerged from the room and exchanged a look with the men below. "I'm so sorry, guys. I can't believe he's closing it down!" he said as he descended the stairs with Chelci behind.

"You're sorry?" Morgan said. "I'm sorry for you! This was your creation. You built this from nothing!"

"It's alright," Veron said. "I guess it was time to move on. What are you two going to do?"

The men exchanged glances, and Danyel answered first. "Lynette's been trying to convince me to leave the market and move down to the Docks near her. I think this may be a good excuse. I could probably use the money I've saved to open a small bakery there. You know . . . basic stuff. Everyone needs bread."

"Yeah, that's a good idea. What about you, Morgan?" Veron asked.

The grocer was less prepared. His face turned down, and he glanced around at the market's remains. "I don't know," he said in a dejected tone. "This is practically all I've ever done."

Veron perked up at a thought. "Why don't you start your own—" he stopped short as he remembered what happened in the past.

Morgan shook his head at him. "I'm banned, remember. I can't run a business in Karad. Now that Raynor Fiero is baron, I'd say my chances are slimmer than ever. I guess I could go back to the docks." He arched his back and pressed on his hip with his hand. "I'm not sure how well my body would handle it, though."

Veron's eyes suddenly grew wide as an idea came to him. "I've got it!" The other three jumped at the sudden outburst. He gestured between him and Chelci as he said, "Come with us! Come to Felting!"

Morgan jerked his head back as if the idea was completely absurd, but his forehead gradually smoothed out the wrinkles.

"I'm serious!" Veron insisted. "We can help you find something. You can start fresh! You could open a grocery or even an entire market! Fiero's the only person who would care about your ban."

"My father is the High Lord of Commerce," Chelci said with a smile. "I'm sure we can work it out."

Morgan's face lightened and eventually grew into an enormous grin. With a hearty laugh, he wrapped both Veron and Chelci up in his arms. "I love it! I could use a fresh start. This could be great for me." He glanced at what remained around the market. "I can sell off what I have left here and use the money to get started in Felting."

His friend's smile filled Veron with excitement he hadn't felt in a long time. The idea of Morgan joining him in Felting warmed his soul.

"What do you think Brixton's up to?" Danyel asked.

"Yeah, something is up with him," Morgan added.

"As far as he's aware, we're still supposed to marry in a few weeks," Chelci said, "unless . . . the way he talked, I'm not sure that's part of his plan anymore."

Veron paced away, holding his chin as he thought aloud. "We know he and his father are working with Bale. We know Bale wants to take over Feldor. And we know they think I'm dead."

"Why do they think you're dead?" Danyel asked.

"Because they killed me," Veron said casually, causing Danyel and Morgan to jerk their heads.

"It's a long story," Chelci added.

Suddenly, Veron gasped and turned with a start. "They think I'm dead! Why didn't I realize it before? They're going to attack, now!"

"Karad?" Morgan asked.

"No . . . Felting!" Veron walked back to the group quickly as he continued, "Bale already controls Karad, even though no one realizes it. Fiero and Billings are with him. I bet they march together against Felting, and it sounds like they're leaving tomorrow!"

"Surely, Felting is ready for that, right? They have walls and an army of their own," Chelci said.

"They're not ready," Veron confirmed. "We met about it two days ago. Half of the lords don't believe he'll attack, and those that do are expecting a weak force. And none of them have any idea when it will be."

"Brixton joined with Bale. That's why he's not returning," Danyel said.

"Still, he seemed hesitant," Morgan added. "Like he was unsure."

Veron looked urgently to Chelci. "We've got to warn them. And we've got to go, now." She nodded, and Veron turned back to the men. "I'm sorry, but we can't stay."

"I understand," Morgan said. "The kingdom needs you. Give me a couple of days to sell my stuff, then I'll come down and join you."

"You better make it fast. Get there before their army does, or you may not get in. Come to the Marlow house when you arrive." After addressing Morgan, Veron walked to Danyel and heartily embraced him. "Good luck with your girl."

After Morgan and Danyel forced them to accept some fruit and bread for the road, Veron and Chelci mounted back up. They dodged people in the streets as best they could until they reached the South Gate. With the city behind them and the wide-open road ahead, Veron glanced at Chelci. *I don't want to drag her into this . . . but I sure am glad she's with me.* She returned his gaze with a warm look of affection.

"Are you ready?" Veron asked. Chelci nodded. They both turned their heads facing up the road and kicked their horses into a gallop.

39

Warnings and the Truth

Veron and Chelci stormed up the Marlows' drive. They rode through the night, pushing the horses, and arrived in Felting early the next day. Veron allowed his horse to cool off a moment while he walked Chelci inside.

"Chelci! Veron! Back so soon?" Chelci's father said, looking up from a book as they entered the sitting room.

"We had to rush back. We found out something, and Veron needs to warn the king," Chelci said.

"Bale is coming," Veron added. "Well . . . at least we're pretty sure he is, and he's coming with Karad's army."

"Like you mentioned at the meeting?" Darcius said.

Veron nodded, but a tightness formed in his stomach before he exhaled a loud sigh. "I still don't have any proof," he said as his eyes lost focus. "It's just my word. I can't tell the king more rumors."

"But, surely, he needs to hear this," Chelci said.

"What did you hear?" Darcius asked.

Veron slumped and relaxed his shoulders. "We didn't actually hear anything. Only that Brixton is leaving Karad." He turned to Chelci and shrugged. "So, what do we do now?"

"Stay for a meal," Darcius suggested. "The kitchen staff is cooking something up, and I would love the company."

Veron sighed, frustrated by the futility of their rushed return. "Sure, that sounds good."

Chelci lightly rubbed her hand across his shoulder. "I'll be back. I'm going upstairs to clean up."

"So, how was Karad?" Darcius asked as Chelci left and Veron took a seat.

"It was short—unnecessarily so, apparently. I did get to see a few old friends though."

"Veron, I'm so sorry about what happened since you came here . . . all of it. Luciana handled servant hires. I never thought twice about how she did it or where they came from. I think I found it easier to stay aloof."

"Thanks. I understand," Veron said. "And I'm sorry about what happened to your wife."

"Thank you," Darcius replied, staring vacantly toward the window and nodding slowly. He wiped his eye for a moment and then turned to Veron. "You know, I'm thinking of stepping down from my position as High Lord of Commerce."

"Really?"

"I never wanted all of this," he said, holding his hands up as he looked around the house. "Luciana always pushed me to do more, but I never desired it."

"What would you do then?"

"I'm not sure yet. Maybe open up a shop of some sort. Talk with people all day. I think I'd enjoy that."

A clamor came from above as someone ran down the stairs. Moments later, Chelci burst into the room, breathing heavily.

"What is it?" Veron asked. She held up an envelope with a broken seal of wax and an unfolded letter.

"Oh, yes, that letter arrived for you earlier today," Darcius said. "I left it on your bed. What is it?"

"Veron," she said. "We need to see the king . . . now."

Veron's first visit to the castle had only been a few days before, but its grandeur was already lost on him. Conversely, Chelci walked the halls wide-eyed with her head on a swivel. They weaved through the maze of corridors and many flights of stairs, arriving at the king's private study. A guard stepped aside as Veron and Chelci approached.

"Veron!" King Wesley said, opening his arms and standing as they entered the room. Quincy Hilliard, one of the other advisors, sat next to him. "I thought you were away another couple of days. And Chelci Marlow! What a surprise!" The king turned to Veron and spoke in a mock whisper. "Is this the young woman you mentioned?"

Veron felt a flush creep up his neck, and he glanced at the floor. "Uh . . . yes, Chelci and I are . . ."

"Together now," Chelci finished.

"Yes," Veron confirmed with a sideways grin.

"Good for you both," Wesley said.

"But that's not why we're here, Your Majesty," Veron said. "Bale is coming—right now."

The king stiffened. His face narrowed into a piercing gaze. "You're certain of this?"

"I am. We overheard Brixton Fiero, the baron's son, talking to others in Karad. We concluded Bale is about to march on Felting."

"More speculation, just like before," Quincy said. "We can't act on hearsay." With a smirk, Veron turned to Chelci, who handed the letter to the king. "What's this?" Quincy asked.

Wesley read aloud.

Dearest Chelci,

I know you and I have had our differences. At times, I've struggled to control my temper and rein in my ambition. Over the last several weeks, I've faced decisions that challenged me in unimaginable ways. I hope you can understand my intentions were always to do what's right. I don't know if you're aware, but our kingdom is secretly being invaded by Edmund Bale from Norshewa. It shames me to admit he partnered with my father, among others. He has plans to conquer Feldor and all of Terrenor. He and my father have asked me to take part. He has promised me fame and glory, but over time, I've realized some things cannot be bought—namely, pride and self-conviction.

Bale wants me to use my connection with your father to spread false information. Although he believes I will do this, I have no intention of doing so. His men will leave their camp on Marketday—likely the day you receive this letter. They will march through the forest to avoid detection and will take several days to get to Felting. They hope to attack before the city realizes their presence and sends for reinforcements.

I want to ensure Felting takes any necessary actions to stop him. Please communicate it with whoever you feel appropriate. I hope my actions redeem some of the mistakes I've made in the past, and I hope you can understand there is goodness in my heart.

Yours truly, Brixton

PS. I heard about Veron's death, and I want you to know I am truly sorry. Even though I fought him, he was always a loyal friend. I hope I can live to be half the man he was.

"What if it's a ploy?" Quincy asked with a red face. "Could they be baiting us into leaving Karondir defenseless so they can attack there?"

Wesley turned to Veron and lifted his eyebrows as if to pass the question along.

"I don't think so," Veron replied. "I know Brixton well, and I don't think that's what he's after."

The king nodded. "I agree. Karondir is strong enough to stand even with a mere hundred soldiers remaining." He turned to Quincy. "Send a bird to Karondir, immediately. Tell them we need ten thousand soldiers within two days. Then send word to the Council. I want a meeting tonight." Quincy bowed and left the room. The king turned back to Veron and Chelci. "Thank you for bringing this to me. I'm sorry we didn't act sooner, Veron. It wasn't that I didn't believe you, but we must be cautious when making decisions affecting the entire kingdom."

"I understand."

Returning to his chair, Wesley tapped his chin. "Why does Brixton think you're dead?"

Veron pursed his lips as he glanced at Chelci. "Oh . . . well, remember how I told you Bale wanted me dead?" The king nodded. "He sent men to kill me the other night at the Marlow house."

"I'm guessing they weren't successful?"

Veron let out a short laugh. "They thought I was dead. I believe that's why Bale is attacking now—because he thinks I'm gone."

The king leaned back and stared down his nose. Veron adjusted his stance, wishing the man would say something or look away.

"But you lived . . . when they thought you were dead. And now here you are, completely uninjured? Would it have anything to do with the medallion around your neck?" the king asked.

Veron's mouth turned up at the corner as his hand reflexively pressed against the metal object under his shirt. "How did you—"

"I noticed it the night we met in the library." The king leaned forward and extended his hand. "May I see it?"

Veron pulled the medallion out from the neck of his tunic and leaned forward to show the king.

"It's been many years since I've seen one of these," Wesley said with a laugh. "And I thought I never would again. I assume you got it from William?"

His father's name struck Veron like a thunderbolt. His heart thumped in his ears, and his breath grew shallow. "How did you know?"

The king laughed. "Veron *Stormbridge* asks me how I knew. The one with the medallion. The one who dies yet remains unscathed. Please. You said it yourself . . . I'm not *that* old. You look just like your father. So, you can use the origine?"

Veron barely managed a nod.

"Where did you learn it?"

"There was a man in Karad. His name was Artimus—"

"Artimus! How is the old man? Still having kids run around with boulders on their shoulders?"

Veron lowered his head. "He passed away two years ago."

Wesley's face sank. "Oh . . . I'm sorry. He was a good man."

"He was. He saved my life and taught me the ways of the Shadow Knights. Although for most of this season, I couldn't use the origine correctly . . . until a few days ago."

"Until we took the anklet off?" the king asked.

Veron's head shot up. "Yes! How did you know?"

"'Like a metal ring circulates the transfer of energy, your body must exhale its power.'"

Veron's eyes grew wide. "You know the book?"

"Some of it," the king admitted. "While I can't access the origine, I worked closely with the knights. Their training center was just down the street from the castle, but I didn't spend much time with them." Veron's eyes brightened at the mention of their training center. "The metal anklet you wore blocked your energy release. That's why shadow knights can't wear armor or any metal. It halts their abilities."

Veron exhaled a loud sigh of relief. "And I thought I was just losing it. That's great to know!"

"So, Bale wanted to kill you because he thought you were the last shadow knight. With you dead, the prophecy couldn't come true."

"Yeah, I guess," Veron said.

"How do you feel about dying?" Wesley asked.

"Dying?" Chelci asked, looking between the two, her brows knit together.

Veron winced. He had purposely not mentioned it to Chelci.

Wesley cocked his head. "The shadow knight who kills Bale dies in the process. It was foretold in the Dream."

Veron glanced at her, but Chelci's face was frozen. Her jaw was tight, and she stared ahead.

"You didn't tell her about the prophecy?" Wesley asked Veron in a lower voice.

"Chelci," Veron said as he put a hand on her shoulder. She quickly sloughed it off. "It's just an old Dream. It means nothing."

Her frozen exterior shattered as she turned to Veron and shouted, "It means nothing? Is that why you left part of it out?" Her reddened face hardened into sharp lines.

"I'm sorry. I didn't want to—"

"No!" she yelled, held up her hand, and stormed out of the room.

Stunned at the turn of events, Veron looked back to the king and ran his hand through his hair. "That didn't go over well," he said, unsure what to do next.

"What do you think you'll do about it?" Wesley asked.

"About Chelci? I don't know. Just give her time to cool down, I guess. We have bigger things to worry about at the moment."

Wesley walked around the desk. "A man who waits to conveniently address a problem will rarely find the time he needs."

"Yeah, but—"

"We have two days at least before they might arrive," Wesley said, gesturing his head in the direction Chelci ran. "If I've learned anything from the queen, it's that communication can solve a great deal."

"You think I should talk to her?" Veron asked. "Try to explain better?"

Wesley laughed. "I *do* think you should talk. But I suggest *listening* better—not explaining better." The king nodded his head toward the door. "Now, go find her before she gets lost in this place."

Veron left the room, jogging along the hall and down a set of stairs. *She could be anywhere!* He glanced into rooms as he passed, but she was nowhere to be found. When he poked his head into the room with the oval table, a figure on the balcony caught his eye. Chelci stood at the edge, gazing into the nothingness.

A breeze hit him as he passed through the archway. Veron approached with soft steps. "Chelci?" She flinched at her name but didn't turn. "I'm sorry I didn't tell you about the prophecy. I didn't want to worry you."

"You mean you didn't want to scare me off?" Chelci asked to the open sky.

Veron swallowed hard, and after a long moment of silence, she turned. "You're right," Veron said. "I think I was worried if you knew what was supposed to happen to me, you'd leave. I didn't think about how that might affect you, and I realize how selfish it was. To be honest, I don't know if it's true. It was just a woman's Dream, so it may not happen."

"Did your Dream come true?"

Veron pulled at his collar. "Um . . . I guess, mostly, but I thought I was going to die in that fight . . . and I didn't! Who knows what this woman actually saw about Bale." Chelci crossed her arms and maintained the tight look on her face. "I'm sorry my potential death is making you upset."

"You don't get it, Veron. Sure, I'm upset about the possibility of you dying, but I'm even more upset you didn't trust me to handle the information." Veron nodded, then looked down at his feet. Chelci stepped to him and rested her hand on his upper arm. "Veron . . ." She lifted his chin with her other hand to look into his eyes. "You are destined for great things. I knew that from the first night I met you. If someone told me you're the only person in all of Terrenor that could stop Bale, I wouldn't doubt it for a second. If that destiny meant you had to die . . . then I wouldn't want to miss a moment together until then."

Her words were soft, genuine. Her eyes pierced him, and a comforting warmth surged through Veron's body. He stepped in and wrapped his arms around her while Chelci hugged him back. Her head rested on his shoulder, and their bodies pressed together. Veron held tightly.

"I don't know how much time I have, but I agree with you," Veron said. "I don't want to miss a moment together, either."

40

Council Updates

Veron scanned the oval table as the Advisors Council members sat in silence. He had just finished reading Brixton's letter and waited for someone to speak.

"Sounds like a load of rubbish to me." Eldon Crone finally broke the silence. "It could have been written by anyone."

"I have to agree," High Lord Bilton added. "It could be a trap."

"What are you talking about?" Darcius Marlow said, hands wildly gesticulating. "This letter tells us everything we need to know—when they're going to be here, how they're going to arrive, their goals. Why would we *not* act on this?"

"Didn't you say the other day we could trust Raynor Fiero, Darcius?" Eldon asked. "Now you're saying it was all wrong?"

"Well, clearly . . . Yes!" Marlow replied. "This is new information!"

"I still insist Gareth Billings is no traitor," Bilton added.

"And how can we trust this *Brixton* fellow?" High Lord Hampton asked.

"I know Brixton," Veron said, raising his hand halfway. "I've known him for years."

"Great! Because the *gardener* knows him, we should deploy the entire kingdom at his word," Bilton said.

"Veron is a part of this council, just the same as you, Geoffrey," King Wesley said in a commanding voice.

"He's not the same," the High Lord of Defense muttered as he leaned against the back of his chair.

"So, if it's a ploy, what traps should we guard against?" the king asked. The table was quiet as the men glanced between each other.

Unsure if they understood the king's question, Veron spoke up. "You said it could be a trap. What type of trap might be possible?"

"I heard the question, *boy!*" Bilton snapped back.

"Karondir?" King Wesley offered. "You're worried about us leaving them unprotected?"

"Karondir should be fine," Bilton mumbled after a moment of silence.

"Then, what are the traps? What is the downside of responding to this information?" Wesley asked. Again, no one answered. "Karondir has ten thousand men on their way here who should arrive by Halfday." A few men nodded their heads, but several crossed their arms. "Bilton, do you have our defensive strategy ready?"

The High Lord of Defense nodded. "Of course, Your Majesty. We'll use the regular deployment along the water, the walls, and the gates. With the men from Karondir, we'll have *more* than enough."

"Make sure to prepare your men for anything," Veron said. "Bale is smart, and he's bound to come up with something unexpected."

"I'm tired of this *common servant* giving orders!" Bilton shouted as he pounded his fist on the table. "Who do you think you are that you know better than me!"

"I'm just saying . . . hubris can bring down even the most well-prepared army."

Bilton stood quickly, his chair scraping the stone floor as it pushed back. "That's it!" he shouted as he stormed around the end of the table.

"Geoffrey, this isn't necessary," Darcius Marlow said, standing and raising his hands to try and stop the High Lord of Defense. "Veron is just trying to help."

"Yeah? Put a sword in his hand, and I'll show you who's the greater warrior."

"You don't want to do that," Darcius said. "Trust me. I think he'd surprise you."

Bilton pulled his sword from his sheath and glared at Veron. "Oh, really? If you're such a great fighter, come and show me!"

Veron held his hands up. "I didn't say I was—"

"Bilton, come on," High Lord Hampton interrupted. "That would prove nothing. We all know you're the greatest swordsman in Feldor." He leaned toward the rest of the table and softly, sarcastically whispered. "At least that's what he tells us constantly."

The rest of the men laughed, and Bilton's face turned a bright shade of red. He breathed heavily as he stared at Veron, holding his sword out and waiting on a response.

The table fell silent as every man looked at Veron. His forehead pinched together. "I'm sorry if I've offended you, High Lord Bilton. As High Lord Marlow says, I'm only trying to help. I mean no disrespect. If I were able to defeat you, it wouldn't accomplish anything. I must decline."

Bilton howled with laughter. "You think you can defeat me? Come on Veron the Gardener. I think we'd all love to see that!"

Darcius Marlow leaned across the table. "Veron, you don't have to do this. You—"

King Wesley rested his hand on Marlow's arm, stopping him with a tight shake of his head. He glanced at Veron with a wry grin but didn't say anything. Veron looked back to Bilton, who stood with his chest heaving and sword held tightly. Suddenly, Bilton ran at him, and

Veron jumped out of his seat away from the man. A guard handed Veron a sword, which he took and extended toward the charging opponent.

Every man around the table exploded out of their seats. Chairs scraped as they moved out of the way and chattered unintelligibly. Bilton halted his charge and grinned broadly. He paced just out of Veron's reach and swung his sword vigorously several times. Veron held his sword out but stood firm, debating the ups and downs of winning versus losing.

"Take it easy on him, Geoffrey," High Lord Hampton said.

The men continued to mutter to each other as the swordsmen stared each other down. Veron glanced at the king. Wesley smirked and gave a tight nod. *Here we go then,* Veron thought.

Bilton moved first. With a grunt, he swung his heavy two-handed sword toward Veron's shoulder. Pulling a slight amount of origine, Veron deftly ducked under the strike. Bilton stumbled as his blade found nothing but air, but Veron didn't strike back. The high lord's face darkened instantly as he regained his stance. With a second grunt, he heaved the sword from the opposite side toward Veron's midsection. Veron jumped, bringing his feet over the swinging blade before landing softly.

Surprised gasps echoed around the table. "How'd he do that?" a man asked.

"Stop," Veron said. "There's no point to this."

"Are you going to fight?" Bilton asked. "Or are you going to avoid me? You probably don't even know how to use that thing!"

"I know how to use a sword," Veron said, annoyed. "I just—"

"Then show us!"

Veron groaned as he held the blade up. He lunged with enhanced speed. Bilton and the other men appeared like statues while Veron used his weapon, swinging to knock a knob off the high lord's belt.

His work done, he ducked out of reach and released the origine before Bilton even moved his sword. The High Lord's eyes bulged for a moment. He looked down just as his trousers—no longer supported by buttons or a belt—fell to the ground.

Cries of surprise and peals of laughter filled the room. Veron paled. "Oh no! I'm so sorry! We should stop. I didn't mean to—"

Bilton's face turned scarlet, and his jaw fixed into a hard line. "How dare you . . ." With his pants around his ankles, he moved forward with jerking steps as he flexed his arms and swung. "I'll teach you how to—"

Veron pulled heavily from the origine, and the entire room stopped. The advisors' faces were hardened in moments of shock or laughter. One side of Bilton's face was turned up in a snarl. His forearms rippled with enormous muscles frozen in stone. The blade of the sword had nearly reached Veron when he acted. Moving so quickly the men couldn't see, he pried Bilton's sword from his fingers and took it for himself. Armed with both weapons, Veron walked around the backside of the high lord and faced him as he released the energy.

Bilton's arm continued its arc without a weapon. He stumbled and glanced around frantically while the men around the table cried out in surprise.

"Behind you," Eldon Crone said in a wavering voice.

Bilton turned and inhaled sharply as he saw Veron. The whites of his eyes formed a complete circle as his hands shook. Men muttered quietly around the oval table.

Bilton's jaw wavered. "H—how did you—"

Veron didn't wait for the sentence to finish before he pulled from the origine one last time. He rushed in, a breath away from the high lord's face, and held both swords crossed against his neck. When he released the energy, the room was silent. For a moment, Veron wondered if he still used the origine, but Bilton's ragged breaths proved otherwise. The man extended his chin as he swallowed hard with a fixed jaw.

"I said, stop." Veron stared into the man's eyes. The others were slack-jawed and wide-eyed. A chuckle came from King Wesley at the end of the oval. He smiled, his head bouncing in time with the laughter.

Veron stepped back and relaxed the swords. He turned Bilton's sword around and extended the hilt. The high lord exhaled, and his chest deflated as he took his sword back, arm shaking. Veron handed his to the guard before heading back to his seat.

He plunked his hands down on the table with a thud as he turned to the king.

"Well," Wesley said in a cheery voice. "Where were we?"

The room exploded with questions. Veron glanced around but couldn't distinguish one voice from another. While the cacophony continued, High Lord Bilton shuffled around to his seat, holding his pants with one hand and sword with another.

Finally, Wesley held his hands up to regain control of the room. "Quiet down, men!"

Veron glanced around the table as the noise faded. Every pair of eyes settled on him as the men struggled to understand what they had seen.

"As you can see, Veron here is not merely a servant or a gardener. He is not a random person off the street. Veron is a shadow knight." Gasps echoed around the table. "He is the last one of the elite group of warriors, and he is the only one able to stop Edmund Bale."

Veron slid his hand down the smooth, stone wall. His feet felt like lead, unable to move. The Shadow Knights' training facility sat just down the street from the castle. His torch lit the rusted front door, hanging open a crack and beckoning him to enter. His heart thudded.

The Shadow Knights cloak rested heavily on his shoulders. Forcing his legs to move, Veron pushed the door, and its metal hinges creaked in protest. Veron glanced back to King Wesley, who wore plain brown linen clothes to blend in with a crowd on the street. Five soldiers stood several steps behind him.

"Go ahead," Wesley said, pointing his torch toward the door.

A musty smell filled Veron's nose as he stepped into a long hallway. Walking down it, he discovered sparse bedrooms adjoining the passage. The furniture was humble. Covered with dust and cobwebs, the beds and desks reminded him of the servants' rooms at the Marlow house.

Through an open doorway along the hall, Veron entered a large room filled with tables and shelves. *This must be the common room.* The long tables could seat sixteen or more people. A counter with shelves and an empty basin filled one wall. A quiet fireplace sat against the other one. Ashes sat undisturbed, where they'd likely remained for years. The empty room, glimmering from the torch, gave Veron an eerie feeling, and he shuddered as he hurried to leave.

As he reentered the hallway, Veron remembered Artimus' words about finding his father's body there outside the common room. He scanned the hall until his eyes locked on a pale stain. Approaching cautiously, he bent to touch the floor. The stone's grit rubbed harshly against his fingertips. The stain of blood, faded over time, brought a catch to his throat as his eyes watered. *Would this have been Father? Or maybe the men he took with him?*

"Is it what you expected?" Wesley asked, standing to the side, giving him space.

"It's—" Veron glanced around and froze as he looked at the bloodstain. "It's grim."

"We haven't used it since the attack."

"Did you know my father?"

"William?" Wesley said. "Not well. I knew who he was and what he looked like, but Artimus was the only one I met with regularly. Is this where he . . . ?"

"I think so," Veron said as he stared at the stain. "Did you see the bodies after the attack?"

The king shook his head. "My guards whisked me away after Artimus told us about the raid. Plus, we cleaned up in a hurry. We thought it best to keep the whole thing a secret."

"What do you mean?"

Wesley exhaled heavily. "I've always had a lot of opposition as king. The Shadow Knights played a large role in helping keep peace and order in the kingdom. They helped keep troublemakers in check." He hung his head. "We didn't want to broadcast the fact they were gone, so we covered up the attack. We had some soldiers take care of the bodies and kept it quiet."

Veron's eyes widened. "Is there a grave? Could I see it?"

The king shook his head. "They burned the bodies. I'm sorry." Veron clenched his jaw as he nodded. "Come on," Wesley said as he grasped Veron by the shoulders and led him along the hallway.

At the end of the passage, a door led to an outdoor courtyard. Dirt covered the ground of the square area. In the dark corner, two large, beat-up logs hung from chains. *This is where they trained!* Veron imagined ten men and women spread out in the courtyard, practicing their skills.

The king crossed the courtyard and climbed a flight of steps on the opposite side. Veron followed until they emerged on top of a short wall surrounding the center. The wind whipped against him, billowing his black cloak and rustling his hair as his torch flickered. Leaning against the wall, Veron gazed into the city dotted with lights.

"I miss the knights," the king said. "They helped enforce laws and quash uprisings. Ever since they died, I've felt Feldor steadily slipping away. Those problems you mentioned the other day? I see them every day, but I hit dead ends when I try to fix them."

Veron squirmed and avoided looking at the king. "I'm sorry for being so blunt when we met. If I'd known I was talking to you—"

"Don't apologize, Veron. You were right. Everything you said is something I want to change, but I need help. Around fifteen years ago, I enacted the Fair Wage Edict. It ensured we paid the people of the city a wage they could live by."

"It didn't work?"

The king scoffed. "Some people weren't happy about it. It worked for a while, despite the high lords' and merchants' criticisms. The Shadow Knights helped. They even thwarted a couple assassination attempts. Once the knights were gone, the opposition was too great. Employers didn't want to pay high wages because they wanted to keep the money for themselves, so they banded together against me. I could either revoke the edict or deal with the consequences."

"What consequences?"

"If they didn't kill me first, they were going to choose a new king, and *that* king would revoke it. Keep in mind, I'm not king for life—only as long as the high lords approve of me. I figured I might as well make the change myself. That way, at least I'd have a chance to try something new. Ever since then, I've been fighting uphill." Wesley turned around to look down into the courtyard. "One day, I'd love to see this courtyard filled with shadow knights again."

Veron felt a catch in his throat. "But if I'm supposed to die fighting Bale . . ." He trailed off, avoiding the thought.

"I know. It's just a wish," Wesley said before turning to Veron. "I'm not sure what's coming in the next few days, but I'm glad to have you here, Veron. Your father would have been proud to see you now."

Veron beamed at the compliment. His gaze drifted past the training center to the towering castle beyond. From its sides, the city wall spanned from river to river, defending the city from the north. Somewhere beyond the wall, Bale and his army headed toward him. Veron inhaled deeply and blew out a smooth, even breath. He had a destiny to fulfill, and he aimed to be ready.

41

Unexpected Discovery

ensen steadied himself with his staff as he padded through the woods. Finley followed behind, matching his steps. A branch snapped in the distant darkness, and the two halted. Bensen bent his ear toward the sound, but nothing rewarded his effort.

"Are you sure we haven't already covered this area?" Finley whispered after Bensen resumed walking.

"Yes, *again*, I'm sure," Bensen replied in a hushed voice and stepped over a fallen branch.

"I thought we'd passed that bog before."

"You're thinking of the one by the old live oak tree. We're at the eastern end of the swamp now."

"Ah, yes . . . you're right," Finley breathed. "They look so much alike."

"Except they're completely different," Bensen mumbled.

As he climbed over a rock, a noise came from the woods to the left. He crouched and held his hand back to stop Finley.

"I heard it, too," the young guardsman whispered.

Bensen raised his hand to his mouth in a cupped shape and whistled a lilting borrellbird call. After a tense moment of waiting, the call echoed back, slightly louder. "That is Brannon and Royce. Come on." Bensen continued walking straight.

"I don't see how you can all keep these sections straight," Finley said. "We'd be all over the map if I were leading."

"And that's why you're here with me." Bensen slowed as they approached a steep rise, leading up a rocky ridge.

"Do we have to climb up there?" Finley craned his neck and trudged along.

"We will, but not yet. First, we need to check out the cave."

"Cave? What . . . Ridgeback Cave?"

"I think that's what you kids call it," Bensen said.

"I used to love exploring there when I was little." Finley stopped with a shuffle of his feet. "Wait. You don't think the valcor's in there, do you?"

"We won't know until we check."

"I'm *pretty* sure someone checked weeks ago."

"And we're going to check again." Bensen felt along the rocky wall as he traversed along the slope. Eventually, his hand sank into a depression at waist level. He'd found what he wanted. "You want to go?"

Finley's eyes seemed to glow in the moonlight as his lids opened wide. "Seriously? Do I *want* to go?"

"You *do* have *two* legs, you know."

Finley glanced down at his legs. "Yeah, but . . ."

Bensen sighed after a moment of silence. He tossed his staff against the rock wall and took the coiled rope off his shoulders, setting it on the ground. "Fine. I'll go. Hold this."

Finley held a candle while Bensen lit it using flint. The light glowing, he bent to his knees and shuffled to the entrance. The cave's opening stretched barely as wide as his shoulders.

Sliding face-first with the candle in front of him and his sword scraping the rock, Bensen wormed his way through the narrow opening. He heavily favored his left side and pushed his body along with his good leg as his warm breath bounced off the rock walls. After a bit, the passage opened, and he was able to stand, using the wall to steady his footing.

Bensen held the candle in front of him. The inadequate light barely illuminated the area around him while blackness lurked just out of the flame's reach. A musty scent filled his nose as he breathed in deeply. Somewhere beyond the light, a steady drip fell into a puddle. Around him, rock and mud covered the floor and walls.

"There's no way a valcor could fit through here," Finley huffed as he pulled himself through the tight area and rolled into the open space.

"You'd be surprised what animals can squeeze through," Bensen said as he took a few more steps deeper into the darkness.

"Do we need to search this whole place?"

Bensen extended his arm and panned around. "No. If the valcor came in, we would already know."

"Because . . . it would have eaten us by now?" Finley asked, his voice quivering.

Bensen chuckled. "No. Because we would have smelled it. Let's go . . . back outside."

"Argh! Why did I crawl through there if we're just turning back around?"

"I never said you had to follow me."

The cold hit as Bensen exited the cave. After the tight crawl, he wiped the sweat off his forehead and pulled his village guard uniform closer to ward off the chill. He blew out the candle, grabbed his rope and staff, then looked diagonally up the rocky slope. "Let's go."

It was difficult to stay quiet as the two summited the ridge. Finley panted heavily, preventing Bensen from hearing any noise from the surrounding woods. Loose rocks skittered down the slope, announcing their presence to any beings in the area. When they finally arrived at the top, Bensen continued without resting.

"Do you . . . think we'll . . . find it tonight?" Finley asked between breaths.

"Shhh," Bensen whispered, putting a finger to his lips. "You've got to be quieter."

"Sorry," Finley whispered back. "But . . . do you?"

Bensen dropped down off the end of a large, flat boulder and kept walking. "It's the third night in a row we've searched, and we haven't found it yet."

"So, our chances aren't good?"

"Our chances get better every night because of the grid the teams are using. It's got to be out here somewhere, and eventually, we'll find it."

"Unless it moves around," Finley said. "You know . . . Every night in a different hiding place—avoiding the areas we're about to search."

"I think you're giving it too much credit. We start from its old nest at the molopyr tree and search the woods in sections—five groups each night—as many nights as it takes," Bensen said as he stopped, resting his hand on a thick tree trunk.

"What's this?" Finley asked. "A special tree?"

"This is the end of our grid. Now, we head back." Bensen passed Finley at an angle, returning to the side of the path they just traveled.

After a few minutes walking, they arrived back at the top of a different part of the ridge. The moon lit up the smooth, precarious path down. "Keep your body low," Bensen said, using his staff as he crouched and shuffled down the slope.

Finley followed, continually knocking loose rocks that bounced off Bensen before continuing their journey down the ridge.

"So, you think we're gonna find it soon," Finley said. "What are we actually gonna do with it?" Bensen tried to ignore the question and focus on his footing, but Finley was insistent. "I mean . . . you fought it with two legs and almost died, and you're one of our best swordsmen. How are you and I supposed to kill this thing? You only have one leg!"

"Don't worry about that," Bensen said. "We need to find it first."

Finley nervously laughed. "Uh . . . yeah, but . . . *that's* worrying to me."

"When we find it, I'll take care of it."

"I don't mean to be rude, but . . . that thing ripped your leg off with its monster claw. Your sword just bounced off it, right?"

"Yeah, but Chelci found a way."

"Okay, sure . . . We'll make sure to ignore its massive body and dodge its claws of death and only stab *inside* of its mouth."

"As I said . . . I'll take care of it."

Suddenly, Bensen stiffened. He heard something and paused, his body angled on the slope. Rocks somewhere in the distant darkness tumbled down the ridge.

"What's that?" Finley whispered. A group of voices carried over the barren rocky incline. "Is that Royce and—"

"Shhh," Bensen hushed. "No one from our village would be out here." On the opposite side, more voices carried down the slope. "Come on. Let's get down."

Bensen resumed his downward climb at a quicker pace. When they had almost arrived at the bottom, rocks bounced down the ridge from directly above, and Bensen gave up any attempt at a slow, careful descent.

When they arrived at the flat ground at the bottom of the ridge, men's voices surrounded them. Bensen spun, considering who they could be and wondering the best path to take.

"They're all around us," Finley whispered. "Who do you think they—"

"Hey!" a rough voice shouted as three men emerged from the darkness.

Bensen spun in their direction. The men wore matching red-and-black soldier uniforms laden with weapons and packs of gear. They looked tired, as if they'd traveled a long distance. All three unsheathed their swords simultaneously.

"Get behind me," Bensen ordered Finley, who complied without argument. The instructor drew his weapon and leaned on his staff as he stared down the men.

"Kill them," one of the soldiers ordered.

Bensen dropped his staff and held his sword with both hands, crouching on one knee. His wooden leg prevented full movement, but he could still fight. The men advanced.

Bensen knocked a sword out of the way and dispatched the first man with a quick jab to the gut. The second traded a few blows until Bensen hit his weapon away and scored him across the chest. Meanwhile, Finley engaged the third soldier. He backpedaled while the man in red and black pummeled him until Bensen stabbed the attacker in the side. The man cried out as he fell. While the three bodies writhed on the ground, inquisitive voices shouted from every direction.

Bensen spun, but there was no way out. "Hurry," he said, picking up his staff and loping along the bottom of the ridge as quickly as he could while holding his sword at the ready.

Another soldier materialized from the darkness. "Hey, who are—" he started with a growl before Bensen cut him off with a quick strike from his sword.

Bensen scraped the rock face with his staff as he hurried.

"Find them! We can't leave them alive!" a voice shouted behind him. Bensen glanced over his shoulder where two torches approached through the gloom.

Panic crept in as Bensen sensed soldiers hemming them in. *Come on, where are you?* he thought as he reached out to feel the rock. A torch ahead signified there was nowhere to go. Suddenly, his hand felt the depression.

"Go! Get in!" he shouted to Finley, who hit the ground and immediately began to crawl. Bensen spun, watching the torches approach while he waited for Finley's legs to clear. When the soldiers had nearly arrived, he knelt to the ground and dove headfirst into the black space. After a few moments of frantic pulling and writhing, he sensed the room open up. Bensen rolled away from the tight entryway and collided with Finley, who didn't protest. He lifted his sword and turned toward where he came from, but the room's pitch blackness wouldn't confirm exactly where to look.

"Where'd they go?" a voice said, bouncing through the cave opening.

"I heard 'em just a moment ago."

Bensen panted and tried to remain quiet. Slowly, a red glow materialized in the narrow passageway ahead.

"Whoa! Do you think they went in here?" a voice asked, causing Bensen to clench his jaw.

"Yeah, I bet they're hiding. Go find them and kill them."

"Are you crazy? I'm not crawling through there."

"What? Are you afraid?"

"I don't think I can fit. If you're so brave, why don't *you* go?"

Neither voice spoke for a moment. Bensen trained his ear, listening for the sound of a body scraping its way through the tunnel, but nothing came.

"We don't even know they're in there."

"You're right. They probably went somewhere else."

Bensen laughed to himself. *They don't want to be run through with a sword while stuck in a tiny passage.*

"Come on," a new voice said. "Leave 'em."

Bensen and Finley deeply exhaled. Footsteps outside the cave sounded for a moment then faded as the red glow gradually disappeared. Bensen made them wait. When he felt it had been long enough, he went first, squeezing his way out. Leading with his sword, he paused when his head poked outside to listen. *Nothing. The soldiers are gone.*

Bensen and Finley approached the molopyr tree where four groups of guardsmen milled about, waiting on them. A lone torch lit the space, resting in the crook of a branch. Bensen shuddered. He remembered almost nothing about the night of the attack weeks before, yet being near the tree still made him sweat.

"It's about time," Russell said. "We were about to go after you."

"You see anything?" Aleks asked.

"No valcor, but we did run into an army of Norshewan soldiers," Bensen replied. The men around all quieted and stared.

"Norshewans?" Russell repeated. "What were they doing?"

"Marching through, it seemed. None of you saw them?" The crowd of men looked between each other and shook their heads.

"How many?" Russell asked.

"There was no way to know. It was too dark. At least hundreds . . . possibly thousands."

"Why would they be here?" Aleks asked.

"How would they *get* here?" Royce added.

Bensen shrugged and looked at Russell. "Marching to Felting, I guess. They must have come from the north."

"Where our hunters disappeared," Russell added after a pause. "Are you two alright?"

Bensen glanced at Finley before nodding. "Yeah, we're fine."

"Bensen and I took out six of them with our swords," Finley said. "Then we hid in a cave while dozens tried to get to us, but they were too afraid and gave up."

"So, what do we do about them?" Aleks asked.

"Norshewans on this side of the mountains is a bad omen," Bensen said, looking at Russell with eyebrows lifted.

Both men stared for a long moment until Russell finally spoke. "We don't do anything," he said. "We don't bow to the crown of Feldor. They don't protect us, and we don't pay taxes to them. It's not our problem. Come on. Back to the village."

Bensen gazed toward the dark woods to the south. He gripped his sword's hilt, breathed deeply, and exhaled. Finally, he turned to follow the rest of the men back to Nasco.

42

War Drums

Veron sat at the oval table dressed in his Shadow Knights cloak. The fabric fell loosely from his shoulders and draped to the floor. He leaned forward in his chair to give space for Farrathan, resting in its sheath over his shoulder.

The glances coming his direction carried a fear and respect he'd not seen in previous Advisory Council meetings. Quincy Hilliard and Eldon Crone sat close to the king, as if proximity would make him weigh their input more heavily. High Lord Bilton paced to the side, avoiding any eye contact with Veron.

"So, how many do we have now?" King Wesley asked.

"Nearly ten thousand have arrived from Karondir, the last trailing in this morning. That brings us to around eighteen thousand able-bodied men," Bilton said.

"Good . . . Good. Any sign of Bale yet?"

"No, Your Majesty. The roads are empty, and our scouts have spotted nothing in the woods."

"I still don't like it," Eldon said. "We moved most of Karondir's defenses because of a letter, and no one's even seen the enemy yet."

Veron bristled at the advisor's dismissive attitude. "Would you rather wait until the army arrives and *then* come up with a plan?" he asked pointedly.

"I think we've been wise to take the steps we have," the king said.

The others did not argue, and Veron sat a little taller in his seat. "When they arrive, they'll attack quickly," Veron said.

"I agree," Quincy chimed in. "They're expecting the element of surprise on their side and won't give us the chance to mobilize or gather reinforcements."

"We'll be ready," Bilton said in a low voice.

Wesley stood. He looked antsy, as if tired of waiting. "How are the men deployed?" he asked as he walked to the center archway. Deep shades of red and purple lit up the late afternoon sky through the opening.

"Three thousand guard the docks," Bilton said. "We *hope* they'll attempt to breach the city there. If so, it will be a quick battle. Ten thousand line the walls, and the remaining soldiers wait just inside the gates."

"Is there a chance they lay siege and wait us out?" Eldon asked.

Bilton shook his head. "It's unlikely. The rivers and land are too much to guard. Plus, they'd expect us to send word to Karondir and Tarphan as soon as they arrived. While waiting on us to give up, twenty thousand men would quietly surround them."

"Men! Come!" King Wesley said sternly, facing the balcony.

The words' authority sent a shiver through Veron. He rose with the others and walked to the balcony. Stepping outside, his stomach dropped as he took in the sight. Men streamed from the woods. The gleam of metal reflected the setting sun as the ranks formed into tight lines facing Felting's wall.

The other two advisors' jaws hung slack. "They're here," Eldon said in a wavering voice.

Wesley turned to Veron. "Where's the best place for a shadow knight?"

Veron set his jaw, preparing for the eventuality of facing Bale. "As long as they're outside the city, I thought I could walk the walls and help where needed?" He glanced at Bilton. "If that's okay with you, High Lord?"

Bilton lifted his chin and returned the gaze for a long moment. "Of course. We welcome the help."

The king nodded. "See to it, then."

Bilton's eyes narrowed as he looked past the walls. "Is that it?" he asked. The stream of soldiers had stopped. They formed into ranks, and Bilton moved his mouth silently as if counting in his head. "There can't be over five thousand."

"That doesn't make sense," the king said. "Didn't they have at least eight thousand? What about the five from Karad? If they're attacking together, shouldn't they have around thirteen thousand?"

"How would they expect to get in?" Quincy asked. "They can't breach the gates with such a meager force."

"In Karad, Fiero let them in the walls through a secret gate," Veron said. "Are there any secret entrances?"

"Yes, there is one in Felting," King Wesley said. "But Fiero and Billings wouldn't have access to it."

"If their force is so small, maybe they aren't aligned with Karad after all?" Eldon sneered.

Veron's heart raced. *What are they up to? Where would the rest of the men be?*

"I bet they don't even attack," Eldon added. "They're probably a distraction while the larger portion heads to Karondir!"

King Wesley stepped closer to the edge, narrowing his eyes as he stared. The group was silent as the wind whipped across the balcony. Veron strained his ears as a sound slowly built. At first, it was too muffled and distant to make out, but soon, it was unmistakable. The deep thrum of war drums echoed against the stone walls. A chant built as the Norshewan soldiers joined in, beating their weapons against the ground.

"Send the word, Bilton," the king said. "Close the gates. Ready the men. It begins." Bilton scurried through the archway, shouting orders.

"I'll go to the walls," Veron said.

The king nodded solemnly. "If you run into Bale . . ." Wesley paused as Veron's stomach turned. "Good luck."

The city wall was thick. Men lined the front of the battlements, three to every crenel with more behind. The line of blue-and-gray Feldor uniforms stretched as far as Veron could see while he walked along. Ahead of him, a tower rose above the main gate. Dressed in the Shadow Knights cloak with his sword slung on his back, men stepped aside as he approached. While appearing confident, his stomach roiled as he climbed the narrow stairs to the tower.

At the top, older men twice his size continued to make way as Veron walked to the front. He placed both hands on the ancient stone wall and stared ahead. Bale's army looked larger from near the ground. The drums continued to pound, and the men chanted, but so far, no attack came. *Where is Bale?* he thought as he scanned the ranks. The men were too far away to tell.

Veron turned to the dozens of men manning the tower. "Where are you all from?" he asked the group closest to him.

"Karondir, sir. I just arrived this morning," the first soldier said in a thick accent. The rest replied in turn.

"Karondir."

"Here in Felting, sir."

"Felting."

"Karondir."

Veron walked closer to the group. "What's your name?" he asked the first man.

"Jamie, sir."

"How long have you been in the army, Jamie?"

"Six years. Baron Devenish himself trained me."

Jamie's beard reminded Veron of someone from Karad, which helped him realize how important their mission was. They weren't only defending Felting. All of Feldor and even Terrenor was in jeopardy.

"Veron," a voice said, turning him around.

"High Lord Bilton!"

The high lord walked out of the mass of men and peered over the front of the wall, avoiding eye contact as he spoke. "I've been harsh on you the last week, and I'm sorry. You were right, and I'm glad to have you here."

"I'm glad to help," Veron said, basking in the acceptance as he stood slightly taller. "So, what do you think about this?" he asked, waving toward the opposite army.

Bilton breathed quickly through his nose. "Unless they have double this hiding in the woods, defending the walls should be simple. What do you plan to do if they attack?"

Veron looked around. "I'll do what I can. I'll stay on the walls for now."

"The men are in awe of you," Bilton said, nodding toward the other soldiers. "Word travels fast. To most of them, shadow knights are a thing of legends." Veron noted the men around him. Mouths hung open and several whispered between themselves. "Would you say something?"

"Say something?" Veron repeated.

"To the men," Bilton motioned around them. "Usually I would, but I think they would find you inspiring."

Veron nodded and looked around. To maximize visibility, he jumped onto the edge of the wall and steadied himself against the merlons with his back to Bale's army. "Men of Felting, thank you for standing up to defend your city," he said in a loud enough voice to be heard, even over the drumming. "Men of Karondir, thank you for coming. Edmund Bale is an enemy who does not know mercy. He is bent on conquering this land and turning us all into mere pawns for him and his empire. This must not happen!" Veron grew increasingly bold as he spoke. Many of the soldiers nodded their heads and shouted in approval.

"I've met Bale," Veron projected his voice even louder. Men from the lower walls looked up toward the tower. "I looked him in the eyes, and you know what I learned? He's scared! He's afraid of death and defeat! He's merely a man, and you have the advantage! You hold the walls secure and outnumber them three to one! But don't for a second think they won't put up a fight, because they will! So when they come—and come they will—stand your ground. Let's turn these invaders away . . . for your families! For yourselves! And for Feldor!"

The soldiers roared. They waved their swords and clanged them against their shields. For a moment, the rousing cry of Felting drowned out the sound of the Norshewan army. Veron smiled broadly as he looked at the men. They were strong, ready.

Bilton nodded slowly with a reserved smile. "Thank you for being here," he said before clapping Veron on the shoulder and turning to leave.

As the men's cries died down, a new sound sent chills through Veron. A piercing horn sounded from the opposing forces. Veron turned around, propping one foot on the top of the wall. The sea of black, red, and silver below moved as one, beginning with slow, deliberate steps before speeding up to a run as they approached the wall.

Veron reached over his shoulder and slowly removed Farrathan from its sheath. Holding the sword with both hands, Veron stood in a crouch and waited for the army below.

Chelci jerked her head to the sound when the drums began. They were distant but strong.

"The army's arrived," her father said.

Chelci picked at her plate. She had eaten a few small greens and nibbled a piece of bread, but her mind was elsewhere. Veron was out there . . . somewhere. *I know he can handle himself, but . . . if that prophecy is accurate . . .* She tried all day to steady her mind, but the drums made distraction impossible.

"I'm sure he'll be okay," Morgan said after swallowing a chunk of bread. "If I've learned one thing from the six years I've known Veron, it's that he always comes out on top."

"It seems like you made it here just in time, Morgan," her father said. "You wouldn't have been able to get in the city now."

"I'm lucky. I traveled as quickly as I could. Thank you again for taking me in, High Lord Marlow. I doubt grocers are your usual guests," Morgan said. "I'm eager to work hard, but until I get established, your hospitality is much appreciated."

Darcius fixed his mouth into a line and nodded. "My daughter and Veron have taught me a lot in a short amount of time. Chiefly among them is to not overlook someone based on what they do."

There was a commotion outside the dining room, and all three heads veered in that direction. In a moment, the door flew open, and an out-of-breath, soaking-wet young man with blond hair entered the room.

"Brixton!" Chelci yelled as she stood. "What are you doing here?"

"I'm sorry, he burst past me," Jensen said, trying to pull the young man back.

"It's okay, Jensen," Darcius said, dismissing the servant.

"I'm so sorry to burst in, but I had to—" Brixton stopped mid-sentence when his eyes landed on the middle-aged man sitting next to Chelci. "Morgan?"

"Brixton," the grocer said coldly.

Brixton's mouth remained slack, having seemed to lose his line of thought.

"It's over between us, Brixton," Chelci said, crossing her arms. "I will not be marrying you."

"You—" Brixton's forehead creased as he reeled. "That's . . . That's okay. It's not why I'm here. Morgan, how are you—?"

"Wait!" Chelci yelled. "How did you get into the city? I'm sure all the gates are blocked."

"I swam the river and climbed a wall. Then I came straight here."

"What wall?"

"Chelci, stop it! There's no time!" Brixton yelled, silencing everyone in the room as he continued to pant. "Did you get my letter?"

"Yes . . . I did. Thank you for that. I warned the king."

"Good. It's not enough, though. Bale is here, and he's changed his plan. King Wesley won't be prepared."

"They received reinforcements from Karondir," Darcius said. "The city is well fortified. How will they not be prepared?"

"Originally, *I* was supposed to let them in," Brixton said to Darcius. "Apparently, there's some . . . secret gate or something. They wanted me to threaten to kill Chelci unless you showed me where it was and unlocked it." Chelci stiffened and leaned closer to Morgan, prompting Brixton's eyes to grow wide. "I'm not doing it!" he blurted as he took a step backward and held his hands up. "I don't even *want* to know if there's a gate. But I was with them in camp when I overheard them talking."

"Talking about their plans?" Darcius asked.

"Yes. I thought I could thwart them by relinquishing my role, but apparently, they made other arrangements as a backup."

"Which are . . . ?"

"They have someone on the inside. Edgar . . . Edwin . . . something with an E . . . Crone."

"Eldon Crone?" Darcius said.

Brixton's eyes lit up. "Yes! That's him! I'm not sure who he is, but if I can't let the army in, Crone's supposed to assassinate the king."

Chelci gasped.

"Eldon is one of Wesley's top advisors," Darcius said. "I'm sure he's with him right now. The king needs to hear this!"

"Can you warn him?" Brixton asked.

"Yes, I can," Darcius pushed his chair back and stood. "And you're coming with me. Chelci, Morgan, stay here, and don't leave the house! I'll be back soon."

The ground rumbled as the army ran toward them. All around Veron, soldiers unleashed arrows from the ramparts that whistled as they sought their targets below. Several found their marks, but most landed harmlessly in the dirt. The invaders continued. When they arrived at the wall, ladders emerged from the ranks and quickly slung against the top of the battlements. Veron jumped back from the wall to avoid getting hit as one rammed against the tower.

Using the smallest bit of origine, Veron lifted the hooks that had fallen to hold it in place and pushed the ladder. The wooden structure flung through the air, sending the men flying to the ground below. Behind him, two other ladders leaned against the wall, and the Felting soldiers struggled to free the hooks and knock them down.

"Move!" Veron shouted as he quickly slid in front of one. Again, he lifted the hooks and flung the ladder through the air. On the opposite side of the tower, a Norshewan soldier arrived at the top. Felting defenders jabbed at the man but kept missing. *Come on, guys.* When Veron arrived, he cut the man down with one swing from his sword. The ladder jerked as his blade splintered the wood. Veron glanced down to see five men hanging from the rungs, fighting to hold on. Using his sword to hit it again, the ladder spun sideways, and they all fell to the ground.

"Come on, men! Knock the ladders down as soon as they arrive!" Veron yelled to the men, frustrated he was the only one who seemed able. He glanced at the lower walls. The men below struggled. Several Norshewan soldiers had already breached the top, and the Felting soldiers ineptly fought back.

Veron leaped from the top. The wind pulled his cloak, flapping behind him as he fell. He crashed with strengthened legs on the narrow stone battlement. Feldorian and Norshewan soldiers alike froze, stunned at his abrupt arrival, but Veron didn't hesitate. He spun, knocking down every red-and-black uniform in sight with his sword. Dodging between the fellow defenders, he ran along the wall, pushing back each and every ladder.

Finally pausing to catch his breath, Veron looked behind as he panted. The wall was clear of enemies for the moment, but in the field beyond, the soldiers continued to advance. Shouting filled the air, and some enemy movement caught his eye. Soldiers parted as a clump of men carrying a large battering ram ran toward the tower. Inside the walls, a mass of Feldorians stood behind the gate, pressing against the wooden doors.

An earth-shaking crash filled the air and shook the structure underneath his feet. Veron reached out to steady himself and keep from falling. The gate's massive wooden crossbar splintered, sending the defenders reeling. *On their first ram? How is that possible?*

After running down the stairs, Veron sheathed his sword and sprinted down the stone street to the gate. "What happened? How did it break?" he shouted to a man with a thick beard with his back pressed against the door.

"I don't know!" the man shouted back. "Some men just left to grab the spare! We never thought we would need it! Help us until they get back!"

Veron leaned into the wooden doors just as a second crash landed on the other side. Even with the origine, the force knocked him and the others onto the stone street. Quickly, they scrambled to their feet and leaned again into the door.

"We can't hold it!" the bearded man yelled. "They're gonna break through!"

Veron steadied his breath. He knew what they needed. As he left the door, the bearded man called to him. "Come back! We need everyone!"

Veron looked at the man. "Get the new brace. I'll buy you time." The bearded man's eyes slowly widened as Veron faced the wall steps and ran, taking them two at a time. He pumped his legs, propelling him to the top. He heard his breath as he tuned out the rest of the battle. When he hit the top step, Veron pushed off with all the strength he could muster and pulled his sword out of its sheath. His momentum sent him sailing over the top into the air beyond.

Veron's stomach jumped as he fell toward the earth. Thousands of soldiers, wearing armor and brandishing weapons, waited below. The company holding the battering ram readied to attack but faltered when they spotted him flying through the air.

When Veron hit the earth, the impact's shock knocked over the nearby men, and his sword went to work. The Norshewans fell quickly, unable to react to his lightning-fast attacks. He ducked under an axe and stabbed its bearer in the chest. An arrow whizzed toward him, but he dodged and grabbed the arrow out of the air. Holding it by its shaft, he stabbed it into the vulnerable neck of the closest enemy. When the entire battering ram company had fallen, he still continued his attacks. His muscles were taut and head was clear. Every swing of his sword sent multiple men flying. He stabbed and twirled, leaving a field of blood and bodies in his wake. A sweet stench rose from the field, multiplied by his enhanced senses, and a hint of copper settled on his tongue. When he finally paused to breathe, the Norshewan soldiers kept their distance. Veron stood between them and the gate, but no one dared approach.

"We're good!" a muffled voice called through the gate. "The beam is in place!"

Veron bolstered his legs to jump. When he landed back on the wall, the surrounding men simply stared. Their swords dangled limply, and their jaws hung slack. Veron gave a slight nod as he walked down the stairs, gasping for breath to slow his pounding heart.

He crossed the street to lean against the opposing building. Resting his head against the wall, he took several deep breaths before focusing on the fight again. On the battlements, Norshewan soldiers arrived once more from new ladders, and the men from Felting struggled to push them back. Invaders struck down several blue-and-gray uniforms. Some defenders turned and ran. Veron clenched his jaw. *What are they running for? They hold an elevated position against a vastly outnumbered enemy!*

A growing yell drew his attention to the gate just before the wooden structure shuddered under the weight of another attack. Like before, the large wooden brace shattered, and the gate behind hung askew. *What's wrong here? How are they entering so easily?*

Veron glanced atop the tall tower over the gate. Freshly placed ladders leaned against the wall and a stream of Norshewans surmounted the top. Jamie, the familiar soldier he spoke with, was still there. He pushed against the attackers, but it did little good. *It's like they're not even trying.* Jamie lunged and stabbed with his sword. *What is he—?*

Veron froze. A thought as sharp as a bolt of lightning hit him. His breath caught then quickly became ragged. The blood pulsing through his body felt like ice, and his stomach turned as the pieces came together.

Oh, no! We're in trouble! Veron staggered away from the wall before he turned and ran.

43

Plans Exposed

Brixton followed Darcius Marlow as they wound their way through the castle. Dead faces in paintings frowned at him as they passed. Brixton shrugged off the uneasy feeling as he struggled to keep up.

Twenty armed men followed—Felting soldiers they picked up as they approached the castle. Darcius said it was wise to have support.

As they climbed the stairs, Brixton began to sweat. *I wonder if this Eldon person will even be there? Am I doing the right thing?* His stomach turned as he considered the consequences of betrayal.

After crossing a long hall, Darcius led them into a large chamber with an oval table. Passing the table, they walked outside through an archway to a balcony. The sun had nearly set, and a reddish glow covered the city below. Brixton swallowed hard as he took in the sight of the attacking army pressing against the city walls.

"Darcius, what is this?" The voice drew Brixton's attention. A man that could only be King Wesley stood, surrounded by two older men. The king's eyes scanned the soldiers as they spread out on the balcony. "What's going on?"

Brixton tried to shrink back to the wall, but his feet remained frozen solid. *It's too late to back out now.*

Veron burst into the sitting room, and Chelci and Morgan jumped. Chelci's sword hung on her hip, and her hand instinctively moved to grab it.

"We've got to go!" Veron said.

"What's wrong?" Morgan asked, setting down a candlestick he had grabbed.

"What happened?" Chelci added.

Veron breathed heavily as he rushed to explain. "It's the soldiers. There's no time. The city is lost. We've got to leave."

"What do you mean?" Chelci asked. "What's wrong with the soldiers?"

Veron exhaled slowly to steady himself. "The soldiers are fighting with Bale." Chelci and Morgan stared blankly. "The Feldorian soldiers . . . inside Felting . . . are fighting with Bale," Veron clarified.

Morgan's brow wrinkled. "What do you mean? How's that possible?"

"Father said most arrived this morning from Karondir," Chelci said. "How would they be fighting with Bale?"

Veron shook his head. "The men who arrived. The ten thousand reinforcements we received . . .They're not from Karondir. They're from Karad."

Silence filled the room.

"They're from Karad?" Morgan repeated. "How do you know?"

"I recognized one of them," Veron said. "I couldn't place him at first, but I'm sure he's a soldier from Karad."

"But that doesn't mean for sure that—"

"They're not fighting, either."

"What do you mean?" Chelci said.

"They're not even trying. They're allowing Norshewa over the walls and through the gate. The men act as if they're fighting for Feldor, but they're not. I even saw one stab another soldier from Felting when he thought no one was looking."

"But how is that possible? Father said they sent birds to Karondir, and they—"

"I bet you they never made it."

"You're saying Bale's army was ready and intercepted the birds? But how would they even know we would—" Chelci stopped as her eyes grew. "Brixton!"

Veron nodded. "Exactly. His letter wasn't to warn us to get reinforcements. It was to give the Karad and Norshewan army an excuse to be invited inside the walls, posing as relief from Karondir."

"Oh, no!" Chelci said. "King Wesley!"

"The king will be evacuated as soon as they realize the walls have fallen. He'll be alright." Veron beckoned them with his hand. "Come on. Let's go!"

"Veron, we've got bad news," Morgan said. "Brixton was here."

"What? What did he want? Where is he?"

Morgan and Chelci exchanged a glance. "Father took him to see the king," Chelci said.

Veron blinked several times, then snapped into motion. "I've got to go, now! You two, wait here and stay safe. I'll be back as soon as I can."

"What's going on? Where are you going?" Chelci asked.

"I've got to stop Brixton," Veron said.

"Stay with us," Chelci said, pulling on his sleeve. "Brixton's given us enough grief. Let him be."

Morgan nodded along. "Yeah, he's going to expose a traitor. Chelci's father will make sure nothing bad happens."

"He's not going to expose a traitor," Veron said, his voice turning low as he locked eyes with Morgan. "Brixton's going to kill the king."

Veron turned from their stunned looks and ran. Chelci's voice called after him as he exited the house and descended the front steps. He glanced over his shoulder to see her emerge from the front door, running after him.

"Go back, Chelci! Stay with Morgan!"

"No," she yelled without breaking stride. "I'm coming with you." Her sword swung at her hip, and her eyes held a fierce determination.

Veron sighed as he slowed for a moment and allowed her to catch up. Truthfully, he was glad to have her. The two turned up the drive and ran toward the castle.

Brixton fought to keep his legs from shaking as he stared at the men and soldiers around him on the balcony.

"You've been betrayed, Your Majesty," Darcius Marlow said, out of breath from the steep climb.

"Betrayed? What do you mean?" the king replied.

"One of your closest men has deceived you." Darcius stared at the advisors. "Should I tell him, Eldon, or would you like to?"

The older advisor's face twisted as he glanced at the others turning to him. "I don't know what he's talking about!" he said as he took a step away.

Darcius stepped forward. "He's been working with Bale."

A scoff erupted from Eldon. "Preposterous!"

"He was going to kill you, Your Majesty," Darcius added. Eldon's jaw dropped as he stared back at the high lord.

"Is this true, Eldon," the king asked.

"No! He's making this up!"

Darcius looked to Brixton. "Tell them, Brixton."

Brixton swallowed hard as all eyes turned to him. "Um . . . It's true," he said shakily. "I've been spying on Bale, and I heard him speaking about the plan. Eldon Crone was going to kill you, Your Majesty."

Several Felting soldiers surrounded the advisor and held him tight. "This is absurd!" Eldon yelled. "I demand proof!"

A soldier pulled a long knife from a sheath hidden on Eldon's hip, underneath his clothes. "What's this?" King Wesley asked as the soldier handed him the weapon.

"That's my knife!" Eldon protested. "I *always* carry it with me!"

"You disgust me, Eldon," Darcius said as he got into his face. "And to think of all the years you've sat in that room and advised—"

The high lord's words were cut short as Eldon freed his hands and forcefully pushed him. Darcius fell to the stone and skidded away, grimacing in pain. The soldiers recaptured the free arms and tightened their grip on the advisor.

"Are you okay?" Brixton said, extending his arm to help the high lord up.

"Yes, I'm fine," Darcius said.

Brixton leaned in close, while the rest of the men's attention focused on the advisor. "Don't speak. Get ready to run," he whispered urgently into Darcius's ear.

The high lord's face twitched in a tight expression as his brows narrowed. "What do you—"

"Shhh! I mean it! Get ready!"

None of the other men paid attention as Brixton walked slowly backward, holding Darcius' confused gaze. Turning around, he took in the scrambled confusion of soldiers, advisors, and the king shouting insults at each other, but the words never reached him. His mind was a muddled mess of thoughts and screams. A dryness covered his throat, but he had no intention to speak. His eyes grew blurry, and he blinked to clear them.

As he stepped across the balcony, he drew a dagger from his belt, gripping it tightly with his sweaty palm. His pulse pounded thickly in his ears. He was an arm's length away. Flexing his legs to keep them from shaking, Brixton braced his foot and lunged, plunging the knife deep into the king's back.

Wesley cried out as he fell to the ground, and his advisors froze wordlessly in their places. Brixton looked behind him, where Darcius stood in stunned silence. "Go," Brixton mouthed silently. The high lord took two hesitant steps backward before he ran through the archway into the room beyond.

A few of the Felting soldiers jumped into action immediately. They lunged toward Brixton but fell to the ground before reaching him, cut down by fellow soldiers' swords.

As the king sputtered on the ground, desperately grasping at the legs of his stunned advisors, the remaining soldiers joined Brixton and surrounded the three men. Some removed their outer garments to show the red-and-black Norshewan uniforms underneath.

"Excellent work, Brixton," a deep voice said from the tallest of the soldiers. The man removed his helmet to reveal his dark black hair and an unmistakable scar along his face. Brixton bowed promptly to the King of Norshewa.

"Bale!" King Wesley cried as he coughed blood onto his clothes.

"I was always clear about my intention to take over Feldor. Too bad you didn't take me more seriously," Bale told the dying king with a smirk before turning to Brixton. "You said you could do it, and you proved yourself. I had my doubts about your idea to warn them with a letter, but it worked perfectly. As promised, you will have a place by my side."

"Thank you, Your Majesty," Brixton said, fighting the queasy feeling in his stomach.

"As for you," Bale said, turning back to Wesley as he unsheathed his sword. "I will take over your pathetic kingdom and turn this land into the greatness it once was. Feldor used to serve Norshewa, and so it will be once more."

"You'll ruin this land with your selfishness and greed, Bale!" Wesley painfully spoke through a bloody coughing fit.

"Don't worry, *Your Highness*," Bale said. "I will keep your people working. They will find themselves plenty busy as they come to Daratill and build a new palace worthy of my greatness!"

Brixton turned his head while Bale's sword jabbed toward Wesley's neck. Jeers from the soldiers drowned out a gurgling cry. Bale wiped his sword off on the king's pants.

As Bale's laughter died, he turned to the advisors cowering behind the king against the wall. "Cyrus, what should we do with them?"

Bale's captain stepped forward and dangled his sword toward the men. "I'm sure they'd want to join their king whom they've served so faithfully." The soldiers all joined in an evil laugh. Cyrus sheathed his sword then grabbed the older advisor with both hands.

"No! What are you doing?" Eldon whimpered. Cyrus pulled the old man roughly toward the balcony. "Please! No, I can—" Eldon screamed as his body flew over the low railing into the darkness beyond. His cry gradually faded, replaced by a faint thump.

Another soldier repeated the process with the next advisor, sending him flying into the void amidst wails of protest. The soldiers' laughter echoed off the stone walls, but Brixton's stomach churned.

While the men gathered around Bale to congratulate him, Brixton walked to the edge of the balcony and leaned over the low railing. He looked for the remains of the men, but the darkness hindered his view. He shuddered as he imagined the broken bodies somewhere far below.

When he turned around, Brixton froze in place while his heart leaped into his throat. A silhouetted figure with bushy hair and a dark cloak stood in the archway, holding a sword. *No! It can't be!* He dragged his dagger out of his belt and extended it with a shaking hand. He hoped it was only a ghost or some mind trick, but in his gut, he knew the truth—Veron was alive.

Veron's anger seethed as he took in the scene. Surrounded by soldiers, King Wesley lay motionless next to a growing pool of blood. To the side, Brixton wavered at the edge of the balcony, eyes locked on him. Chelci rested her hand against his back, giving him a feeling of comfort.

"Brixton," Veron growled as he walked forward slowly, holding his sword out. "What have you done?"

Brixton's face was pale. He looked as if he wanted to flee but had nowhere to run. A gasp sounded near Wesley's body. Veron turned as a tall soldier in a Norshewan uniform straightened and held up his sword. Veron's breath caught, instantly recognizing the King of Norshewa.

"Bale!" he said, turning toward the man who held his destiny. Veron nodded to King Wesley's body on the ground. "Is he dead?"

Bale extended his neck and took a hesitant step backward. "Your *friend* killed him."

Veron paused and looked back as Brixton hung his head. He tightened his grip on the sword and turned to Bale. "Sorry to disappoint you, Bale. You may have killed King Wesley, but this is where your story ends."

Bale set his jaw. With a flick of his hand, he pulled a knife from a sheath and flung it through the air. The blade whistled as it spun, growing ever closer. Veron grabbed the hilt, stopping it in midair, the blade a hand's length away from his face. He tucked it into his belt without a word while the king's shoulders fell.

Soldiers moved to surround Bale. In a moment, a dozen men stood between him and Veron. Although Veron wasn't fully rested, the origine surged inside of him, begging to be used. *Is this it?* he thought. *Is this where the Dream is fulfilled?* He hesitated. Bale had nowhere to go, but his men stood in the way. Veron held his sword up straight and steeled himself. *I know what I must do.*

Suddenly, a cry sounded behind him, drawing his attention. He spun halfway, keeping Bale in partial view. Brixton stood in front of Chelci and pressed his knife to her chest, pinning her to the stone wall.

"Brixton!" Veron roared. "Leave her out of this!"

"No!" Brixton yelled in return. "You don't want to hurt her, do you?"

Chelci looked around frantically, but the knife halted her.

"Go, now! Come back with one hundred men! Move!" Bale shouted to one of his soldiers, who immediately disappeared through one of the arches. "Brixton, take her away and kill her if he does anything to me!"

Veron's heart raced. His breath became ragged as he snapped his head between the two sides of the balcony. "Brixton, don't do this!" he said with a tinge of desperation.

Chelci tensed as Brixton turned her shoulders, pressing the knife against her back and holding onto her collar as he pushed her forward. "You shouldn't have come here, Veron!" he shouted as he passed under the arch leading into the meeting room beyond.

"Brixton!" Veron's shout received no reply. He spun to Bale, his heart pounding even harder. The king stood still as stone, staring back. *I have to defeat him,* Veron thought. *But—* He glanced to where Chelci had just disappeared, getting farther away by the second. *She needs me!* Veron turned back to Bale. The Norshewan and his men all tensed as they held up their weapons and tightened the circle around their leader. Veron raised his sword then pulled at the origine, desperate to achieve both of his goals.

The shadow knight lunged, trying to strike Bale quickly, but too many bodies blocked the way. He turned his attention to the soldiers at the front, dodging their swords to grab their bodies and fling them across the balcony. The other soldiers reacted slowly, but their swords and bodies filled the gaps, providing him new targets. Veron knocked a sword out of a man's hand and slashed another's chest through his armor. Other soldiers replaced the fallen, and Bale remained just out of reach.

Veron paused and stepped back, taking a moment to rest. He gasped for breath as Bale's remaining men collected themselves and formed a tighter barrier. Veron peeked at the door and imagined Brixton dragging Chelci through the castle. He turned back to Bale and lifted his weapon, but after a moment of hesitation, he exhaled and unleashed a primal yell of frustration before turning and running after Brixton.

44

Escape

Chelci stumbled down the hall, trying not to trip as Brixton recklessly pushed her forward. The point of the knife pressed against her back, forcing her forward. They turned down corridors and descended steps. As they passed a large banquet hall on the right, Chelci decided to act.

Dropping to the floor mid-stride, she extended her legs, tripping Brixton who was unprepared for the sudden movement. As he flailed on the floor, she scrambled to her feet and dashed into the banquet room.

"Chelci!" Brixton shouted.

Chelci grabbed the large, wooden door and pulled with all her strength. The door groaned as it swung close. Just before the gap disappeared, a boot planted itself at the bottom, stopping the door's path.

"Let me in!"

"No!" Chelci yelled, leaning her body into the wood and straining with all her might.

Brixton pushed back, and Chelci's hope sank. He was much stronger than her. The door lurched as he rammed his body against it. Despite Chelci's attempts, the opening widened. Finally, his body almost through, she abandoned the effort and left the door, running into the room and putting the long banquet table between them.

"Chelci, it's over," Brixton said as he approached the table, holding his knife out. "There's no use in running away."

"Ha!" Chelci scoffed. "You know it's not over. I saw that look on your face when Veron arrived. He's going to show up here any second, and you don't want to be anywhere around me when that happens!" Brixton's eyes narrowed, but he didn't reply. "Why'd you do it, Brixton?"

"Why'd I . . . ?"

"Lie to me! Kill the king! Betray your country!"

Brixton sighed as he moved around the end of the table. "You wouldn't understand."

Chelci pivoted opposite him as she made her way to the other side. "I wouldn't understand how your preoccupation with money and power results in decisions opposed to what you know is right?" Brixton's eye flinched, and Chelci continued. "Or that you're so caught up with impressing your father you'll do anything to get his attention?"

"You don't know me!" Brixton shouted before jumping on the table and walking toward her.

"No, I don't," she said. "But Veron does. Brixton . . . this isn't you!" Perspiration dripped down her forehead. She wiped it away as he grew closer. There was nowhere to go. Desperate to get away, Chelci ran toward the door, but Brixton jumped down from the table, grabbing her arm. She instinctually sprang like a coiled serpent. Her fist collided with his face, and his nose crunched.

"Argh!" he yelled, managing to hold onto her arm while pressing his other hand against his face. Blood poured from his nose. "You'll pay for that!" he screamed as he abandoned his nose and stabbed wildly in her direction.

Chelci met his arm with hers. She deflected the blade safely out of reach and followed with a swift knee to his gut. Brixton groaned, and his knife clattered to the floor. As he bent to reach for it, her quick kick sent the weapon skittering to the far end of the room.

Brixton looked up with malice glowing in his eyes and blood dripping from his nose. Chelci inhaled sharply but didn't give up any ground. His fists clenched, and a growl steadily grew. With a furious yell, Brixton attempted a flurry of blows, but Chelci was prepared, blocking punches and kicks with the trained skill of a Nasco guard. When he tried to grab her arm, she spun and kicked his legs out from under him, sending him to the ground with a loud thump.

"Chelci!" A faint voice called somewhere in the hallway. "Where are you?"

Chelci looked to the open door and yelled back, "Veron!"

A scuffling sound turned her back around. Brixton had found his feet and disappeared through the smaller door on the far side of the room. She had no desire to follow.

"Chelci!" Veron cried as he entered the room, running to her and holding her in a tight embrace. "What happened? Where's Brixton?"

Chelci nodded toward the door after pulling away. "You missed him. He just ran through there."

"Are you okay? Are you hurt?"

She shook her head. "I'm fine. How about Bale. Did you kill him?"

"I couldn't get to him quick enough. I tried, but left to find you."

"Veron! You shouldn't have worried about me. Bale is much more important!"

"Not to me, he isn't," he said. Chelci's mouth curled up. "But if you're okay now, I need to hurry back. Maybe I can—"

An army of footsteps silenced him. Chelci and Veron pressed against the wall, and she leaned forward to peek into the hall. In a moment, a steady stream of soldiers ran past, led by the soldier on the balcony from earlier—the one who went to get one hundred men.

Veron sighed and lowered his head as the sound of men faded. "I think I missed my chance."

Chelci lifted his chin until their eyes met. "It was foolish to come after me, but thank you for doing it." She squeezed his hand before looking toward the smaller door across the room. "Do we need to do anything about Brixton?"

Veron exhaled slowly. "No. He's gone, and we should be, too." He pulled her arm gently as he moved toward the main door. "Let's go."

Keeping an eye out for soldiers, Veron navigated through the city back to the Marlows' house. He only relaxed after entering the gate.

"What happened?" Darcius asked, jumping up with Morgan as Veron and Chelci entered the house. "Are you okay?"

Chelci nodded. "We're fine, Father. Brixton betrayed us though."

"I know. He killed King Wesley!"

"Yes, we arrived just after," Veron said.

Darcius' eyes widened. "What about Bale? Did you . . . ?"

Veron hung his head and muttered, "No, I tried but—"

"He saved me, instead," Chelci interrupted.

Morgan laughed softly. "Yeah, he has a habit of doing that."

"So, what do we do now?" Chelci asked. "Bale will look everywhere for you!"

"I agree," Morgan said. "He's not gonna stop until you're dead."

Veron nodded solemnly. "I need to get out of the city. Bale will be protected by half of his army by now."

"I'm coming with you then!" Chelci said.

"Me, too," added Morgan.

"No, it won't be safe wherever I am. You should both stay here."

Morgan took a few steps to a desk, grabbed three bags, and handed one to Chelci and Veron. "Sorry, Veron. You're not getting rid of us that easily."

"What's this?" Veron asked, holding the bag up.

Morgan shrugged. "I've been getting ready . . . just in case."

Chelci hefted her bag over her shoulder and looked at Veron. "It's settled then," she said.

Breathing a sigh of relief, Veron accepted his friends' willingness to join. He turned to Darcius and raised an eyebrow. "If we all run, they're going to question you."

"I'll be fine," Chelci's father said, dismissing the idea with a wave. "I'm too old to go traipsing around and hiding. Plus, as far as any of them know, you're just a troublesome servant who stole my daughter away. You all go."

Chelci hugged her father while Veron inspected the bag. "Food, water skins, flint, and a few candles," Morgan said. "And in yours . . ." He rapped on a solid item at the bottom. "Your book."

Veron smiled and grasped his friend on the shoulder. "Thank you, Morgan. I'm so glad you're here."

When Chelci finished telling her father goodbye, she rejoined the others. "So, how do we get out of the city?" she asked. "I'm sure the gates are crawling with Norshewan and Karad soldiers."

Her father lifted a finger. "I have an idea."

The streets were dark, and every door and window was shuttered tightly. Shouting and the clashing of metal echoed down the streets, but Veron had trouble placing where it came from. Several times, their group ducked into an alley to allow a group of soldiers to run past. Bodies of dead men, women, and even children littered the streets. Veron's stomach turned at the sight of unrecognizable bodies. They passed several buildings engulfed in flames while families cried helplessly outside.

"Come on, we're almost there," Darcius said, waving them forward as Veron stopped to stare.

The group crossed through Turba Square with Morgan bringing up the rear. He led a horse by its reins, laden with their supplies. Vendor carts were abandoned in the desolate square. Food and goods were strewn about in the open as if the sellers had suddenly vanished.

Just past the square, Darcius ducked off the main street at a cistern that supplied water to that section of the city. Arcs of water fell through holes in the wall, waiting to be caught by hands or vessels. Below, a stone basin collected it in a large pool. From one end, water poured into a lower basin on the ground where the horse bent to drink as the group paused.

Darcius squeezed through a narrow opening to the side of the wall and removed a key from his pocket. Just past the cistern waited a rusted, metal door. After fumbling with the lock, the door swung open with a loud creak.

"Follow this passage. It's cramped, but Fred should fit," Chelci's father said as he patted the horse on its neck. "At the end, there's another door where you can flip a latch on this side to get out."

"How did you know about this?" Chelci asked.

"All the high lords know . . . in case we ever need to escape."

"Where does it exit?" Veron asked.

"By the river, upstream from the city. Keep in mind, once you go through this door, you won't be able to get back in."

Veron nodded. He looked at Chelci and Morgan, standing straight with determined looks on their faces. "Are you sure you want to do this?" he asked. Chelci groaned as she stepped past him and ducked into the passage ahead of both men. Veron laughed as he turned to Morgan. "I guess we're doing it, then."

"After you," Morgan said, pointing with his arm.

Veron stepped through the doorway as he held up the lantern. A chill sent a shiver through his body as a musty scent tickled his nose. The slow trickle of water surrounded him. After a moment, the loud clang of metal thundered through the passage as the door closed.

There's no turning back now.

45

Hiding with the Past

Veron held Fred's reins as they slowly navigated the trail through the woods. Around him, the dense foliage was quiet—a far cry from the bustling city life he'd grown up in. Just ahead of Veron, Chelci and Morgan walked side-by-side, talking. Although he hated to upend their lives for his sake, their presence comforted him. He was glad they insisted on coming. They had spent two nights in the woods, taking turns staying awake to keep watch. So far, no one seemed to be on their trail.

As he walked, Veron's eyelids drooped. It was early evening, exactly two days since they had left Felting. The lack of sleep and long days of walking wore on him. *Come on, Veron. You're a shadow knight! If Chelci and Morgan can do this, surely you can.* The full moon above barely filtered through the thick branches of the surrounding trees.

"Are you sure you know where you're going?" Veron asked.

Chelci slowed as she turned to look back at him. "I sure hope so. Otherwise, we could be lost in these woods forever!"

Her mischievous grin didn't set him at ease, but the wink told him it was best to simply trust her. "What about you, Morgan? Did you ever venture out here?" Veron asked.

"When I was young, on my parents' farm, I used to hunt with my father. We came into the woods, but never this far south."

The trail widened, and Veron walked alongside Chelci. "Thanks for coming with me . . . both of you," he said, leaning forward to see Morgan. "I don't know what's going to happen, or how long it will take. But I can't imagine doing it alone."

"I wouldn't be anywhere else," Chelci said.

"Are you kidding?" Morgan added, extending his arm and taking Fred's reins for his shift. "This is way more exciting than selling vegetables!"

"What do you think is happening in Felting, now?" Chelci asked.

Veron looked ahead, up the trail. "With Wesley dead and Bale's army in control, they'll probably set up a new government. From what I heard, it sounded like Bale may place Raynor Fiero in charge."

Morgan uttered a cry of disgust. "I'll hide in the woods for a lifetime just to get away from that man."

"Brixton is probably emperor of commerce, or whatever silly title Bale gives him. I'd guess Bale will probably set his sights on Karondir soon or maybe go straight to Tarphan. From what I hear, they barely have an army."

"So, what do we do? How long should we hide?" Chelci asked.

Veron glanced down at his black cloak and the Shadow Knights symbol. It reminded him of his job, his destiny. "I'm not sure yet. We need to give him time to let his guard down. Then, attack him when he least expects it. We also might need to find help, but I'm not sure how. For now, we just need to wait."

Ahead, the path angled uphill, and two glowing lanterns became visible through the trees. "Shh . . . we're here. Keep your voices down as we approach," Chelci said.

Veron watched his steps, walking with Morgan just behind Chelci. Suddenly, the trees thinned, and a row of wooden houses emerged from the darkness on top of a short hill. The lanterns set back from the edge of the woods gave a warm, glowing feeling. Chelci held up her hand, prompting Veron and Morgan to stop at the bottom of the hill. "Wait here," she whispered. Veron didn't argue as Chelci scurried up the slope.

"Halt!" a voice called out as a dark figure emerged from the shadows to confront her. Veron tensed and rested his hand on the hilt of the sword over his shoulder. From a distance, he watched helplessly as the two silhouettes met. The shadowy forms embraced in a brief hug. Veron relaxed his shoulders and released his breath.

After a moment, the other figure walked away, and Chelci motioned them to join her. "Who was that?" Veron asked as they reached a well-worn path at the top of the rise.

"Just a friend," Chelci said. "Come on. This way."

Veron followed as she walked down the path. Away from the woods, rows of houses became visible with dirt paths running between them. Soon, Chelci stopped in front of a house with a light shining in the window.

"Is this it?" Veron asked.

Chelci took a deep breath and released it but didn't answer the question. She stepped onto the front porch. Wooden boards creaked beneath her, announcing their presence. Morgan tied up Fred to the wooden railing, and he and Veron waited just off the porch.

Chelci raised her hand and hesitated before knocking, as if something held her back.

They heard steps inside before the door opened. Warm light spilled through the open doorway as a robust woman with curly hair filled the frame. Veron tensed as a loud cry came from the woman. His muscles contracted, but the woman immediately wrapped up Chelci in an enormous embrace. An excited white dog wagged its tail and danced around her legs.

"Elise—er . . . Chelci! I can't believe it! It's you!" the lady shouted with joy. Another pair of footsteps filled the room. "Come in, come in!"

Chelci turned and motioned for Veron and Morgan to follow, and all three entered the cozy home. Inside the house, Chelci exchanged a stiff hug with a middle-aged man who was friendly though not gushing with emotion.

"What are you doing here?" the woman asked as she rubbed Chelci's shoulder.

Chelci glanced back at Veron and Morgan. "We needed a place to go. Guys, this is Nevi and Russell." Veron gave a slight wave. "Bale has taken over Felting, and we needed to escape."

"Bale?" another voice said from the back of the room. Veron glanced behind the crowd to see a man with a coiled rope around his chest struggle to stand. Once upright, he walked to Chelci, limping heavily.

"Bensen! It's so good to see you," Chelci said as she hugged him. After a moment, she stopped and jerked back. "Your leg! What . . . ?"

The man smiled and bent down to knock on the lower part of his leg. "Aleks' father helped build me a replacement. It's not what it used to be, but it's better than nothing." The man looked in Veron and Morgan's direction. "Who are your friends?"

Chelci stepped back and pointed to them. "This is Morgan. He recently moved from Karad to Felting."

Morgan gave a shy wave. "It's nice to meet you all."

Chelci smiled broader as she motioned to Veron. "And this is—"

With his guard down, Veron was not prepared for what happened next. Before Chelci could introduce him, Bensen moved in a flash. He pulled a knife from his belt and lunged across the room to pin Veron against the wall, holding the blade to his throat.

"What is this?" he yelled, grabbing Veron's cloak.

"Bensen!" Chelci yelled. "Stop! What are you—"

"Where did you get this from?"

Veron was so shocked at the man's response he was momentarily frozen. The people in the room stared at him, looking just as confused as he felt. As it finally dawned on him that a man held a knife to his throat, Veron pulled from the origine. The people in the room seemed to freeze as he moved with a speed and power none could match. He hit the man's hand out of the way, clearing the weapon from his neck and knocking it to the floor. He pulled on the origine once more and lifted his foot to kick the man away

As he lifted his foot, the frozen man suddenly moved. He grabbed Veron's foot mid-air and twisted, sending Veron twirling in the air and collapsing to the floorboards.

What's happening? Is it not working again? Veron thought. He pulled more origine as he stood and faced the man. The rest of the people remained frozen, but Bensen matched him, move for move. Veron punched, but the man blocked. He tried to knock the man's legs away, but Bensen deftly jumped over the attack. Before he could think of what to do, Bensen dove at him, catching Veron in the mid-section. The two men tumbled to the ground. Veron used origine to push him away, but the other man countered his strength.

Veron rolled over and got on top, fighting to push Bensen's hands away. Through the struggle, his Shadow Knights medallion came free and dangled. When the man saw the metal object, his eyes widened. With one strong effort, he pushed Veron away, and both men scrambled to their feet.

Thankful to catch his breath, Veron released his hold on the origine, and the rest of the room caught up. Veron chanced a glance at the others. A line of slack faces stared in disbelief.

"Where did you get that?" Bensen growled at him, pointing at the medallion. Veron didn't respond as he pulled Farrathan out of the sheath over his shoulder and held it toward the man. Bensen inhaled sharply as his eyes widened at the sight of the sword.

"Who are you?" Veron asked. "How did you do that?"

"This is Bensen," Chelci said, pleading. "He's a friend. Stop this, both of you!"

"I go by Bensen—" he glanced for a moment at Chelci before turning back to Veron. "But that wasn't always my name. I took it when I arrived here in Nasco thirteen years ago."

Veron stared at the man—tall and strong, despite his lean frame. His thick, dark-brown hair fell shaggily across his face. A tingling feeling ran up Veron's spine as something gnawed at him.

"What's your name?" the man asked weakly.

"His name is Veron, and he's a good man," Chelci pleaded. Veron didn't take his eyes off his opponent.

The man's shoulders relaxed, and his arms seemed to shake. He stood up straight as he spoke. "I knew a Veron once . . . many years ago . . . back when I went by the name William."

Bumps formed across Veron's arms and legs. His jaw hung loose as he stared at the man. *His eyes. His nose. His face. He looks like—*The sword fell limply from Veron's hand, clattering to the floor as he hesitantly stepped forward. "Father?"

The Shadow Knights Trilogy concludes in Shadow of Destiny. Pre-order on Amazon today!

I'd love to hear what you thought! Send me a message at michaelwebbnovels.com/contact, and I'll reply as soon as possible!

For behind the scenes writing updates, follow @michaelwebbnovels on Instagram or Facebook.

Acknowledgements

First off, I'd like to thank the readers of The Last Shadow Knight. It was your eagerness to find out more of the story that encouraged me to finish Rise of the Shadow so quickly! I was not prepared for the incredible reception it received, and now I'm more motivated than ever to keep the books coming! To my Alpha readers . . . thank you Johnny, Debbie, Brian, and Eli for your help out of the gate in shaping the story and helping me to see the flaws that needed fixing. A big thanks goes to my developmental editor, Dan, who took the story, characters, and flow to the next level! Next, I couldn't have polished it like it is without my Beta readers. Thank you Jan, Tara, David, and Sara for the time and detail you put into your work! Ian, thank you for your detailed line and copy edits that really helped fix mistakes and smooth out the story. Additionally, I want to recognize and thank RJ, Nicole, and Avery. It's possible that you all have been more excited about my writing progress than even me! Your excitement is motivating and inspiring! Finally, thank you Julia! You encouraged and supported me every step of the way! No one brags about me more than you, and I couldn't do what I do without you behind me!